Praise for *Our Own Private Universe*

"An important and heartfelt contribution to contemporary teen lit about queer women: hopeful, realistic, and romantic, Talley's newest is sure to satisfy."

—*Kirkus Reviews* (starred review)

"This pitch-perfect romance is all heart, touching on serious issues but never becoming too heavy, and will be a strong addition to any teen collection."

—*School Library Journal*

"Reminiscent of Sara Ryan's *Empress of the World*, Talley's latest is a sweet love story about discovering who you want to be with and, more important, who you want to be."

—*Booklist*

Praise for *What We Left Behind*

"This title is a must-read for high school Gay Straight Alliance members.... Toni's genderqueer identity contributes a fresh perspective to LGBTQ fiction."

—*School Library Journal* (starred review)

"Talley continues to tackle tough issues with unvarnished honesty.... Well-intentioned and sympathetic."

—*Booklist*

"Characterization is poignant and razor-sharp... Emotionally astute."

—*Kirkus Reviews*

Praise for *Lies We Tell Ourselves*

"[A] well-paced, engrossing story.... A beautifully written and compelling read."

—*School Library Journal*

"A well-handled debut."

—*Booklist*

"A piercing look at the courage it takes to endure...forms of extreme hatred, violence, racism and sexism."

—*Kirkus Reviews*

"This is a meaningful tale about integration."

—*VOYA*

"*Lies We Tell Ourselves* might be fiction, but the story is true—and it's one we should never forget."

—*NPR*

Also available from Robin Talley

Lies We Tell Ourselves
What We Left Behind
As I Descended
Pulp

OUR OWN PRIVATE UNIVERSE

ROBIN TALLEY

Recycling programs
for this product may
not exist in your area.

ISBN-13: 978-1-335-01336-1

Our Own Private Universe

Copyright © 2017 by Robin Talley

All rights reserved. Except for use in any review, the reproduction or utilization
of this work in whole or in part in any form by any electronic, mechanical or
other means, now known or hereafter invented, including xerography, photocopying
and recording, or in any information storage or retrieval system, is forbidden
without the written permission of the publisher, Harlequin Enterprises Limited,
22 Adelaide St. West, 40th Floor, Toronto, Ontario M5H 4E3, Canada.

This is a work of fiction. Names, characters, places and incidents are either the
product of the author's imagination or are used fictitiously, and any resemblance to
actual persons, living or dead, business establishments, events or locales is entirely
coincidental.

This edition published by arrangement with Harlequin Books S.A.

For questions and comments about the quality of this book, please contact us
at CustomerService@Harlequin.com.

® and TM are trademarks of Harlequin Enterprises Limited or its corporate affiliates.
Trademarks indicated with ® are registered in the United States Patent and
Trademark Office, the Canadian Intellectual Property Office and in other countries.

Printed in U.S.A.

For all those who stare at the stars.

PART 1

Kiss

CHAPTER 1

THE STARS ABOVE me danced in the cool, black Mexico sky. So I started dancing, too.

My body buzzed with the lingering vibrations from all those hours of flying. The music poured through my headphones and straight into my soul. I twirled, I soared, my head tipped back as I watched the stars.

I'd never seen a sky like this one. All my life I'd been surrounded by cities. Lights had shone on every side of me, drowning out the world.

I never realized that before. Not until I came here.

Here, in the middle of nowhere, all the light came from above. The sky was pure black with a thousand dots of white. Millions, actually, if I remembered Earth Science correctly. The air above looked like one of those lush, incomprehensible oil paintings my mother was always staring at whenever she dragged us to a museum back home.

I wanted to float up among those stars.

Nothing to think about. Nothing to do but soak it in and watch them shine.

The song's beat pulsed through me. It was my favorite—

well, one of my favorites. It was the one I'd never told anyone about because I didn't want to deal with the looks I'd get.

Listening to it without dancing was impossible.

With my headphones on and my eyes on the sky, my
body in constant motion, I was oblivious to the world on the
ground. So I didn't know how long Lori had been trying to
get my attention before I felt her sharp tug on my arm.

"Hey!" I lowered my gaze to meet my best friend's. She
winced.

"You don't need to yell." Lori rubbed her ear. "I'm right
here."

"Sorry." I pulled off my headphones.

"You always shout when you wear those. One day you're
going to do it in the middle of church and get kicked out."

"I never wear headphones in church. Mom would slaughter me."

"Yeah, well, I'm going to slaughter you right now if you
keep acting so antisocial. What are you doing out here all by
yourself?"

"Oh, uh." I glanced back across the darkness toward the
courtyard I'd abandoned. The house where the party was
being held was on the far edge of town, backing up into the
empty hillside. Behind me I could hear the sounds of voices
and laughter and faint faraway music floating out over the
walls. "Sorry. I guess I forgot."

Lori laughed. "You're lucky you're hot, because you can
be a total weirdo when you want to be. Come on, we should
mingle."

Right. I was supposed to be trying.

I followed Lori across the hills and through the courtyard's
tall, swinging wooden door. We passed a few people gathered
along the back wall and went up to a table where some chips
were set out next to flickering decorative candles.

At least half the party was gathered around the table, talking and rubbing their eyes. We hadn't all taken the same flights, but everyone had been on at least two planes today, and most of the group looked like they still felt dizzy.

Someone had set up their phone to play music through its little speaker. The melodies were tiny against the open dirt and dotted sky beyond the courtyard walls.

I said hi to the people I knew from church. Lori chattered at everyone, flirting with the guys and fiddling with the bracelet that dangled from her wrist. It was one I'd made. Our allowances were pathetic, so Lori and I made jewelry to sell at school.

I wasn't sure if saying hi to people and following Lori around officially counted as trying. Maybe it was something close, though. Something closer than dancing by myself under the stars.

But, God, those stars. I had to fight not to let my gaze drift back out into the open air.

Trying wasn't optional, though. Not this summer.

Because, well. I had this theory.

Granted, all I ever had were theories. That was the whole problem. My life, all fifteen years of it, had been all about the hypothetical and never about the actual.

I was a hypothetical musician (I hadn't played in more than a year). I was a hypothetical Christian (it wasn't as though I'd tried any other options). Despite the age on my birth certificate, I was essentially a hypothetical teenager, since *real* teenagers did way more exciting stuff than I ever did.

But as of this summer, there was one particular theory that was taking up way more space in my brain than I had to spare.

To be honest, my theory was mostly about sex. But it applied to life in general, too. If I wanted to have an interesting life—which I did—then there was no point sitting around debating everything in my head on a constant loop.

If I wanted my life to change, then I had to *do* something. Or at least *try*.

And it was now or never. This summer, the summer we'd come to Mexico, was the time to test out my hypothesis.

The problem was, I was really good at sitting around and debating things in my head. Trying stuff? Actually *doing* it? That wasn't really my jam.

Lori was different, though. She wasn't any better than me at doing things, but she sure loved trying.

"We've *got* to go to the welcome party tonight," she'd whispered to me that afternoon, seconds after the bus dropped us off at the church. "How else are we going to meet all the new guys?"

"I am absolutely not in the mood for a party," I whispered back as I helped her haul her stuff inside. I'd already decided that, due to jet lag, my theory could wait at least one more day for testing. "I'm all woozy. Like I'm still on that plane, the one that kept shaking around."

It had taken three different planes followed by a four-hour bus ride to get from home, in Maryland, to this tiny town somewhere way outside Tijuana. I'd never flown before, and now that we were on steady land all I wanted to do was put on my pajamas, go to bed and sleep until noon.

Except it turned out we didn't have beds. Just sleeping bags lined up on the cement floor of an old church.

I didn't have pajamas, either. The airline had lost my suitcase.

So I gave up fighting it. My theory was getting tested, jet lag or no jet lag.

"The new guys are going to be incredible," Lori had whispered to me as we walked to the party with the others.

"They're going to be exactly the same as the guys we already know," I whispered back.

"Not true. These guys are way cooler. Much less boring."

"How could you possibly know that?"

"Look, I'm an optimist, okay?"

For the next month, the youth groups from our church and two others would be working together on a volunteer project. All Lori cared about was that we'd be spending four weeks with guys who weren't the same seven guys we'd been hanging out with since we were kids.

I didn't see what was so bad about the guys at our church. Sure, most of them thought of me as a dorky, preacher's-daughter, kid-sister type, but, well, that was pretty accurate. And I'd never been great at meeting people. I wasn't shy or anything. It was only that sometimes, with new people, I didn't know how exactly to start a conversation. I liked to listen first. You could learn a lot about someone that way.

The welcome party was at one of our host families' houses. The local minister's, maybe. But all the adults—my dad and the other ministers and chaperones, plus our Mexican host families—spent the whole time in the living room, which meant the forty-or-so of us from the youth groups had the outdoor courtyard to ourselves. That was a good thing, since whenever the adults were around I could hardly understand what anyone was saying. I'd gotten an A in freshman year Spanish, so I thought I'd be able to get by in Mexico all right, but we hadn't even made it out of the Tijuana airport before I'd found out the truth. The woman at customs had asked me a question and the only part I understood was *por favor*. So I stared at her with my head tilted helplessly until Dad whispered for me to unzip my purse so the woman could check it for bombs or whatever.

Along the back wall of the courtyard, where the adults

couldn't see them from inside, a handful of people had started dancing. I turned back to Lori and stole a chip out of her hand. She pushed her long, curly blond hair out of her face and raised her eyebrows at me.

"See, aren't you glad we didn't skip this?" Lori lowered her voice. "The guys on this trip are already way more interesting than our usual crowd."

She meant that they were older. Lori and I were the only two sophomores who'd been allowed to come on this trip. The others were mostly going to be juniors or seniors in the fall. Some, like my brother, Drew, were already in college. Lori and I got special permission because my dad was our church's youth minister, and he and Lori's aunt Miranda were both chaperones on this trip.

"Why are you so into meeting new guys, anyway?" I asked Lori.

"I don't know. I just want to expand my horizons. Have something new, something that's all mine. You know what I mean?"

I nodded. It sounded like Lori was testing a theory of her own.

We fell into silence. A new song had come on, one of the big songs of the summer that had been playing in every store back home for weeks. Half the group was up and dancing. One of the guys from our church and his girlfriend were swaying slowly with their arms wrapped around each other, even though the song was a fast one.

"Do you want to go dance?" Lori asked.

I gave her a weird look instead of answering. Lori knew very well I never danced in front of people.

I tilted my head back to get another look at those stars. They swam dreamily in the sky.

"Stop looking up so much," Lori whispered. "Your neck

is already freakishly long. People are going to think you have no face."

"My neck is not freakishly long," I said, but I lowered my chin anyway.

Two white girls I didn't know were half dancing, half standing in the darkest corner of the courtyard. One girl had hair so short you could see her scalp and leather cuffs with silver buttons on both wrists. The other girl had dark hair that curled around her ears, heart-shaped sunglasses perched on her head, a tiny silver hoop in her nose and a quiet smile that made me want to smile, too.

"Aki, you're staring," Lori said.

"Sorry." I looked away from the girls.

"Do you like one of them?"

"No."

"It's okay if you do. You can tell me."

"I don't. I was distracted, that's all."

Last year I told Lori I thought I might be bi. Ever since, whenever she saw me looking at a girl, she asked if I liked her. Lori didn't get that sometimes it was fun just to notice people without having to think about whether you liked them or not.

The girl with the sunglasses turned toward Lori and me. Oh my God. She wasn't that far away. Had she heard us? I was going to kill Lori.

The girl was still smiling, though.

She was cute, but she made me nervous. I wasn't used to looking at girls that way. Being bi, just like the rest of my life, had always been mostly hypothetical. I scanned the crowd, trying to look for a guy who was equally cute.

"Is there anyone here you might like?" I asked Lori.

"Maybe." She nodded toward a super-tall blond guy drinking from one of the frosted glasses our host family had set out. "What do you think of him?"

I studied the guy. He had to have been a senior, at least. He had a T-shirt with a beer company logo and he was laughing loud and sharp at something his friend had said, his mouth open so wide I could see the fillings in his back teeth.

"He looks like a tool," I said.

"Whatever, you think everybody looks like a tool."

The girl with the sunglasses was coming toward us. She was even cuter up close.

Oh, *God*.

"Look who it is," Lori whispered.

As though I hadn't already seen her. As though she wouldn't see Lori whispering and think we were incredibly obvious and immature.

"Hi." Somehow, the girl was now standing in front of us, her head tilted at a startlingly attractive angle. "You guys seem cool. I'm Christa."

I had no idea what to say. I shoved a chip in my mouth.

"Thanks." Lori glanced over at me. "I'm Lori."

"Hi, Lori." The girl turned toward me, expectant, but I was still chomping on my tortilla chip. I probably looked like the biggest tool in Mexico.

But Christa didn't seem bothered. "What church do you guys go to?"

"Holy Life in Silver Spring," Lori said. I swallowed, nearly choking. Lori ignored me. "What about you?"

"Holy Life in Rockville," Christa said, her eyes still on me. Then she turned back to Lori. "Does your friend talk?"

Lori nudged me.

"Um. Hey." I was positive there were chip crumbs on my face. Would it look weirder to leave them there or to wipe them away? What if I was just paranoid and there *weren't* chip crumbs on my face, and it looked like I was wiping my face for no reason like a total loser? "I mean, hi."

My face must've been bright red. Why was Christa still looking at me?

"What happened to your girlfriend?" Lori asked, tilting her head toward where Christa had been dancing before.

"She went out around the back to smoke." Christa lowered her voice and added, "And she's not my girlfriend."

"Smoking is revolting," I said, because I didn't want to say anything about whether Christa did or didn't have a girlfriend. Or whether she might want one.

"For real, right?" Christa said. "I try to tell her, but some people, you know?"

She smiled at me. I smiled back. There was a pink streak in her shoulder-length hair that I hadn't noticed before. She was wearing jeans and a yellow tank top, and her sneakers had red hearts drawn on the sides with a marker. I'd never known it was possible for a person to look as cute as Christa did.

"I'm gonna go get more salsa," Lori said.

I shook my head at her frantically. I couldn't do this by myself.

Lori only grinned and left. Christa stayed where she was. Damn it.

"So, what's your name?" Christa asked me.

"Aki."

"That's pretty."

It was so hard not to giggle. But I managed to keep my face relatively composed as my insides jumped for joy.

"It's short for Akina," I explained.

"Akina." I liked how she said my name. She pronounced it slowly, as though it was some spicy, forbidden word. "That's even prettier."

Was this flirting? I'd never really flirted before. Sure, I'd hung out with guys, but they never told me my name was pretty. Instead they made stupid jokes and then looked really happy when I laughed.

Was it even okay to flirt with a girl here? If someone saw us, would they be able to tell we were flirting from across the courtyard? Or did flirting just look like talking?

And if Christa *was* flirting, what made her think I wanted to flirt back? Was it something about how I looked? What I was wearing? Did she know I wanted her to flirt with me?

Did I want her to?

If she was really gay, she probably had a girlfriend back home. I didn't know if I was ready to have a girlfriend. I'd never even had a boyfriend for longer than a couple of weeks.

"Wait... Aki?" Christa cocked her head, as if she was studying me. "Aki from Silver Spring. I've heard about you."

"Yeah?"

Oh.

My stomach tensed. This cute girl, the first girl ever to flirt with me, knew exactly who I was.

Of course she did.

I was the black girl with braids. I was Pastor Benny's daughter. Everyone in all of the Holy Life community knew who I was. I was one of a kind.

But then she said, "You're like a really talented musician, aren't you?"

And my stomach didn't know whether to twist tighter or do flips in the air.

"I. Um." I didn't know what to say.

"I've definitely heard about you." The smile spread wider across Christa's face. "You play a bunch of instruments, right? And you write music and you sing? My friend went to a service at your church where the whole choir sang something you wrote. He said it was gorgeous and that everyone cheered and talked about how amazing you were."

That had been during Advent in eighth grade. The piece we performed was the same one I'd used for my audition for MHSA. Even thinking about it made me want to throw up.

But this girl. God, this girl was so amazing.

And she was staring at me as though she thought I was amazing, too.

So I nodded. "Yeah, that's me. It's not that many instruments, though. Mainly I play guitar. And a little piano."

Okay. So that wasn't totally true.

But it wasn't really a *lie*, either. It was just an inaccurate verb tense. I *used* to do that stuff, after all. If I'd said *played* instead of *play* it would've been a 100 percent accurate statement.

Either way, it totally didn't count as lying.

Either way, I was glad I said it the way I did when Christa beamed at me in response.

"Oh, wow! That's so cool." Christa nodded over and over again. "It's so neat to meet someone else who's seriously into artistic stuff. I'm not anywhere near your level, but I'm an artist, too. I do photography sometimes."

"You do?" I seized on the chance to talk about something that wasn't me and music. "What kind of photography?"

She took out her phone. "Most of it's on my Instagram, but..." She sighed. I understood. We'd all gradually realized on our bus ride into town that our phones didn't work here. No service. We could play games and take photos, but no internet, no texting. It was like missing an arm.

Christa swiped through the photos on her phone. I tried to crane my neck to see them, but she held it out of my reach. "No, no don't look at that one, that one's awful. That one I need to crop. That one's not—hey, actually, you can look at this one. This one's good."

I leaned in until my face was only inches from hers. I had

to force myself to focus on her phone screen instead of the soft, warm scent of her skin.

I didn't know anything about photography, but even so, I could tell it was a good photo. It was better than any pictures I'd ever taken with my phone, anyway. It showed a kid's bare feet hovering in midair over a pool of water on a bright green lawn, as though the kid had been in the middle of jumping into the puddle when the phone was taken. You could see individual ripples and the reflection of the kid's toes in the water.

"I really like that," I said. "Are those your little brother's feet?"

"Yeah. At least the little demon is good for something."

I laughed and reluctantly stepped back from her phone.

"Do you go to King?" I asked her.

King was the big public high school in our area. My brother had gone there, but Lori and I went to Rowell, a tiny private school. There were only twelve people in our grade.

Christa nodded. "I do."

"Do you know Eric?" I asked. "He's the president of our youth group. He goes to King, too."

Crap. I should've just stayed quiet. Things had been going great when we were looking at her phone, but now I was asking her the most boring questions ever. Why couldn't I think of something cool to say? Christa was going to think I was boring with a capital *B*.

But she didn't look bored.

"Sure, I know Eric. He's okay." She tilted her head to one side. "For a straight, privileged white guy, you know?"

She laughed. I did, too.

Her saying that had to mean she was gay. Or bi, at least. She must be into girls one way or another. Right?

"I don't know what you mean," I said, trying to be clever and praying it was working. "I have lots of friends who are straight, privileged white guys, and I'm totally okay with them. I think they should have equal rights, just like the rest of us."

Christa laughed again. Her eyes crinkled up, as though she actually thought I was funny. "As long as they don't flaunt it, right?"

I laughed again. Christa slid her shoulder up against the wall right next to me and leaned forward until her face was only inches from mine.

My heart thudded in my chest. I was too nervous to look back at her.

I did it anyway.

Maybe *this* qualified as doing something.

I could barely remember what we'd been talking about, so I was halfway relieved when a smiling black guy I didn't know came up to us. "Christa, are you bothering this nice young girl?"

I wished he hadn't called me *young*. Or *nice*. Those two words added up to the opposite of *sexy*.

"I don't know." Christa turned toward the guy, then looked back at me. Her light brown eyes glimmered in the dim light. "Am I bothering you, Aki?"

"No," I breathed.

The guy and Christa both laughed, and she introduced us. His name was Rodney. He went to the same church as Christa, and they were both going into their junior year at King. I was surprised Christa was only one year older than me.

The three of us sat down on the tile patio and Rodney grabbed a pile of chips for us to share. I took an inventory of the courtyard while Rodney and Christa talked about their friends from school. I counted only five black people, including Rodney, my brother, Drew, and me.

I wondered if that was why Rodney had come over to talk to us. There were plenty of black people in our part of Mary-

land, but most of them went to all-black churches. Only a
handful of black and Hispanic families went to our church,
and I figured the same was probably true at Christa and Rodney's, too. The other church who'd sent their youth group on
this trip was in Harpers Ferry, West Virginia. I didn't know
much about West Virginia, but from what I did know, I had
a feeling that church was all white, all the time.

Rodney wasn't bad-looking. I probably should've been excited that he wanted to talk to me. But all I wanted was to be
alone with Christa again.

Other people came over to sit with us. Christa kept saying stuff that made everyone laugh, me especially. Then the
group got so big that a bunch of different conversations were
going on at once.

A short white guy came over and sat down next to me.

"Hi." He waved awkwardly. "I'm Jake. I go to Holy Life
of Harpers Ferry."

"Hey, Jake."

Jake, it turned out, was really, really chatty. He kept trying
to ask me questions about the people who went to my church
and about the national conference that was coming up at the
end of the summer for all the Holy Life churches. I knew absolutely nothing about the conference, so I mostly nodded
while Jake talked.

It actually turned out to be kind of cool hanging out with
new people—people who didn't automatically see me as a
music-dork preacher's kid—but even so, I couldn't focus. I
wanted to talk to Christa again. She was funny. And I liked
how her eyes caught the light.

Lori came over and motioned to me, so I apologized to Jake
and got up. It was good to have an excuse to get away. It was
hard to think clearly with so much happening around me.

I followed Lori through the courtyard's tall, swinging

wooden door. A patch of gravel ran behind the row of houses and faded into dirt as the hills rose up behind the edge of town. Lori and I walked out a few yards past the gravel into the pitch-black night so we could talk without anyone hearing us. It took all my energy to focus on Lori instead of those stars again.

She wanted to tell me about the blond guy she'd spotted earlier. She'd found an excuse to talk to him. It turned out his name was Paul, and he went to Christa's church in Rockville.

"He's going to be a senior at King," Lori said. "He has a car and everything. A Toyota."

"Do you like him?"

"Uh-huh. He's really cute and funny. Plus, older guys are more mature, you know?"

"Do you mean *mature*, like, emotionally, or *mature*, like, he's done it?"

"Oh, shut it." Lori giggled. I did, too. "I took a picture of us goofing around. Want to see?"

Lori took out her phone and showed me a poorly framed photo of her and Paul sticking their tongues out at the camera. It made me think of Christa and her gorgeous photography. I flushed, glad it was dark so Lori couldn't see.

"Do you think you'll ask him out or something?" I said.

"I don't know. What is there to even do around here? Maybe we'll just hang out at the volunteer site. And find someplace to sneak off to when the time is right."

We both laughed again.

We were supposed to start work tomorrow. None of us were sure exactly what that meant. We'd come here to do construction on a church that the local congregation had already started building. None of us knew the first thing about construction, but my dad and the other chaperones said they'd teach us. I only hoped they didn't make me climb ladders. I was afraid of heights.

My back felt stiff from sitting on the ground, so I stood on my tiptoes and stretched my arms over my head, arching my spine so my braids hung straight down. This time, I couldn't resist gazing up at the stars. They were closer out here than they were within the stone courtyard walls.

In that moment, it felt like we were the entire world. Just me and those gorgeous stars.

It was colder out here, too, away from the lights of the houses. We weren't really in the desert, even though that was what I'd expected when I signed up to come to Mexico. Here there were trees and stuff, and it had been hot during the day but not *that* hot. Now that it was dark, it was only sixty-something degrees.

I lowered myself back down from my toes and rubbed my bare arms, wishing I'd worn more than my T-shirt and jeans. Then I remembered my missing suitcase. I didn't have anything else *to* wear.

"We're going into town on Saturdays, right?" I asked Lori. "Maybe you and Paul could do something while we're there."

"Or maybe you and that girl could." Lori smirked.

"Oh, whatever." But I couldn't help smiling.

I wasn't sure if lesbians even went on dates. Did anyone, really? I'd been on one official date in my entire life, to a dance at a school I didn't go to with a blue-haired guy who threw up because he drank a beer.

I'd wondered what it would be like to have a real boyfriend. Maybe a girlfriend, too. Someday.

Just the idea of a girlfriend seemed like it was from a whole different life. I mean, even if Christa *had* been flirting with me back in the courtyard, that didn't mean she actually wanted to go out with me. She must've been able to tell I didn't know anything about being gay.

Heck, she probably thought I was straight. I might as well have been, for all I'd done so far.

Was Christa bi, too? Maybe she was into Rodney. Or someone else. Maybe she hadn't really been flirting with me at all.

"So do you like her?" Lori asked me.

"I don't know," I said. "Maybe?"

"I knew it!" Lori pumped her fist. "I could so tell when you were looking at her before."

"It doesn't matter. She isn't interested."

"How do you know?"

I shrugged. There was no reason someone like Christa would want someone like me. I'd never even kissed a girl.

It wasn't as if I didn't *want* to. Lately, kissing was all I thought about. Boys. Girls. My daydreams didn't discriminate.

That was where my theory had *really* gotten started.

Christa had probably kissed tons of girls. And done more than kiss.

I'd been daydreaming about *that* a lot lately, too.

"You're smiling again," Lori said.

"Oh, shut it. Hey, do you think—"

Before I could finish, Lori clapped her hand over my mouth and held her finger to her lips, her eyes bulging. Now that we were quiet, I could hear it, too. Gravel crunching behind me, then footsteps on the dirt.

"Hi, you guys," a voice said.

I turned. It was too dark to get a good look from this distance. But I knew it was Christa.

"Hey there." Lori was grinning, as usual. "I'm glad you came out here. I wanted to ask you something."

Oh, *no*. I was too far away to elbow Lori, so I glared at her. She ignored me.

"Shoot." Christa was close enough now that I could see a design on the inside of her wrist. It looked like a tattoo, but I could've sworn it wasn't there when I'd seen her in the court-yard earlier. It was purple. Some kind of complicated knot.

Lori lowered her voice. "You're into girls, right?"

My eyes jerked up. I couldn't believe Lori said things like that. I would never say something like that to someone *she* had a crush on. But Christa didn't seem to mind.

"For sure," she said. "But don't tell my parents, okay?"

"Deal." Lori laughed. "So what kind of girls do you like? You know, generally. Tall, short, long hair, short hair…"

Christa glanced over at me. I tried to smile, but my face felt all wobbly. I shifted from one foot to the other. Why did Lori have to be this way? *Why?*

"I think," Christa said slowly, "right now, if I were to de-scribe exactly the kinds of girls I like, I'd say…tall, with long hair, in braids. With big dark eyes and pretty smiles. Oh, and I especially have a thing for preacher's daughters who wear vintage hip-hop T-shirts."

I beamed and tugged on one of my braids. I'd worn my fa-vorite Usher shirt on the plane. It was only three years old, so it didn't exactly qualify as vintage, and Usher wasn't so much hip-hop as R&B with some light hip-hop influences. But I did not care even the tiniest bit about those things right then.

"And I like girls with nose rings who draw stuff on their wrists," I said. It wasn't the cleverest thing I could've come up with, but the truth was, just saying "I like girls" took so much out of me, I didn't have energy left for cleverness. It was the first time I'd admitted it to anyone but Lori.

Now I was definitely doing something.

Christa took a step toward me. Someone else was coming through the swinging door, but I didn't look to see who it was. I didn't want to see anyone but Christa.

"That's truly excellent news," Christa said. "Because I happen to believe that the process of creating is what makes people interesting. Any kind of creating, I mean, but let's be honest—music is the best art there is. It's the purest. And, well, I'm actually a little obsessed with musicians. It's kind of my thing."

My stomach tightened again. I could tell from her voice that Christa was joking, at least sort of. But now I really wished I hadn't messed up my verb tenses earlier. I'd already promised myself to never again create so much as a single note.

But with the way Christa was looking at me now, I knew there was no way I was ever going to tell her that.

And that meant I was now most definitely lying to her. About something she seemed to care about a lot.

I swallowed and dropped my gaze down to my feet.

"Er, I mean, sorry, Lori, no offense." Christa turned her still-joking voice to my best friend. "I don't know if you're an artist. It's totally okay if you're not."

"I make jewelry," Lori offered.

"That totally counts!" Christa turned back to me, smiling. I met her eyes, folding my shaky hands behind my back. "Anyway. I have to go, because I promised my friends we'd go back early to claim the best spot for our sleeping bags. But can I come find you tomorrow?"

"You most definitely can." My palms felt all tingly. I couldn't believe I was talking this way, as if this conversation was no big deal at all.

"Excellent," she said. "Maybe you could play me something, if you have anything recorded? Or even just sing something? Is that weird of me to ask?"

"Um." I could feel Lori's quizzical eyes on me. I silently begged her not to give me away. I hadn't sung since my MHSA audition, not even in the shower. Not even in church when the rest of the congregation opened their hymnals. But how could I tell Christa that now, after she'd just said you had to create art to be interesting? "I, um—"

"You coming, Christa?" someone said behind us. It was the girl with the short hair Christa had been hanging out with at the beginning of the party.

"Yeah." Christa smiled at me, then ducked her head. I smiled back at her goofily. Then she turned around and was gone.

"Wow." Lori was already by my side as Christa and the other girl disappeared through the swinging doors. "You were wrong. She *definitely* likes you."

"I guess."

Lori let out a mini squeal. "And you like her."

I shifted again. "I guess."

Lori's eyes shone. "And what was all that about you singing for her tomorrow?"

I scrubbed my face with the heel of my hand. "That part is...actually kind of a problem. She'd heard I did music stuff, and I didn't tell her I'd quit, and somehow it turned into this."

"So you're, what—pretending you still do all that stuff?" Lori's forehead wrinkled. "I mean, there's no way she won't find out. Everyone from our church knows how obsessive you are about not ever singing or anything. Your brother talks constantly about how he wants you to get back into music."

"I know." I scrubbed my face with my hand again. "Listen, promise you won't say anything."

"Yeah, of course." Lori's lip quirked upward. "Wouldn't want the truth to stand in the way of true love. Or true hooking up, at least."

I forced a laugh. Yeah, I wanted to hook up with Christa. The more I thought about it, the more I wanted to. In fact, standing in the dark, watching her walk away, I realized *exactly* how much I wanted to.

But was she only into me because of a lie? Because she thought I was some amazing artist, when in reality I'd proven to be anything but?

I didn't know what to think. I'd never dealt with anything like this before.

There was only one thing I knew for sure.

What I'd done tonight definitely counted as doing something.

So far, my theory was proving 100 percent correct. Doing stuff was a *lot* more fun than not doing stuff.

And, yeah, maybe some of the stuff I was doing wasn't completely honest. But I'd deal with that later.

First, I needed to focus on testing out my theory some more.

Because now that I'd met Christa, there was suddenly a *lot* of stuff I wanted to do.

CHAPTER 2

"I CAN'T BELIEVE we have to sleep in there." My paint-brush glided down the back wall of the church, leaving a thick wet trail of primer. "For a whole *month*."

"I know," Lori said. "I feel stiff all over."

"The adults totally get to sleep in beds. And take *showers*. In *houses*, even."

"My aunt said we're staying in the church because we're young and our backs still function. I told her my back wasn't going to be functioning after this, but all she did was laugh."

The night before, we'd slept on the floor of the town's old church. The pews had been stacked along the walls to make room for the mats and sleeping bags we'd brought from home. My suitcase full of clothes was still somewhere in the Dallas airport, so I was stranded in Mexico with nothing but my duffel with my sleeping bag, a toothbrush, and some under-wear, plus the clothes I'd worn on the plane. Lori had lent me an old pair of track pants and a long-sleeved T-shirt to wear today, but I was a lot taller than Lori, so my ankles, wrists and part of my stomach were bare.

Plus, we had to shower outside in these camp shower things

the chaperones had brought. They were basically really small tents with a bag of tepid water at the top that sprinkled on you if you pulled a cord. That morning I'd showered for about sixty seconds while a line of girls huffed and waited for me to finish. The experience had left me feeling decidedly unfresh.

Not that it mattered, given that our agenda for the day consisted of manual labor in an un-air-conditioned cement building. We were painting the town's new Holy Life church. When it was done, this one would replace the old building where we were camping out.

"Is this how we're supposed to do it?" I lowered my brush and frowned. The church walls were tall, probably twenty feet high, so we were only painting what we could reach. Our little patch of white primer looked kind of pathetic.

"Who knows?" Lori dabbed her brush in the paint tray. "Just keep going."

I'd tried to pay attention during that morning's painting lesson, but I'd been standing toward the back of the group, and Christa was at the front. I kept craning my neck to get a better look at her.

I hadn't seen her after the party. By the time we got back to the old church someone had hung up a tarp to separate the boys' half of the floor from the girls', but the single lightbulb that lit the whole room was on the boys' side. Our side was a strange dark cave, quiet except for a few people whispering and swarms of mosquitoes buzzing past the windows. There was no way to spot Christa in the dark. Plus, every time I saw a shadow move I was positive it was a snake. (I had a thing about snakes.)

"So, question." Lori painted another slow, uneven line. "Regarding your new paramour."

"She's not my paramour." I smiled.

"Only a matter of time, babe." Lori glanced at me with her

eyebrows raised. "But what's your dad going to say about you being gay? I mean, bi?"

I'd carefully avoided thinking about that. I returned my focus to my paintbrush. "I don't know."

"What about your mom? And your brother?"

"Come on, they don't all have to know everything. Mom isn't even here."

"Ooh, so you and that chick are going to sneak around Mexico having secret liaisons under preacher daddy's nose? Gnarly."

"*Liaisons?*" I laughed. "*Gnarly?* What is this, 1980?"

Lori laughed, too. "For real, though. If you're not having secret liaisons, what are you going to do, lesbian it up right in front of everyone?"

I shifted again. "I met this girl five seconds ago. Nobody's lesbianing anything yet. Besides, I still like guys."

Lori tried to arch one eyebrow, but she couldn't do that very well, so her face just wound up amusingly strange and contorted.

"You know what I really want to do this summer?" she said. "Have a fling."

I laughed. "What kind of fling?"

"You know, where you have a boyfriend, or a girlfriend or whatever, but only for the summer. You hang out, you hook up, and at the end of the summer you go back to your regular life. Short, meaningless, but fun."

"What's the point of that?" I said. "Don't you want a regular boyfriend?"

"Yeah, sure. But this summer is our perfect fling opportunity. Most of the guys here go to other schools, so we'll basically never see them again. The girls, too."

Hmm. "I sort of see what you mean."

"I know what we should do." Lori put down her paintbrush and grinned at me. "We should *both* have a fling. Let's make a pact."

I laughed again. Lori and I used to be really into pacts. When we were younger we'd make pacts to eat the exact same number of conversation hearts at the Valentine's Day party, or to include the word *hickey* somewhere in our fifth-grade Life Science reports. In middle school, Lori was obsessed with having her first kiss, and she got me to make a pact that we'd each kiss someone before the end of the school year. But when I kissed Tim Mayhew at the school Chrismukkah party that December, she'd been furious. I'd actually forgotten about the pact by that point—I only kissed Tim because he came up to me at the party wearing one of those mistletoe headbands all the guys had that year and I liked the way his green eyes locked on mine when he smiled—but Lori remembered everything. She said I'd violated the pact because we were supposed to have our first kiss at the same time, even though I didn't remember agreeing to that part at all. It turned out to be fine because Lori kissed Barry Tuckerton at his New Year's Eve party the next week, but I still felt kind of bad. Barry Tuckerton's breath smelled like cheese.

"We should do it," she said. "For real. Come on, it'll be fun."

I thought about Christa's face again. Her voice. *I especially have a thing for preacher's daughters . . .*

"Yeah. Let's do it." I was getting excited now. "Okay, rules. We'll each hook up with someone—um, how about three times? Three's a good number."

"Okay," Lori said. "And it doesn't have to be that girl and Paul—it can be anyone. Also—wait, how are we defining *hookup*, exactly? Is kissing enough, or does it have to be more?"

I acted surprised, even though I'd been wondering the same thing. "Wow, that's—um. Do you really think—"

She started laughing. "Kidding. Of course kissing counts. I mean, that's all either of us has done before, right? But whatever we wind up doing, we have to tell each other every last, sweaty detail, the way we always do. So, are we both in?"

She held out her hand, her little finger curved up, for our standard pact-agreement pinkie swear.

I glanced around the cavernous space of the church. I didn't see any sign of Christa now, but I remembered how she'd smiled at me in the dusty shadows the night before.

I'd have given anything just to have her smile at me that way again.

I grinned and linked my finger with Lori's. "I'm definitely in."

"Hate to interrupt your girl talk, ladies, but you have too much paint on your brushes, there." Lori and I turned slowly. Dad's voice had come from far enough behind us that I was pretty sure he hadn't heard anything, but still, when a parent sneaks up on you, it's almost never a good thing. Especially when you've just finished making a pact that involves kissing other girls. "When you load paint onto your brush, you need to tap off the excess on the edge of the pan, this way."

Dad took Lori's brush and demonstrated. Globs of paint dripped off the brush. I could tell he was right, but I rolled my eyes anyway. Dad loved nothing more than telling me I was doing something wrong.

"Thanks, Benny." Lori smiled as he handed her back the brush. She never understood when I complained about my dad. Her own dad had moved out when she was in elementary school, and she hardly ever saw him. She was supposed to spend a few weeks with him every summer, but her summers were always so packed with activities that it usually only wound up being a weekend trip. Maybe she didn't realize how annoying dads could really be.

"You ought to be using rollers, though." Dad stroked his chin. "I'll see if I can pick some up in town. By the way, Aki, want to come talk to me for a sec?"

I groaned under my breath and followed Dad outside. The sun charged straight into my eyes, so I pulled on my baseball cap. My brother, Drew, and bunch of people were digging a ditch for the new fence, and they all had giant sweat stains under their armpits. I was glad I'd gotten an indoor job. Our whole family sweated a lot, me included, but Dad and Drew got it the worst.

"How are you liking Mexico so far?" Dad asked me, wiping the back of his neck.

"It's okay. You didn't tell me we'd be sleeping on a cement floor."

Dad chuckled. "Why did you think we told you to bring sleeping bags?"

"I thought we'd go on a special camping trip or something. For, like, one night."

"Well, don't worry. Sleeping on the floor will build character." Dad chuckled again.

"Whatever." Mom and Dad both loved to say anything Drew and I complained about would "build character."

"Listen, there was something I wanted to talk to you about," Dad said. "You remember that our first Holy Life national conference is coming up?"

I nodded. Jake, the guy from Harpers Ferry, had said something about that at the party last night.

Some of my friends at school thought our church was weird, but it wasn't, really. Holy Life started out in Maryland after a couple of nondenominational churches decided to start doing some activities together. Then some churches in other states joined in and even a few in other countries, like this one here in Mexico. Holy Life churches aren't the kind where preachers talk constantly about how abortion is evil and how we should all vote Republican or anything, though. I mean, some people at my church probably *do* vote Republican, but mostly we don't talk about that stuff. Instead we get together for picnics and ice-cream socials, and on Sunday mornings we sing hymns and listen to sermons about whatever Jesus did that week.

But now the different churches were trying to get more officially organized. Everyone had been talking about the conference since Christmas, but I'd sort of tuned it out. Usually, if I paid attention to church stuff, it was because I'd done something wrong that week and knew I should pray about it so I wouldn't feel guilty.

"Well, the delegates who'll be at the conference are very interested in this trip," Dad said. "It's the first time we've brought multiple churches together for an overseas mission project."

"We didn't come over the sea to get here," I said. "It's more of an over*land* project."

Dad ignored me. "I'll be giving a presentation about this trip at the conference, and one of the things the delegates want to hear will be how we worked with the local congregation. Since you volunteered at that clinic last summer, I thought you and some of your friends might want to take on a side project here with the local kids."

A side project? Dad wanted me to do *more* work? "What kind of project?"

Dad shrugged. "Whatever you think they might enjoy. Could you teach them a praise dance or a worship song?"

"*Dad.*" I side-eyed him. After a moment he gave up and looked away.

My parents knew very well that I'd stopped all that. I didn't sing in the church choir or the school chorus anymore, and

I'd dropped out of the dance class I'd enrolled in the summer before.

I was done with music. After what had happened with MHSA, there was no way I could ever go back. Mom and Dad may have thought they were dropping subtle hints when they asked me to lead a worship song or left a brochure for my old music camp on the kitchen table, but I knew exactly what they were trying to do, and it wasn't going to work. I'd made up my mind.

No more spending hours with my stupid guitar. I played lacrosse now, and I'd joined the math team, too.

No more music camp, either. I'd signed up to come on this trip the same day our church's lead pastor announced it was happening. Mainly so my parents would stop bugging me about music camp.

"Well, maybe you could all do a presentation together at the end of the summer," Dad said.

"Ugh, do we have to?" That would be even worse than doing a song. I hated standing up in front of people and just talking. In class, whenever we got assigned to do a presentation, I begged the teacher to let me do a separate extra credit project instead. In church I always kept my head down when they asked for volunteers to read Bible verses.

I didn't want to present. I wanted to *perform*. But I wasn't good enough for that, apparently.

"Well, it could be anything to keep the kids engaged," Dad said. "What did you do at the clinic?"

"Crafts, mostly." Last summer, after I'd dropped out of music camp at the last minute, I'd wound up volunteering at a health center in downtown Silver Spring for people who didn't have insurance. I'd thought I was going to learn how to bandage people's cuts and test them for viruses and stuff—I'd signed up to work there because I was into math and science, after all—but instead I was a glorified babysitter for the little kids in the waiting room. On my second day I brought in craft supplies from home and the next thing I knew, I was the most popular volunteer in the place. All the kids wanted me to show them how to make my special paper airplanes that were guaranteed to fly in loop-di-loops. "But I don't have any craft supplies here, except for the jewelry materials Lori and I brought. Those are for us, though."

Lori and I had been making jewelry since middle school. I'd found some bead patterns online and gotten obsessed with them. I loved anything that involved neat, orderly rows and following a bunch of steps to get it right. Lori and I started wearing our jewelry to school, and soon people were asking if they could buy it. We wanted to sell it online but our parents were afraid people would try to take advantage of us. Parents had no idea how the internet actually worked.

"Well, we could reimburse you for the materials," Dad said. "I guess it's my fault for not mentioning this before we left home. I thought you could do a dance or something that didn't need supplies."

"*Dad.*" I groaned.

Dad rubbed his neck again. "For the jewelry, do you think you could have them make Christian-themed pieces? You know, cross necklaces, that sort of thing?"

"Sure." I didn't know if we had any cross-necklace supplies, but Dad would probably forget he'd asked me that anyway.

"Good. Well, this is an excellent plan. You can start today after lunch. I'll talk to Carlos about rounding up some of the girls and I'll swing by to take photos of you for my presentation."

"Today? Wow, okay." It was a good thing we'd brought the jewelry stuff in Lori's suitcase and not mine.

I went straight back in to tell Lori while Dad stayed outside to help with the fence work. I was trying to figure out how many supplies we'd brought with us and how we were going to teach jewelry making to a bunch of kids whose language we didn't speak when I saw that a girl in a bright pink hat had taken my spot by the wall. She and Lori had their backs to me, and they were talking and laughing as they painted.

It was Christa. I recognized her by the pink streak in her hair. Which clashed horribly (and, somehow, adorably) with her hat.

I stopped walking. Suddenly I was…what? Afraid? Nervous? Jealous?

What was I supposed to *do*, exactly? What should I say? The night before everything between us had just sort of fallen into place, like magic.

But that night had been special. That night, *I* was special. Today I was regular old Aki, with too-short track pants and smears of white paint on my hands.

Lori bent to dip her brush into the pan and saw me. She waved. "Aki! Look who came to help!"

Christa's face broke into a grin as she turned around. Her heart-shaped sunglasses dangled from a string around her neck. "Sorry! Did I steal your brush?"

She reached up to adjust her hat. There was a speck of white paint on the side.

That's when I realized it wasn't a hat. It was a beret.

A raspberry beret.

Wow.

Not only did Christa own a raspberry beret, she'd *brought it with her to Mexico.*

I didn't know a single fellow Prince fan who was younger than my mother. It was as if Christa had been custom-made for me.

Just like that, things were easy again.

"Yeah." I grinned. "But I guess I'm willing to share."

"Okay." Christa held out the brush to me. "I'm a big fan of sharing, myself."

I took the brush from her and smiled when my fingers met hers on the handle. It was the first time we'd touched.

And I was certain it wouldn't be the last.

CHAPTER 3

"WHAT DID YOUR dad want?" Lori asked.

I was still grinning at Christa. "What?"

"Your dad? He took you outside for something?"

"Oh, yeah." I forced myself to turn toward Lori. "He wants us to make jewelry with the kids here. I told him we'd start after lunch today."

"'We'?" Lori paused her painting mid-brushstroke. "Who, you and me?"

"Yeah. He said we should do some kind of side project and I told him we already had the supplies. They're going to reimburse us."

"Oh. So we're doing this for the whole trip?"

"I don't know," I said. Christa had found another paintbrush somewhere and was dipping it into the pan. When she bent over I could see her bra strap peeking out from the neck of her tank top. "I guess?"

"All right." Lori looked out the window, studying the yard critically. "We can set up over there if someone can loan us a blanket for the kids to sit on. During lunch we'll need to go back to the old church to get supplies and plan what we're going to do. Will they give us a translator or something?"

"Um," I said. Christa was wearing sweatpants. How was it fair for anyone to look that cute in sweatpants? "I don't think so."

"So we're teaching a bunch of kids in a language we barely speak how to make the jewelry designs it took us two years to learn?" Lori narrowed her eyes.

Christa reached up to paint a new section of the wall. The movement made her tank top ride up. Her skin was tan under the hem of her white shirt. I could see her belly button. She'd drawn a star around it with a purple marker. I wondered how it felt to touch her there.

"Actually, never mind." Lori handed me her paintbrush. "I'm going to go see if they need help outside."

"See you later, Lori," Christa called after her.

"Yeah, see you."

I leaned down to dip Lori's brush into the pan, making sure to tap off the extra paint. When I glanced up, Christa was watching me. I looked away so she wouldn't see me getting flustered.

After a minute, I stood back up and we painted in silence. I snuck glances at Christa every so often. The third time I looked her way, she was watching me, too.

"I thought you'd be wearing another vintage T-shirt today," she said, nodding at my outfit.

"Oh, yeah. Well, actually the shirt I had on yesterday was from his 2014 tour so it isn't vintage, it's…" I trailed off before I said something totally nerdy. "But anyway, I don't have any of my other clothes here. They lost my suitcase on one of the planes."

"Oh, that sucks." Christa made a sympathetic face, her lips turned down. Once again, I wanted to touch her. "Let me know if you need to borrow anything. I mean, you're about two feet taller than me so my stuff probably wouldn't fit you, but still."

I imagined putting on Christa's sweatpants. My skin, right where hers had been.

I needed to change the subject before I had a total meltdown.

"That's a great beret," I told her.

"Thanks." She touched it, spreading the white paint farther along the side of the hat. "They said we should bring a hat, since we'd be painting, so I went to the thrift store. I thought this one was hilarious. I wear a lot of funky stuff, but I never heard of a bright pink beret before."

"Well, it's a raspberry beret," I said.

Christa blinked at me.

"You know," I said. "The Prince song?"

"Oh." Her smile faded. "Do you mean the singer Prince? The guy from back in the eighties or whenever?"

All right. Okay, so she wasn't a fan after all.

Well, most people our age weren't weirdo Prince obsessives like me. This didn't have to be a bad sign.

I recalibrated.

"Yeah." I tried desperately to think of something new to ask her. "So, um, did your parents make you come on this trip? Or did you beg them to let you? It seems like everyone's either one or the other."

Christa gave me a sudden sharp look. At first I thought I'd said something wrong, but then her face softened. "I guess it was my parents' idea. Pretty much whenever there's a church trip anywhere, whether it's counting cans at the food bank or painting walls in Mexico, they sign me on without even asking me about it first. All they care about is church."

"I hear you. My family's pretty hardcore about church, too."

"Yeah, I'd guess, with your dad being a youth minister and all."

"It's annoying. Some days I think I'd rather just be a heathen, you know?"

For a second Christa got that sharp look again, but then she laughed. "Most of my life consists of trying not to let my parents know about my heathen ways."

For some reason, that sounded really sexy. I flushed and looked away.

"How did they react when you got your nose ring?" I asked.

"They flipped. They tried to order me to get rid of it, but I refused, so they grounded me for two months. They thought I'd change my mind and take it out, but it was nothing I didn't expect. I mean, if I'm totally honest, the main reason I got it in the first place was to piss them off."

"Wow. You went through all that just to annoy them?"

"Well, at first. But now I think it's legitimately awesome." Christa turned so I could see the ring glint in the light from the window. It was really simple, only a little silver hoop, but it made her look amazing. Rebellious. Hot, too.

Okay, she probably would've looked hot anyway.

Crap, I was getting flustered again. I had to distract her so she wouldn't see what a fail I was.

"Are you allowed to get paint on it?" I asked her.

"I don't know. Probably not?"

"Then look out!"

I reached up with my paintbrush like I was aiming for her nose. She squealed and jerked back, reaching out to steady herself, so I tapped her bare elbow with the tip of my paintbrush. "Got you!"

"Hey!" she pulled her arm away, laughing. "What, are polka-dotted elbows the new trend?"

"Sorry! It was an accident." I held up my hands in fake

shock/apology. "Besides, I mean, you're into art, right? Consider it an artistic statement. An accidental one, I mean."

As soon as I'd said it, I wished I hadn't. I didn't want to remind Christa about the art thing. The guilt from my lie the night before rose up in my throat.

"Well, I suppose accidents do happen..." She lunged toward me with a cackle and painted a streak across my bare wrist. It looked like I'd been slashed by a snowman.

"That was *so* not an accident!" I tapped her cheek with my brush, leaving a tiny white dot. Behind it, she was blushing.

"Hey!" She shrieked and bopped her brush onto my nose.

"What are you guys *doing* over here?" We both turned, hiding our brushes behind our backs. My brother stood behind us, holding a dirt-caked shovel over his shoulder. He chortled when he saw me. "Sis, you look like a shrink-wrapped Rudolph."

I rolled my eyes at Drew and bit back a snappy reply. I was trying to be slightly less snarky to him than usual, which was hard.

Drew and I had always been close, especially when we were younger. But things changed when he left the private school we'd both gone to since kindergarten and transferred to the public high school. He liked going to school with more people, he said, and getting a chance to play on a bigger basketball team. He was always bringing his new friends home.

After I didn't get into MHSA, I asked my parents if I could transfer to Drew's school instead. They said no. Dad thought I wouldn't like it as much as Drew did, but I never knew how he was so sure about that. It wasn't as though *Dad* had gone there.

Drew's life in high school, as far as I could tell, was basically perfect. When he got to college, though, things changed. I hadn't realized how much until the day before in the Tijuana airport.

When we'd landed in Mexico and gone to pick up our bags, everyone had grabbed their suitcases off the turnstile right away except for me. The bags kept going around in their loop, and mine kept not showing up. Dad went ahead with the others and told Drew to wait with me until my suitcase showed up.

For a while my brother and I talked about the usual stuff. Dumb TV shows. Basketball. How annoying Dad had been on the plane with the way he kept trying to read out important geographical facts about whatever we were flying over— *The Gulf of Mexico didn't even exist until the Late Triassic period! Did you know that, kids?*

Then out of nowhere, Drew said, "Okay. Listen. I've got to tell you something."

I looked away. I was certain this would be more of the same.

After I didn't get into MHSA when I first auditioned at the end of eighth grade, everyone I knew—but Drew most of all—kept nagging me to audition again the following year. It would be my last chance, since MHSA didn't let anyone in after ninth grade.

They had tons of different programs—acting, singing, dancing, visual art, instrumental music—but I'd auditioned for the music composition program. I brought my electric guitar and played them the best piece I'd ever written. Then I got a callback where I had to sight-read and play my piece on the piano, which was harder. Two weeks after that, a slim envelope appeared in the mailbox with a single sheet of paper inside. "Although you show significant promise, we are unable to admit you to the Maryland High School for the Arts at this time." It might as well have said *You're a giant loser. Buh-bye.*

"You're amazing at guitar," Drew kept saying when this year's audition season was coming back around. "Why do you have to get in for composition? They have a regular music program. All you have to do is play them one of those Prince guitar solos you're always practicing at home. Those judges will throw down their stupid scorecards and *beg* you to come to their big nerdy art school."

I didn't bother explaining that there weren't judges or scorecards—just a single bored teacher with a simpering smile—or that the idea of getting into MHSA just to play an instrument made me want to cry. *Anyone* could play guitar. I'd been doing it since I was a kid, when I first picked up the choir director's old acoustic while Mom and Dad were in one of their endless meetings at church.

I loved playing, sure—I loved it even more once I started taking actual lessons, and especially once I started picking out my own songs on it for the first time—but I didn't want to get into my dream school for something that came so easily it was basically one step up from breathing.

I wanted to get in because I was special. I wanted to get in because I could do something, *create* something that no one else could. And I wanted to spend four years learning how to do it better.

Prince wrote a song every single day of his life. I'd only written a handful, but even my very best song wasn't good enough to get me past the starting line.

There was no way I was going to put myself through that a second time.

So that's what I thought Drew was going to talk about in the airport that afternoon. I thought he was going to berate me again for throwing away my greatest opportunity ever, blah blah blah.

I folded my arms and braced myself. Then he surprised me.

"This past semester wasn't so good," Drew said. "I didn't let anybody see my grades, but listen—Sis, they were bad. Really bad."

"What?" I'd known Drew had some problems with his first semester of college—he'd gotten a D in his required math class, which was weird because he'd always been good in school when he was younger—but he'd done okay in his other subjects. "How bad?"

"Academic probation bad." Drew swallowed. "I'm going to have to take pretty much everything over again."

"*Everything?* Are they holding you back?"

Drew shook his head. A new load of suitcases came across the belt, but my bag—purple with red flowers—was nowhere in sight. "It isn't the same as high school. You don't get 'held back.' But it's the same idea."

"Wow." I was still struggling to get my head around the thought of Drew failing. My brother had always won at everything he'd tried. "Dad is going to freak."

"You can't tell him, okay? Promise you won't tell him." I'd never seen that look on Drew's face before. Drew was usually a cheerful guy, always making other people laugh. But there was no trace of a smile on his lips now.

"Yeah, yeah, of course. So what are you going to do, take all the same classes when you go back again this year?"

"Maybe." He tugged on his ear. "If I go back."

It took me a second to understand what he'd said. When I got it, I whirled around to face him, the hunt for my suitcase forgotten. *"If?"*

"Calm down, Sis." Drew held up his hands. "You don't need to turn into a banshee on me."

"Are you talking about *dropping out of school*?" He might as well have said he was considering Satanism. All Mom and Dad had been telling us since birth—probably even longer; they probably told us while we were still in utero—was how important our educations were.

"I don't know." Drew ran a hand over the back of his head,

the way he did when he was anxious. Dad did that, too. "All I'm doing is considering my options."

I stared at him, my jaw on the floor. How long had he been thinking this? I'd thought I knew everything about my brother. I thought his life was golden.

"Listen, for real," he said. "Promise you won't tell Dad."

"Of course I won't." I was offended he'd even ask. Drew and I had been keeping each other's secrets forever. "But tell me when you decide, okay? And if you need help in math, I can tutor you."

Drew laughed and elbowed me. "I'm not getting tutored by my kid sister."

"Whatever, I'm better at math than you. Even college math."

"Yeah, okay, genius." Drew scanned the belt again. "Also, Sis, I hate to say this, but I don't think your suitcase is here."

"Oh…crap."

We went to the airline counter to tell them about my suitcase. Drew had to do most of the talking, since his Spanish was better than mine. Then Dad came back to check on us and we didn't have another chance to talk about what Drew had said.

But I kept thinking about it. My brother—dropping out of college? Mom and Dad would never let him. They'd *kill* him.

"We're priming the wall," I told Drew now, since I couldn't say any of that.

"Yeah, looks like it's getting there." Drew eyed our white patch, which still looked really uneven. "You're Christa, right? From Rockville? I'm Drew, Aki's brother."

"Hi." Christa stifled her giggles. She set her paintbrush back in the pan and tried to wipe the paint off her elbow. "I hate to tell you this, but your sister is kind of a meanie."

"Oh, I'm well aware." Drew grinned at her. Christa was still rubbing at her elbow. God, she was cute. "By the way, Sis, your clothes don't fit."

"They're Lori's clothes, genius."

"Right, your suitcase." Drew scratched his head. "I've got some stuff you can borrow if you want."

"Drew, you're, like, a guy."

"Oof. Harsh." He clasped a hand to his heart. I rolled my eyes again. Drew turned back to Christa and pointed to the patch of wall she'd been painting when I came in. "Hey, Christa, did you paint this section?"

"I sure did."

"I figured," Drew said. "It's the only part that looks halfway decent."

"Hey!" I reached out to swipe Drew with my paintbrush, but he stepped away in time.

"Come on, Aki's section looks great," Christa said. I beamed, even though she was totally lying.

"Had you painted before you came here?" Drew asked her.

"Yep. Well, I've painted one room, anyway."

"Your room at home?" Drew asked.

"No." Christa bent down and wiped her paintbrush on the edge of the tray. "I helped my boyfriend paint his room at his dad's house."

"Your ex-boyfriend?" I asked, thinking I'd misheard.

Christa stood up, biting her lip. "Uh, no. Current."

I dropped my brush. Paint splattered onto my pants. Drew jumped out of the way to avoid getting hit.

"Hey, you three!" one of the pastors from the West Virginia church called over. "No roughhousing!"

Christa stood up straight. When she called back to the pastor, her voice was totally different than it had been when she was talking to us. She sounded calm. Demure, almost. "We're very sorry, sir."

The pastor came over to us, looking with a frown at our uneven paint job. "I don't think it's really going to take all three of you to finish what's left of that wall. You two are Benny's kids, right?"

Drew and I nodded, keeping our sighs to ourselves. Preacher's kids never got a break.

"Come out here and we can get you to work on the ditch." The pastor nodded to Christa. "You can finish up that wall on your own."

"Yes, sir," she said, still in that strange voice.

Stop, I wanted to say to Christa. *Wait. Tell me what this means.*

"Come on, Sis," Drew said. Preacher's kids did as they were told.

I tried to catch Christa's eye before we left, but she didn't look my way. She'd already turned back to the wall.

She was out of sight long before I'd stopped shaking.

CHAPTER 4

I POKED THE rice with my fork. It looked like rice, anyway. It was hard to tell. There was all sorts of…*stuff* in it. Beans, and other things I didn't recognize.

Mexican food in actual Mexico, it turned out, wasn't anything like the Mexican food at Taco Bell. Everyone around me was gobbling down whatever was on their plates, but I preferred to be sure I knew what, exactly, I was putting in my mouth.

Lunch had been torture. We'd split up into groups and gone to the local families' houses to eat. A nice Mexican lady kept putting more and more food on the table in front of me, but all I could do was nibble on some corn. Then I'd gotten a lecture from Lori's aunt Miranda about being respectful of local cultures.

At least for dinner we didn't have to eat in people's houses. Instead we were sitting at a row of picnic tables near the church. A whole team of ladies had set out big bowls full of rice and vegetables and tortillas and stuff. It was really pretty outside at this time of day, right when the sun was going down. Beams of light shone through the scraggly trees that dotted the hillsides to the west. Plus, this time I didn't have to worry about getting a talking-to from a chaperone about what I was eating. The adults were at their own table, so far away we could barely see them.

A big pile of toast stood in the middle of the table, still in a plastic bread wrapper. I grabbed three slices. Maybe I could make it through four weeks in Mexico eating nothing but corn and prepackaged toast.

"Hi, Aki." Jake, the guy I'd met at the party last night, swung into the seat next to me.

"Hi." I tried to smile through my mouthful of toast crumbs, but I could feel my face arranging itself into an embarrassing half smirk instead. "Did your day go okay?"

"Yeah. I'm beat, though."

"I know. Me, too."

I tried again to smile, but it still wasn't easy.

I hadn't seen Christa all afternoon. Not since the "boyfriend" thing.

She'd *told* Lori she was into girls. Sure, maybe she was bi, but still—why had she been flirting with me last night if she already had a boyfriend?

All afternoon I'd worked outside, digging that stupid ditch with Drew and the others. When the work day ended I waited for Christa to come out so we could talk, but I never saw her. She must've been avoiding me.

I'd thought this summer was going to be when my life actually started to happen. Now I was right back where I'd started.

"I didn't know Benny was your dad," Jake said.

"Yep." I leaned over the table for more toast. "Want any?"

"Yeah, thanks. That stuff is great." Jake held out his empty plate. A fellow picky eater. "Hey, cool bracelet."

"Thanks." It was one I'd made last year, when Lori and I

were into embroidery. It was emerald with white stitching that said, *Music should be your escape.* "It's a Missy Elliott quote."

"Super cool," Jake said. I could tell he had no idea who Missy Elliott was. "So, he's going to be a delegate at the national conference, right? Your dad, I mean?"

I shrugged. "All I know is that he's going. He wanted to take some pictures to show there."

Dad, true to his word, had rounded up half a dozen girls from the local church for our first jewelry-making workshop. They'd been gathered on a blanket near the work site waiting for Lori and me when we got back from lunch with our supplies. Dad was already taking pictures. The girls were mostly around seven or eight years old, and I couldn't understand a single word they said. Lori managed to talk to them, though. She and I had taken the same Spanish class with the same teacher and gotten the same grades, but Lori was the only one who could say more than "¿Hola?" and actually have people understand her. We'd planned to make beaded safety-pin bracelets, but the girls had trouble getting the tiny beads we'd brought onto the pins, so Lori told them to stick with fastening the safety pins together to make loops. The girls loved it. They'd kept giggling and stringing safety-pin chains around my arms. One of them thought my baseball cap was so cool I wound up trading it to her for a safety-pin necklace.

The problem was, now we were out of safety pins and I had no idea what to make with them tomorrow. Plus, Lori was irritated with me. She'd had fun with the girls, but she kept complaining that she was having to do all the work since she was the only one who could talk to them. I thought I'd helped plenty, so whatever.

"No, he's definitely a delegate," Jake said. "He's on the list on the conference website."

"You got onto their website?" I put my toast down and

turned to Jake. "Do you get internet on your phone here? Can I borrow it?"

"No, I, uh." Jake scratched the back of his neck. "I printed out the list of delegates before I left home."

I smiled again. "You're really into this conference thing, huh?"

"Yeah, our little Jakey's a big old nerrrrrrrd," the guy sitting across from us said, dragging out the word in a way that I was sure he found hilarious. This guy looked older, maybe Drew's age, and he was wearing a T-shirt with an American flag on it, even though we weren't in America. "He'll talk to anybody who'll listen about that stuff."

I didn't like the way the guy was grinning at Jake. I didn't like the way Jake was staring down at his toast, either.

"Do you go to the church in Harpers Ferry?" I asked the guy across the table.

"Yep." He waved his fork at me. "I'm Brian."

"I'm Aki. I go to Silver Spring."

Brian frowned at me. "How do you spell your name?"

I sighed. "A-K-I."

"Oh," Brian said. "So it's Ahh-kee?"

I sighed again. This had been happening my entire life. I told someone my name, and they told me I was pronouncing it wrong.

It was my brother's fault. When I was born, he was four and still learning how to talk. (When I told people this story, I always said he was actually still learning how to talk now, but if Drew was nearby that was a good way to get a sharp elbow in my rib cage.)

My parents had just brought me home from the hospital. They put my baby carrier on the floor next to Drew and told him I was his new sister, Akina. Drew didn't even try to say my real name. He pointed at little me, turned to Dad, and said

"Ack-ee?" Apparently the way he said it was so cute, Mom and Dad decided to call me that from then on. Thus sentencing me to a lifetime of explaining myself to dudes like Brian.

"Ack-ee," I corrected him.

"Oh." Brian looked confused. I might as well accept that no one around this place was ever going to learn my actual name.

One of the nice Mexican ladies who'd served our meal came over to clear our plates away. I jumped up, ready to help her, but she laughed and put her hand on my shoulder, pushing me gently back onto the bench. The same thing had happened at lunch. I'd always been taught to help clean up when I was someone's guest. One more adjustment to get used to.

The sun was almost down. Seeing the church ladies in their dresses carrying our plates inside reminded me that I hadn't cleaned up after work today. None of us had, but still, I felt scuzzy and sweaty in my paint-spattered, too-small clothes.

(That was another thing Lori was annoyed at me for. I'd gotten paint and dirt on her clothes. But what was I supposed to do? I didn't have any of my own clothes, and everyone got paint and dirt all over *everything* today.)

I stretched my arms over my head. Once dinner was over we had to go to vespers. Every single night we were here, the chaperones would take turns leading us in prayers and songs so we could reflect on the work we were doing. I'd never been much for reflection, but I was a preacher's kid, and I could play along with the best of them.

"Hey!" I yelped suddenly. Someone was tickling my armpit.

At first I thought it was Brian, and I was ready to yell louder if I had to, but when I turned, Christa was there. "Oh. Sorry! Hi."

"Hi." Christa pulled her hand back. She was giggling again. "I couldn't resist. You do that a lot, you know?"

"What, stretch?"

"Yeah. Is it because you're tall? Do you need to flex your limbs and stuff?"

Christa was smiling, but I didn't smile back. I wasn't going to act as if everything was normal.

"No," I said. I decided to head her off before she could ask any of the other questions everyone always asked me, too. "And no, I don't play basketball."

"Sorry." Her smile faded. "I didn't mean to..."

"Hi." Next to me, Jake stuck out his hand. "I'm Jake. You're Christa, right?"

Christa's head swiveled toward him. "Uh, yep, that's me. Hi, Jake."

"Want to sit with us?" Jake scooted over on the bench to make room.

"No, thanks." Christa fumbled with her hands. "Listen, Aki, do you want to go somewhere for a second?"

I glanced around the table. Jake suddenly seemed very absorbed in his food. No one else was paying attention to us.

I followed Christa around the corner of the house. We couldn't go far, not with vespers in a couple of minutes.

The view back here was incredible. On the bus ride in from Tijuana the day before we'd mostly seen hills and sparse trees and a pretty, golden landscape. Since we'd arrived in this tiny town, Mudanza, we hadn't seen that much besides houses and churches. But now Christa and I were standing on the town's northern edge, with Mudanza on one side of us and empty country on the other. Ahead of us were hills, valleys and trees as far as the eye could see, with a painted pink sky to frame it all.

Christa was walking toward the hills now, into the last sliver of sunlight. It shone on her dark hair and reflected off her long bead necklace. She was wearing a fresh, clean T-shirt that clung to her body and jeans that looked brand-new and paint-free. She must've changed for dinner.

She turned around and smiled at me over her shoulder. "I missed you this afternoon. I mean, I wound up less covered in polka dots compared to this morning, so there's that. But it turns out painting by myself is way more boring than getting polka-dotted by cute girls."

I stood motionless. "You didn't tell me you had a boyfriend."

The smile fell from her face. We'd passed the peak of the hill. When I looked back, I couldn't see the rest of our group. We were alone out here.

"I—" She paused and took a breath. "I'm sorry. I didn't mean to tell you that way. It sort of slipped out."

"Slipped *out*?" How could she be so casual about this? And right after she'd said that thing about getting polka-dotted by cute girls that made my insides want to melt? "Who is he?"

"His name's Steven. He goes to a private school in DC. I met him at drama camp a few years ago. He's a really talented actor."

"Oh." I tried to stick my hands in my pockets, but Lori's track pants didn't have pockets. I stuck my thumbs in my waistband as though that was what I'd meant to do all along.

I didn't know what I was supposed to say. Christa had flirted with me, but it wasn't as if she owed me anything. If she'd flirted with me even though she had a boyfriend, he was the one who had a right to be annoyed about that, not me.

Plus, I wasn't exactly in a position to be self-righteous about telling the absolute truth. Not when I was still straight-up lying to her by acting like I still did music.

The boyfriend thing hurt, though. A lot.

We'd made it to a little valley between two rows of hills. They were sort of hills-slash-sand dunes, now that I looked closer, with trees scattered along the peaks. We couldn't even see the town behind us anymore. We'd barely come any distance at all, but it was as if we'd gone straight into the wilderness. It was cool enough that for a moment I stopped thinking about how upset I was.

"Wow," I said. "It's gorgeous out here."

The sun was almost down. Everything was gray and hazy. All I could see were sand and hills, trees and sky.

And Christa. She was gorgeous, too. She was biting her lip and brushing her hair out of her face and looking at me with her steady brown eyes and I wanted... I didn't even know what, exactly. I just *wanted*.

"You'd like Steven," Christa went on. "He's really smart and funny. Open-minded, too."

"Great."

"Yeah. We're actually a really modern couple. Steven hates all those old-school rules about how relationships are supposed to work, and I do, too."

"That's great." I wished she'd shut up about Steven.

"Everyone's stuck in this 1950s mentality," Christa went on. "As if people still 'go steady.' I mean, what a boring idea, that you're supposed to be with one person all the time and never so much as *look* at anyone else. Haven't we evolved past that as a culture?"

I was about to reach my breaking point with this conversation. "What are you talking about?"

Christa looked down at her hands. "The thing about Steven and me is that we're taking a break for the summer."

"A break?" I watched her closely. "What does that mean?"

"You know." She met my eyes for a second and then looked away, her shoulders shifting. "We don't believe in that old-fashioned rule about how you always have to be totally monogamous. It isn't human nature, you know? So, since I was coming down here, we decided we'd take the summer off from our relationship. So we could see other people for a little while. If we wanted to, I mean."

"Oh." *Ohhhhh.* "So you mean—he was your boyfriend up until this week, and he'll be your boyfriend once you get back home, but right at this moment, you're boyfriend-free?"

She nodded. "That's the general idea."

"Why didn't you tell me about him last night?" My annoyance was fading fast, but I tried not to let it show. This kind of changed everything.

She bit her lip. "I'm sorry. I should have. Steven and I agreed before I left town that we'd both be totally up front about the whole thing so no one gets the wrong idea."

"And what would the *right* idea be, exactly?"

She looked back up at me, her mouth set in a straight line. "The right idea would be…that even though I technically have a boyfriend, I could still like a girl. A particular girl, I mean."

My chest felt fluttery. Damn it. I was supposed to be mad at her.

Also, this meant Christa was definitely bi. The same as me. I'd hardly known any other bi people.

"I mean." She stepped closer. "You know my thing for artist types. Because as it happens, there's this one artist girl, a musician in fact, who I happen to like a lot. But only if she's okay with the temporary thing, since that's all I can do. And only if she likes me back."

This time, I was the one who looked down at my hands. She was being honest with me, but I wasn't being honest with her. She still thought I was an artist type, like her. And like the super talented actor that was Steven.

"Because the thing is," she went on. I glanced back up. She was still biting her lip. Was she nervous? Did Christa *get* nervous? "I mean, if that particular musician girl *did* like me back, then, well, we're here in this totally new place, where we hardly know anyone. Where we can basically start a whole new life, just for ourselves, just for these next four weeks. No one even needs to know about it. It could be our own private universe. And then once we get on the plane at the end of this trip, we go back to the real world."

Christa tugged at her shirt again. She looked so awesome, especially next to me in my paint-splattered pants. Had she changed her clothes because she knew she was going to see me?

I looked away again so she couldn't tell I was smiling.

Christa had a boyfriend. If we really did hook up, a little summer thing was all we could have anyway. We'd say goodbye at the end of the trip with no harm done. It would be a fling. Exactly like the one Lori and I had fantasized about that morning.

Maybe it wasn't even a big deal that I'd lied about my music. It wasn't as if Christa and I were getting married. For a summer fling, getting all the details right didn't matter quite so much.

This was my chance to see if I really liked girls. It would be an experiment. The coolest experiment ever.

Suddenly I felt very sophisticated. Or, as Christa had said, modern. Why *should* we have to stick to rules about monogamy that some old white guys made up a million years ago? We were young. We should be having fun.

Christa was looking at me expectantly.

"I…um…" I sounded horribly inarticulate after all that amazing stuff she'd said about universes. "It would be a total secret, right?"

Christa nodded. Good. I couldn't picture going up to Dad after he was done leading us in one of his long, rambling prayers at vespers and telling him I was bisexual. Or anything-sexual.

Come to think of it, we were probably already late for vespers. Oh, well.

Christa was still watching me. Waiting.

I took a step closer to her. She looked right at me. The smile was in her eyes as much as her lips.

Oh, God. We were going to kiss.

I thought I'd be nervous, but I wasn't.

I felt awesome, actually. Better than I remembered feeling in, well, ever.

So when Christa stepped toward me, I didn't wait. I leaned over and pressed my lips against hers.

I could feel her smiling as she kissed me back.

And...oh.

She tasted like the sky.

Kissing her felt sweet and strong and urgent all at the same time. As though we were made to kiss each other.

We didn't bump against each other awkwardly, the way I usually did with boys. Instead we kissed gently. Slowly.

I'd never kissed anyone that way before. As though it really meant something. I wasn't sure *what* it meant, exactly, but I didn't care.

After that things got kind of—well—intense. She ran her hands along my back. I played with her hair. It turned out the pink streak wasn't real. It was just clipped in, as I discovered when I accidentally pulled it out. We both giggled at that, but only for a second, because kissing required every bit of attention we had.

When we finally pulled apart, I felt breathless and raw, and it was getting dark. I should've been worried—we were late for vespers, and we were out in the middle of nowhere in a foreign country—but my heart was beating too hard to focus on anything but Christa.

She looked as if she felt the same way. Her cheeks were

flushed, and her eyes sparkled. Our arms were still wrapped around each other, and our breasts were touching through our clothes. I thought again about that bra strap poking out from her tank top earlier. I was getting flushed, too.

"We should go to vespers," I said. "Dad will notice if I'm not there."

"Okay."

But we didn't let go.

I closed my eyes, but I could still see the stars overhead.

"We should, um." I tried not to think about how she felt. "We should go."

We kissed again. And again after that.

The stars were all around us, spinning, whirling, carrying me off with them into the sky.

By the time we finally left those hills, kissing Christa was the only thing I ever wanted to do.

PART 2

If I Was Your Girlfriend

CHAPTER 5

"SO DID YOU full-on hook up or just make out?"

"Shut it, Lori!" I darted my head from side to side. No one was close enough to hear, but still. "Discretion, please!"

Lori laughed. "I need to know if it counts toward the tally. Three hookups, remember?"

"Well, this definitely counts as one."

"Mmm, I'm not sure. Did you only go to first base?"

I put my hands on my hips, tucking the ball of pale purple thread I was untangling into my palm. "That's none of your business!"

"Yeah, right." Lori laughed again.

She had a point. I'd been dying to tell Lori what happened ever since Christa and I stopped kissing last night. Actually, maybe even before that. I vaguely remembered looking forward to telling Lori about kissing Christa while I was still actively in the process of kissing Christa.

But I had to wait. By the time we got to vespers that night the meeting was already halfway over, and there was no chance to talk. Christa and I had slunk in through the shadows from the candlelight while Señor Suarez played hymns on a beautiful old twelve-string guitar. We'd kept our heads bent as if we were praying. Dad didn't say anything about it, so he must've thought we were there the whole time.

All through the prayers and the singing, it was impossible to act normal. I kept running my fingers over my lips and sneaking glances at Christa. She was glancing at me, too.

After vespers, we all walked back to the old church in a big group. Then we waited in line to use one of the two indoor toilets. (Everyone hated the porta-potties. Some of the guys had started peeing outside so they wouldn't have to wait in line. It was so gross.)

After that we went to bed in the dark again. All around us, people talked and laughed and acted as if it were any other night. For them, I guess it was.

Now, finally, I had my chance to tell Lori all the details. We were sitting on the blanket outside the work site. In a couple of hours we'd meet with the local girls and teach them a simple lanyard knot to make friendship bracelets. That should keep them busy for a few days at least. We had to sort the thread first, though. It had come out of Lori's suitcase pocket in a big tangled pile.

"It's weird," I said. "This is the first time I've ever seriously been into a girl, and the thing is, I don't remember ever liking a guy as much as I like her. So what's that about? I mean, I *could* be just as into a guy, right? I've been into guys before, but not this much. What I'm saying is, this doesn't mean I'm not bi anymore, does it?"

I'd never thought this much about what it really meant to be bi. I should probably be talking to Christa about it instead of Lori, since Christa would relate more, but I couldn't exactly analyze our relationship with *her*.

I'd already told Lori all about Christa's boyfriend situation, though, and Lori, at least, seemed to think it was perfectly normal. Apparently her mom was always watching some old TV show where couples were constantly taking breaks and having flings and fighting with their significant others about it. Once Lori told me that, I actually felt weirdly better about the whole situation.

"Well?" I asked Lori now. "What do you think?"

Lori looked up from the threads that wound between her fingers. "I've got to be honest, Aki, babe, I didn't quite follow all that."

"It's only—I should know by now, shouldn't I? If I'm straight or gay or bi or, I don't know, whatever? I mean, I'm fifteen already. If I haven't figured this out yet, am I ever going to?"

Lori frowned. "I don't know. I think I've always known I was straight. I never thought I might be anything else, at least. Well, there was that girl at camp one time who I thought I had a crush on but we were, like, eight, so..."

"Yeah, see? You're supposed to have always known. Crap. What if I never hook up with a guy again? Then how will I be sure?"

Lori put her thread down. "Don't you want to hook up with *her* again?"

"Oh, well I mean, yeah, of course. I'm only thinking ahead."

"Since we've only been here for a day, I'd recommend concentrating on the girl at hand." Lori poked through the pile to find the blue strands. "You know you're a total badass, by the way. Going to first base lesbian-style your very first day in an exotic land."

I grinned. "No one's ever called me a badass before."

"Get used to it, badass." Lori bumped my shoulder, making me drop the lanyard strands I'd been sorting. I bumped her back. "Now I've gotta get moving on my own end of the bargain so we can both be badasses."

"Yeah? With who? Paul?"

"No, actually, I'm—"

"Wait, Paul's a badass? Since when?"

A shadow loomed over us. I looked up slowly, worried one of the chaperones had caught us cursing.

Nope. It was Christa.

I beamed up at her.

"Hiiii." I could hear the breathiness in my voice but I was helpless to make it go away. Next to me, Lori chortled.

"Hiiii," Lori whispered so only I could hear.

I bumped her shoulder again. "Shut up."

"No, Paul's not a badass." Lori giggled. "We were just talking about how last night—"

"Shut *up*." I bumped her shoulder harder this time, but Christa didn't seem fazed.

"So, uh." Christa twirled a lock of hair around her finger. I still couldn't get over how cute she was. "What's with all the thread and whatnot?"

Lori told her about the jewelry project while I kept smiling dorkily.

"We're sorting this stuff now," Lori said when she was done explaining. "You can help if you want."

"Sure, totally." Christa dropped down next to us on the blanket. Her jeans were caked with dirt. She must've been working on the fence. I was trying to stay away from both dirt and paint since I'd had to borrow clothes from Lori again. But that meant I couldn't do any actual work, so I'd been alternating between setting up for the jewelry class and walking around acting as if I had somewhere to be.

Christa pulled some thread out of the pile and tried to straighten it out. I watched her hands move, her fingers running delicately over the strands. Her palm had a blue and purple design on it today. A sun and moon drawn in marker. It was cool that she did that sort of thing. She had a true artist's spirit. Not like me. I couldn't remember the last time I'd created something new.

I reached out and stroked her finger with mine. Then I got nervous—what if she thought that was weird?—and pulled away. I dipped my hand back into the pile to get more lanyard thread instead.

Christa reached into the pile, too. Her fingers slipped under the tangles of thread until her hand was touching mine.

I bit the inside of my cheek to keep from smiling too obviously. It didn't work.

"You guys." Lori laughed. "You are *way* too cute together."

"Lori! Shhh!" I tried to put my hand over her mouth, but she pulled away, laughing.

I gave Christa a sheepish grin. She snickered.

"I'm not a fan of the word *cute*," Christa said. "Little kids are cute. I prefer to associate myself with more mature words. Let's say *charming*."

"*Sweet*," I suggested.

"*Adorable*."

"*Delightful*."

"*Quixotic*."

"*Quixotic?*" I tilted my head down at her. "I don't think that means the same thing as *cute*."

"To be honest, I'm not sure exactly what it means, but it's a cool word anyway. You and me, we're the quixotic-est."

My chest got warm when she said that. Before I could think of a witty rejoinder, I saw a new figure coming toward us. Jake, with a paper and pen in his hand.

"Hey, you guys." He squatted down on the ground across from us. He looked nervous. "I came to see if you wanted to sign my petition."

"A petition? What's it about?" I craned my neck, but he was

holding the paper too far back for us to see. I'd signed online petitions before, but I didn't remember ever seeing an actual physical petition.

"It's for one of the planks they're voting on at the national conference," Jake said. "I'm trying to get a core mass of youth to sign on before I present it to the delegates."

"'A core mass of youth'?" I eyed Jake warily. I couldn't imagine getting worked up over anything that included the words *plank* or *delegates* or *national conference*. Social Studies class was my daydreaming time.

"Which plank is it?" Lori asked. Jake handed her the paper, and Christa and I leaned in to look.

Lori read it out loud. *"Resolved: To recognize and perform marriages between same-gender couples."* She looked up at Jake. "This is about gay marriage?"

"Yeah." Jake's head bobbed eagerly, but his hand trembled where he held the pen. "Holy Life is finally putting together an official, national policy on whether to perform wedding ceremonies for LGBTQIA people."

Lori counted the letters off on her fingers. "Lesbian, gay, bi, trans, queer—wait, is it queer or is it something else?"

"It's queer or questioning." Jake turned pink. "And inter-sex and asexual."

"I'll definitely sign that." Lori grabbed the pen and scribbled her name. "It's dumb that they're even having to vote on this."

Jake looked like he wanted to kiss Lori. "Thank you. Wow, thank you so much."

"Who else has signed it so far?" I asked.

"Well." Jake pointed down at the paper. There was only one name at the top of the list. "Just me, actually."

"Are we the first people you've asked to sign?" Lori frowned.

"Uh." Jake rubbed the back of his neck. "I asked some people from my church, but they weren't up for it."

"What, like that guy Brian from last night?" I shook my head. "Don't worry about him. He's a tool."

"I would never have asked Brian." Jake shook his head. "I asked Hannah, and Olivia, and Emma. None of them wanted to put their name down."

"What? *None* of them? That's so dumb." Lori waved a dismissive hand in the air. "Don't let them get to you. We'll all sign it."

"Uh." Christa drew back, hooking her thumbs into her glittered belt. "I'm really sorry, but I can't. If my parents found out, I'd be in huge trouble."

Lori stared at Christa, openmouthed. I did, too, at first. Then it occurred to me that maybe I should be careful myself. I didn't want to deal with my parents on this, either.

"Whatever," Lori said. "Everyone from our church will totally sign. Right, Aki?"

"Uh. I don't know."

I studied the petition in Lori's hand. I didn't exactly keep up with church politics, but even before I figured out I liked girls, I knew it was stupid for there to be rules about who could get married and who couldn't.

"I don't know if everyone will sign it," I said, reaching for the pen. "But I will."

Jake grinned. "You rock, Aki."

"Why does *she* rock?" Lori asked as I signed my name. "What about me?"

"You both rock, but it especially rocks for her to sign it 'cause her dad's a minister. And a conference delegate."

"So?" I handed the petition back to Jake. I was getting nervous now. Who did he plan on showing this to?

"It's cool, that's all." Jake tucked the petition back into his bag. "You sure you can't sign, Christa?"

"I'm sure." Christa climbed to her feet. Some of the glitter from her belt had fallen onto our blanket. It shimmered. "I'm going to see if they need help outside. See you guys later."

She left, and Jake followed her, waving thanks to Lori and me. As soon as they were out of earshot, Lori turned to me, her voice lowered to a whisper that was approaching a hiss.

"Why won't she sign the dang petition?" Lori looked incredulous. "You have to support gay marriage if you're a gay *person*, right?"

"I don't know," I said. "It's complicated. She doesn't want her parents to know."

"So what? Your parents don't know you're gay, but *you* signed it."

"I'm not gay," I whispered back. "I think maybe I'm bi, that's all."

"'Maybe'?" Lori whispered. "What, now that you've finally actually *done* something with a girl, it's 'maybe'?"

"No. I don't know." I sighed. "That's complicated, too."

"I don't see what's complicated. She's gay. She should sign a stupid gay rights petition."

"She's not gay. She's bi."

"You know what I mean."

"All I'm saying is, there's a difference." I dump the last lanyard threads into their piles. I was getting annoyed.

"I mean, okay." Lori looked halfway contrite. "I know. But I don't see what the big deal is about signing this petition thing."

"Well, yeah, because you're straight. You can't get what it's like for Christa and me."

Lori got quiet after that.

Soon the kids started showing up for our jewelry class, and Lori and I had to stop talking. But our class that day wound up being scary. We were halfway through teaching friendship knots when Guadalupe, one of the little girls, started hacking out of nowhere. I could tell it was an asthma attack because I'd seen the same thing happen to a boy at the clinic last year. That kid had sucked on an inhaler until he was fine, but when I looked around frantically for Guadalupe's inhaler, it turned out she didn't have one. I took her over to a cool spot under a tree and tried to soothe her until her breathing started to calm down a little. After that I tried to go find her parents but she wanted me to stay and help her finish her friendship bracelet instead. Kids were so weird.

For the rest of the day, Christa was super quiet. I could tell she was upset. I tried to talk to her at dinner, but she barely answered me. Eventually I gave up and sat alone at the long table, eating toast and acting as if I wasn't totally depressed.

Vespers was even worse.

Like the night before, we met in the minister's living room, piled on the floor in rows while the adults sat on the couches above us. First we watched the news on TV for a while, even though we couldn't understand it since it was in Spanish. The chaperones had this thing about us "not losing sight of what's happening in the wider world," but I thought it was mainly because they didn't have service on their phones, either, and they were desperate for information. That night, the news showed a sad story about some really young American soldiers who'd been killed overseas and how their families back home were coping. We all got depressed even without totally understanding what the news anchors were saying.

I think the chaperones must've realized the news was kind of a downer, because Dad turned the TV off quickly and went straight to leading prayers and songs by candlelight. The local minister's wife, Señora Perez, was trying to teach us songs in Spanish while Señor Suarez played his gorgeous old guitar. That part might've been kind of fun if I wasn't sitting right across from Christa. She studiously looked around in every direction but mine.

"Let's sing 'If I Had a Hammer,'" Dad said from the couch. The other adults in the room laughed. The rest of us groaned. "If I Had a Hammer" was this old, boring song that people like my grandad loved.

We started off in those droning voices you have to use when you sing old-people songs. When we got to the end of the first verse, Drew hopped to his feet and went to stand next to Señor Suarez. When the second verse started—it's about what you'd do if you had a bell instead of a hammer (I told you this song was dumb)—Drew held up one hand as if he was dangling a bell, then pretended to whack the invisible bell with a stick. We all giggled through our singing. As the song went on, Drew kept banging on the bell, and his gestures got more and more elaborate. He pranced around the room while everyone laughed even harder. I rolled my eyes so hard they nearly fell out of my head when Drew got to the next verse, about what you'd do if you had a song, and he started waving his arms dramatically, opera singer–style. Everyone was laughing so hard they could barely sing.

Everyone except me. I watched Drew carefully, and after the first verse, I could tell his heart wasn't in this little show.

There was something behind his smile. A glimpse of what I'd seen that day in the airport.

He wasn't enjoying this. He was only playing the part.

He made everybody else believe it, though. Dad was watching Drew with an indulgent tilt to his head. If I'd acted like that much of a fool during vespers, Dad never would've let me hear the end of it.

Drew's life had been perfect when he was my age. He'd done well in school, he'd had a ton of friends, he'd played ball, and he'd always been grinning about something. But all that had changed when he started college. I should've figured out that something was up, but I hadn't even known there was a problem until he broke down and told me. I was too obsessed with everything that was wrong in my own life. I hadn't even really thought about Drew's.

It hurt, now, to think about what a bad sister I'd been. I turned away so I couldn't see him.

Maybe by accident, or maybe not, my eyes landed on Christa.

This time, she was looking at me, too.

She looked away just as fast. But I knew I hadn't imagined it.

Dad dismissed us when the song was over, and we all climbed to our feet and started down the dark path to the old church. Everyone was still laughing and talking about how hilarious my brother was. I walked with Lori and our friends, but I never stopped watching Christa. She was walking alone at the edge of the group.

Above us, the open field of stars stretched for millions of miles. Trillions.

In two minutes, we'd be inside the church, under the dark, thick ceiling with everybody else. We'd use our shaky flashlight beams to find our spots. On the girls' side of the room, everyone had laid their sleeping bags perpendicular to each other so our feet wouldn't wind up in each others' faces. It hadn't worked. Worse, now that we'd been here for a few days, I was smelling more than feet.

I didn't want to be in that room. I wanted to stay out here. Under those stars.

With Christa.

We were almost at the church by the time I screwed up the courage. I tried to act casual, sidling up next to her with my hands tucked into the pockets of my borrowed jeans.

Christa glanced at me, but didn't say anything.

"Hey," I said.

She didn't meet my eyes. "Hey."

After another minute of walking in silence, I said, "Did I do something wrong?"

"No."

"Is this because of Jake's petition? Are you annoyed that I signed it?"

"No." She looked away. "I wish I could have."

"Well." I didn't know what to say. I wished she'd signed it, too. "Do you seriously think your parents would find out?"

"I don't know." She shrugged. "But they could. It's easier when I'm at home. They don't have a reason to question whether I'm straight or not, you know? But with me down here..."

Right. She meant that back home, her dumb boyfriend Steven made her life easier.

I didn't want to hear any more about how great Steven was. It felt as if she'd picked him over me before I'd even had a chance. Maybe she thought I wasn't worth bothering with after all. The most we ever could've had was a summer fling, after all.

I was so frustrated I could've yelled. Instead I swallowed hard.

Maybe this was going to be it for me. One night. One kiss. That was the whole story of my big summer lesbian experiment.

"Well if your boyfriend's so great, what am I even doing here?" I said.

"Shhh." Christa wrapped her arms around her chest and swiveled her head from side to side. Checking to see if anyone was listening, probably. I tried to think back to see if I'd said anything incriminating.

Wait, though—*incriminating*? Not wanting your family to

know was one thing, but Christa was acting as though there was something wrong with just talking to me. Even though the night we'd met, she'd been the one acting all flirty.

"This isn't about him," Christa whispered. "We're taking a break, remember? I'm only saying that it's really convenient when I don't have to worry about my parents finding out I'm, you know, not completely straight."

"Would it be so terrible if they did? I mean, they're going to have to know eventually, right?"

I realized as I said it, though, that her parents *didn't* have to find out, not ever. That was the thing about being bi. If Christa only ever told them about going out with guys, she really could keep it a secret forever.

I guess that was true for me, too. I'd been thinking of coming out to my parents as inevitable, but maybe it wasn't. Maybe I could stay hidden, too, if I wanted to.

Did I want to?

"You don't understand." Christa turned to look me right in the eyes. "My parents aren't cool the way your dad is. After I first got my period, my mom sat me down and gave me a speech about how I had to make absolutely sure I never had sex, because if I got pregnant, they wouldn't support me. That's literally what she said. 'We won't support you.'"

Wow. I couldn't imagine my parents saying anything that awful. Not that they'd love me getting pregnant or anything, but they'd help me if it happened, I was sure of that much. "Have they said specific stuff about what would happen if you were gay?"

"No, but I can guess. They won't let my brother and me watch any shows with gay characters, even stupid sitcoms. They say shows like that 'promote an amoral agenda.' Once when I posted a photo I took of a crowd on the Fourth of

July that had two men holding hands in the background, they confiscated my phone and took down my whole Instagram account until I promised to delete the picture."

"Wow. I'm sorry. That's really awful."

"Yeah. That's why I'm so obsessive about this stuff. If they found out I liked girls, they might—I don't even want to guess. Ground me forever? Refuse to pay for college? Honestly, I don't know, and I really want to make sure I don't find out."

Now I felt bad for being annoyed at her.

We were almost at the entrance of the church. Only a few people were still outside, and they were all way too engrossed in their own conversations to listen to us.

"Look." My heart was pounding so hard it was embarrassing. "I— Look, you know... I like you, okay? And it's okay if you don't actually like *me* that much. I mean, I know you already have a boyfriend and everything—it's only that last night I thought maybe you kind of did, you know, like me. So..."

Christa stopped walking. I stopped, too. She stared at me.

Then she looked around. Almost everyone had disappeared into the darkness of the church.

Christa grabbed my hand and ran, pulling me behind her.

I stumbled after her, trying to figure out what she was doing, trying to figure out how to ask. Then she pulled me behind the dark church wall and kissed me, hard.

It was totally different from our kisses the night before. Those had been slow and warm and sweet.

This one was fierce. Visceral.

It took me a second to start kissing her back, but once I did, I couldn't stop. She was delicious. She was incredible. And for that moment, she was all mine.

She pushed me against the cement wall. It was hard and cold against my back. Somehow that felt incredible, too.

We were crushed together, her hand tight on the back of my neck, my hand on her hip holding her in place. I'd never kissed anyone like this before. As if I was kissing her with my whole body.

Somewhere in the back of my brain, I knew that anyone could walk out and see us at any moment. That idea only made me wrap my arm around her waist and hold her even closer.

She slid down so she was kissing my neck, moving back to my ear. The sudden shock of air on my lips was so intense that I had to do something. Say something. I murmured, low, unintelligible words. I wasn't even sure what they were. *Oh, my God,* maybe.

That tiny murmur must've been what snapped her out of it. Christa pulled back a few inches, her eyes blinking into consciousness.

I gazed back at her. I don't know how my face looked—I felt lost, dazed, unfocused—but hers was beautiful.

Her eyes tore away from mine, darting left, then right. There was no one around.

"We should go someplace else," Christa whispered.

I nodded. "There are hills around here, too."

So we walked out into the dark hills that rimmed the town. I reached for her hand, the muscles in my fingers twitching, afraid she'd pull away.

She didn't. She jumped as I slipped my hand into hers, but then she intertwined her fingers with mine and squeezed.

And somehow, it was everything, that single squeeze.

That squeeze meant I hadn't made this up in my head. This weird thing that I felt—I didn't know what it was exactly, but now I knew she felt it, too.

We climbed the hill into the little valley. Our little valley. I slipped my arms around her neck and she kissed me, again, slower and lighter than before.

We didn't need to hurry. We had all the time there was.

Maybe—just maybe—this wasn't only an experiment. Maybe this was something else altogether.

Maybe it was even something real.

CHAPTER 6

"¡OYE, MIRA POR AQUÍ!"

"¡Volver!"

Two boys, maybe nine years old, were shouting to each other across a dusty street, kicking a soccer ball back and forth between them. A third boy joined in and they took off down the block. My friends and I ducked out of the way just in time to avoid getting slammed by either a ball or a kid.

"Ah-ki!" someone shouted. At first I thought it was one of the girls from our group—half of them still pronounced my name wrong—but it was Juana Suarez from our jewelry-making class. We'd started having lunch at the Suarezes' house every afternoon, and Juana's mom was an amazing cook (that was according to Christa—I was still mostly sticking with my toast). Her dad played the guitar for us at vespers, and he was teaching Juana to play, too. She'd explained that to Lori and me one afternoon by singing a hymn and accompanying herself on air guitar. It had been adorable, but I'd had to resist the urge to correct her technique.

"Hola, Juana." Now that I'd been in Mexico for a week, I

could say a few words in Spanish without feeling like a complete fail. "¿Cómo estás?"

"Bien." Juana didn't seem to think my speaking two complete sentences in Spanish was quite as big a deal as I did. She grabbed my hand and tugged me toward where the other kids were playing in the street. "¡Vamonos!"

I laughed and swatted away a buzzing mosquito. "No puedo." I pointed to the light blue dress I was wearing, trying to show her that I didn't want to get it dirty. Which was true. I'd borrowed it from Lori, and it was the first time all week I'd worn something that I didn't expect to get covered in paint.

Juana pouted at me for about half a second. Then she dropped my hand and ran after the ball.

I laughed again. Then I must've forgotten where I was, because I started to reach for Christa's hand. At the last moment I settled for smiling at her instead.

We were walking into town with a dozen or so people from different youth groups. It was Saturday, and we had the morning off. This afternoon we had to be back at the Perezes' house for some kind of dance performance, but for now, we were free.

We hadn't really gone anywhere but the old church, the work site and Reverend Perez's house the whole time we'd been in Mudanza. The town was small, but still big enough to get lost in, so the chaperones had told us to make sure we traveled in groups today. In the few blocks we'd come so far, all we'd seen were a lot of gravel roads and squat buildings with pink walls and corrugated metal roofs. Oh, and two more churches.

Christa and I were near the front of the group. She had two cameras hanging from her neck, a fancy digital one and an old-fashioned one that took black-and-white photos. She'd worn a dress today, too—it was black and fit snugly around her waist—with three strands of gold Mardi Gras beads wound around her wrists.

Most of the girls in our group had dressed up. It was the first chance we'd had since the welcome party to look halfway decent. I'd even borrowed some of Lori's mascara. I didn't wear makeup much back home, but now that I was sort of dating someone, I figured I ought to make an effort.

Except Christa and I weren't dating. She was already dating someone else. The two of us had just been sneaking off into the hills behind the church to hook up on a nightly basis.

Well, but still.

"Hey, puppy!" Lori called out to a dog trotting along the sidewalk near us. Christa stopped walking and lifted her camera to take the dog's photo. Lori stooped to pet it, but it ran away before she could get close.

"I wouldn't pet any stray dogs in Mexico," said Sofía, one of Drew's friends. She was tall, Hispanic and intimidatingly pretty. "You never know who's got rabies."

"You can tell if dogs have rabies," I said. "They foam at the mouth and stuff."

"Not always," Sofía said.

"Yeah, you can't always tell with dogs," Drew echoed. I was positive Drew didn't know if that was true any more than I did, but I knew how it was when you liked a girl.

"There's a chicken up ahead," Christa said, clicking away on her digital camera. I thought she was kidding, but I looked and, sure enough, a chicken was wandering around between two houses. Just hanging out, as if it had nothing better to do. "Should we check it for diseases to be safe? You never know with chickens."

Lori and I laughed. Drew covered his mouth, but I was pretty sure he was laughing, too.

We'd reached the end of the block, where the kids were kicking the soccer ball around. Two of them stopped playing and turned to watch us.

I wondered how we looked to them. A huge gang of mostly white people walking along their dusty road on a Saturday morning, all dressed up as if we were going to a party.

"Sure, I'll sign it," Gina said behind us. At first I thought she was talking to me—Gina went to our church back home, and she hung out a lot with Lori and me—but when I turned, she was talking to Jake. "You got a pen?"

"Yep. Thanks, Gina. You're awesome." Jake passed her a pen and paper. Gina stopped walking and held the paper against the nearest pink wall, scribbling her name on it.

"I thought it was mostly over," Becca said to Jake. I'd only talked to Becca once or twice before. She was white, and she went to Christa's church. "The war, I mean."

"We still have troops stationed over there," Jake said. "The plank they're voting on calls for us to withdraw all US military from the region except humanitarian aid missions."

I interrupted them. "Wait, is this a different petition from the one before?"

"Yeah." Jake pointed to the paper. "This one's on whether Holy Life will officially call for an end to the war. Want to sign?"

"Wait, it's my turn next." Becca took the pen from Gina. Jake grinned.

"Are you still doing your other petition?" I asked him.

"Yeah, but this one's gotten way more signatures." Jake looked massively pleased with himself. I was impressed, too. I hadn't thought many people would be willing to sign a petition over something as random as church policy.

"What's the other petition on?" Gina asked.

"Marriage," Jake told her. "There's a plank to make it so Holy Life ministers can perform same-sex weddings."

"They can't already do that?" Becca handed the pen to another guy so he could sign. Jake looked happier than I'd ever seen him.

"They can, but it isn't officially recognized by Holy Life national if they do," Drew said.

It was weird to hear my brother talking about this. He'd had a ton of friends in high school, but none of them were gay. Or if they were, he hadn't mentioned it.

Maybe that was why I hadn't told him about Christa. I was used to telling Drew pretty much everything—I'd even told him about the dumb pact Lori had gotten me to make, about both of us having a fling this summer, and I'd stood there and acted like it didn't bother me when he laughed so hard his face looked about to fall off—but I'd kept this part secret. I didn't know how he'd react. His whole high school world was all about super hetero dates with pretty girls and parties with his ball-playing friends. When I was a kid I used to be so jealous.

Maybe I still was. It was frustrating sometimes, going to my tiny school where I'd known everyone since we were little. My plan had always been to transfer to MHSA for high school, but then I got rejected.

I'd dreamed of spending my high school years becoming a real musician. Instead I wasted ninth grade doing nothing but hanging out with Lori, doing the same things we'd always done.

I wasn't a kid anymore. I was running out of time to start doing cool things.

Well, I was doing something this summer, at least. I smiled at Christa, who was adjusting something on her black-and-white camera. She glanced up and met my eyes. Then we both ducked our heads before anyone could notice.

"I heard they aren't sure if the marriage plank is going to pass," Sofía said. "There's a lot of controversy."

"That's ridiculous." Lori huffed. "Why does anyone even care if gay people get married? What business is it of theirs?"

"Well, it's caused big problems for some denominations," Jake said. "Whole national church groups have split in half because they couldn't agree on whether to recognize same-sex marriages."

"For real?" I'd never heard that before.

"Yeah." Drew looked at me like I was dumb. "It was all over the news a few years ago."

"Jeez," Gina said. "How do you guys think your dad's going to vote on it?"

"Uh." I had no idea. I knew Dad would vote to end the war—he and Mom hated everything to do with the military; they'd even tried to get a religious exemption to keep Drew from having to register for the draft when he turned eighteen—but I'd never heard him talk about the marriage thing.

Drew shrugged at Gina. "I don't know."

"A lot of black people don't support gay marriage," Becca said. "Church people especially."

Everyone got quiet then. I had no idea what Becca was talking about.

"My dads told me that," she said, when she realized we were all staring at her. "They're gay, so they should know."

"That's completely not true," I said. "And if your gay dads told you that, they—"

"Hey, I think this store sells that toast you're so obsessed with." Christa tapped her finger on my arm kind of hard. That was the most she'd ever touched me in front of other people, so it was enough to shut me up. "Want to go see?"

She was right. We were in front of a tiny grocery store with a sign in the window for the brand of toast I'd been eating to the exclusion of almost everything else since we'd come to Mexico.

"Okay," I said. Becca was eyeing me. I really wanted to keep talking about her dads (and to ask what it was like to have gay dads in the first place), but Christa was probably right. That conversation wasn't going to end well.

The store was tiny. When Christa and I ducked inside, we took up nearly all the available space. A woman was sitting behind the counter, reading a newspaper. I smiled and said, "Hola," but I was too anxious to try to say anything else.

The store definitely sold toast, but I didn't see the point in buying any since our hosts put it out at every meal we ate. It felt like we should buy something, though, so Christa found a pack of ponytail holders and went up to pay, fumbling in her purse for the pesos we'd all gotten at the airport. I walked around, gazing at the shelves of canned vegetables, then caught a reflection in the store window that said *Salud*. *Salud* meant *health*. I turned around.

Across the street was yet another one-story cement building. A stone fence stood around it, and the front of the building was plain except for the painted words *Casa de Salud* above the door. In my head, that translated to *house of health*, but it probably sounded cooler in Spanish.

The name made it sound like the building was some kind of doctor's office, but it didn't look anything like the clinic where I'd volunteered back home. This place looked old and deserted.

I'd seen doctors' offices in Tijuana when we drove in from the airport. They'd looked pretty similar to doctors' offices back home—neat and shiny, with giant signs announcing the doctors who worked there and what their specialties were, in Spanish and English.

Maybe there was a big, shiny doctor's office in some other

part of Mudanza. I was still curious about the Casa de Salud, though.

"I'm all set." Christa pocketed her ponytail holders. "Sure you don't want to grab some toast, seeing as how nothing else in the whole country is edible for you?"

"Oh, whatever. Listen, do you want to go check out that building across the street?"

"What? Oh, uh." Christa craned her neck to read the sign, then looked at me quizzically. "Sure."

"I only want to stick my head inside. See how it looks."

Christa reached for her digital camera and followed me across the street, through the opening in the stone fence and up to the front door of the Casa de Salud.

The door swung open. Christa lowered her camera. Inside, the building looked just as old as it had outside, but it was far from deserted. In fact, all I could see no matter which way I looked were people, waiting. There must've been at least thirty of them, mostly women and kids, swatting at the mosquitoes that buzzed around them.

There were only a few chairs, so most people were sitting on the floor or standing. At first I couldn't see what they were waiting for, but then I spotted a desk strewn with papers in the far corner of the room. Behind it was a door that must've opened into another room. A young woman in a button-down shirt sat behind the desk, talking to a woman with a baby on her lap. The baby was crying. The woman behind the desk was trying to explain something, but the woman with the baby was arguing with her. I wished I could understand them.

An older woman came up to Christa and me, speaking rapid Spanish. She was wearing a stained gray sweatshirt and holding a jar of bandages, and she didn't look particularly happy to see us. I dipped my head in an apology and murmured "Lo siento" before backing out the door with Christa.

"Did you see any medical equipment in there?" I asked when we got outside.

"Some bandages, I think?" Christa glanced back over her shoulder. "Most of the equipment was probably in the other room. That must be where all the doctors and nurses are."

I had a feeling that wasn't the case.

The clinic where I'd volunteered back home wasn't anything fancy, but it was neat and mosquito-free. And it had rooms full of equipment. Machines that the orderlies wheeled around. Drawers and drawers full of medicine and syringes.

I didn't know what to think of any of it. Maybe I should ask Dad. He probably understood it all better than I did.

"I think we lost them." Christa pointed up the street. We could still see the rest of our group, but they were so far ahead of us now, we couldn't tell who was who.

I didn't actually mind, though. There was only one person I'd been looking forward to spending time with today, and she was standing right in front of me.

"Well." I turned to meet Christa's eyes. "If they're that far off, I guess there's no point trying to catch up."

Christa smiled.

"I'm quite confident," she said, "that we can have a lot more fun on our own."

CHAPTER 7

WE SPENT THE rest of the morning exploring the town by ourselves, stopping so Christa could take photos whenever we saw something interesting. And now that I was actually paying attention, there was a lot of interesting stuff. Mudanza was beautiful, with the hills in the distance and wide, open streets. Everyone we saw smiled and waved at us. One man even tipped his hat. When Christa asked a few women standing in front of a shop if she could take their photo, they beamed and twisted into so many different poses Christa finally had to tell them she was running out of storage space on her camera.

I asked her questions about the photos she was taking, and it turned out that was really interesting, too. She had a whole method she'd learned from classes and from reading tons of articles online.

"This camera shoots on film," she told me, holding up the old black-and-white camera. "I only have so much film, so I have to be really choosy about what I shoot. I'm using it for artsier shots, where there are cool shadows and stuff. Those are the ones I want to print out and play around with in the darkroom once we get back home."

"Darkrooms are still a thing?"

"Yeah! I mean, not many are still around, but my school has a tiny one in the art department. They have a way fancier one at the school I wanted to go to, but my parents wouldn't let me apply. Hey, did you ever think about going there? Your parents would probably be cool with it. It's called MHSA, the Maryland High School for the Arts. It's a public school, so it's free, but you have to apply, and they only take the very best. They have lots of different programs. Visual art, theater, music."

Sweat broke out along the back of my neck. I should've known this might come up. "I, uh…"

I could tell her the truth. This would be the perfect time to tell her the truth.

But I didn't want her to know I was so bad at writing music that I hadn't even gotten in. Besides, I'd have to admit I'd lied to her, and right when things were going so well between us.

Plus, why did it even matter? We were only having fun. She didn't need to know my whole life story.

"I've heard about it, but I decided not to apply." I rubbed at the sweat on the back of my neck, but that didn't help because now my palms were sweating, too. "I read that their music program was all about rote learning and that it totally stifled creativity."

I actually had read that, after I got my rejection letter. On a message board for other people who'd gotten rejection letters, too.

"Oh, that's too bad." Christa seemed to believe me. Whew. "Hey, do you want to go into any of these shops here? I think we're right in the middle of town."

We were walking down a little strip lined with stores on both sides. I nodded and we went into a couple of them. One was another grocery-type store. One looked like a bookstore but it turned out to have nothing but religious pamphlets, in

Spanish, of course. There was a tiny shop that had a sign about computers and internet, and Christa nearly hyperventilated at the idea of getting on Instagram, but it was only open in the afternoons. I asked Christa if she wanted to chat with Steven the next time we could get online, but she shook her head.

I wondered if she'd tell him about me someday. I wondered how I'd feel if she did.

We saw more kids playing in the street, too. All the kids seemed to play in the street here, even though I couldn't see their parents anywhere. There were hardly any cars driving around, though, so it was probably all right.

I asked Christa what music she was into.

"You're going to think it's horribly uncool," she said. "You know about all the funky, different music, and all I know is what comes up on my playlists."

"That's okay," I said. "I swear I don't judge musical taste. *Any* musical taste."

"Okay, fine." She covered her face with her hand. "Don't laugh, but my all-time favorite is… Taylor Swift."

She peeked out between her fingers, like she thought I was going to make fun of her.

"I think Taylor Swift is awesome," I said honestly. "I mean, I think pretty much all music is awesome, but she's got some great stuff. I especially love her early songs, when she was still country."

Christa wrinkled her nose. "I never listen to those. Country music is so cheesy."

"No, no, there's a lot of really cool country music out there. Here, listen."

I pulled up one of my country playlists and held my phone up between our ears. For a while we walked along quietly, each of us straining to listen through my phone's tiny speaker.

It was too hard to walk and listen at the same time, so we gave up after a few minutes, but that was okay.

"So is that your favorite kind of music?" she asked. "Country?"

I laughed. "No, but the truth is, I don't really have a favorite kind of music. Just favorite artists."

"Who's your all-time favorite? Do you have a playlist for that, too?"

I hesitated. Talking about Prince felt weirdly personal. No one ever seemed to understand why his music mattered so much to me. Hardly anyone knew what my favorite song was—only Mom and Dad and Drew, since I played it so much there was no way they could avoid it. It was the song I'd listened to the night we arrived, when I'd danced alone out in those hills before Lori dragged me back to the party.

"I don't have one all-time fave." Ugh. The more I lied to Christa, the more I hated myself for it. "But what else are you into besides Taylor Swift?"

Christa told me more about the music she listened to while she cooked or worked in the darkroom. It was all dance music, the kind I rocked out to when I was alone, too. Soon Christa was pulling up the songs on her phone and singing along while we both howled with laughter.

Talking about music seemed to make something shift between us. Soon we started talking about our actual lives back home, which we'd never really done before. It was the first time we'd hung out together when all we could do was talk.

Christa asked me how it was being a preacher's kid. I told her about how everyone always thought I was totally innocent and boring, and I asked about her family. Both Christa's parents had gone to Princeton, and now they worked for the federal government.

"Their work hours are totally bizarre," she said. "They almost never both make it home for dinner on the same night."

I couldn't imagine that. Both my parents worked from home most of the time. They were always around. "Is it weird?" I asked her.

"Nah. My brother and I are used to taking care of ourselves. Plus, this way I don't have to worry about anybody looking over my shoulder."

We talked about school. I wasn't surprised to hear that her huge public high school was really different from my tiny school—pretty much every school was—but I was surprised when she talked about how competitive things were, like grades and sports.

"We didn't even have tryouts for lacrosse at my school," I told her. "The coach knew I could play from gym class so she asked if I wanted to join the team."

"I barely made it onto the softball team last year," Christa said. "Then I wound up quitting because I hurt my shoulder. But it was okay because that way I could get my nose ring without having to worry about getting hit in the face with flying sports equipment. Besides, I was never that into softball. It's such a stereotype, you know?"

"Wait, what's the stereotype?"

"You know, how all lesbians are supposed to play softball and listen to the Indigo Girls. As though we can't be into whatever we want, the same as anybody else. Not that I'm a lesbian, but you know what I mean."

"Oh." I hadn't known that stereotype was a thing. I'd listened to the Indigo Girls when I was in elementary school and going through my nineties phase. Had that meant something? "Yeah, I mean, obviously."

"Besides." She sighed. "Everyone at my school is obsessed

with doing every activity so they can put it on college applications."

"College. God, I've barely even thought about it yet."

"It's all my parents will *let* me think about. When I was a kid, I told them I wanted to be a chef when I grew up, but they told me cooking is a hobby, not a career. It's the same with photography. They want me to keep taking photos, especially when there are contests I can win because they think it'll look good on college applications. But according to them, if I don't have a perfect grade point average every semester, I might as well give up on everything else."

"That sucks. I'm sorry."

"Thanks." Christa shrugged. "It'll be nice to go away somewhere, though. Start fresh. Mom and Dad want me to go to an Ivy. Well, really they want me to go to Princeton. They keep talking about how two women Supreme Court justices went there, but as far as I can tell, being a judge only means having to wear seriously ugly robes and be mad at everybody all the time. Anyway, I don't care where I wind up for college as long as it isn't too close to here. I mean, to home."

"Yeah, I know what you mean. Lori's mom is always trying to get her to go to UMD, but she wants to go somewhere warm, like Florida."

"Florida could be fun. Or California."

"Wow. I've never been that far from home. Until now, I guess. Have you?"

"No, this is the first time I— Hey, wait." Christa looked up at me suddenly, in that way she did that made me feel light inside. "Stop right where you are. Don't move."

"What?" I froze. Was there a snake nearby?

"For real, don't move." Christa lifted the black-and-white camera to her eyes, and I relaxed.

"I never said you could take my picture," I said, but I was teasing, already making my usual selfie smile.

"I never ask." She smiled, too, and snapped the camera thingie. "Okay, this time don't smile. Stand the way you were standing before."

I tried to remember how I was standing before, but I hadn't been paying attention. She must have thought I did it right, though, because she snapped the camera thingie two more times. I remembered what she'd said about only taking a few shots with that camera because she didn't want to run out of film, and I preened a little, knowing she'd used three whole shots on me.

"Let's get a photo of both of us together," I said. "We can use your other camera if you want to save film."

"Oh, no." Christa made a face. "I don't believe in selfies."

"You don't?" I'd never heard anyone say that before. Even my dad, who thought the word *selfie* was hilarious, was a huge ham who'd steal the phone out of my hand to snap a photo of himself holding a foot-long hot dog he'd just grilled. When I finally got my phone back, I'd have to go through and delete them all. My father was seriously so embarrassing.

"It's almost impossible to make selfies come out right," she said. "Framing *is* photography, and you can't frame a shot if you can't even hold your arm steady."

"You should get a selfie stick!"

I grinned. Christa gave me a mock-withering look, then grinned back. "I'm going to pretend you didn't just say that and change the subject. How long have you and Lori been friends?"

I laughed. "Forever. Or since fifth grade, anyway. That was when Lori moved to Maryland. Her aunt Miranda went to our church, so Lori's family started going there, too, and our moms bonded right away. That's how she and I got to be friends."

"And you've been best friends the whole time?"

"Oh, yeah." I told Christa the story of our first-kiss pact, and Tim Mayhew and Barry Tuckerton. Soon we were both laughing so hard we could barely stand up.

"You've gotten better at kissing since then," Christa said.

I flushed. I wished I could kiss her then and there. "I sure hope so."

I wondered if she was thinking the same thing, because she looked away quickly after that. We were both smiling, though.

"How about Lori?" she asked. "Does she get up to a lot of kissing of her own?"

"Not that much, I guess. She hasn't gone out with that many guys."

"Are she and Paul a thing?"

"Nah. I mean, I think she's into him, but I don't think anything's happened."

"That's good. Tell her he's sketchy. He steals from the collection plate at church."

I laughed. "What for?"

"Who knows? But he brags about it at school. He volunteers to pass the plate and then pockets half the cash. Someone told me he uses the money for drugs, but I think he probably only buys stupid T-shirts. Every time I see him he has a new stupid T-shirt."

"Well, she's going to be disappointed," I said. "She was pretty into him."

Christa looked confused. "Does she even know him?"

"Not really. She gets crushes on guys from afar a lot. Most of the time nothing ever happens. The guys don't really notice her, and she doesn't do anything except watch them from across the room and stuff."

"Huh. That's kind of sad."

"Nah, I think she's just nervous."

Christa grinned. "You weren't nervous the night you met me."

Wow. Did she seriously think that? I threw on what I hoped was a confident look. "I guess I don't find you that intimidating."

She laughed. "I like confident girls."

She looked into my eyes the whole time she was talking, but she was biting her lip again. I smiled and ducked my head.

"Hey, let's stop for a second," she said. We were on our way back to the Perez house, walking alongside a waist-high stone wall. Christa dug in her purse and pulled out a green Sharpie. "I have an idea."

She bent down against the wall, not seeming to care that she was getting dust on her black dress. She crossed one leg over the other, crouched and started drawing something on her ankle with the marker. I tried to see what it was, but she held her other arm up so I couldn't get a good look.

Finally she put the cap on the Sharpie. This time she hadn't drawn a design. She'd written the word *QUIXOTIC* in flowery letters running up the back of her calf.

I wanted to squeal. Instead I put two fingers on my lips to hide my grin. "Can I borrow a marker?"

"Sure." She fished in her purse again and passed me a blue one. I sat down on the ground next to her and tried to write *QUIXOTIC* on my leg, too. It didn't come out as cool-looking as hers—I didn't have as much practice at this, so my letters wobbled—but I loved that we matched.

Christa took a photo of my leg with her digital camera and tilted her head, her smile radiating warmth. I wanted to plant a kiss on her right there in the wide-open Mexican daylight. Instead I smiled back.

I liked her. God, I liked her so much.

"We'd better go." She looked at her phone. "The dance performance starts soon."

I climbed to my feet and reached for her hand to help her up, then reluctantly let go.

"Hey, Cee!" someone called from the far side of the street. Christa turned and waved, wearing a very different smile from the one she'd just given me. "You want to hang with us tonight? We've got the party right here!"

Paul and three other guys I recognized from Christa's church were walking in the opposite direction, holding cardboard boxes on their shoulders. The one who'd yelled was named Nick, and I was pretty sure the other two were Will and Tyler, though I didn't know which was which. Every time I saw them they were together, usually snickering at something on one of their phones, if they weren't making fart noises.

"Nah, I'm good," Christa called back. "You think you got enough?"

"Hey, yo, this stuff's got to last!" Paul slapped the cardboard box on his shoulder with a thump.

Christa laughed and waved again as the guys left.

"Do they know they're going the wrong way?" I asked Christa.

"Probably." Christa watched them disappear around the corner. "They're such losers. I mean, they're nice guys and all—I've known them since we were kids—but to them, the whole point of being in Mexico is that they can buy beer. They say no one here checks IDs."

I looked back at the group. They were far away now, but when I squinted, I could see the logos on the cardboard boxes they were carrying. Christa was right—it did look like beer. "So, what, do they sit around and drink all day?"

"I think mostly they drink at night. Some girls hang out with them, too."

Oh. I wondered if I should be jealous that I'd never been invited. Not that I especially wanted to spend time with a bunch of drunk guys I didn't even know. "Did you want to hang out with them tonight?"

"Not if *you* want to hang out with me, I don't."

That brought my smile right back up.

The sun was high above our heads. There was something amazing about walking out here in the open with Christa, talking about our day-to-day lives. Up until now, so much of our world had been about silence. The two of us alone together under those amazing Mexican stars.

We were among the last ones to get to Reverend Perez's house. We went straight around to where everyone was gathered in the courtyard, passing the spot where we'd talked that first night. It might as well have been a hundred years ago.

When we walked through the gate, Dad came straight up to us. His presence broke the spell I'd been under spectacularly.

"There you are." Dad looked a little frazzled—probably because he was annoyed at me for being almost-late—but he smiled at Christa. "Did you girls have a nice time in town?"

"Oh, yes." The voice Christa used for my dad was decidedly formal and fake. The same way she'd talked to that West Virginia pastor on our first day of work. "Everyone's so friendly here."

"Good, good," Dad said. "Aki, may I have a word, please?"

A tiny note of panic flared up in my chest. He couldn't know, could he?

No. We'd been careful. We'd—

Well, except that one night, outside the church. God, that had been amazing. But that was days ago. If he'd heard about that, he'd have said something before now, wouldn't he?

I was still freaking out when Dad pulled me into a corner of the courtyard and said, "I wanted to check in and see how you're doing. We haven't really seen much of each other this week."

He didn't seem angry or concerned. He still had that frazzled look in his eyes, though. I tried to force the worry out of my face.

"Oh, I'm good," I said. "I'm having a lot of fun."

"I'm glad to hear it," Dad said. "I've noticed that in vespers sometimes you look a little distant."

Well, that was because every night during vespers, all I could think about was sneaking off afterward to make out with Christa. The last thing I cared about was listening to praise songs. I couldn't very well say that to Dad, though.

"I'm just tired," I said. "I'm not used to doing this kind of work all day."

Not that the work was so hard. I mean, I spent my days painting and making jewelry with Lori and the girls. But Dad seemed to buy my explanation.

He turned to face the courtyard. The youth groups were settling into chairs and mats on the ground. The dancers, mostly girls around my age who went to the local church, were getting set up at the front toward the house. They wore old-fashioned white dresses that were long and flowy. Their hair was pinned up, and their faces sparkled with makeup and gold jewelry. They looked amazing.

"Yo, Benny! How's it hanging?" two Harpers Ferry guys called from the front row. Dad waved to them. Everyone here called my dad Benny. It had been weird to hear at first. At home, Mom called him Benjamin, and I had always been under strict instructions to call my friends' parents Mr. or Mrs. Whatever. But after years of youth group meetings, I was used to Dad being Benny.

"It seems as though you're making friends," Dad said.

"Oh, yeah. There are lots of awesome people in the other youth groups."

"I'm glad. That's part of why we're on this trip. The Holy

Life churches have operated separately for years, but we're try-ing harder now to bring everyone together."

"Oh." I yawned. "Because of the conference?"

"No, it's the other way around. The conference is part of the larger effort toward improving our overall community structure."

I nodded as if I were really interested in talking about this. Then I remembered what I'd wanted to ask him.

"Hey, so, I saw something today," I said. "There was a doctor's office in the middle of town, but it was pretty run-down. Do you know if that's the only doctor in Mudanza or if, maybe, I don't know, this was the old clinic and there's a newer one a few blocks up or something?"

Dad shook his head. "Can't say I know the answer to that. Why do you ask, sweetheart?"

I shrugged. "Well, I had fun last year working at the clinic back home. I guess I wondered if maybe they needed volun-teers here, too."

"Well." Dad passed a hand over his hair. "Well, Aki, you're already busy all day with work on the church and your jew-elry class project. But if you're curious about the doctors here in town, we could always ask Carlos."

"Carlos? No, Dad, it's okay, we don't need to—"

Dad wasn't listening. "Carlos! Do you have a second?"

Carlos was up at the front, setting up the sound equipment and chatting with Lori, but when he heard Dad he trotted over to us, smiling broadly. He was in his twenties, and he was the one member of the Mexican church who spoke En-glish well enough to translate for us. He was a nice enough guy, and a lot of the girls in our group whispered behind their hands about how cute he was. But my dad was so embarrass-ing when he got this way.

"Carlos, my daughter here is interested in learning more about the Mexican health care system," Dad said.

"That isn't what I asked," I muttered.

"Of course," Carlos said. He *was* pretty nice-looking, now that I was paying attention. "How can I help you, Aki?"

I explained about seeing the Casa de Salud. I didn't mention the part about it looking kind of old. I didn't want to insult Carlos's hometown.

"Are there other doctors' offices in Mudanza?" I asked him.

"Are you sick?" Carlos looked concerned. "We could find someone to drive you in to Tijuana tomorrow. I know an excellent doctor there."

"No, no, I'm fine." I stretched my arms over my head, trying to show him how healthy I was. "I was only wondering."

"Ah." Carlos nodded. "The Casa de Salud is all we have here in Mudanza. The big cities have more doctors, but in this part of Mexico, the smaller towns only have a clinic. The government assigns doctors to work in the rural clinics for their fifth year of medical school."

"Only one doctor for the whole town?" I said.

"There's also a nurse, and a helper," Carlos said. "We share the doctor with the clinic in Cedro, the town nearest to here. But the doctor is often away on other work, as well, so it can be difficult to get in to see him. Tijuana is better."

"How many people live in Mudanza?" I asked.

"About five hundred, right, Carlos?" Dad said. Carlos nodded.

That made one doctor for a thousand or so people, counting the other town. A doctor still in med school, too. I had no idea how many patients my doctor saw back home, but I didn't think it was a thousand.

What did people do here if they got seriously sick while the doctor was in the other town? And what if they got cancer or had heart problems like my grandad? Did everyone really drive all those hours to Tijuana to go to a decent doctor?

I wasn't sure how much people here drove, though. I hardly ever saw cars on the road. Reverend Perez had a truck—we'd seen it parked behind his house—but it looked really old. I couldn't imagine driving it all the way to Tijuana.

The dance was about to start, though, so I whispered thanks to Carlos and went to join the others. Christa had saved me a seat. I sat down next to her on a mat, spreading my skirt out over my knees.

Carlos went up to the front to welcome us and introduce the dancers. It turned out the lead dancer, a gorgeous woman named Alicia, was his wife. I'd heard he was married, but the whispers I'd heard from the girls in our group were that people in Mudanza got married really early and he and his wife were more friends than anything else. Looking at Alicia, though, I wondered if that was just wishful thinking on the girls' parts.

Carlos clapped really hard when the music started and Alicia walked out front. The girls held their long skirts in their hands and swung them around as they danced, their feet moving in complicated steps. I felt like I was going to trip just watching them, but the dancers smiled, as if this were as easy as walking.

I wished I'd learned to dance for real. I'd always loved dancing, but all I could do were silly moves I copied from music videos and practiced alone for my laptop camera. I'd been supposed to start dance classes the previous summer so I could get ready for MHSA, but I'd canceled them, along with everything else, when I didn't get in.

My jealousy ran deep as I watched the local girls. I had a feeling none of them had ever taken a single dance class. They were naturally talented. But for me and my music, even after studying and practicing for years, my own talent still wasn't good enough.

Tears burned at the backs of my eyes. That part of my life was over. My future wasn't going to be what I used to think, but I'd accepted that. I had to move on.

I glanced back at Christa to distract myself. She was looking at me, too.

I forced down the memories as my stomach rolled in giddy anticipation. The only future I needed to think about was tonight.

CHAPTER 8

VESPERS WERE CANCELED for the night. Dad told us to rest up for church in the morning instead.

Apparently, church was going to be in the same room where we slept, so we'd have to get up before dawn, get dressed, move our stuff out of the building, take down the camp showers and set up the pews. Then we had to come sit on them with everyone else for the service. Which we wouldn't understand because it would be in Spanish.

And I'd thought having to get up on Sunday mornings for church back *home* was annoying.

But no vespers meant more Christa time, so we didn't waste a minute. As soon as dinner was over, everyone spread out into groups around the outdoor tables, talking and laughing and trying out the dance steps we'd seen that afternoon, but Christa and I wandered off toward the hills, carrying a couple of extra mats and checking to make sure there was space between us so no one would think anything was up.

We passed Nick and Paul and their group stumbling off in the opposite direction, cans of beer held over their heads. They seemed to be having a contest to see who could burp the loudest. Christa and I rolled our eyes and kept going toward the trees.

It was a warm night. When we made it over the first row of hills and into our grassy valley we spread out the mats and sat down, leaning back on our elbows to watch the sunset.

"This might have been the best week of my life," I said as the sun dipped low.

I felt anxious as soon as the words were out of my mouth, but then Christa said, "I know what you mean," and I relaxed again.

I wanted to lean my head against her shoulder. Could I do that? Would she think it was weird?

Whatever. I did it anyway.

She didn't seem to mind. In fact, after a minute, she leaned against me, too, and slid her arm in next to mine.

We slunk down lower, watching the sun until it was nothing but a memory above the scraggly treetops.

Then we kissed. I wasn't even sure who started it this time. We were touching, and then we were turning. Our faces met. Then our lips.

Kissing Christa was so different from kissing anyone else. It wasn't because she was a girl, either. It was because I cared about her more than I'd ever cared about anyone.

We kissed, and kissed. I lost track of how long we'd been out there. The night was still and quiet, and I could feel how warm and soft Christa was through her clothes. Just when I was wondering what she felt like underneath, she was rolling on top of me, her body pressing into mine.

Our kisses weren't gentle, friendly kisses anymore. These were fiery and hard, both of us breathing fast and messy. I wrapped my arms around her back and pulled her against me as tightly as I could. I felt warm between my legs.

We kept kissing and moving together until the moon was

high overhead. It had to be getting late. I pulled back from Christa a little and opened my eyes. She looked flushed and sweaty. Above her I could see the tree line and the stars.

"Somebody might notice we're gone," I whispered. I didn't know why it seemed necessary to whisper, but it did.

She nodded. Slowly, she pushed herself off the ground, separating her body from mine. It felt strange to have space between us. To be just me, not part of me-and-her.

Christa glanced toward me. Her mouth curled up in a not-quite-laugh. "Your mascara is, um." She bit her lip. "Having some problems."

"Crap." I licked my finger and tried to rub under my eyes. "Does that help?"

"A little. Don't worry, it's so dark no one will notice. Do I look normal?"

"Uh. Your dress is kind of rumpled."

We both laughed. "Yours, too," Christa said. "Maybe we should—"

A rustling sound came from the hill above us. We froze.

Was it my dad? One of the other chaperones?

It could be anyone, really. We were out in the Mexican wilderness.

I forced my head up, my heart pounding even harder than it had when Christa was on top of me.

The rustling came again. It was definitely footsteps, on the side of the hill farther from the town.

I looked. It wasn't Dad. It was—

It was some kind of animal.

Christa sucked in her breath. The thing on the hill seemed to be a really big dog, except I'd never seen a dog like that before.

"Is that a *coyote*?" Christa whispered.

I didn't know. I'd only ever heard of coyotes from cartoons. But the dark shape at the top of the hill wasn't anything close to the animated versions. It had sharp ears and claws we could hear scrabbling in the dirt. Even though I couldn't tell in the dark, I was sure it had sharp teeth, too.

"What do we do?" I whispered. Christa shook her head. We were city girls, both of us. "Does it know we're here?"

"Do you think we can make it up the hill to the other side?" she whispered.

"I think we'd better try."

"Let's go slow. Maybe it won't see us that way."

We grabbed the mats and started to climb as quietly as we could. I wanted to run, but whatever that thing was, I was positive it could outrun us if it wanted to.

A scratching sound came from the valley behind us. Christa gasped. I clapped my hand over my mouth to keep from yelling.

We made it over the crest of the hill, and this time we did break into a run. My sandals didn't let me go very fast, but I was still faster than Christa. I kept looking over my shoulder to make sure she was there, but she was, running flat out in her flip-flops.

When we were almost to the church I turned around. Christa was still running, but I didn't see anything in the dark behind her. I motioned for her to stop and we dropped into silence.

The thing wasn't chasing us anymore. Maybe it hadn't been after us to begin with.

But even so.

"Holy hell," I whispered.

Christa clutched her chest, her breath coming in heaves.

That coyote-thing had been terrifying. But part of me was still a little relieved it hadn't been Dad catching us in the act.

Either way, our private little valley wasn't so private anymore.

CHAPTER 9

THE TINY BIT of Spanish I'd picked up over the past week counted for nada when I tried to follow Reverend Perez's sermon that Sunday morning. So I spent the service bowing my head when everyone else did and trying to think of places where Christa and I could hang out at night now that the hills had been overtaken by wild animals.

I kept getting distracted, though. Thinking about Christa's lips. About how the sensations from last night had lingered in my body.

I'd kissed guys before, sure, but it had never felt this way. Kissing Christa sent an electric current running through my veins. I wondered if the people sitting in the church pew with me had ever felt anything like it.

I glanced from side to side. Lori was sitting on my left, Drew on my right with Sofía on his other side. Christa was three pews in front of us, wearing a purple fedora. Next to her was Madison, the girl she'd been dancing with the night we arrived.

From now on, it looked like Christa and I would be stuck meeting indoors. But I didn't know how we'd find a place where we could be alone. We worked all day, surrounded by a million people. At night, in the church, we were equally surrounded.

Although...the church was only full after dark. All day long, while we were at the work site, it just stood here, empty.

It wasn't as if we could sneak away from the work site, though. Someone would notice. Besides, the whole point of being in Mexico was to do our volunteer work.

Maybe we could sneak away in the evenings. During vespers? No, Dad would notice. But maybe at supper. The chaperones ate together. Dad probably wasn't paying much attention to me at meals or he would've said something about me only eating toast.

It could be cool to hang out in the church alone with Christa. Before the sun went down, it would be gorgeous in here, the light filtering in through the windows. And there would be plenty of sleeping bags around if we needed to lie on something.

Mmm. Last night was the first time we'd ever actually been horizontal together. That had rocked.

At the altar Reverend Perez said something and raised his hands. In one movement, the congregation stood, and I scrambled to my feet.

After another silent prayer, people started gathering up their things. Apparently church was over. I hoped no one would ask me what I'd thought of the sermon.

Lori and I followed Drew and Sofía down the aisle. Everyone was hanging around outside, talking and laughing, the local congregation and our group all mixed in together. Next to me, Sofía smoothed out her short, flowered dress, laughing at something Drew had said.

I wondered if she and Drew were serious. I'd thought Drew would have a hundred girlfriends in college, but he'd spent most of his freshman year either at work or in his room with the door closed. I wasn't sure when he actually spent time with his friends. Or if he even still had friends.

"Any word yet on your suitcase?" Lori asked me. It felt weird, talking to her about other stuff when I hadn't told her yet what happened with the coyote. Up until now, she'd heard about all my hookups with Christa—I'd already fulfilled my end of the summer-fling pact and then some—but I wasn't sure I wanted to tell Lori about this time. I kind of wanted to keep some things between me and Christa now.

"It's at the airport in Tijuana," I told her. "Carlos said they're hoping someone can drive over this week to pick it up."

I knew Lori was tired of me borrowing her clothes. I was tired of it, too. They weren't *me*, and besides, they never came close to fitting. Plus, I'd gotten my period, so I'd had to use Lori's tampon supply, too.

By the way, having your period when you had to wash out your underwear every night, and you were stuck sharing two toilets with forty people? Was pretty awful.

Today Lori and I had traded the dresses we'd worn on Saturday, since Lori had only brought two dresses to Mexico. It was a little weird knowing she was wearing the same clothes I'd had on last night when I was out in the hills with Christa.

Speaking of which, I wanted to tell Christa my idea, about meeting in the church in the evenings. I craned my neck, but I didn't see her.

"Yo, Sis." Drew waved a hand in front of my face. This clearly wasn't the first time he'd tried to get my attention. "You coming?"

I pushed his hand away. "Coming where?"

"Lunch. Remember? We're supposed to meet Dad."

"Oh, right." The Suarezes had invited Dad, Drew and me

to Sunday dinner at their house. Another hour of picking at my food and not understanding a word anyone said.

We said goodbye to Lori and Sofía and found Dad near the edge of the crowd with Señor and Señora Suarez. Juana, the girl from my jewelry-making group, was their daughter, but she didn't usually eat with us at lunch during the week, so she was hilariously excited that we were coming over today. As we walked to their house she kept running around us in circles, chasing her two younger brothers, then giggling and looking back to make sure we appreciated the show. Her hair was up in a complicated braid that must've taken ages to get right, and dust had already started accumulating around the hem of her pristine white lace dress, but no one seemed to mind.

Drew had taken more Spanish than I had, so he talked to Juana's parents as we walked. I hung back with Dad. He'd done a year abroad in Greece in college, so he was great at telling stories about Zeus and Athena, but no better than me at talking to the Suarez family.

"Dad, can I ask you something?" I said while the others chattered incomprehensibly.

"Of course, sweetheart." Dad didn't look at me, though. He was gazing off into the hills.

"Are you—do you know how you're voting at the conference? On, you know, the different planks?"

I didn't want to say the words *gay marriage* to him. Well, really I didn't want to say the word *gay*.

"Not yet." Dad was still staring into space. "Our congregation won't meet to finalize our plans until August."

"The congregation has to meet?" I scratched a mosquito bite on my shoulder.

"Yes. I'm representing Holy Life of Silver Spring, so we'll all decide on our votes together. And sweetheart, are you wearing bug spray like we told you to?"

"Yeah, yeah."

"Anyway, as a delegate, I'm hoping we'll vote in favor of the anti-war plank." Dad turned to face me then. "I don't see how we, as Christians, can decide otherwise."

"Me, neither." We were all pacifists in the Simon family. When I was a kid, I thought everyone was. I was shocked when I got to school and met kids who didn't think war was so terrible, or who played games where they pretended to shoot people.

Dad rambled for a while about how the voting worked. What would I say if he mentioned the marriage plank? Would I try to persuade him to get the congregation to vote yes on that, too? What if he didn't want to?

I'd never heard him mention feeling one way or the other about gay marriage. We didn't really know any gay people. I mean, there was one guy at my school, Marcus, who everybody said was gay because he wore really tight pants, but I didn't know if that counted.

When we got to the Suarezes' house I tried to follow Juana's mother into the kitchen to help, but she waved me away the same way all the ladies did when they served our meals. I sighed and wandered back to the front room.

"Ah-ki," Juana called. She was running around the dining table setting out plates and silverware. Usually at lunch my friends and I ate in the living room, where there was more space, but today it looked as if we were sitting with the family. "¡Vamanos!"

She said other words, too, but *vamanos* was the only one I could understand. All the kids said it when they wanted someone to come with them.

I thought she was asking me to help her set the table, but Juana took my hand and tugged me past the couch where the adults were gathered, down a narrow hallway and into a tiny room with a small bed tucked into the corner.

The room was bright and airy. The small window was open, and sunlight gleamed over a neat pink bedspread. A soft gray doll with beady black eyes sat propped up against the pillows.

"Es muy bueno," I said, wishing I knew the word for *room*.

Juana rattled off a bunch of commands I couldn't understand in Spanish. She kept pointing at me, then at the floor by the foot of her bed. Finally I got that she wanted me to sit down. I thought she wanted to play a game, but instead she grabbed me by the shoulders and twisted me around. I laughed. For a little kid, she sure was good at going after what she wanted.

Then she sat on the bed behind me and grabbed at my hair. Oh, okay. I knew about this from church camp. Everybody loved to touch black girls' hair.

It didn't bother me with Juana the way it did with the blonde girls back home, though. For all I knew, Juana had never even seen black people before my group showed up here. I sure hadn't seen any other black folks walking around Mudanza.

Juana grabbed at my hair and started pulling it back into some sort of style. I'd gotten my hair done in braids before we left home so it would be easier to deal with down here, but after a week of tying them back with ponytail bands, I'd left them hanging loose that morning for church. I couldn't see what Juana was doing, but it felt as if she was trying to wind the hundreds of tiny braids into one thick braid. I tried not to wince as she tugged at my scalp.

Maybe I could ask Juana what she thought of the health clinic here. She must've gone there for shots and when she got colds and stuff. I wondered why her friend Guadalupe hadn't gotten an inhaler there yet.

"Juana?" I said. "Ah… ¿usted va al doctoro?"

Juana giggled. "¿'Doctoro'?" she repeated.

Maybe *doctoro* wasn't the word. "Uh…al Casa de Salud?"

"¿Qué?" Juana tugged at my scalp again.

I tried again. "El Casa de Salud. ¿Qué, uh, qué vas—"

"There you are, Sis."

Juana paused in her yanks. I twisted around to see Drew standing hunched over in the doorway. He was so tall he took up most of Juana's room.

"Is lunch ready?" I asked him.

"No, not yet. Actually I, uh, wanted to ask you something." He turned to Juana with a big, charming smile. "¿Qué pasa, señorita?"

Juana giggled at him but didn't answer. She went back to pulling on my hair.

Drew's smile faded as he turned back to me. Suddenly he looked hesitant. He kept glancing at Juana. Well, she wouldn't understand him, if that was what he was worried about.

"Come on in." I motioned for him to close Juana's door. "There's space over there where you can sit."

Drew gave Juana a big wave as he crossed the room in three strides. She giggled and went back to winding my braids together. Drew settled down into the space under the window, folding his long legs underneath him awkwardly.

We fell into silence. Juana yanked on my hair. I tried not to wince.

"So, uh, I don't know how to say this," Drew said after a long moment.

I sat up straight. Panic glided slowly into my chest. "Just say it."

"There's a, uh…" He cleared his throat and glanced back at Juana's closed door. When he spoke again his voice was so low I had to strain to hear him. "Look, I heard something and I kind of want to know if it's true. About you and…that girl, from Rockville."

Oh, God. We'd thought we were being so careful.

It was impossible to tell what Drew was thinking. He wasn't smiling, but he didn't look as though he was about to throttle me, either.

Should I lie?

I never lied to Drew. I hadn't since we were little kids. Once in kindergarten I'd taken his favorite basketball jersey to wear as a Halloween costume and got grape jelly on it at lunch. I tried to hide it for the rest of the day, then I cried about it all night. Finally, the next morning, I showed it to him. He laughed and told me not to worry, that he got stuff on his jerseys all the time and it would wash right out. From then on I'd always told Drew the truth, even if it meant he gave me a hard time about it.

"It's true," I said softly. I twisted around to see if Juana understood what we were talking about, but she was looking down at my hair, a determined expression on her face. She shoved my head back until I was facing forward.

Drew looked up at the window at the foot of Juana's bed. "I heard a couple of days ago. I didn't think it was for real at first because I thought you'd have told me. But then yesterday I saw how you two were with each other, and—I wasn't so sure."

I wondered how he'd heard a couple of days ago. I wondered what Christa and I had done yesterday that made him believe it. "Yeah."

He stood. It wasn't easy, in that tiny space. He leaned into the corner, turning to gaze out Juana's window. "I wish you'd have told me sooner."

"It only started since we got here."

He turned back and met my eyes. "That's not what I meant."

I knew what he meant.

I wanted to tell him I was bi, not gay, like he probably thought. I wanted to tell him I hadn't really been sure, not until this summer. But I couldn't say any of that. I didn't know how well sound might carry in that house.

"Did you think I wouldn't be cool with it?" he said. "Because I am. I mean, you're my baby sister and you shouldn't be doing any of that crap with anybody anyway, but, well. You know what I mean."

"Yeah." I held out my hand to Drew. After a moment he leaned forward and took it. "I know what you mean. I didn't think you wouldn't be cool with it. I—look, I don't know. I had to figure myself out first. I'm still figuring myself out."

He let go of my hand. "I didn't enjoy hearing about it from other people. That's all."

"Who'd you hear it from?" My heart was pounding, but I wasn't sure I really wanted to know the answer.

"Just…people." He shrugged. "I've got to admit, I was freaked at first. Maybe I was dumb, but I had never thought about it being a possibility, you know?"

My heart sank. That was why I hadn't wanted to tell anyone. "You were freaked?"

"Kind of. But then I thought some more, and I talked to Sofía, and—"

"You told *Sofía*?" Oh, lord, if even Sofía knew…

"Yeah. She told me I was stupid to be weird about it, and this was totally normal, and it's the twenty-first century and all. She was right. I mean, you know, whatever, right? Different strokes for different folks."

I laughed. Then I sniffled. I hadn't realized how relieved I felt. Or how afraid I'd been.

"Just, look, promise me one thing," Drew said.

"Of course." In that moment, I'd have promised to do his math homework for the rest of my life if he asked.

"Promise you won't tell Dad. Or Mom, but especially Dad. He—I don't think he'll take it well. You know, he's old-fashioned, being a minister and everything. He thinks you're still his baby girl."

I sat back against the bed. Behind me, Juana huffed and pushed my head forward again.

"You think he'll—" I swallowed. "Be upset?"

"I don't know. They're voting on that thing at the conference, and I think he might vote yes, but he also might not. If he finds out about this, that might make him start seeing things differently, you know?"

"For real?" That was basically my worst fear. "You think he'd be so freaked he'd vote against marriage?"

"I don't know. Us kids, we grew up in the modern times. But Grandma and Grandad, they were old-school Bible thumpers. I think Dad is, too, deep down. This news might crush him. I'd be really careful if it were me."

He thought this would *crush* Dad? God, what was I going to do?

Maybe I should go back to being straight. It wouldn't be that hard. It wasn't as if I wasn't into guys at all.

But... Christa.

"Okay." I swallowed again. "I won't tell him."

"I mean, you know how they are," Drew went on. "Mom and Dad both. All they want us to do is church, church, church. I swear, if Holy Life had a school they would've sent us both there."

"But lots of people are way churchier than we are. Half the kids from Harpers Ferry—"

"No, that's not what I mean. It isn't just religion for Mom and Dad. They've kept us so massively sheltered. You especially, but it was the same for me up until I switched to public school. The only reason they sent us to Rowell was because it was so tiny it was easy to keep an eye on us."

I shook my head. "I'm not sheltered."

Drew dropped his head. "Do you even know what a big deal it was for them when you auditioned for MHSA? Dad was dead set against it at first. Mom spent months talking him into letting you."

I stiffened at the mention of MHSA, but I hadn't known that. "He never said anything to me."

"Yeah, they don't like for us to see them disagree. But they really wanted you to stay at Rowell. They were rooting for you to get in, of course, but I think they were relieved when you didn't audition again last year." Drew fixed me with a look. "Like I said, they really want you where they can keep an eye on you."

"Well, I don't care." I shifted on the bed. Juana punished me with an extra-sharp tug. I sat up straight. "And I don't want another lecture from you about why I should've auditioned again."

"Don't worry, I'm not going there." Drew raised his hands in the air. We'd done that since we were kids, to ask the other one to back off. Then his voice got serious. "I'm only saying, I think the reason Mom and Dad—but especially Dad—are this way is because of Uncle Andrew."

"For real?" We'd hardly ever talked about Uncle Andrew before. He was Dad's little brother, but he died before Drew and I were born. He'd had cancer or something.

"I think him dying made Dad paranoid, and now he's obsessed with making sure you and I are safe all the time."

"Come on, Drew, maybe you're overthinking this."

"Maybe you're underthinking it."

Juana yanked on my scalp again. I changed the subject.

"Have you decided yet what you're going to do in the fall? Are you going back to school?"

Drew looked down again. "I don't know. I was actually looking at maybe signing up for the army, but—"

"*But?*" I nearly screeched. I used every muscle in my body to force myself to stay still, even though I wanted to leap to my feet. "*But?* Drew, Dad would *kill* you. You *know* how he and Mom feel about the military."

"It's my call, not theirs." Drew's voice was so low I had to strain to hear him. "Anyway, whatever, it was a dumb idea."

"I'll say it was." At least Drew had thought better of that one. I couldn't believe he'd even considered it.

"Drew?" Señora Suarez's voice called from the other room. "Aki? Juana? Dinnertime!"

Señora Suarez's English was a hundred times better than my Spanish. Juana let go of my braids and I stood up slowly. Tears pricked at the backs of my eyes.

"Hey, your hair looks really nice," Drew said.

I felt the back of my head and touched a nice, neat braid. "Gracias, Juana. Es muy bueno."

Juana giggled. I realized *"Es muy bueno"* was basically the only thing I'd ever said to her.

Drew and Juana went down the hall. I started to follow them, but I paused in the doorway first. I needed to breathe.

I just came out to my brother.

Up until today, I'd barely even thought about how coming out would feel, but telling Drew—that made this bigger than it was before. This wasn't only a thing that existed solely between me and Christa in our tiny little world anymore.

I really was...not straight. Or something.

I couldn't tell Christa about what had happened. She'd be so upset.

But—was Drew right, with what he'd said about Dad? Would he really be crushed if he knew?

That idea made *me* feel kind of crushed.

This was too big. I didn't know how to deal with it. I couldn't.

But now I had to go out there and act as if nothing had happened.

So I smoothed out my borrowed dress and slid a smile onto my face. I closed my eyes, breathed in and opened them again.

I followed Juana into the dining room and took the empty seat next to Dad. After everyone had sat down and Señor Suarez had said the prayer, Señora Suarez started right away piling beans and vegetables onto my plate before I could even say "No, gracias."

Suddenly there was a huge pile of food in front of me and no prepackaged toast in sight. I fiddled with my fork, wondering if I could somehow shove this tower of nutrients under my napkin without Señora Suarez noticing.

No one else was hesitating, though. Drew was shoveling food into his mouth and making "Mmm" sounds as though he hadn't eaten in weeks. And even Juana's littlest brother, who couldn't have been more than three, was digging into his plate of beans like he was at Baskin-Robbins with an ice-cream sundae.

Okay. Fine. One small bite of beans probably wouldn't kill me.

I scooped a tiny helping onto my fork—two beans' worth—and lifted it to my lips. It actually smelled kind of good.

I hesitated another moment before I realized Juana was watching me. I couldn't back out now.

I slid the fork into my mouth, trying to act like this was totally normal, as if I ate this kind of food every day. Then I had a shocking realization.

Señora Suarez's food was good.

It was better than Taco Bell. It was a *lot* better than toast.

I forgot Juana was watching me and dug into those beans. I even tried the veggies. They were good, too. Everything was especially good together.

I ate everything on my plate and helped myself to more. I wondered what else I'd been missing out on because I'd been too scared to try it.

I ate my food quietly and watched Drew smile fake smiles at Dad and the Suarezes. He and I were the same in so many ways. We were both good kids. Preacher's kids.

Kids like us didn't have secrets. Kids like us knew better.

Girls like me smiled politely and always did the right thing. Girls like me definitely didn't sneak away at night to do things that would crush their fathers.

And if they did, girls like me knew how to keep it to themselves.

PART 3

Somewhere Here on Earth

CHAPTER 10

I DIDN'T SEE Christa when we got back to the old church, but she had to be somewhere. The pews had been moved back against the walls and the tarp that broke the room in half had been hung up again, but it was pulled over to one side. Everyone from all three youth groups was talking in little groups, still in their church clothes.

An excited buzz hung in the air. Something had happened.

"Aki!" Jake called from the far side of the room. He was sitting next to Lori, a pile of beads spilled out onto the pew beside them. "Over here!"

I swept my eyes across the room one last time, but Christa wasn't inside. So I made my way over to Lori and Jake, stepping carefully over a group of Harpers Ferry boys playing games on their phones. I pinched my skirt hem to make sure they couldn't see up my dress.

"Where've you been?" Lori asked when I reached them. She and Jake were sorting beads by color. Lori had been doing most of the planning for our jewelry lessons lately.

I sat on the floor in front of them and started sorting out the green beads, humming the Destiny's Child song I couldn't get out of my head. "I had to go have lunch at the Suarezes' with Dad and Drew."

"Yikes," Jake said. "Did they let you get away with only eating toast?"

"No, but actually the food was pretty decent."

Jake shook his head, as though he was disappointed in me.

"Did your dad tell you about Texas?" Lori asked.

"Nope. What about Texas?"

"You didn't hear? It's all everybody's talking about." Jake sat up straight. I couldn't tell which was more exciting for him, getting people to sign his petitions or being the first to know the gossip. "The weekend after next we're all taking a bus ride to some college in Texas, and we're going to stay there for two nights!"

I sat up, too. "Wait. College? Are we staying in dorm rooms?"

"Precisely," Lori said. "With actual beds. And doors. And *showers*."

"Why are we going up there?" I asked, the wheels in my brain beginning to whirl.

"Some youth Bible festival they want us to go to." Lori shrugged. "I guess a bunch of churches are sending youth groups from all over the US. There's some famous preacher who's going to talk, and there's a concert by that Christian rock band people are into."

I had no idea which Christian rock band people were into—my musical landscape didn't extend quite that far—and I'd listened to more than enough preachers to last me until I was in college myself. But I'd listen to a hundred bands and preachers if it meant I got to share a dorm room with Christa.

"You said we're staying overnight?" I said. "*Two* nights?"

"Yes!" Jake was close to jumping out of his seat. "We're taking the bus up on Friday, then we'll spend the night in the dorms, then the festival is all day Saturday so we have to spend *another* night, and then we drive back the next day. It's going to be the coolest *ever*."

"Did they say anything about assigning roommates?" My imagination was racing far ahead. Crossing the border.

What would happen if I got to share a room with Christa?

What did I *want* to happen?

I tried to focus on finding the green beads, but it wasn't happening.

To be *truly* alone with her. The idea was exciting and terrifying all at once.

It was so much fun, feeling this way. When I'd hung out with guys before, it was always kind of cool to make out, but I never looked forward to it every second of the day the way I did with Christa. Maybe that meant I was more gay than bi.

"No," Jake said. "Everyone's already pairing off, though."

"Gina asked me to room with her," Lori said. "But I told her you and I always room together on trips."

"Oh," I said. "Uh, actually, maybe you should room with Gina after all. I might need to—uh."

Lori's face fell. But—she'd understand once she'd thought about it, wouldn't she? Dorm rooms only had two beds. At least, they did on TV.

"Does Christa know about the trip?" I asked. "I didn't see her when I came in."

"She was here when they made the announcement," Jake said.

"But now she's hanging out with her ex." Lori jerked her thumb toward the door leading out behind the church.

"Her ex?" I tried to look where Lori pointed, but I didn't see anyone. "What ex?"

"You know. Madison, from her church. They've been outside since we got back from lunch."

"She used to go out with *Madison*?" Christa had never said anything about them being a couple.

"Aw, that's so cute," Jake said. "You're jealous."

"Jealous?" I tried to act shocked. "That's ridiculous. Why would I be jealous?"

"Because your girlfriend might like another girl?" Jake was visibly struggling not to smile.

"My—" I turned to Lori, my throat tightening. "You *told* him?"

"Uh, she didn't have to tell me anything," Jake said. "Relax. Pretty much everybody's known for, well, a while."

I turned to Lori, horrified. *"What?"*

Lori raised her eyebrows sky-high. "You seriously didn't know?"

"Oh, God." I rubbed my forehead. "She's going to kill me."

"It isn't only *your* fault," Jake said. "You guys are, um, really obvious. You go off together every night. Also, this guy from Rockville was going around saying he saw you and her kissing on Tuesday after vespers."

That explained how Drew found out, at least. "Do you think Christa knows?"

"Well, you didn't." Lori shrugged. "And, well, sometimes she seems kind of oblivious, so maybe not?"

This wasn't helpful. I stood up. "See you guys later."

"Have fun." Jake didn't bother to cover his smile this time.

I sighed and stepped back over the gaming boys on my way out the church's back door.

It took me a while to find Christa and Madison. They were standing far behind the church, at the base of the row of hills. Christa was still wearing the fedora she'd had on during the service. Madison was holding a cigarette. I'd forgotten she smoked.

To be honest, I'd barely thought about Madison since that

first night. Christa hardly ever talked about her. But Madison had super-short hair and wore board shorts everywhere, even to church. Now that I thought about it, she was such an obvious lesbian.

As I got closer, I could hear them arguing but I couldn't make out the words. What did it mean when your new kinda-sorta-not-really summer girlfriend had a secret fight with her ex?

"Fine!" Madison tossed down her cigarette and ground it out under her sneaker. Then she must've realized she was standing in pristine Mexican nature because she picked up the butt and put it in her pocket.

When she turned around, she looked straight at me. I wished I could disappear.

Madison gave me a disgusted look and walked away toward the street.

Christa turned to look at me, too. Her face was blank. Now I *really* wished I'd disappeared.

She shoved her hair out of her face and ambled toward me.

"Hey, Aki." She was trying so hard to sound casual. It didn't work. "How's it going?"

"Uh." I looked pointedly at Madison's retreating back. She was probably too far away to hear us now. "You tell me."

Christa kept her eyes on me. "Look, she gets that way sometimes. It's her thing. She's the queen of mood swings."

"What does that make you?" I said. "The ex-king?"

Christa opened her mouth, then closed it. It was strange seeing her at a loss for words.

"Look," she finally said. "The thing with me and her was over so many millions of years ago."

So it was true. "You never told me there was a thing between you and her."

"That's because it doesn't matter. Seriously, we were only kids, and it lasted half a second. I barely even remember it."

I didn't see how it was possible to barely remember going out with someone. Especially a girl. Did that mean someday Christa would barely remember me?

Christa reached out to link her fingers with mine. I pulled away.

I wanted to ask if she knew our secret was out. I wanted to tell her what happened with Drew.

Instead I said, "I wish you'd told me you'd already had a girlfriend. You might as well have straight-out lied to me."

I wondered if she could hear the guilt in my voice.

I was angrier at myself than I was at her. I was the one who'd really lied. Who was still lying to her now.

"I didn't lie," she said. "I just didn't mention it. Because what happened with me and her seriously wasn't a big deal. Besides, it's not as if you're jealous or anything, are you?"

"No." I didn't even know if I was, but saying no seemed important right then. "It's only that *I* haven't. Had a girlfriend. But I'm not jealous. Not of Steven, either."

Christa looked away. "Good. Because there's nothing to be jealous of. Anyway, look, Madison and I were fighting because she asked me to room with her in Texas, and I said no."

"Oh." She did? Hmm. "All right."

"I was going to ask if *you* wanted to. Be my roommate, I mean."

It was only two nights at some youth retreat thing. But it felt as though she was asking for something a lot bigger.

Not to be her girlfriend. I was a summer fling, and that was it. That was all either of us had wanted. Christa was already someone's girlfriend. Or at least she would be once we got home.

Besides, *girlfriend* was an official word. A public word. Madison might have been her girlfriend, but I never would be. Being a girlfriend wasn't the same thing as sneaking off into the hills to be alone under the stars.

But the stars were all Christa and I had. That, and now an empty dorm room somewhere in Texas.

And that was plenty.

"Yes," I said. "Let's do it."

I blushed. She did, too. The pink on her cheeks gave me the courage to say what I wanted to say next. "And by the way, regarding tonight. I had an idea."

A smile spread wide across Christa's face.

That night, we didn't waste a second.

As soon as the others left for dinner, I went into the bathroom and Christa stayed back, pretending to look for something in the row of suitcases that lined the back wall of the church. When we were sure everyone else was gone, I came back to the girls' half of the room, behind the tarp. We built a tent out of mats and sleeping bags, laughing and shushing each other as we stacked layers on top of layers.

We crawled inside our little cave, and as soon as we were hidden, we started kissing right away. The kissing was amazing, but we figured out fast that it was way too hot to be under a sleeping-bag tent. Besides, everyone was long gone by then. So we crawled out and lay on top of the pile of mats and bags. We rolled onto our sides, facing each other. Our noses touched, and we giggled.

"I'm sorry I was weird earlier," I said.

"It's okay," she said. "I get weird, too."

I wanted to ask again if she knew that our secret was out. I wanted to ask what had really happened between her and Madison.

But I didn't want to waste time. And I didn't want to make that smile fade.

So I kissed her again instead.

We kissed slowly. It was incredible, knowing we had at least an hour to ourselves, that we didn't have to worry about anyone seeing us or anything scary happening.

Christa ran her fingers up and down my side, making me shiver. I liked it this way, when we were just barely touching. But I liked it when we did more, too.

Her hand crept up my stomach, over my dress, sliding over my breast. My breath caught. I didn't know if I was ready for this, but I didn't stop her. Instead I pushed myself forward, pressing into her touch. I wanted to feel her, too, so I reached up and stroked her through her dress. Under it I could feel her bra, and under that was *her*, warm and solid and real. That was when I forgot how to breathe altogether.

She moved down to kiss my neck, and I couldn't reach her anymore, but that was okay. She kissed down my chest to the neck of my dress, her hands squeezing both of my breasts. It felt better than anything had ever felt in my entire life. The only sounds in the world were the mosquitoes buzzing softly in the trees outside. I stroked Christa's hair and kissed her forehead and thought, *So this is what it's like.*

I felt that warmth between my legs again, and I wanted her to touch me there, too. Soon, maybe. Not quite yet. But at least I had one new thing for my tally.

I reached for her again. I wanted to touch her with nothing between her skin and mine. I wanted to—I didn't know exactly what I wanted. I wanted everything.

That was when the tarp rustled behind us.

Someone else was here.

CHAPTER 11

CHRISTA AND I sprang apart. She grabbed a sleeping bag and yanked it over us.

I froze. It was too dark to see Christa's face, but I could feel her shaking.

We waited. At first we didn't hear anything else. Then, right when I was starting to relax, a guy's voice called out from the other side of the tarp. "Hello? Who's in here?"

Apparently there was no use being quiet.

I scrambled around in the dark, fixing my clothes. I tried to straighten my bra but my hands were trembling. I wanted to whisper something to Christa, but if I did whoever was on the other side of the tarp was bound to hear.

Christa was trying to straighten her clothes, too. When the guy called out again, in shaky Spanish this time, his voice was wobbly. He sounded more scared than we did. "¿Quién está ahí?"

I let out a tiny, hysterical giggle.

I couldn't help it. I knew this was serious, and someone was about to catch us "in flagrante delicto," as my mother would say, but—come on. I was going to second base with my not-girlfriend in the middle of a church in Mexico right before vespers, and this guy on the other side of the tarp was afraid of *us*?

My heart was still pounding from what we'd been doing before. I wondered how far things would've gone if we hadn't had to stop. I wondered how far I'd have let them.

"Aki?" the guy called. "Is that you?"

Christa's eyes were so wide it was scary.

I peeked out from around the edge of the sleeping bag. I couldn't see the guy—he must've still been on the other side of the tarp. I climbed to my feet, checking to make sure my clothes looked normal. My braids had half-fallen out of the arrangement Juana had made, so I quickly yanked them loose so it wouldn't look as though I'd been rolling around on the floor. Even though I had.

"Yes, it's me!" I called. "I was, uh—taking a nap. I'll come out."

I ran over to the edge of the tarp before the guy could pull it aside.

It was only Jake. Thank God.

"Oh, okay," he said. If I looked disheveled, he didn't seem to notice. "I wondered why you weren't at dinner."

"Yeah, I needed to crash." It took Herculean effort not to double-check that I was really wearing all my clothes. "I was about to get up for vespers, though."

"Well, I brought you something." Jake held out a web print-out, a single page from a long document. I tried to focus on the words, but my heart was still throbbing in my ears. I could hear Christa rustling on the other side of the tarp, and I prayed Jake didn't notice.

"What is it?" I asked him.

"It's another plank they're voting on at the conference in

August. I knew you'd been asking about the health care system here, so I thought you'd be interested."

Oh, right. I held out the paper, but it was too dark to get a good look. The headline Jake had circled stood out clearly, though: "Global Health and Welfare Ministries." Below that were a few dense paragraphs I couldn't read in the dim light.

"It's about—" Jake cut himself off midsentence when the rustling from the other side of the room turned into soft footsteps. He cast his eyes toward the tarp, his forehead creased. When he looked back at me, his face shifted from alarm to amusement. He'd figured it out.

"It's about health care, right?" I said loudly as Christa tiptoed to the back door. "Cool. We should probably be on our way to vespers, right? Let's walk and you can tell me all about it."

I kept babbling, and Jake didn't stop me. To my huge relief he didn't say anything about Christa. I didn't want *this* to be the way she realized our secret was out.

Jake and I went out the front door. I wished I'd been able to get in front of a mirror before reentering the world, but at least it was getting dark. Hopefully I didn't look as though I'd just been hooking up with my secret summer fling.

"So what is this?" I held out the paper again, but my hands were shaking so hard I couldn't follow the words.

"Basically, it says Holy Life encourages people to support foreign aid for health care, and that we think the US government should up its foreign aid budget. There's a whole bullet point in there on why it's important to support better health care systems for developing countries."

The tiny Casa de Salud flashed in my memory. Maybe I couldn't do anything to help the people in Mudanza this summer, but if this resolution passed, all the Holy Life churches could help clinics like the Casa de Salud. "Do you think the plank will pass?"

"No clue." Jake shrugged. "I only read up on the marriage resolution."

"Well, maybe I'll start a petition on this one. It can't hurt, right? Plus, it won't be hard to get signatures. I mean, it's about international aid. This won't be controversial. Just look where we are."

"Yeah, probably not," Jake said. "The only controversy talk I've heard about is on the war and the gays."

"That's for sure," Lori said. I hadn't even seen her come up alongside us. A few other people were walking along the path now, too, heading toward vespers. "The gays are definitely the only thing I hear about anymore."

"Shh, Lori." I glanced over my shoulder. "Keep your voice down."

"Sure, sure." She didn't look at me. "By the way, I meant to tell you, I'm out of clothes."

"What do you mean, you're out of clothes?"

"I mean, between the two of us we've literally worn all the clothes I brought with me. I've only got one outfit left for tomorrow. Everything else is dirty."

"Oh." I didn't exactly love wearing Lori's clothes, but they were all I had until my suitcase showed up. Which, at this rate, could be never. "What am I supposed to wear, then?"

"I don't know. Figure it out?"

I stopped walking. So did Jake. After a minute, Lori turned around.

"Look," she said to him. "Aki and I need to talk about something."

It was obvious Jake wanted to stay and get the gossip. But he nodded and went back to join the others on the way to vespers.

"Yeah, so." Lori glanced behind us to make sure no one

was in earshot. "Look. I know you told your girlfriend about our stupid first-kiss pact. And my pathetic crush on Paul, too."

My stomach flipped. "I wouldn't—Lori, I swear, I never said you were pathetic."

"Aki, I *heard* them. That guy from her church Rodney was telling one of the Harpers Ferry guys. They said I had some little-kid crush on Paul but I was too scared to talk to him. They looked right at me, laughing."

"When was this?" I prayed it happened before yesterday. Then it couldn't have been Christa's fault. We'd only talked about Lori when we were hanging out in town.

"Just now. At dinner. Rodney said he heard it from Madison and she heard it from Christa."

Oh, God. I'd told Christa all that stuff was a secret, hadn't I?

Well, but either way, shouldn't she *know* that when I tell her something, she shouldn't repeat it to her ex-girlfriend?

Except, it wasn't as if *I* was her girlfriend. Maybe she wasn't obligated to keep my secrets. It wasn't like we were ever going to see each other again once we left Mexico.

"Uh." I swallowed. I had no idea what to say to Lori. "They must've heard it from someone else."

"Save it." Lori pulled her hair back roughly into a lopsided ponytail. "I don't care anyway. I moved on from Paul a long time ago."

"You did?"

"Don't act so surprised." Lori hunched forward, clasping her elbows. "You aren't the only one who can have stuff going on."

"What stuff? Wait—Lori, did you hook up with someone?"

She looked away. "Not like you have time to care."

"What? I totally care. I care so much, are you kidding? Who is it? What happened? Tell me everything."

"Why should I? You don't tell me everything. Even though that was part of the deal, remember?"

Oh. Right. I'd sort of stopped giving Lori the play-by-play of everything that happened with Christa and me.

"Well, I mean, I may not mention every detail anymore, but you don't really want to know it all, right?" I said. "I mean, you're not interested in stuff with girls. *You're* not bi."

"Nope." The sarcasm in Lori's voice was thicker than usual. "Guess I'm not as cool as you."

"Come on, you know I didn't mean it that way. Anyway, who did you hook up with? Is it one of the Rockville guys?"

Lori was walking faster now. I jogged to keep up with her. "No."

"Harpers Ferry?"

"No."

"Wait, you mean it's one of the guys from *our* church? I thought you said they were all boring."

"They are."

She was basically running now. I worked hard to keep pace. "Wait, so—who the heck is it, then?"

Lori sighed. "I seriously can't tell you. We can't risk anyone finding out."

"I'm not *anyone*. I'm your best friend, remember?"

"Okay, well, *best friend*, if you're not going to tell me everything about your life I don't see why I should have to tell you about mine. Besides, I swore I wouldn't tell a soul. There's too much risk of someone overhearing in this tiny town, and if that happened his wife would find out for sure."

I stopped walking.

"His *wife*?" I stared at Lori, sure I'd heard wrong, but she looked right back at me, her lips set in a thin line. She'd stopped walking, too. "I thought you were hooking up with one of the youth group guys."

"Yeah, right." Lori scoffed. "Why would I want one of these losers when I can be with someone who's actually got his life together?"

"What, someone who's *married*?"

I stared at Lori, waiting for her to tell me I'd misunderstood. She looked right back at me.

I swallowed. "Who is it?"

Lori bit her knuckle.

I tried to think. One of the chaperones? But they were all people's dads. Plus they were all really old. If Lori was going to hook up with someone who was married, it would be someone young. Someone more or less normal.

"Oh, God." I didn't want to think it was true, but they were talking the other day, and... "It's—is it Carlos?"

Lori smiled slowly.

"Oh, God," I said again, because Lori really didn't seem to be joking.

"Promise you won't say anything." There was a strange look in her eyes. It was freaking me out.

"How *old* is he?"

"Not that old. Seriously, I need you to promise. If you tell your dad, my whole life will be over."

I hadn't even thought about that, but— "Maybe we *should* tell my dad. He'd know what to do. Seriously, Lori, this is really weird. I get that you're into older guys, but this one's so old he's *married*."

"You can't tell!" Lori swiveled her head from side to side, panic creeping in her eyes. "Aki, please, please promise me you won't. God, I knew I shouldn't have told you."

I shook my head. "It just isn't right. His wife is so sweet. It's such a mean thing to do to her."

"No, no, it's fine. She's seeing someone else, too. Please, I'm begging, don't do this to me." Her chin shook. She looked so scared. "I can't believe you'd even think about telling your dad. I haven't told anyone about you and Christa."

"That's totally different."

"Not really. You're with someone you don't want your parents to know about, same as me."

I swallowed. "Is he nice to you? Is he, you know, normal?"

"Of course he is. You know him. He's a good guy."

I'd met Carlos a few times, sure, but I certainly didn't think he was a good guy now that I was hearing this.

"It's so sketchy," I said. "He's *so* old."

"Only a few years, really. In Mexico it's not a big deal to date someone a few years older than you."

"I bet it's still a big deal if that someone's married."

"Come on. They didn't even want to get married. Their parents made them. He says they'll probably get a divorce soon."

I couldn't look at Lori. "It doesn't seem right."

"Just, please promise me you won't tell. You keep my secrets, I'll keep yours. *Please?*"

She looked at me, her eyes wide, her hands wrenched tight in front of her. All I could see was the Lori who'd been my best friend since we were kids. I'd already told one of Lori's secrets, and look how that turned out.

"All right," I said. "I promise. But this still isn't right. You have to end it before it goes too far."

"How far is too far, exactly?"

"Lori. Come on." We locked eyes. "Tell me you haven't."

She stared back at me for a long moment. I finally exhaled when she said, "I haven't."

"Good. That's good."

"But you've changed, Aki. You used to have my back."

"I still have your back, but come on—"

"You're a different person down here." Lori pressed her lips together tightly. "I think about you and her sitting around making fun of me, and it makes me want to throw up. You start hooking up with somebody for, what, a week, and suddenly you know everything there is to know about sex, and this random girl is more important than your best friend."

"She isn't." I swallowed. "We don't make fun of you. I'd never do that."

"Yeah, okay." Lori looked down. Her chin quivered. "I've barely seen you since we got here. You stick me with this stupid jewelry project and you barely even help—"

"I totally help!"

"And all you want to talk about is her. All you want to *think* about is her. Then you tell her about this thing we did and suddenly it's all a big joke. Well, whatever. What I have going on is a thousand times better than what you and her have."

"*No.* What you're doing is wrong, Lori. Come on. You've got to see that."

The look in her eyes was dead serious. "If you don't have my back, I don't have yours. That's how it works."

"I *do* have your back, just not on this one thing. Look, let's go talk to someone—I bet your aunt Miranda will know what to do if we only—"

"No! God! You promised you wouldn't tell and now you want to go tattle on me to Miranda?"

"No, that's not what I said, I—"

"Forget it." Lori looked up. There were tears in her eyes. "Forget all of it. You can borrow your stupid girlfriend's clothes from now on."

Lori turned around and walked alone into the dark.

CHAPTER 12

THREE DAYS WENT BY.

Lori and I didn't speak. When we saw each other, we turned and looked away. In our jewelry lessons, we sat on opposite ends of the blanket and divided everything in half without a single word. As though we didn't even know each other.

I'd barely gone twelve hours without talking to Lori since we were kids. I hadn't realized how much I counted on her. I'd listen to the guys in our group telling dumb jokes and I'd already be rehearsing in my head how I'd recount it all to Lori.

Then I'd remember I couldn't tell her. I was on my own.

It wasn't as if this was the first time we'd argued. There was the Barry Tuckerton thing in middle school, of course. And once last year on a field trip, Lori had gotten bored and told three of our friends this made-up story about some guy she'd supposedly hooked up with, and I was annoyed at her about it, and we argued in hushed tones for the whole bus ride home. By the time we got back to school, though, we'd pretty much forgotten the whole thing.

This was different. This was...painful.

This was my best friend, gone. It felt as though a part of myself was gone with her.

I didn't even really have Christa to talk to anymore. There was nowhere it was safe to be alone. We hadn't kissed since the night Jake caught us. We still had lunch every day with the rest of our group at the Suarezes' house, but lately Christa had started spending most of lunch going back and forth to the kitchen. At first I thought she was avoiding me, but then I realized Señora Suarez was teaching Christa how to make Mexican food. Christa's face, whenever I saw her at lunch, was either screwed up in concentration as she tried to get the beans right or blushing when Señora Suarez pointed at something she'd done and said, "¡Bueno!"

Every now and then, when no one was around, Christa and I would smile at each other. Sometimes we'd touch hands.

I'd started borrowing her clothes, too. They didn't fit me any better than Lori's had, but wearing them was exciting, and it was kind of a turn-on. Which was nice, since hand touching wasn't exactly what I'd had in mind when I pictured my summer fling.

I'd been spending more time with Gina and our other friends, and with Jake, who I was really starting to like. I'd even hung out with Drew and Sofía some, and to my surprise, that was actually fun.

Drew looked at me differently now, as though he was seeing me for the first time. At first he kept giving me weird looks, like he expected me to start doing, I don't know, overtly lesbian stuff right in front of him. But eventually, when he saw that I hadn't shaved my head or tried to make out with Sofía or anything, he seemed to calm down. But the best part was, it turned out Sofía was a fellow Prince fan. I didn't tell her just how into him I was—it was too embarrassing to admit that I used to dream about growing up to *be* Prince, or that my favorite song was—well. But either way, Sofía knew a lot about him, and soon we were analyzing the differences between his eighties albums and his later stuff and reenacting all those weirdly cryptic interviews he used to give so often that Drew had learned to groan and wander off whenever we got going.

Still, though, as I sat in vespers that night, trying to sing along in Spanish to a song about Jesus being the king of my life, all I could think about was how my summer had been ruined before it could even get going.

Up until I got to Mexico, the idea of having a girlfriend—even a kinda-sorta-not-really-because-she's-with-someone-else-but-still-kinda girlfriend—was this faraway idea I'd thought about with words like *maybe* and *someday*. I'd imagined an older version of me, in college or something, who was so mature that dating a girl would be no big deal. Back then, I figured that if I ever really hooked up, or even had sex, with a girl, that it would all fall into place easily.

In reality, nothing with Christa and me was easy. I hadn't thought about how hard it would be to keep things between us secret. Maybe if we were back in Maryland where we could be alone—where we had actual houses or even cars—things would be different. Here, though, everything seemed to be a problem.

Next to me, Jake wiggled his eyebrows at the King Jesus song. I laughed. At least I had one friend who things weren't complicated with.

Jake started lip-syncing along to the song with really exaggerated movements. He basically unhinged his jaw on the last, big *"Jesus!"*, silently howling at the ceiling. I choked down my laughs so Dad wouldn't notice.

Then I spotted Nick and Tyler across from us. Nick was imitating Jake, his own *"Jesus!"* howl directed at Tyler, who was laughing a lot louder than I had. Soon I noticed other people watching Nick and laughing, too. When I glanced back at Jake, his face had collapsed.

Everyone was clapping now that the song was over. I held out my hands so Jake would know I was clapping for him as Lori's aunt Miranda, that night's vespers leader, gave the closing.

"Now we depart with the holy spirit in our hearts," she intoned.

"Amen," we all chorused.

I climbed to my feet and held out my hand to help Jake up. I was about to tell him not to worry about Nick and his dumb friends when I heard someone else come up behind me. I couldn't see who it was, but Jake said, "Hey, Christa."

"Hey, Christa," I echoed. When I turned, I was startled to see her only inches from me.

"Hey." She half smiled as she bit her lip. "I was wondering if we could talk?"

Everyone was still milling around Reverend Perez's living room. The adults weren't paying any special attention to Christa and me, but we were getting stares from some of the others. Christa didn't seem to mind, though.

"Sure," I said. "Let's go."

As soon as we got outside, Christa started walking to the long tables under the trees where we'd eaten dinner. People would see us there, but we'd be too far away for them to hear us talking. I turned to say goodbye to Jake, but he'd already slipped away.

Christa lowered herself onto one of the benches. I made sure I left space between us as I sat next to her. She pulled her digital camera out of her bag.

"Turn to your left," she instructed. "Look at the sky, the way you were doing a second ago."

I turned, a smile climbing onto my face before I could stop myself.

"No, don't smile. Look neutral."

I had no idea what that meant, but I tried to look blank. Christa grabbed my chin, making me giggle, and turned my head a little farther to the left. Then she let go.

"Okay," she said. "Make your expression serious."

"I'm trying!" But I couldn't stop giggling.

She giggled, too, but she started taking photos anyway, the camera clicking away just out of my view. Finally I managed to smooth out my face. She took more shots, then got down on the ground to take photos of me from below.

"This is getting weird," I said.

"It's okay, I got what I needed." She climbed back onto the bench beside me. "You should really be an art model. You have the coolest face. All these incredibly interesting angles."

"Uh. Thanks, I guess?"

"Oh, it's definitely a good thing." She tucked her camera back into her bag. "When you're a rock star, you'll be on all the magazine covers. The celebrity photographers will love you."

I covered my face with my hand. "I'm not going to be a rock star."

"That's not what I've heard. Hey, when we can finally get online, you've got to play me some of your songs. Since I can't convince you to sing for me."

Some of my songs were probably still online. I hadn't listened to them since middle school, though. I could only guess how crappy they'd sound now.

"Maybe." As always, I changed the subject. "So, this is kind of nice. I'm not used to sitting someplace like this, where people can see us together."

Christa tilted her head backward. The motion made her shiny dark hair slide off her shoulder and curl against the back of her neck. I traced the line of skin there with my eyes. I imagined reaching over and lifting her hair off her neck. Running my fingers along the curve of her shoulder blades.

"It makes me nervous, though," she said. "After what happened last time."

Okay, we probably shouldn't have tried to hook up in the church where everyone we knew spent half their time. That hadn't been my brightest idea.

Still, though. There was something about the way she talked about it. As though she was ashamed of me. Or of what we did together.

Maybe she wasn't that far off. After all, if my dad found out, apparently he'd be crushed.

I didn't want to think about that anymore.

So I said, "Lori isn't speaking to me."

Christa looked up, her mouth in an O of surprise. "What happened?"

"She—" I hesitated. I wanted to tell her everything, but Lori had sworn me to secrecy, and even if we weren't friends anymore, I wasn't about to betray her again. "She's mad at me. I guess word got out that she liked Paul."

"Well, that's not your fault." Christa shrugged. "That's how it is in these kinds of places. Everybody knows everything that's going on. She'll get over it in a couple of days."

"It's already been a couple of days, and she isn't over it yet. And, look, it is my fault. She heard Rodney telling some guys he'd heard about it from Madison."

"Madison?" Christa's forehead creased.

"Yeah. You told her, right?"

Christa looked away. "She wouldn't tell anyone. I trust Madison."

"She definitely told them. Lori heard them laughing about it."

Christa shook her head. "It couldn't have been her."

"No one else knew. Besides, you shouldn't have told her."

"You—" Christa looked away. "You never told me it was a secret."

Crap. I hadn't? "Still. You should've known. I thought I could trust you."

Christa drew her shoulders up. Then she hung her head. "I'm sorry. You *can* trust me. Listen, I'll talk to Madison. She'll be sorry, too. I know Lori was your best friend, and it really blows when something like this happens."

Is, I wanted to correct her. Not *was*. Lori and I were best friends right now.

But what if that wasn't true? What if this was the end for Lori and me?

"Anytime you need to talk, I'm here," Christa said. "I mean, it's hard because we can't really be alone, but if you're, you know, missing your BFF, I get it. I've been there. It's the worst."

"Thanks." It was hard to stay annoyed at her when she was being so nice. "Well, actually, I do have something to tell you. Something kind of big."

"What is it?" She touched her pinky to mine. I felt warm all over, even though I was nervous, too.

"I—um. I told my brother."

Christa's head shot up. Her hand fell away from mine. She clearly knew exactly what I meant. "Why?"

"Because he asked me, and he's my *brother*. I'm not going to lie to him."

Christa's face was scarlet. "What if he tells someone?"

"He's not going to tell anyone."

Christa turned away, staring off into the clusters of people lingering around the edges of the Perezes' yard.

"Does your dad know?" Christa's hands trembled in her lap.

"Of course not. Drew won't tell him. He promised."

I didn't mention what Drew had said about Dad being crushed. Telling Christa would only make it more real.

She dropped her face into her hands. "This is exactly what I was afraid of."

I sighed. "I'm glad Drew knows. He was fine with it, and now I don't have to worry about keeping a secret from him. It's better this way."

Christa lifted her head. "I told you, I can't risk my parents finding out."

"I know, but no one here is going to tell your parents. Not my brother, not our friends and not any of these random people from West Virginia. It's seriously going to be fine." I swiveled around on the bench, staring down at the surface of the table. I traced a swirl in the cracked paint with my finger. "And I kind of wish you could be happy for me about telling Drew. Because that was a pretty big deal for me."

We sat in silence. I traced the swirl in wider and wider circles and kept my eyes on the table, trying not to think about what Christa might say. How her voice might sound.

I could feel the stars watching us overhead. I wondered if there were people watching us, too.

"I am happy for you," she said, finally. "That's awesome, about your brother. I just…can't imagine what that would be like. That's all."

I didn't know how to answer her. So we sat there in the dark, in the still silence, until I felt something touch my finger.

I looked down. My hand had been resting on the bench beside her, and now her fingertip was brushing the edge of my wrist. I ached to move closer, to slip my hand into hers.

"I'm sorry I'm so complicated," she whispered. Her finger traced the outside of my hand. I wanted to put my arm around her. To kiss her, right there. "The only thing I know for sure is that this summer, I want to be with you. Sometimes I wish

I could make everything else go away and have it only be you and me in our own little world."

I closed my eyes. Those words.

I never knew how much words could mean.

"I want to be with you, too." I kept my eyes focused on our hands. If I looked into her eyes, I was pretty sure I'd collapse. I didn't think it was possible to feel this many things at once and still be sitting here like a normal person.

"I think that's all that really matters." Christa was still whispering. "We can figure the rest of it out. We've got to be careful, but what matters is that we make the most of the time when we *can* be together."

I nodded. "It's worth it."

I wanted so badly to kiss her. I settled for stroking her finger instead.

She wanted to be with me, and I wanted to be with her.

And that was it. *That* was what mattered.

CHAPTER 13

MAYBE WE COULD meet at the work site, at night.

Except it smelled like paint in there. And it was so big. Totally exposed. At least in the old church there was a tarp to hide behind.

Maybe we could go into town? There didn't seem to be many streetlights in Mudanza. We could hide and kiss in the shadows.

But we wouldn't be safe outside. Anyone could stumble across us. And who knew how far the coyotes roamed?

Besides, kissing wasn't enough anymore. Now that we'd gotten started, I wanted to go forward, not back.

I could see the pink streak in Christa's hair over on the far side of the group. She was walking with her friends, snapping photos every so often, but I resisted the urge to look her way. It had been almost a full week since we'd last kissed—three days since she'd said those words, *I want to be with you*—and I ached to touch her again.

We had to find a place. Soon.

But it was Saturday afternoon, which meant we were walk-

ing into town, and Christa and I were studiously pretending
to ignore each other, just as we'd planned.

Not that anyone seemed to notice. Everyone was too caught
up in their own dramas.

The latest development was Nick and Emma, who were
walking at the front of our group. The rest of us were behind
them, whispering at the sight of their linked hands. As of yesterday, the last I'd heard was that Nick and *Hannah* were a
thing. Maybe that was why Hannah was walking at the very
back of the group, surrounded by three of her friends, holding her hand in front of her face.

Jake, meanwhile, was rambling to me about his latest petition.

"I thought it would be a no-brainer," he said. "I mean,
we're *in* Mexico. The plank isn't calling for full amnesty. It's
only saying we should support the immigrants who are already here. I mean, there, back home. But I haven't been able
to get anyone to sign except you and Lori."

I nodded absently. I barely even saw Lori anymore. Outside
our jewelry classes, she was almost never around.

She was still furious with me, though. Her eyes blazed every
time they met mine. Sometimes I worried she was so mad
she'd do something to get back at me. Like tell Christa I'd
lied to her about MHSA. Or, even worse, tell her about our
summer-fling pact and the hookup tally we'd kept.

I shivered. I never should have agreed to the pact in the
first place. I wouldn't have if I'd known how things would
turn out. What I had with Christa wasn't something to giggle over anymore.

"What did the others say when you asked them to sign?"
I asked Jake.

"The same crap people say back home." He shook his head.
"One girl said she'd never support giving immigrants jobs be-

cause her dad lost his job years ago, and the reason he couldn't find a new one was because the government was letting immigrants have all the jobs."

I rolled my eyes. Jake rolled his, too. Then he stumbled and nearly fell onto me. "Ow."

I grabbed his arm. "You okay?"

Jake straightened up. "Yep."

"What happened? You tripped?"

Jake glanced behind him. "Yeah, I tripped."

I looked back. Tyler and that guy from Jake's church, Brian, were watching us and guffawing behind their hands.

Had they tripped Jake on *purpose*? What were we, eight?

"Who are you rooming with?" a girl asked behind us while Jake and I walked in silence. We were almost at the downtown area now, where the shops were. We'd come later in the day than we had last week so we could spend the morning in an orientation session for the trip to Texas next weekend. Mostly the session had consisted of praying, again, some more.

"I'm supposed to be with Emma, but I want to change," another girl answered. "She talks in her sleep and it's so embarrassing."

I tried to tune them out. I'd heard at breakfast that Lori and Gina were sharing a dorm room.

It didn't feel right. Lori and I had been roommates on every trip since we were kids.

Even though I'd much rather room with Christa. Obviously.

"Who's your roommate going to be?" I asked Jake.

"No idea." He nearly stumbled again, but there was no sign of Tyler or Brian this time.

I changed the subject. "Is it true that the only votes at the conference that people care about are the ones on gay marriage and the war?"

"Well." The lines around Jake's mouth faded. "To be honest, I didn't read *that* much of the conference forums. I was mostly into making sure people voted the right way on marriage. But from what I saw, people are talking about the war more than anything else. Marriage was a distant second. I didn't see a lot about any of the other issues—even though so much of this stuff, like immigration, is so important. I wish I'd paid more attention to it before."

"Is that why you're putting out all these petitions?" I fanned out my shirt against the heat. It was one of Drew's jerseys. I'd wound up borrowing some of his stuff after all, and I'd forgotten how comfortable his shirts were. I used to wear his clothes all the time, when I was little and thought Drew was the coolest person who'd ever been invented.

"I guess." Jake frowned. "The more I think about it, the more I realize *all* these issues are important, you know? Plus the war, well. I know it's a big deal, but it feels a lot farther away. I mean, there are fifty kids in my school who immigrated in the last couple of years. They aren't all Mexican, but most of them came in through Mexico."

I nodded. "You're right. It's weird people aren't talking about this stuff more."

We'd reached downtown Mudanza. Smaller groups were starting to peel off to go into the tiny stores or wander down the narrow alleys. I turned in the direction of the internet place I'd spotted last week. Jake turned with me.

Crud. I should've seen this coming.

"What's down here?" Jake glanced from one side of the street to the other.

"Uh." We were still a few blocks away, but if I told him where I was going, he'd want to come, too. "Actually, it's kind of—private."

"Private?" Jake's face clouded up again, the way it had when

I asked who he was rooming with in Texas. "What, are you meeting up with your other friends?"

For a second, I just stood there with my mouth flopping open. Then I had a brilliant idea.

"Actually, I'm meeting up with…well…" I lowered my voice to a whisper. "You know. Christa."

I shrugged in a way that I hoped looked suggestive.

"Oh!" Jake's eyes widened. Then he laughed. "Okay. Guess I shouldn't crash that party."

"Yeah, that'd be awkward." I could feel my face flushing. If only I really *were* going to a clandestine meetup with my not-really girlfriend.

What I was actually doing was far less sexy. It was almost the opposite.

"All right. Guess I'll see you back at the church later, then." Jake looked lonely as I waved goodbye. Poor dude.

I was almost at the internet place, praying it was open, when Juana stepped in front of me. She was holding a soccer ball and wearing a dusty purple dress. She grinned, her mouth showing a wide row of bright, uneven teeth. Even though I was worried about running out of time, I couldn't help grinning back. "Hola, Juana."

"¡Hola, Ah-ki!"

She then proceeded to rattle off a bunch of sentences in Spanish I couldn't understand.

I waved my hands in the air, trying to look helpless. She laughed. Then she dropped the soccer ball and played air guitar, the way she had during jewelry class. She tilted her head to one side and closed her eyes as she air-strummed. It was adorable. When she opened her eyes, she pointed at my chest and said, "¡Para usted, y sus amigos! ¡Esta noche!"

I was pretty sure that meant "For you and your friends tonight." But I still didn't understand what she was talking about.

"¡Gracias!" I said. You could never go wrong with *gracias*.

Juana smiled and ran away, kicking the ball ahead of her, stirring up more dust. I waved and turned back to the internet place.

When I pushed through the rickety glass door, the store was empty aside from a girl sitting behind the counter who not that much older than Juana. There were four computers sitting in two rows back-to-back. Big, boxy monitors on top of big, boxy hard drives.

I smiled at the girl. "Hola."

"Hola." She said a bunch of words I didn't know. I held out my hand with a few pesos, hoping she'd get the idea.

The girl smiled, took one of the bills out of my hand and gave me some coins. Then she scribbled two numbers on a piece of paper—"1, 30"—and handed it to me.

The computers had signs on them with numbers. The one farthest from the door was labeled "1." She was telling me to use that computer, for...thirty minutes?

"¿Treinta minutos?" I asked her, pleased with myself for remembering the words.

The girl nodded, looking equally pleased.

I sat down at the ancient computer and pressed the power button. The monitor blinked to life. I opened a browser window and glanced back at the desk, but my new friend had gone over to the door to talk to another girl. I couldn't understand what they were saying, but there seemed to be a lot of giggling involved.

Well, I had to get started. Even if it was embarrassing just to type the words.

I went to the search box and put in "Do lesbians use condoms?" Then I reached up to cover the screen with my hand, even though no one was around to see.

But I needed to know this. And there wasn't anybody I could ask.

The results took forever to load, and the first few that came up were strange. They were from different forums, and they used a lot of words I didn't want to click on. *Dildos*, for example.

I'd seen a wooden dildo in health class once. They made everyone practice putting a condom on it. It was gross. I had no idea how anything like that was supposed to be sexy.

The sex-ed presenter told us all about different kinds of protection, but she didn't say anything about gay sex. I knew it was important to be careful when you had sex with guys because you could get pregnant or get diseases. But how were you supposed to use a condom when there was nothing to put it on? Could two girls even give each other a disease?

It was mortifying to think about. Up until this summer, I'd always thought of sex in kind of vague terms. I figured I'd do it someday, and I'd understood the basics, sort of. But now I needed to get a lot more practical about things. I had a feeling real sex wasn't going to be the way it was in all those Prince songs, where you and a girl you barely knew just went for it in a barn or a corvette or wherever was handy. Not that I might not want to do that kind of thing someday—never say never—but I didn't want it for my first time. I wanted it to feel right. And with Christa, it did.

What had surprised me the most about what we'd done so far was how...*normal* I still felt. I mean, we'd done stuff I'd never done before with anyone. Certainly not with a girl.

Before, I'd thought it would make me feel different. Like more of an adult. Instead I basically still felt like me. Except a version of me who knew what it was like to touch a girl's boobs.

It wasn't what I'd expected at all.

Anyway. I scrolled through the search results and clicked

on something called "How to Practice Safer Sex for Lesbians." That sounded promising.

I could tell as soon as I clicked through that the website was meant for teenagers, with lots of bright colors and funky graphics. I almost closed it—I didn't need to read another lecture from someone like the lady who made us touch the wooden dildo—but I saw a headline halfway down the screen that said "Safer Sex: Why Lesbians Need It Too." When I clicked through, the beginning of the article made me squirm.

Sex education usually focuses on one kind of sex only: The kind involving a penis penetrating a vagina. That's why most sex-ed classes focus on protecting vaginas from penetrating penises. But even when there are two vaginas on the scene and no penis in sight, trust us, those vaginas still need protection from each other.

Whoa. I looked over my shoulder. Then I sat up and twisted around so I had a clear view of the door. If someone came in I'd pretend I was checking my email.

Women who have sex with other women don't have to worry about pregnancy (unless one of those women has a penis—see our section on safer sex for transgender and nonbinary folks here), but they're susceptible to sexually transmitted infections, just like everyone else. That means they need to use barriers to protect them both.

I'd never heard of "barriers" before, not in a sex context anyway, but I kept reading, and soon I got it. Using barriers just meant putting something in between you and the other person during sex, the same idea as a condom. The article talked a lot about gloves and something called a *dental dam*.

I tried to imagine making out with Christa while wearing gloves. It didn't sound very romantic.

But the more I read, the more it started to make sense. Gloves weren't for making out. They were for doing stuff down there with your fingers. Dental dams were for doing stuff down there with your mouth.

Wow. I squirmed harder.

Where was I supposed to get dental dams and gloves, though? The shops in Mudanza seemed to mostly sell canned tomatoes.

I opened a new search window and typed in "where to get dental dams." A bunch of ads popped up for websites where you could order them. I pictured a box of dental dams showing up on the front steps of the church where we slept. Then I clicked on a link to another teen sex-education site. It said you could get dental dams for free at Planned Parenthood or at a community or university health center.

Hmm. I doubted I'd find dental dams at the Casa de Salud in Mudanza, but I *was* going to a college campus next week.

The rest of the article on the website was really long, and it had illustrations. I scrolled past those fast. The words were embarrassing enough. Then I got to a section called "Talking with Your Partner about Sex."

Many people say they're afraid to practice safer sex because they're too nervous to bring it up with their partners. Although this is a common concern, it's dangerous. You're putting your own and your partner's health at risk if you're too bashful to talk about safety.

Oh. Now I felt bad for being embarrassed.

The door to the shop opened and closed. The girl and her

friend must have finished gossiping. I scrolled down farther on the page.

There were links to a bunch of other articles. One said "What Is Bisexuality?" I clicked on that, even though I already knew what bisexuality was. It was pretty obvious. When I read the first line of the article I nearly closed the window.

A bisexual person can feel attraction to people of more than one gender.

I mean, duh.

Then I skipped down a couple of paragraphs and saw this:

One common myth is that bisexual people must be in simultaneous relationships with both men and women to be sexually satisfied. Another is that bisexuals are promiscuous. In fact, many bisexual people may be perfectly happy in monogamous relationships.

Well, that was interesting. All I'd heard anyone say about being bi was that guys thought it was hot for a girl to be bi. I was pretty sure it had something to do with porn.

Last year, when I first started thinking I might be bi, I'd looked at some porn videos. They were disgusting. It had almost been enough to make me think I might not be into girls after all. Then I overheard some guys talking about porn at school and I realized that the porn I saw on the internet, even the lesbian porn, was supposed to be for guys, not girls. That's why the stuff I'd found was gross—it wasn't the real thing.

There were a lot of other articles on the website that looked interesting—there was one called "Are You Ready for Sex? A Relationship Checklist"—but my time was running low. I'd have to come back to the site later.

"Treinta minutos," the girl said from the desk. I figured she was telling me I was out of time, but when I looked up there was a man standing at the desk, taking a piece of paper from the girl. Uh-oh.

I closed the page and brought up the browser history so I could clear it out. It took way too long, though, on that slow connection. I tapped my fingers on the counter anxiously.

The guy sat down at the computer at the far corner from mine and started typing fast. He was wearing a baseball cap and sitting hunched over the screen, the same way I was.

My computer finally finished deleting the history. I grabbed my purse, ready to speed out of that place, when I realized the guy in the cap was—"Drew?"

My brother swiveled in his chair, blocking his screen with his broad shoulders. "Hey, Sis. Just checking email."

"Yeah, me, too." Crap, now I wished I really *had* checked my email. Then I had an idea. "Hey, do you have a roommate yet for Texas?"

Drew side-eyed me. "No, but—uh, listen, Sis, I don't think us rooming together is a great idea. I know we used to do it at Grandma's, but—"

"Oh, no, I'm not asking for me. I was wondering if maybe you'd be up for sharing with Jake? He doesn't have a roommate yet, either, and he's really cool. The other guys from his church are all big jerks."

Drew glanced back toward the screen. "Yeah, sure, whatever. I can't talk right now, though. Need to write to my professor about a class."

My mouth dropped open. "Does that mean you decided to go back to school?"

He looked away. "Maybe. I don't know. See you later, okay?"

"Okay. See you."

I waved to the girl at the desk and left, the glass door swinging closed behind me. The street was empty except for a couple of Mexican women talking in another store's doorway.

For a second I felt lost. I'd never been downtown by myself before. I almost wanted to go back inside and wait for Drew to finish his email so he could walk with me.

No. I should stop being a baby. I looked toward one end of the street, then the other. I'd come from the right. It would be easy enough to retrace my steps back to the church.

Once I started walking, it was actually kind of nice to be alone. I might be in a foreign country, but I could still take care of myself.

I followed the road back toward church, stepping carefully over the holes in the pavement in the too-small flip-flops I'd borrowed from Christa. Images from what I'd read swarmed through my skull.

I hadn't realized lesbian sex was so…complicated. Up until now I'd sort of been doing whatever felt natural. Kissing, and touching. One thing had seemed to lead to another. It was strange to think about "going all the way" when everything felt like a logical progression.

One more week. In Texas, I could get the stuff we needed. And then…if we wanted to…

Yeah. I needed to make sure Christa and I had a dorm room to ourselves.

I was still smiling when I got to the work site. The rest of the group wouldn't be back for another hour. Señora Perez was out front talking with Aunt Miranda and some of the other chaperones. Dad was there, too, organizing painting supplies.

"Yo, Dad!" I jogged up to him.

Dad smiled. "Been a while since you last shouted 'yo' at me."

"Yeah, well." I grinned at him. "I wanted to ask you something."

"Shoot." He stood, dusting off his jeans.

"Are we supposed to put our names down somewhere for roommates for the trip to Texas next week?"

Dad laughed and reached into his backpack. "I suppose we could start. Gotta say, if I'd known you kids would be so excited about that trip, I'd have set one up for every weekend."

Wow. How different would this summer have been if Christa and I could've had a dorm room to ourselves every single week? More than just this trip—my whole *life* would be different now.

Dad pulled out a notebook and pen. "So, will you and Lori be roommates, same as always?"

"Oh, uh, no." My grin faded. It hurt, literally, to talk about Lori. A persistent, stabbing pain in my side. "Could you put me down to room with Christa Lawrence from Rockville?"

Dad glanced down at me. "Is everything all right between you and Lori? I noticed you haven't been talking to her as much as usual."

"Yeah, uh." The day before I'd seen Lori next to a truck full of paint cans talking to Carlos. He'd waved at me, but Lori looked at her feet. I didn't wave back. "We're having, you know, one of those things girls have where they're weird with each other. It'll be fine."

Dad's eyebrows quirked, but he seemed to accept my explanation. "All right. You and Christa, then."

"Can you also put down that Drew is rooming with Jake Spotswood from Harpers Ferry?" I might as well set things up so Drew couldn't back out.

"All right." Dad scribbled on the pad. "Glad to see you're both getting to know kids from the other churches."

"Thanks." I watched Dad shove his notebook back into his backpack. "How come you didn't go into town today?"

"Well, keep in mind, I can go into town anytime I want." We started walking down the gravel road. Dad was heading for a pink house with a big brown dog lying in the sun on the front walk. "It's one of the perks of being a grown-up."

I rolled my eyes. "Where are we going?"

"To the Riveras' house. That's where I'm staying, remember? With Pastor Dan."

"It's so not fair that you get to sleep in a *house*. In a *bed*."

Dad chuckled. "Well, it's actually a couch, and if it makes you feel any better, I'm sleeping on the floor right now so your poor friend Rodney can have it."

"Oh, right." The chaperones had told us a million times before we got here that we could only brush our teeth with bottled water. Even one drop of the water that came out of the faucets in this part of Mexico could make us sick. But Rodney had forgotten, I guess. He'd come down with a serious case of what Miranda called "Montezuma's Revenge." He'd moved in with Dad and Pastor Dan for a couple of days so he could run to the Riveras' bathroom when he needed to. Whenever we saw him at meals, he only picked at his food, and his face was scarily pale.

"I thought the Riveras had a guest room," I said.

"They have a guest house out back, but the power there isn't reliable, so we've been camping out in their living room, same as you."

"'Camping out' in a living room is totally different from having to use a collapsible shower in a field," I said.

Dad chuckled again. He seemed to be in a better mood than he had been lately. "So did you get the information you needed? About the health center?"

I stopped walking, panic in my throat. How could he know I was going to get dental dams at the college health center? I hadn't told a *soul*.

Then he looked at me expectantly, and I remembered. The Casa de Salud. Whew.

"Not really," I said. "I mean, it sounds as though the health care system here has a lot of issues. And Jake told me something about a plank on international health care at the conference that might help. But I don't know what to do about any of it. Jake keeps starting these petitions but he can't get anyone to sign them, so I don't know if that makes sense or not, and..."

I trailed off. I hadn't realized I'd been thinking about this so much.

Dad bent down to pat the sleeping dog and opened the front door. I followed him inside. No one else seemed to be home. The Riveras had a pretty living room with soft-looking couches and windows that let in so much light it felt as though we were still outside.

"You know, I hadn't thought about the global health care resolution that way, but your friend Jake might be right," Dad said. "Let me see if I can find the materials on that. I brought a lot of the conference documents down here with me. I don't know when I thought there would be time to read."

Dad pulled a suitcase out from behind an end table and flipped it open. He tossed aside a pile of wrinkled T-shirts. Mom would've been furious to see he hadn't been trying to keep anything folded at all.

"Um, Benny?" I jumped. Rodney was standing in the hallway. I hadn't even known he was in the house. He looked paler than the last time I'd seen him, and he was bent over, clutching the small of his back. "Can you come here for a sec?"

Dad straightened up. "Sure, Rod. Be right there. Aki, sweetheart, there's a bunch of papers at the bottom of the suitcase. See if you can find the background materials I brought with me on the conference planks."

"What, you mean right now?"

Instead of answering me, Dad took off down the hall after

Rodney. I held my nose and reached into the suitcase for the sheaf of papers. Everything was crumpled.

The top papers were all about our travel arrangements for this trip—plane ticket confirmations, super boring stuff. I was flipping through it, looking for anything about the conference, when I saw the photo.

It was tucked between two stacks of papers, but it wasn't crumpled at all. That was because it was in a protective plastic sheath. The photo looked old, though, like Dad had been carrying it around for years.

At first I thought it was a photo of Drew, but I realized quickly that wasn't right. The guy in the photo looked about Drew's age, but his eyes weren't as crinkled as Drew's, and the corners of his lips didn't turn up quite as high. And he was wearing a T-shirt Drew didn't own for a band I'd never heard of.

As Dad's footsteps echoed back down the hallway, I realized who it was.

My uncle Andrew. Dad's brother. He was about Drew's age when he died.

"Sorry about that," Dad said. I fumbled through the papers, sliding the photo back where I'd found it. "Did you find the materials?"

"Oh." I tried not to look guilty. "Uh, no."

"Give it here."

I handed Dad the stack, wondering if he was hiding the photo of my uncle on purpose. Did he carry it everywhere he went?

I gazed out the back windows while Dad looked through his documents. The Riveras had a courtyard, like the Perezes did, with a wall around it. Behind the courtyard, I could see the guest house. It was tiny—probably a bedroom and nothing

more. The curtains were open. I could see straight through
to the other side, where a door stood ajar.

Hmm.

"Found it." Dad handed me a couple of pages. "This is the
background on the international health care plank we're voting on. Want to read through it and tell me what you think?"

"Oh." I hadn't expected homework. "Do I have to?"

"Well, you said you weren't sure what you could do to help.
So here's one thing."

I tucked the papers under my arm, gazing out at the guest
house again.

"I'm pleased to see you're interested in this," Dad said. "Let
me know your verdict, all right?"

"All right. Hey, I should probably get back. I need to talk
to Drew about something."

"Sure thing." Dad let me out of the house with a wave.

I left and went down to the end of the block in case anyone
was watching. Then I cut around behind the row of houses
and doubled back, staying close to the hills where Christa and
I had spent so much time in that first week.

Sure enough, the Riveras' guest house door was standing
open. Only a little way, but it would be enough.

The curtains were open on this side, too. Inside the room,
I could see the dim outline of a low bed.

If the power didn't work out there, that meant the lights
wouldn't, either. No one would be able to see inside the room
when it was dark out.

Wow. *Wow.*

I couldn't wait to tell Christa.

CHAPTER 14

I HAD TO wait through the whole afternoon *and* dinner *and* vespers before I could tell her.

To make things worse, vespers was extra-long that night. And extra-annoying. Nick and Paul and their friends Will and Tyler had apparently spent the entire day drinking, and they kept burping loudly whenever the chaperones weren't paying attention. And I'd gotten stuck sitting on the floor right in front of them.

I kept trying to inch away from them so I wouldn't have to smell their burps. After I inched away for the third time, while one of the Harpers Ferry chaperones was droning on about the importance of being open with God about our sins, I heard a sudden burst of laughter behind me. I turned to glare. Will started giggling again as soon as he saw my face. Then Tyler said, "What're you looking at us for? I thought you were a muff diver."

The laughter after that was so loud the chaperone had to interrupt his talk and tell the guys to be quiet. I turned back around, my face burning.

The guys were just being jerks. I knew what they'd said shouldn't bother me, but it did.

Plus, I didn't want Christa to hear them saying that kind of stuff. She was sitting on the far side of the room with Madison, and I didn't think she'd heard, but I didn't want to take that chance.

Maybe she'd had the right idea about keeping things secret.

"All right, y'all," Lori's aunt Miranda called from the front of the room. "It's time for the singing."

Usually everyone would groan as soon as one of our chaperones said the word *singing*, but since it was Aunt Miranda, people just nodded, looking bored. She was younger than most of the chaperones, and she wore hippie-type clothes like crocheted vests and scarf-headbands. She was black, too—she and Lori's mom were only half sisters; Lori and her parents were as white as Elmer's glue—and sometimes she tried to be all buddy-buddy with me, as though we were two black girls together against the world. As if I'd forget she was so old and dressed like a weirdo.

"Guess what?" Aunt Miranda said. "We have a special helper here this evening, don't we?"

Everyone shifted in their seats to see the "special helper"—Juana. She was sitting next to Señor Suarez, holding his twelve-string guitar.

My dad was on the other side, smiling at her encouragingly. He and Drew had been hanging out at the Suarez house a lot lately, practicing their Spanish and stealing extra bites of Juana's mother's cooking.

Señor Suarez gestured for Juana to begin. Her forehead was wrinkled, and her fingers shook as she lined them up on the neck of the guitar. Now I understood what she'd been trying to tell me earlier that day—that tonight, after her long hours of practice with her dad, she was finally going to play for us.

I was amazed, honestly. I couldn't imagine learning to play a twelve-string at her age. My guitar teacher at school wouldn't even let me try until eighth grade.

But Juana seemed to know what she was doing as she strummed the first notes. It was a song we'd sung at vespers a few times. Her version of the song was simpler than the complex cords her father usually played, but it was beautiful all the same. Señor Suarez led the singing, but instead of paying attention to the lyrics, I watched Juana play. She was a beginner, that much was clear—some of the chords didn't sound quite right, and she was concentrating a little too fiercely on the movements of each finger—but her eyes were shining. She loved music just as much as I had at her age.

Suddenly, my hands itched to touch those strings. I hadn't picked up a guitar in more than a year, but now the memories flooded back. I'd loved the tautness of the strings under my fingers. The steady weight of the strap across my back.

I wanted to feel what Juana was feeling. I wanted it to all be fresh and new again.

No disappointment. No resentment, either. Nothing but a world full of open possibility.

When the song ended, I started clapping, hard. We didn't usually applaud at vespers, but people joined with me anyway. A few even let out little *woo hoo*s for Juana. She grinned at us, her face alight.

I was startled when she climbed down from the couch, passed the guitar carefully to her father, ran over and hugged me. I laughed, though, and hugged her back. For the first time in years, I remembered what it was like to get that excited over playing. When it's not about hitting every note perfectly or impressing anyone—it's just about the joy of the song.

Señor Suarez stood, smiling down at Juana, and led her

outside as Dad and Reverend Perez launched into the closing prayers.

After ten minutes of monotonous pastors praying in simultaneous English and Spanish, they finally dismissed us. Everyone climbed up off the floor, stretching. I leaped to my feet and made a beeline for Christa.

She was already in the doorway next to Madison. Her eyes sparkled in the reflected light from the candles that dotted the room. Even her glitter headband seemed to take on an extra shine.

"So, I have news," I told her. "Kind of a lot of news."

Madison was watching us. I tried not to let that bother me. It wasn't cool to get jealous just because your sort-of-but-actually-not-really girlfriend was hanging out with her ex.

I still kind of wanted to shove Madison, though. Or maybe just pinch her.

But I'd be mature about it. It would only be a tiny pinch. On, like, on her elbow or something.

Christa glanced at Madison. That only made me want to pinch her more.

Finally, Christa turned back to me and jutted her chin toward the door. I got the idea and followed her out of the Perezes' house and halfway down the block.

She and Madison walked together. I stayed twenty feet behind them, my eyes shooting daggers into the back of Madison's neck.

Finally the crowd started to thin out as people wandered back to the church or drifted off in twos and threes. Christa slowed down, then stopped. Madison leaned in to say something to her, then walked away toward the church.

Christa was alone in front of me. Now that I wasn't distracted, she looked astonishingly pretty against the dim lights in her pale purple dress. Something was written across her left arm in a dark blue marker, but I couldn't read it from this distance.

She turned around and smiled. I smiled back, trying to forget about Madison. There were too many good things to focus on the bad ones.

As I got closer, I could read the letters on her arm. *QUESTION STABILITY*, it said. I liked that idea.

I liked the dress she was wearing, too. It was a tiny bit tight around the waist, and the hemline showed more of her legs than I was used to seeing. It was tight around her chest, too.

The clothes I was wearing were hers. I'd borrowed a long skirt (that wasn't nearly as long on me as it probably was on her) and a sleeveless top that buttoned up the front. I'd never seen her wear either one before. She must've brought more clothes with her than Lori had. I'd brought a bunch of clothes of my own, too, if my suitcase would ever get here, but for now I didn't mind wearing Christa's. It made me feel closer to understanding what it was like to be her.

"So," Christa said when I got close enough to smile back at her. "What's the big news?"

Oh, right. I grinned. "I asked my dad if we could be roommates next weekend in Texas, and he said yes."

Christa's eyes widened. "That is so awesome."

"Yeah." I was so glad to hear her say that. "I thought so, too."

"I mean, to have some time for just us? That'll be perfect, right?"

"God, yes."

She reached out as if she was going to take my hand. Then she glanced to the side and pulled back.

"Also." I kept going, before she could say anything. "I found a place for us to go. Here, I mean."

"What?" Christa's head swiveled back toward me. "Wait, do you mean—*tonight*?"

"Yeah." I was smiling so hard I was afraid my jaw was going to fall off.

I told her about the guest house. Her eyes widened even more.

"How far is it?"

"A couple of blocks. We can walk out back behind the houses, toward the hills."

Christa turned and started walking so fast I started laughing.

"It's going to be dark," I said. "Do you think we should get a flashlight?"

There were lots of flashlights back at the church. We'd been told to bring them along with our sleeping bags. We used them if we needed to get up at night to go to the bathroom.

"Wouldn't they see the beams?" Christa said. "They'd think someone was breaking into their house."

"Well, that's kind of what we're doing." We both giggled. "Hmm, do you think there are still candles left from vespers? We could put them on the floor way below the windows. The light would be so faint I bet they wouldn't see it."

"That might work."

We went back to the Perezes' house. I'd thought it would be deserted, but the adults, my dad included, were still standing around talking in the front yard. The door was wide open. Beyond it we could see the empty living room with the candles still laid out.

"My dad is here," I whispered. "You go in without me."

"I'm not just going to wander in there by myself," Christa whispered back. "They'll all think I've lost it."

So we went in together. I made Christa stay on the side closest to my dad, and somehow we made it into the living room without anyone looking our way. As soon as we were inside, I erupted into a new round of giggles. Christa looked annoyed at first, but then she started giggling, too.

I grabbed three candles and slipped them into the pocket of my skirt. Christa hunted around for a lighter and found an almost-empty book of matches on an end table. Then we bolted back toward the door.

And ran smack into Aunt Miranda.

"Aki?" Miranda took a step back and looked me up and down in my borrowed clothes. Then she turned to Christa. "What are you two doing here? It's your bedtime."

"Oh, uh." Crap, why didn't I think of an excuse before we came in here? "I was looking for my dad. I need to ask him a question."

"He's right out here." Miranda pointed over her shoulder. "I'll go get him."

"Wait, no, uh." What was I supposed to say? "Actually, never mind, I figured out the answer."

Miranda didn't look terribly convinced. "In the past ten seconds?"

"Uh. Yeah." Crap, crap. "I was trying to think of what to get him for Christmas, but now I have an idea."

"Christmas? Wow, you plan early." Miranda folded her arms. Her lip twitched. "So what are you getting him?"

"Um. It's a surprise." I turned to Christa. Her mouth was in a tight, polite smile, the same way she looked whenever an adult was around. "I guess I've got Christmas on the brain. Earlier some of the Harpers Ferry guys were singing 'Feliz Navidad' and—"

"Actually, I retract my question." Miranda held up her hand. "I don't want to know."

I could've sworn she winked at me.

"All right." I ducked past her, Christa right on my heels.

"But listen, Akina?" Miranda said. I turned around. "Let's

catch up sometime soon. Come find me during the lunch break when you get a chance, okay?"

"Okay." I'd say anything to get out of that room.

"And as for tonight…" Miranda must've seen the guilty look on my face because she said, "Try to stay out of trouble, all right?"

I nodded, not meeting her eyes.

Christa and I ducked through the front yard fast so Dad wouldn't see us. When we got around the corner and were safely out of sight, Christa's polite look slipped away and we both tried to muffle our laughter.

"We've got to keep going!" Christa whispered. "They'll hear us!"

We crept around to the backs of the houses and made our way toward the Riveras'. I was getting hiccups from trying so hard not to laugh.

But I was also starting to get nervous. If this plan worked, we were about to be alone in a room with a real bed for the first time ever.

What were we actually going to *do*? The stuff I'd read about sounded cool but also kind of scary. It was hard to imagine doing something like that in real life.

A yelp came from behind us. I jumped and grabbed Christa's arm, ready to run in case it was another coyote. Then I realized that had been a distinctly human yelp.

"Relax," Christa whispered. "It's only Nick and the guys."

I followed her gaze. It was hard to see them in the dark, but five or six houses down, Nick, Will, Tyler and a couple of other guys were horsing around, throwing something back and forth between them. Probably more beer.

"They're idiots," I whispered back.

"Nah, they're drunk, that's all. Anyway, don't worry about them. Let's go."

We could see the guest house now. In the dark, we couldn't see into the windows at all.

"What if there's someone inside?" I whispered. We probably didn't need to whisper—there didn't seem to be anyone in hearing distance—but whispering was the sort of thing you did when you were sneaking around.

"If there was someone inside they'd have turned on the light," Christa whispered back.

"Dad said the power in there was spotty."

"Oh. Well, let's listen at the door before we go in."

We crept up to the entrance. The guest house was pink, but in the dark it looked gray, and the window showed nothing but blackness. It was tiny—there couldn't have been room for much more inside than a bed. The door was still ajar.

We crept toward it and crouched below the window. My heart pounded. I didn't know if I was afraid someone was inside or if I was afraid of going in there and doing...whatever we were going to do.

A minute passed. Then another.

Christa still hadn't spoken. I wondered if she was as nervous as me.

Finally she said, "I think we're safe."

I pulled the door open one inch, then two.

Nothing happened. The guest house was dark and empty.

Christa fumbled for a match, and I pulled a candle out of my pocket. It took her three strikes to get the match lit. She held the flame low as I slid the door open enough for us to squeeze through.

Inside, Christa set the candle on the floor. The flicker of light it gave off was barely enough for us to see a tiny bedroom. The bed looked lumpy but the blanket seemed clean and fresh.

Best of all, the curtains were thick. I drew them quickly

on both windows. Now we wouldn't have to worry about anyone seeing us.

When I turned around, Christa was looking right at me, smiling nervously and smoothing out her dress.

The whole world was ours. Or at least this little corner of it.

I cupped the back of her head in my palm and drew her toward me, but she moved even faster, closing the space between our lips so fast I giggled again. We kissed, and kissed, and kissed—and then we were falling back, back, until we landed on the bed. Sure, it was lumpy and the pillows felt like sacks full of rocks, but it was still my very favorite bed in the history of beds.

We kissed, and giggled, and rolled around and kissed some more. Then the kissing got deeper, and I rolled on top of her, and the giggling stopped.

I touched her through her clothes. She felt incredible. Then I slid my hand inside the neckline of her dress. Her skin was soft and warm. I reached down to cup her breast inside her bra, and she sighed. I loved the way it sounded, and the way she felt. Touching her with nothing between her skin and mine was new and strange and wonderful.

Christa closed her eyes. Her face looked so peaceful. I kissed her, and she parted her lips to kiss me back. I slid my hand over to her other breast, and she sighed again. I slipped my hand out from under her dress and ran it down her side to her hip, and then down farther, to brush against the hem of her skirt and her bare leg below it.

My heart was beating faster. I was nervous, but I wanted to be close to her this way.

We'd only ever touched above the waist before. But I didn't think she'd stop me, and she didn't. I reached under her skirt hem, just an inch. Then I slid my hand up as far as I dared, to the top of her thigh. Her skin was so soft and smooth. Touching her under her skirt felt so intimate, even if I wasn't touching her *there*.

Christa surprised me then. She rolled me over onto my back and climbed on top of me. She was stretched out, her body touching every inch of me. I kept my hand where it was, on the back of her leg, and she didn't seem to mind.

She kissed me while she fumbled with the buttons running down the front of my shirt. I never usually bothered with buttons—it was easier to pull shirts off over my head—but it was sexy, the feeling of her hands undoing the fastenings, separating the fabric. And when she leaned down and pushed my bra up and started kissing my breasts, that was even better. Her dress was loose around the neckline, so I pushed it down to her waist and took her bra off, too. This was the closest to naked we'd ever been together. It was hot in the guest house, and my skin was dotted with sweat. Hers was, too.

I lost track of time. I couldn't believe how good this felt. How good *she* felt.

I rolled onto my side, wound my arms around her and pulled her tight against me. She started to giggle, but then she saw I was serious, and she stopped laughing. I kissed her hard, leaning in so far she had to bend backward. She made a little sound in the back of her throat that I loved.

I loved this. I loved *her*.

Wait. No. I didn't. What I had with Christa wasn't about love. This was just for fun.

Christa was already with someone else. I wondered if she loved *him*.

But I didn't see how anyone could really love one person and still want to do this with someone else. This was so intimate. So real. And part of what made it feel that way was how much I cared about Christa.

I didn't have time to think about that, though. Right now I had other priorities.

I reached down before I had time to get nervous. I ran my fingers over the front of her dress and between her legs, feeling where she was warm underneath. She drew in her breath.

This was good. No, this was amazing. We didn't have to be in pure, old-fashioned love for this to be the most awesome thing ever.

I pulled on the fabric of her skirt, tugging it up under my fingers, revealing an inch of bare skin, then another, then another. My hands were trembling, I was so scared, but if she noticed, she didn't say anything. She was still kissing my neck. I pulled the hem of her skirt higher and higher, slowly, because I couldn't believe this was actually happening, and then suddenly it was up to her waist. But then I touched her through her underwear and she was gasping, actually *gasping*, and I knew it was real.

I didn't really know what to do, so I just pressed, and moved my hand around in circles, the way I did when I touched myself at night. It must have been the right thing because she started gasping louder. I kept on going, and she kept on moaning, and it was as amazing as before, even though after a while my hand started to ache. Right when I was wondering if I should stop or keep going or what, she made a choking sound and then got quiet. At first I thought I'd done something wrong, but then she was rolling over and pressing me back into the bed, so she must've felt all right about things.

I leaned up to kiss her mouth, and she kissed me back. Fast, hungry kisses. She pulled my skirt up so fast I didn't even know it was happening until I felt her hand on the inside of my thigh. At first I wanted to slow down, to kiss for a little while longer, but then she was touching me, and I didn't want it to slow down. I wanted to keep going. I wanted to feel this way forever.

I'd always thought my first time doing this would be slow and romantic, but it wasn't. It was fast and frantic and still really, really good.

It felt special. As though my chest was going to explode. Just looking at Christa made me happy, and feeling this plus seeing her face over me plus the excitement that I was really doing this, here, now, with her—it was the best feeling ever.

Afterward, staring up into the darkness, I remembered the stuff I'd read about how it was important to talk to your partner about sex before you did it. Oh, well. We could talk later. Anyway, we didn't actually have sex—we only fooled around. Right? What qualified as sex for two girls, anyway? I used to think it was oral sex, but maybe that wasn't right. Christa probably knew. When we talked about it, I could ask her then. She'd probably done it all a bunch of times before.

Anyway, none of that was important now. All that mattered was that I was here with Christa, where I belonged, and that I was utterly, blissfully happy.

This was exactly where I was supposed to be.

PART 4

When We're Dancing
Close and Slow

CHAPTER 15

"WOW." JAKE HELD the paper out at arm's length, studying the careful sentences I'd crafted. "You did a great job."

"Thanks!" I grinned. "I spent practically the whole morning on it. Want to be the second signature?"

"Definitely." Jake took the pen and wrote his name neatly under mine. We were on the road in front of the work site, getting ready to go inside to where the rest of the group was putting up the last coat of paint. "Thanks for giving me the first chance."

"Well, I based it on your petitions." The paper looked a lot better now that there were signatures on it. To be honest, though, when it first came out from the ancient printer at the internet place, I'd already thought it looked good. Dad had given me special permission to go into town so I could put it together.

I'd read the stuff he'd given me and talked it through with Jake. It turned out to be another no-brainer. The global health plank at the conference called for church members to support helping countries that didn't have enough resources to give everyone good health care. It also said we should donate to the Red Cross and other organizations working in countries that were having crises—wars, earthquakes, hurricanes, that sort of thing. I didn't see how anyone wouldn't want to sign on to that.

"How are your other petitions going?" I asked as I sorted through my pens. I wanted to make sure I had enough in case more than one person wanted to sign at the same time. There were only a few minutes left until jewelry class, but I could get more people to sign tomorrow on our bus ride to Texas.

"I got lots of signatures on the war petition." Jake reached out to straighten the hem of my T-shirt. Which was actually his T-shirt. Christa was running out of work shirts, so Jake had lent me his for today. It fit better than I'd expected. Maybe I should start wearing guys' clothes more often. "Immigration is harder, but the marriage petition is the real win. Once those girls from your church started signing it, it really took off. Even some people from Harpers Ferry have signed it now."

"That's awesome!" But I wished Christa had signed that one, too. We'd been meeting in the guest house every night for nearly a week. I'd brought up the marriage petition again, but she said she couldn't talk about it. It was starting to bother me more that she wouldn't even consider signing.

"Yeah, I'm really psyched." Jake smiled. "Uh, by the way, you know. That petition, the one on marriage. You know why I started it, right? Why I got into this whole thing in the first place?"

I had a feeling, but I said, "Why?"

"Well, because I'm, you know." He cleared his throat and glanced from side to side. "You know. I am, too. The same as you and Christa."

I'd suspected Jake wasn't entirely straight, but I hadn't expected him to say so out loud. Up until this summer, I hadn't really known anyone who was bi or gay. Or at least anyone who'd talked about it. I'd always thought it would be weird to hear someone just come right out and say it.

But it didn't feel weird at all, hearing him say the words, watching the nervous smile play on his lips. It felt...normal. Actually, it even felt kind of cool. I'd never had a friend who was like me before.

Everything was changing so fast. The world felt different than it had three weeks ago.

"That's cool," I told him. I took a breath and added, "I think I'm probably bi."

"Yeah, me, too." Jake's head bobbed up and down. He brushed a stray hair out of his face, and I saw his hand shake. "Bi, I mean."

"Awesome," I said. "Do your parents know?"

"No." His hand was still shaking. "No one does."

"Whoa. Am I the first person you've told?"

"Uh, yeah." Jake ducked his head.

"That's so great." I smiled and touched his wrist gently so he'd know I really meant it. His hand was still trembling. "I don't know why people act as if it's such a big deal, you know? I read this theory once that almost everyone is really bi, deep down. Because if everyone's being totally honest, we're all at least a little bit attracted to all kinds of people, right? I mean, the straight girls at school totally talk about which female celebrities they think are hot, and one time I even got my brother to say he thought Prince was kind of okay-looking back in the midnineties."

Jake laughed, and I did, too. It suddenly felt really good to laugh together in that moment. Soon Jake was laughing so hard he was grabbing my shoulder to keep from falling over.

I understood. It was like this big wave of relief had flooded over me, and laughing was the only way to keep from losing it.

"Okay," I said, between giggles. "We have to go inside. I want to get some signatures before I go make jewelry."

I left Jake by the door and strode up to the first group I saw—Rodney, Eric, Sofía and Rosa. They were dipping rollers into pans of yellow paint.

"Hey, guys," I said, pulling out my paper and pens. I still felt high from what had happened with Jake, and I had to stop myself from giggling as I talked. "Want to sign this? It's a petition supporting the international health care plank at the conference."

Rodney bent down to tap the extra paint off his roller. He looked a lot healthier than last time I'd seen him. Montezuma's Revenge must have run its course. "I think I already signed that. Jake brought it around, didn't he?"

"No, this one's brand-new." I held it out so he could see. "Jake's petitions were on other stuff."

"So what's this one about?" Rosa said.

"Global health care." I thrust the paper toward her. "Here, you can read it."

She took the petition and peered down at it. Rodney and Sofía leaned in to look over her shoulder. All of them frowned.

"What does this mean?" Rodney said. "What's it for?"

"It's for helping other countries." Had they not read what I'd written at the top of the page? I'd spent a lot of time getting the words exactly right. "You know, supporting health care and stuff."

"But that's what we're doing here," Sofía said. "We already support helping other countries."

"This is for the US government to support it, though," I said. "To send aid and stuff. For health care."

"But a lot of people don't even have decent health care back home," Rodney said. "My aunt and uncle went bankrupt because they couldn't afford the bills when my cousin got sick."

"This is still important, though." I was getting frustrated. Why wouldn't Rodney look at what I'd written? I'd explained it all so carefully. "You signed the gay marriage petition, didn't you?"

"That was a completely different issue." Rodney passed the petition back to me, unsigned. "I already knew I supported that. I don't get this one."

Rosa and Sofía had both turned away, too. Eric looked as though he was thinking about reaching for the pen, but after a moment he followed the others.

Before I could figure out what to say, Guadalupe came running in.

"¡Ah-ki!" she grabbed my hand. "¡Vamanos!"

I looked at my phone. I was five minutes late for jewelry class.

"Did Lori send you to get me?"

Guadalupe nodded. I sighed and followed her.

The girls were lined up neatly outside, sitting in their jeans and T-shirts with their legs crossed, twisting the wires Lori had set up. She gave me her usual death glare as I sat down. I leaned in to show one of the younger girls how to bend her wire in an S-shape so she could slide the beads on.

"¿Dónde está Juana?" I asked. Juana had never missed a class yet, but she wasn't sitting on our pile of blankets today.

Guadalupe pointed to a grove of trees outside the fence. Juana was hunched over, her face in her hands.

"Is she all right?" I asked Lori. She shrugged.

I wondered if things would be this way between us forever. I still found myself wanting to tell her things, and feeling that ache in my gut every time I realized I couldn't.

But I should check on Juana, so I climbed to my feet. There was something in her lap. As I got closer, I could see it was a piece of wood.

"¿Juana? ¿Qué pasa?"

Juana looked up at me, her face a mess of tears. Without a word, she held out the wood. I took it from her hands.

It was a broken piece of the guitar. Her father's guitar, the beautiful old twelve-string she'd played at vespers on Saturday. The edges were jagged where the piece had been snapped off.

It was from the front of the guitar, where a triangular design had been painted around the sound hole in its center. Up close, I could see the intricacy of the design, worn smooth over the decades.

There was no way this could've been an accident. The whole guitar must have been destroyed.

Horrified, I turned back to Juana. She was crying even harder now. Tears were pricking at my own eyes, too.

That's when I saw the rest of the guitar's remains, scattered around her on the ground. The neck was still in one piece, but it had been ripped off the body of the instrument, loose strings still dangling.

"What the hell happened, Juana? Who did this?" She stared at me. I swallowed, trying to think of the words in Spanish. "¿Quién?"

Juana leaned over to touch the neck of the guitar, stroking the strings.

I closed my eyes, trying to remember. The last time I'd seen that guitar was Saturday night when Juana played for us. And later that night, before Christa and I went into the guest house, I'd seen Nick and the guys tossing something around. I'd assumed it was beer, but it could definitely have been a guitar.

What the *hell*?

Those guys were complete losers. They were nothing but a bunch of drunk jerks who didn't even care about a little girl who loved music. Not to mention getting in trouble for destroying an amazing antique.

And what did I do? Nothing. I saw it happen, and I'd ignored them so I could go hook up with my not-girlfriend.

I looked down at Juana. I didn't know the words for what I wanted to say to her. In English or Spanish. She stared back at me silently, tears still rolling down her cheeks.

I held out my hand. "Vamanos, Juana."

She climbed to her feet, still holding the guitar neck. I stooped down to pick up the rest of the pieces, carefully cradling them in my arms, and motioned for her to follow me.

It didn't take long to find Dad. He was outside the work site's front door with a bunch of the other chaperones, packing up paint supplies.

"Daddy?" That got his attention fast. I didn't call him *Daddy* much. "Can we talk to you?"

He wiped his hands, looking back and forth between Juana and me, his forehead creased. "What's going on, Aki?"

"Something happened to Juana's guitar." I held out the broken pieces for him to see.

"I know." He drew Juana and me aside and carefully took the fragments out of my hands. "Reverend Perez found it in the hills behind his house this morning. It looked as if the pieces had been there for a few days. Such a shame. It belonged to Señor Suarez's grandfather."

I closed my eyes. I felt sick. "Do they know what happened?"

"No." Dad glanced at Juana. I could see him choosing his words carefully to make sure she wouldn't understand. "Unfortunately, it sounds as though in her excitement about performing for everyone, his daughter left it outside the Perezes' house on Saturday night. The next time anyone saw it, it was in pieces. There's no way to know who's responsible."

Poor Juana. She'd been so excited to play for us. She must feel so guilty.

"I know who did it." I reached down to squeeze Juana's shoulder. "I saw some guys that night after vespers. Will, Tyler, Nick and a couple of others. They were tossing something around. I couldn't see what it was at first, but now I'm positive it was the guitar."

Dad's face clouded. "Sweetheart, I'm sure none of the kids from this group would've done something so cruel. They're good Christians, every one of them."

I glanced at Juana again, but she wasn't paying attention to us. She'd taken the neck back from Dad and was trying to straighten out the guitar strings.

"They were drunk," I said. "Maybe they were horsing around and they didn't mean to break it. Either way, I'm positive it was them."

Dad stood up straight, his right hand clenching into a fist. "They were drinking? How do you know?"

"They were drunk at vespers. I could smell it on their breath. They buy beer in town all the time and drink outside at night."

"Aki." Dad shook his head. He had that frazzled look again. "This is a very serious accusation to make."

"It's the truth. Those guys are jerks. They should get in trouble for what they did."

"All right. Thank you for telling me. I'll look into this more. Now you two should both run along back to your jewelry lesson." Dad softly laid his hand on Juana's head. "Lo siento, pequeña senorita."

Juana gave a tiny nod.

Dad went to go talk to Señor Suarez, so I took Juana's hand and led her back to where Lori was finishing up the jewelry class. She glared at me when I sat down, but I ignored her and started cleaning up the supplies. Today I had a good reason to be somewhere else, even if Lori didn't know it.

The girls got up to leave, playing with their new brace-lets. Guadalupe had made an extra bracelet for Juana, and my heart nearly broke in half when I saw Juana's small smile as she slipped it onto her wrist.

Lori folded the blanket and packed it away without looking at me. I reached into my pocket and pulled out the petition.

"Hey," I said. Lori jerked up, surprise on her face. "Do you want to sign it?"

Lori took the paper out of my hand. I watched her eyes move over the sentences I'd written, then Jake's signature and mine below. She silently held her hand out for the pen. I passed it to her and she scribbled her name.

"This doesn't change anything between us," she said as she thrust the paper back toward me. "For the record."

"I know. Thanks for signing it, though. And by the way, I haven't said anything to anyone about, you know."

Lori stared at me. "What, do you want a medal?"

"No. Jeez. Anyway, I still think you should talk to someone about it. If you want, I could mention it to my Dad anony-mously, without giving your name, I mean, and I really think he'd understand, he—"

"No! God!" Lori whipped her head around, her eyes blaz-ing. "Wow, you don't get it at *all*. Do you want me going to your dad 'anonymously' and telling him about my 'anony-mous' friend who's secretly hooking up with an 'anonymous' lesbian?"

I definitely did not want that. "Okay, okay."

"You've gotten so obsessed with that girl you've forgotten how the rest of the world works. Well, news flash—the people you left behind are still living their lives, too. And the sooner you tune in to what's really going on, the better off you'll be."

I had no idea what she was talking about. But I was so

tired of fighting with Lori. I wanted things back the way they used to be.

But, I realized as I watched her walk away, there was no such thing as going backward.

After the day I'd had, it was glorious to escape into the dark guest house.

We went straight from vespers. I tried to forget about Juana and Lori, about everything that was going wrong, and focus on Christa. How she felt. How she moved. How awesome it would be tomorrow, in Texas, when we'd have an entire night to ourselves.

At first, it was easy to forget that other people so much as existed. We kissed, and we did more than kiss, and more still. Every movement, every sensation, every breath was all ours.

After, we watched the shadows play on the wall as the candle flickered down to nothing. We were quiet at first. Then we started talking. We talked about nothing, and everything, the way we'd done every night since we found this place. We talked about our families, our friends. Music, games, movies. Tonight we talked about Harry Potter.

"I always had the biggest crush on Draco," I admitted. "When I was a kid my whole room was covered in pictures of him. One time my brother said he was going to be Draco for Halloween. He found a doofy blond wig at CVS and stole the wand I got online and started going around calling people Mudbloods. He was acting so dumb I burst into tears, because I was only, like, eight. Then he took the wig off and said he was joking and actually he was dressing up as the stupid Falcon. He pulled this bag out from under the bed and showed me how Mom had already gotten him the wings and the goggles and everything. He's lucky I didn't clock him across the head."

Christa was laughing so hard by the time I finished that

story I got worried someone would hear. I tried to *shhh* her but it was hard because I was laughing, too.

"I was into Ron when I was a kid," she said. "I think it was because everyone else fawned over Draco and I wanted to be different. But when I got older I decided I liked Cho Chang."

"Wow." I was impressed. "I don't think it would've occurred to me to like a girl character back then. Now that I think about it, though, maybe I kind of had a thing for Fleur in the movies. I was really into the wedding scene in the second to last one. I watched the dance she and Bill did over and over."

"God, I love that movie."

"Me, too. My favorite thing about that one, though, is the soundtrack. Have you listened to it? They took the score from the earlier movies, when it was all kid stuff, and really messed with it to make it darker. It's awesome mood music to listen to, even apart from the movie."

"You really do like every kind of music, don't you?"

"Mostly. The only thing I don't listen to is Christian contemporary, just because I've never heard any that I really got into. But regular church music is pretty fun most of the time. As long as we aren't having to sing 'If I Had a Hammer' for the forty thousandth time."

Christa laughed. "You never have told me what your favorite song is, by the way."

I shifted. "It's like I said. I don't have one favorite."

"But if you did. If you *had* to pick one."

"For real, I can't." I didn't know why, but I still couldn't tell her. It didn't feel right. "I love too many different songs."

"Then sing something for me." She rolled over and grinned, locking her eyes on mine. "Anything. I want to hear this amazing voice everyone raves about."

"No." I shifted again. Why did she always want to talk about this? "They'd hear us in the house."

"Sing quietly, then." Her voice was teasing, but it only made me more anxious.

"I don't know how to sing quietly. They don't teach you that in choir." Then the words started to spill out, and the next thing I knew, I was telling her what I was really thinking. "Look, singing isn't very much fun for me anymore. Not the way it used to be."

I regretted it as soon as I'd said it. Christa was obsessed with artists, and musicians in particular. That was why she'd liked me in the first place.

She didn't pull back right away. Her eyes widened, though. "Why? What happened?"

"I—" I couldn't tell her about the audition. I'd have to admit I'd lied to her. It would ruin everything. "I don't know. I used to sing, or play my guitar, and I'd disappear into the music. But then I started taking it more seriously, and focusing on technique and writing my own songs, and suddenly instead of playing I was *performing*. It wasn't the same."

Christa was watching me closely, but she didn't look upset. In fact, her eyes crinkled, and she nodded a small nod. As if she...understood, sort of.

I flushed. "Can we please go back to talking about Harry Potter?"

She nodded that little nod again, with a tiny smile to go with it.

"I wish we could get online," she said. "Talking about those movies always makes me want to watch them again. I really want to see that wedding scene now."

"Me, too." I was so relieved she'd let me change the subject, I could've talked about nothing but Harry Potter for the rest of the night. "I loved Fleur's wedding dress so much."

"Was it her you liked or her dress?"

"Huh. I don't know." I frowned. "How do you tell the difference?"

"You got me."

My head was on Christa's shoulder, so I felt her shrug. I reached down to where her arm rested on my waist and slipped my hand into hers. Three weeks ago I never would've dreamed of doing that so casually.

Christa wound her fingers through mine and squeezed. "Oh, hey, did you hear what happened to Nick and Paul and those guys?"

I twisted around to look at her. "What?"

"Somebody found out they'd been drinking since we've been down here, and they're in big trouble. Their parents got called at home—*that* level of trouble. They're permanently grounded for the rest of the trip. They have to do private Bible study every single night after vespers, and in Texas they're going to have to share rooms with the chaperones so they can't sneak out."

"Whoa." Telling Dad had worked. "So did they admit it? About the guitar?"

Christa frowned. "What guitar?"

"Juana's guitar. I mean, Señor Suarez's. Remember, we saw them tossing it around Saturday night, and then this morning it turned up in pieces. I told my dad they broke it."

"You told your dad?" Christa's frown deepened. "Wait, how do you know they did it? We were too far away to see what they were throwing around that night. It could've been anything."

"Come on, it had to be the guitar. Juana left it right outside the house. They probably picked it up on their way to get even drunker."

"I can't believe you're the one who told on them." Christa

shook her head. "Come on, they're good guys. Sure, they drink, but I don't think they'd break a little kid's guitar."

"I never said they did it on purpose. I bet they were just so drunk they threw it into a tree trunk or something."

"Still. I don't think I would've told on them."

I pulled back. "How good of friends are you with them, anyway? Do you hang out with them back home? Is Steven part of their little posse?"

"No." Christa sighed. "Steven doesn't even know them. He doesn't go to our church."

"Oh. Well, anyway, that night at vespers Will and Tyler called me a—something really mean. So I don't really care if they get in trouble, to be honest."

Christa softened. "What did they call you?"

"It doesn't matter. I don't want to talk about it."

My eyes traced the edges of the curtains. A tiny sliver of sky was visible between them. Dozens of stars gazed down on us.

Tomorrow night, Christa and I would be in a dorm room. Alone. For the whole night. Before that, I needed to find my way to the college health center so I could get the stuff I'd read about.

Everything was happening so fast. And yet...not *everything*.

I hated that I was afraid to tell Christa what the guys had called me. I hated that I couldn't say anything back to them that night, because talking back would've meant being honest about who I was.

I hated lying. I hated that I kept lying to Christa.

I didn't want to be like Lori, lying to everyone because she knew what she was doing was wrong. What Christa and I were doing *wasn't* wrong.

"I just can't believe you told your dad we saw them," Christa said. "It's as if you tell your family *everything*."

I pulled back. "I don't tell them everything."

"You told your brother about us."

"That's different. Besides, he already knew."

Christa scooted backward on the bed until she was sitting upright, three feet of space between us. She reached behind her back to hook her bra. "What are you talking about? How did he know?"

Crap. I hadn't meant to mention that. "I think he had, um, a theory."

"How'd he get a theory?"

I didn't see a way out of this. Besides, she was bound to find out sooner or later. "He...heard a rumor."

"A *rumor*?" Christa's eyes bored into mine. Earlier that night, she'd drawn a tiny star at the corner of her eyebrow with a black marker. It had been cute then, but it made her look kind of scary now. "There's a rumor about us?"

"I don't know." I sat up and tugged my shirt down miserably.

"Wait. You told Drew two weeks ago. Are you saying people have known about us for that long?" Her eyes blazed. "Who? How many? Why didn't you *tell* me?"

Because I knew you'd react this way. "I really don't think everyone knows. Word got to Drew because he's my brother, that's all."

"How many people know?" Her skin had gone pale in the candlelight.

"I don't know. Listen, who cares? Just tell them you have a stupid *boyfriend* and they'll forget the whole thing."

I swung my legs off the bed, stood up and straightened out my clothes. I fastened my shorts so fast I missed a button, my fingers fumbling.

"Wait." Christa tilted her head. "Are *you* pissed at *me*?"

"No," I said, automatically.

"You don't get to be pissed at *me* right now. You're the one who lied. You—"

"I didn't lie." Not in the way she meant.

"You should've told me people knew! Not telling is as bad as lying."

She was kind of right, actually. But that didn't make me any less angry.

Why did she get to be in charge of everything? She was the only one who was allowed to have an opinion on whether we told people. And she had stupid, useless Steven, when all I had was her.

Except that I didn't, really. He did.

All I had was what I felt. And feelings didn't count for anything.

"I can't do this." I didn't even know what I meant—that I couldn't stay in the guest house? That I couldn't keep seeing her?

All I knew was that I couldn't keep going like this. One way or another.

Christa's face fell. Then she lifted her chin and set her mouth in a straight line.

"Then don't," she said. "Whatever."

Did she mean that? I swallowed.

"I'm going." I waited to see if she would try to stop me.

She didn't. She only watched, her eyes flickering in the dim light, her mouth still pressed in that thin, even line.

I didn't wait for her to get up. I slipped the burned-out candle into my pocket and pushed the door open, slowly, so it wouldn't creak. When I glanced back over my shoulder, she was still sitting up on the bed, watching me.

I didn't speak as I closed the door behind me.

CHAPTER 16

I'D THOUGHT THIS was going to be the weekend my whole life changed. Instead, Christa wouldn't speak to me.

We were on the bus to Texas and she was three rows behind me, pretending I didn't exist. And to make things even worse, she was sitting with Madison.

"You shouldn't worry about it." Jake pointed to the health care petition in my hand. He thought *that* was the reason I was stressed.

The petition still had just three names—mine, his and Lori's. Desperate to think about something that wasn't how badly I'd screwed up with Christa, I'd shown the petition to a few more people that morning while we waited for the bus. We'd been lined up along the dusty Mudanza road with backpacks dangling from our shoulders and absolutely nothing else to do, but I still hadn't been able to convince anyone to sign. No one seemed to understand what the petition was about, and when I tried to tell them, they still didn't get it.

"It's not a big deal," Jake said. "The ones on the war and marriage both did really well. When we send those off, the conference delegates will see that people our age really do care how they vote. It would've been great if we could've had more issues covered, but even so…"

I nodded, my eyes fixed on the bag under my feet. When I'd packed the day before, I'd left my backpack half empty so there'd be room to add stuff to it. That was when I'd still been thinking about my big plan to go to the campus health center for dental dams as soon as I got off the bus.

Christa was probably going to switch at the last minute and room with Madison anyway. Stupid Madison.

Jake tapped his phone screen. "Hey, it looks as though we're starting to get reception."

"We are?" I lunged for my phone. It had an incredibly weak signal, but that was more than I'd had since we'd left Tijuana three weeks earlier.

Texts started popping up. I tapped through eagerly, but right away I saw that the texts were old. They were from friends back home before I left, telling me they hoped I had a good trip.

"I'm going to the conference website to see if there's anything else we can get people to take a stand on." Jake was excited. "I'm still annoyed the immigration petition didn't take off. Maybe it's too complicated an issue."

"Uh-huh." If my phone was working, Christa's would be, too. Maybe I could text her and explain.

Except…explain what, exactly? I'd meant what I said the night before. I was pretty sure she'd meant what she said, too.

But that didn't mean I wanted things between us to *end*. God, no. Did she think I did?

"That might be the problem with your petition, too," Jake went on. "People didn't understand what you were getting at."

I glanced down at the paper in my hand. Yet another time when I hadn't made myself clear. "I guess. Maybe I didn't explain it well enough. It just seems so obvious to me."

"We need to get people to understand the details." Jake gestured eagerly with his phone. "For all the issues. And it would be way better if we could talk to multiple people at once. That was how I got most of the signatures on marriage and the war. It was when we were all together, walking into town, talking as a group. People were more interested in signing if they knew someone else was signing, too."

"That makes sense." What would I say if I texted Christa, though? *Hey, I still want to be with you, but I'm starting to realize I'm really not okay with keeping it a total secret all the time, and also, it really bothers me that you have a boyfriend waiting for you at home. Plus, sorry I lied to you about a bunch of stuff you still don't know about. Want to have sex tonight?*

Also, come to think of it, I didn't have her number.

"It's so strange that we have to work so hard to make people care about this." Jake was on a roll now. "I mean, look at all these things the delegates are voting on. Climate change. Police brutality. There's even a proposal to eliminate the Department of Education."

"They're voting on police brutality?" I took Jake's phone and studied the list of issues. "Oh, it's actually about whether police should have military equipment. That's really interesting. Whoa, and they're voting on access to birth control, too. And legalizing marijuana. Jake, we should be talking about *all* of this. That's how we get people to see how much this conference matters."

"So what, do we need to have, like, twenty-five different petitions?" Jake frowned.

"No." I was tired of petitions. Besides, I didn't want to distract anyone from how important health care was. "I think we should have a debate or something, where we can tell our side and other people can tell theirs if they want to."

"Did you guys say *debate*?" Rodney twisted around from

the seat in front of me, headphones dangling from his neck. "I do debate at King. Sofía did it, too, last year. Right, Sofe?"

"I did what?" Sofía called from the other side of the aisle.

"You were on the debate team," Rodney called back. "These guys want to have a debate."

"You do?" Sofía was sitting a few rows back, so I had to lean into the aisle to hear her. "What, down here?"

"Um, sure." I looked over toward Jake in the window seat, but he only shrugged, so I kept talking. "It turns out they're voting on a bunch of different issues at the national conference, like on climate change, and on police having military gear, and a lot of people here probably don't know about it. Maybe we should have a debate for the youth groups about how we think they should vote."

"What did you say about police having military gear?" Rodney's eyebrows shot up.

Jake found the page on his phone and showed it to him. Rodney frowned down at the screen. It was so hard not to look behind me at Christa while everyone was distracted.

"Huh. This sounds good, but I wonder…" Rodney took the phone and scrolled down farther.

"So will you guys be debating about everything they're voting on at the conference?" Sofía peered across the aisle at me as though she were seeing me for the first time. It was to-tally different from how she'd looked at me while we were joking around with my brother about Prince. "Is it just going to be you two talking? When are you holding it, anyway?"

"Uh." I looked at Jake again. I didn't really care who talked, or when the debate happened. All I wanted was for people to support the health care plank. And for Christa to look at me again.

"No, it's not just the two of us," Jake said.

"Yeah," I said. "Anyone can pick a topic they want to talk about."

"And someone will be arguing for both sides on all the issues, right?" Sofía was talking faster now. "Because it's not a debate if it's one-sided."

"Well, there is no other side to some of this stuff," I said. "Like marriage. Or the health care plank. It's so obvious they should pass it."

"It's obvious to you, Sis," Drew called from his seat in the back. Wow, was everyone on the entire bus listening to us? "But if you're going to debate it you have to convince other people. Even people who think you're wrong."

I rolled my eyes. "Fine. Both sides."

"So one person argues that they should pass a resolution and the other person argues they shouldn't?" Rodney passed Jake back his phone. "Can I take the pro side for the one on restricting police access to military stuff?"

"Sure." Jake nodded. "We've just got to find someone to take the other side."

"I will," Sofía said right away. "It's always more interesting to argue the con side."

"When is this happening?" Drew said. "We're only in Mexico for one more week."

Jake and I looked at each other. I was starting to get nervous, and I could tell he was, too. Everyone kept acting as though we were in charge of this thing that we'd thought of three seconds ago.

"We can do it next Friday," I said. "The night before we leave. That way people will have time to get their speeches ready."

"How are we going to do research, though?" Rosa had pulled herself up to see us over the top of the seat in front of Jake. "We can't get online."

"We can here." Rodney nodded toward Jake's phone. "I guess we have to research it now, this weekend."

"There's also a computer place in Mudanza," I reminded them. "It's only open in the afternoon, but we could go there on lunch breaks, maybe."

"Can I give the speech on immigration?" Rosa said.

"Sure." I turned to Jake, who looked slightly panicked. "Uh, we should probably start writing this down, I guess."

The only papers we had were the petition forms Jake and I had brought, so we turned them over and used the backs to make a list of what people wanted to debate about. Word spread on the bus. Soon people were calling to us over seats, passing messages or texting to tell us what issues they wanted to claim. We had to turn down five different people who wanted to argue the pro side of legalizing marijuana. Becca had claimed it right away. She seemed to have really strong feelings about pot.

"What about you?" I whispered, as Jake wrote Hannah's name next to the "anti" column for marijuana legalization. "Are you taking the pro side on the marriage one?"

"Uh." Jake's cheeks turned pink. "I'll have to think about that. I don't want—you know."

I nodded. "That's fine. I'm sure we can find someone if you don't want to do it yourself."

"Don't you want to do it?"

"Nah. I'm all over health care. As long as we can get someone to argue the other side."

"You can put me down for that," a familiar voice said from between the seats behind us.

"Lori?" Jake twisted around.

"Hi." She climbed up so we could see her. She'd been sitting way in the back of the bus before, but she must've switched seats with Becca to talk to us. Well, to talk to Jake, since she'd made it very clear for the past two weeks that she was definitely not speaking to me. "I said I'll take the anti on health care."

Jake started to write her name down, then stopped. "But you signed the petition supporting it."

"Yeah, sure. I've always heard that in a debate, though, you need to be able to argue both sides of everything. Lately I've learned I need to get better at defending myself."

I turned around, squaring my shoulders in front of the gap between our seats. I heard her huff behind me, but I ignored it. If she'd only listened to me, she'd have known I was right. She'd have broken things off with Carlos and we could've gone back to normal. I'd have told her everything that was going on with Christa, and she'd have understood. I wouldn't have to be doing this all by myself.

Man, I missed my best friend.

All around us, everyone was still talking about which positions they wanted to take in the debate.

"Hey, that sounds interesting," someone said from behind Lori. I snapped back into my seat when I saw it was Madison. "I'll take the con side on gay marriage."

"Oh, come on, that's silly," Sofía said. "You're—you know."

"What?" Madison said. "Gay?"

Sofía's eyes darted down. As much as Madison annoyed me, I couldn't help being impressed that she had the nerve to be so open about who she was.

"Uh, yeah, I'm aware," Madison said. "That's why arguing against marriage is a cool, mind-expanding thing to do, you know? Besides, not all us queers even want to get married. I don't need any of that patriarchal crap, myself."

Sofía swallowed. Our section of the bus had gotten quiet.

I tried not to look at Christa. I failed. She was slumped

against the wall of the bus, her phone in her hand, but I caught her eye in the gap between two seats.

She was looking straight at me.

I sank back into my seat, my cheeks flaming. I wondered what she was thinking. I wondered if we'd ever be able to get past the things we'd said.

What would happen if we couldn't? Was my big bisexual experiment over?

I didn't want it to be over. I didn't want it to be an experiment, either.

Look at Madison. She didn't have a girlfriend, as far as I knew. But she was still herself. For her, that meant being gay and talking about it without caring who heard.

I wanted to do that, too. The bi version of that, anyway. Maybe not right now, but eventually.

That was when I decided to stick with my original plan. I'd go straight from the bus to the campus health center. Maybe Christa and I would use the dental dams and maybe we wouldn't, but this wasn't only about Christa.

I wanted to have the experience of having sex with a girl someday. And, yeah, I wanted it to be with Christa—but this was about me, not her. My life was bigger than any one person.

Except...wow, I wished she'd look at me.

More people had questions about the debate, so Jake and I were busy for the rest of the bus ride. Soon more than half the people in the group had signed up. I was starting to wonder how we were going to get through all of these speeches in one night. Plus, I had no idea where we were going to do this. Our church was a mess of sleeping bags and suitcases.

We'd crossed the border by then and were rolling past signs advertising fast food and convenience stores, in English. As we got closer, my nerves rolled around in my stomach. How was I even going to find the health center? Would I have to talk to someone when I got there? What would I *say*? "Hi, I'm here to get the lesbian sex supplies, please?"

Soon the bus was pulling through the college's main gate. Everyone was too excited to talk about the debate anymore. Every conversation was about who was rooming together and where people were meeting up after curfew.

The bus slowed to a stop in front of a massive beige-and-brown dorm complex. I swallowed my nerves, grabbed my half-empty backpack and followed everyone else down the steps. Outside, blinking against the sunlight, I saw my dad waving at me in front of a big sign with a campus map.

Great. Exactly the person I most wanted to see before I went off in search of sex gear.

"Hey, sweetheart," Dad said. "I heard you and your friend Jake are putting together a debate about the national conference?"

"Oh, yeah." Was there anything Dad didn't know? I sure hoped so. "We only came up with the idea today on the bus."

"Well, I think it's wonderful." Dad beamed at me, rocking on his heels. "Good on you two for thinking of it. Now, just you let me know if there's anything you need from us to get this going."

"Oh, wow." It hadn't occurred to me that anyone might help us. "Well, we do need a space to have it. Can you think of anywhere?"

Dad nodded. "I'm sure we'll come up with something. Leave that part to me."

"Okay. Thanks."

"Of course. Seriously, sweetheart, I'm really proud of you."

I didn't know what to say. I rubbed the back of my neck and felt my face go red.

"Dad?" I didn't know why the question popped into my

mind at that moment. I just wanted to know. "Why do you carry around that photo of Uncle Andrew?"

Dad looked at me for a long, quiet moment, then blew out a heavy breath. He glanced around us at the people still piling off the bus, then drew me to one side. "Where did you see that?"

"In your papers, that day you told me to look through them." I wished now I hadn't brought this up. I hadn't thought about how Dad might react.

"Right." Dad cleared his throat. Then, finally, he met my eyes. "Well, sweetheart, your uncle Andrew was my little brother, the same as you are to Drew, and I want to keep him with me. He isn't here anymore on this earth, but he's still our family. Do you understand that?"

"Yeah." I swallowed. All I wanted to do now was get out of this conversation. "Thanks for telling me. I think I'm going to go take a walk."

"All right." Dad looked relieved. He patted me on the shoulder. "See you, sweetie."

"Aki, you coming?" Gina called as Dad headed back to unload the bus. "We're getting our room keys."

"Actually, I'll see you guys later," I called back. "I'm just doing something really quick."

"Okay. We're all meeting at the food court for dinner."

"Okay, see you there."

I took a picture of the campus map sign with my phone and took off before anyone else could distract me.

The health center was clearly labeled on the map. And, if I was reading it right, the building was only a couple of blocks from where I was standing.

Oh. I'd expected it to be harder than that.

The nerves fluttered back into my stomach as I started walking. Up ahead, I saw a coffee shop and a drugstore. Suddenly all

I wanted was to buy a magazine and sit down with a smoothie until it was time to meet up with everyone for dinner.

No. I wasn't going to be a baby about this. The website said if you were old enough to have sex, you were old enough to be mature about protection.

The campus was crowded, and by the time I'd walked one block there were people all around me. The event we were here for—an all-day teen Bible festival tomorrow, complete with concerts, workshops and lots of praying—was only for high school students, but most of the people on campus looked too old for high school. They must've been college students who took classes in the summer or something. I felt pleasantly anonymous, walking through a crowd of people who were here for their own reasons that had nothing to do with me.

The health center loomed above me before I'd realized I was even close. It was bigger than I'd expected—a whole building, three stories high, with a big sign out front that said Student Health Services. I'd been stupidly picturing something more like the nurse's office at my school back home. But my school had maybe a hundred and fifty students, and this college probably had fifty thousand.

I peered through the health center doors. All I needed was a second to get myself ready before I went inside. This was no big deal. No big deal at all.

I looked around, expecting to see people staring at me, asking me what I was doing there. But no one seemed to pay me any attention.

A guy came out of the health center's front doors, walking so fast he nearly barreled into me. I stumbled backward and caught myself right before I fell.

"Oh, sorry, sorry," the guy said. He was tall and white, with a backward baseball cap. He pulled out the headphones out of his ears and looked at me earnestly. "Are you all right? God, I'm so sorry."

"I'm fine." My heart pounded, but not because of the almost-falling.

"You going in?" He held the health center door open for me.

"Oh, uh. Yeah." I didn't have a choice anymore. I went in, the door swinging closed behind me, and exhaled, clasping my hands into fists so no one could tell they were shaking.

But now that I was inside, once again, no one seemed to even notice I was there. The health center looked the same as any other office. There were no giant signs saying Considering Lesbianism? Start Here! or anything. Just a long counter and a waiting area with people who looked like college students sitting in chairs, staring down at their phones. Around the perimeter of the room, tables stood with stacks of brochures and boxes.

Bingo.

I walked over to the first table, trying to look casual, as if I was only browsing. The surface was full of brochures about nutrition and eating disorders. Boring. The next table had fliers about mental health and suicide prevention. At the third, I knew I was getting closer. This one had brochures about birth control and sexually transmitted infections. Next to it was a box full of condoms with a sign that said Free—Take as Many as You Need. Below that, it said what I assumed was the same message in Spanish.

I moved on to the next table, sure it would have a box of dental dams to match. But all it had was a stack of information packets on substance abuse and addiction therapy groups. I must've missed the dental dam box.

I circled back around to each table. I checked the corners of the room where there were signs up about why I should join the ultimate Frisbee team and learn to salsa dance. But there were no more boxes of free stuff.

Crapola. What was I supposed to do now?

The website had said you could get dental dams for free at clinics like Planned Parenthood or university health centers. It had seemed so simple when I was reading about it. Was there even a Planned Parenthood near here? Didn't Texas ban them or something?

I had to get out of here and regroup. I needed a new plan.

I was on my way out the door when a woman's voice said behind me, "Hey, are you looking for something? Can I help?"

I wanted to keep walking. Instead a tiny voice in my head told me to turn around. There was a Hispanic woman behind the counter—more of a girl, really; she couldn't have been that much older than me—and she was smiling. "Are we out of something on the tables? We're always having to restock. But I can find it for you."

"Oh, uh—" I fought the instinct to leave again. I moved closer to the counter so I could talk to her without raising my voice. "I'm not sure you have it on the tables, actually."

"That's all right. How can I help you?"

The girl seemed so sure of herself, with her perky brown eyes all lit up. I wondered if she'd ever been fifteen.

"Actually," I said again. I swallowed.

Just say it.

I lowered my voice to just above a whisper. "Do you have any dental dams?"

I waited for the girl to laugh or raise her eyebrows or ask how old I was. Instead she nodded, her smile never wavering. "We do! Wait here, I'll be right back."

When she turned around, I exhaled and let my eyes fall closed. My stomach flopped over and I released my clenched hands.

I'd said the words *dental dams* out loud, to another person. And she'd acted as though it was totally normal.

The girl was back after a minute with a box. She held it out to me and motioned for me to lean in toward her. My heart sped up again. Was she going to ask to see my student ID?

"This is a pack of thirty-six." She was speaking quietly, but I could hear the smile in her voice. "We're supposed to give them out three at a time, so don't tell on me, okay?"

I let out a high-pitched laugh. The guy behind the counter on the far end looked at us, but then he turned back to his computer, not even batting an eye at the box of dental dams in the girl's hand. I grabbed it from her and shoved it in my backpack before anyone else could see.

"Don't worry, I won't," I said. "Thanks."

"You're welcome." The girl beamed back at me. "Have a fun summer."

I zipped up my bag, turned on my heel and charged back out into the sunshine.

I'd actually done it.

After that I figured I could do pretty much anything, so I went to the drugstore and bought a box of disposable gloves and stuck them in my backpack without even worrying about whether the cashier knew what I was buying them for. Why should he care? The girl at the health center was hoping I had a fun summer with my thirty-six dental dams.

I tried to imagine having sex thirty-six times. I couldn't even picture doing it once.

I got a magazine and a smoothie and sat down at one of the coffee shop's outdoor tables. I opened the magazine, but I couldn't focus. I turned a page, then two. Then I gave up and gazed out across the campus, watching people walk from one place to another, going on about their lives, oblivious to the three dozen dental dams hanging out in my backpack.

Across the street, a guy walked out of a building with his back to me, but I recognized that familiar shuffling gait. I checked to make sure my backpack was zipped closed, then I waved. "Drew! Over here!"

At first my brother didn't seem to hear me. He kept looking from side to side. I was ready to shout again when he glanced my way, then strode across the street toward my table.

"Hi, Sis." I motioned for him to pull out a chair, but he stayed standing. He passed a hand over the back of his hair and looked from side to side again. There was a piece of paper in his hand. "You here with anybody?"

I shook my head. "I was desperate for a smoothie. I didn't know how much I missed fast food."

"Yeah, me, too." Drew glanced back the way he'd come. "All right, so... Look, please don't tell Dad, okay?"

"Uh." I glanced at my backpack. Crap. He must've seen me in the health center somehow. "Come on, Drew. I know you think I shouldn't tell him, but I don't know if I—"

Drew glanced over his shoulder again. This time I followed his gaze.

The building Drew had just come out of had a bunch of American flags in the windows. The sign over the door said Army ROTC.

Oh, *no*. "Drew? Why were you in there? Since when do you care about the ROTC?"

I didn't even really know what the ROTC was, except that it had something to do with the military. I'd gotten a packet about it in the mail when I registered for the PSATs, but Dad told me to throw it in the trash.

Drew finally pulled out the chair across from me and sat in it backward with his legs splayed out to either side. "Do you promise not to tell him?"

I swallowed. I didn't know what was about to happen, but I knew it wasn't going to be good. "I promise."

Drew sighed. "I went in there because I wanted to see if I could talk to someone about joining the army."

"Please tell me you're not serious." But it was fully clear from the look on my brother's face that he was. "Drew, Dad is going to *flip*!"

"I'm nineteen. It's my decision, not his." Drew's jaw twitched.

"But *why*? Don't you think war is wrong? That fighting is wrong?" Mom and Dad had been telling us that practically since before we were even born.

"Being in the military isn't only about fighting, Sis. They teach you stuff, like how to do different jobs, that you can use when you get out. It's basically the same as college, except they pay *you* instead of you paying them. And you're learning real stuff that actually matters, not sitting around staring at dumb books that don't mean anything."

I had no idea if what Drew was saying was true. All I knew was that if he joined the military, Dad would never forgive him.

"Mom and Dad are paying for your college, though." I tried to sound rational. So he'd see that he was being anything but. "I know last semester was hard, but why not try it one more time?"

"They're only paying for part of it. The rest is loans I have to pay back. I don't want to spend the rest of my life paying off loans when I don't even like school to begin with."

Drew's jaw was still twitching. He'd thought about this. A lot.

"I bet you could talk to Dad." I had to get my brother to see reason. "After he finished freaking, maybe he could help you figure something out about the loans."

"Well." Drew hesitated for a long moment. "It's too late. I withdrew for the fall semester."

"*What?* When? Since you've been in Mexico? How did you even get in touch with them?"

He turned his face away. "I did it before we left."

I stared at him. "You lied to me. In the airport. You said you hadn't made up your mind."

"I hadn't. Not completely." He hesitated. "Look, you don't have to agree with me, but think about it. This is the first time I'll ever have made a major decision by myself. This is exactly what Mom and Dad *don't* want me to do. Right now it feels as if I'm living somebody else's life."

I swallowed. I knew how that felt, somehow.

Drew looked down at the piece of paper in his hand. "In the ROTC office, they gave me a phone number to start the process of enlisting. I'm calling now. I'll probably start training this fall."

I sat back in my chair. Here he'd acted as though *I* was the one keeping a secret.

"Please." Drew locked his eyes on mine. "You can't tell Dad."

I couldn't believe my brother was making such a huge decision all by himself. "He's going to find out eventually."

Drew stood up. "But you'll keep it quiet, right? You promised."

"Yeah." I shook my head. "This is for you to tell, not me. But you should do it. Soon."

I stood up and hugged him. He hugged me back.

I couldn't remember the last time we'd hugged like this. Like it really mattered.

What if Drew got sent somewhere to fight and he died? What if this was one of the last chances I'd ever get to hug him?

No. I couldn't think that way.

Drew pulled back and half smiled at me. "We need to hang out and play games again. Lately all we have is big talk after big talk."

I laughed. He chuckled with me. "You coming to the food court for dinner?"

"I don't know." I couldn't just go back to my friends and pretend things were normal after this. "I might walk around on my own for a little longer."

"Okay." He pointed to my phone. "Text me if you get lost."

"You don't know your way around, either."

"I'm the big brother. I know everything."

I laughed again. I used to think Drew really did know everything.

But maybe no one knew that much. Maybe everyone was making it up as they went along, the same as me.

CHAPTER 17

MY PHONE DINGED AGAIN, but I didn't look at it. I must've gotten twenty texts in the past ten minutes.

The sun was low in the sky, and I was getting hungry. I'd probably missed dinner at the food court. The truth was, I'd been wandering aimlessly around the campus, and I had no idea where the food court was. There was too much to see to worry about looking at the map.

Everywhere I went, there were college students hanging out. The atmosphere was totally different from my school back home. There, even though we didn't have uniforms, everyone dressed exactly the same, in interchangeable jeans and T-shirts. Here there were so many differences. I saw people in shorts, skirts, jeans, and dresses; sneakers, sandals, and cowboy boots; baseball caps, big floppy straw hats and even a couple of fedoras like Christa's. There were people of lots of different races, too, even though, like at my school at home, most of the crowd was white. Everyone sat in little groups at outdoor tables or alone under trees with books in their hands and phones by their sides.

Everywhere I looked there was another coffee shop or sidewalk café. The buildings on either side of the road were tall and wide. The sorts of places where important professors gave important lectures.

When I went to college, I'd have classes in these kinds of buildings. I'd take notes and learn about complicated subjects. I'd sit at outdoor tables drinking tea and listening to music and talking to my new college friends about all the intricate subjects we were studying. Maybe I'd have a girlfriend, or a boyfriend, and we'd sit under trees together, holding hands and being way too mature to worry about any of the stuff that was making my life with Christa so complicated right now.

Drew didn't want any of that, though. After one year of college he'd rather go to some scary, unknown place and do scary, unknown things.

My stomach growled again. Up ahead was another café with its doors and windows wide open. I checked to make sure I had American money in my purse before I went inside.

It was one of those places where you could design your own salad. I didn't like fancy salads, so I ordered a plain Caesar and potato chips. God, I'd missed American food.

My phone buzzed again as I sat down to eat. I gave up and took it out of my pocket, scrolling as I chewed. There was a long group text thread about which food court place we were supposed to meet at. If I left right now, I'd still be two hours late. Whoops.

"There you are."

Christa slid into the seat across from me. I was so surprised I dropped my fork and had to grab my plastic salad bowl to keep it from tipping over.

"I've been looking all over for you." She retrieved my fork and passed it to me. "Why didn't you answer any of my texts?"

"Sorry." I showed her all the unread messages on my phone. "I needed to unplug for a while."

"It's a good thing you're easy to spot." She nodded toward the shiny blue tank top I was wearing. It was actually her tank top. "I was trying to follow you without being a stalker."

I swallowed a bite of salad to keep myself from smiling at that. "I thought you were still mad at me from last night."

"I sort of am." She shrugged. "But I'd still rather hang out with you than anyone else."

Maybe that shouldn't have made my heart swell up, but it did.

"I know what you mean," I said. And then, because I *had* to talk about it, regardless of all the other stuff going on, I added, "Look, if I tell you something, do you promise not to tell anyone? I mean, for real promise? You can't tell Madison, or *anyone*."

Her eyes flicked down. "Yes, of course."

"Okay." I looked around to make sure I didn't recognize anyone else in the café. Then I told her what had happened with Drew.

By the time I'd finished explaining, I wasn't hungry anymore. I threw out what was left of my salad and we started walking back across the campus the same way I'd come. The sun had set and it was getting cool outside. The paths were lit with hazy street lamps. Even more people were hanging out than I'd seen earlier, standing in groups, talking and laughing. No one seemed to be in a hurry.

"I can't believe he just up and dropped out of college." Christa was eyeing the crowd, the same way I was. "My parents would crucify me."

"Uh-huh. My dad is legit going to kill him."

"Will you tell them?"

"No. I promised Drew I wouldn't." I stuck my hands in the pockets of my denim shorts. They were Christa's, too, of course. They were too short on me, but the cool breeze felt nice on my legs after all those hours on the bus surrounded by stale, air-conditioned air. "It makes me wonder, though."

"Wonder what?" Christa's elbow bumped into mine.

"When I told Drew about me, he made me swear up and down I wouldn't tell Dad. He said he didn't think Dad could deal with the idea. Now I wonder if it was really me Drew was thinking about when he said that. Maybe he knew Dad would be angry about *his* secret, and that's what was really on his mind."

"Hmm." Christa glanced over at me. "Do you think so?"

"I don't know. This is all new territory for me. I'm not used to having secrets." It sounded goofy when I said it that way. I pulled my hands back out of my pockets.

"Will you miss him if he leaves?"

"Yes. God, yes. I mean, he's my brother, so he annoys me sometimes, but he's always been there. I can't imagine the house without him in it."

"I get it. My brother's younger than me, but still, I wouldn't want him going off on his own that way."

"And being here, at a college—that makes this even weirder. I mean, this isn't *my* college, but I keep thinking about being someplace like this someday. All of a sudden I'm obsessed with the future and how different it's going to be. Will I even be the same person then?"

"I know exactly what you mean. My parents and I took a trip over spring break to visit Princeton. I kept walking around all those old buildings, trying to picture myself living there, and I just couldn't. How can you go from living one life to something completely different?"

"No clue." Absently, I took her hand and held it as we walked. "And after four years of college, does your life turn upside down all over again when you graduate? You move someplace else and then you have a job where all day the only thing you do is sit in front of a computer and type things?"

"I think that's even scarier. I mean, my parents have really important jobs. If they screw up, it could be really dangerous. I don't know how you deal with knowing that."

"All I know is I don't want to be a minister, like my dad." I shook my head. "Or a teacher, like my mom."

"Don't you want to be a musician?"

"I used to. Now I'm not sure." I stared off into the distance. "It's weird how what you want changes, you know? Drew used to say he wanted to play in the NBA, but then he didn't make the varsity basketball team in high school, and since then he hasn't really talked about what he wants to do. I guess now he wants to be a soldier."

"I think I—no." Christa shook her head.

"You think you what?"

"Never mind. It's nothing."

"No, tell me. I want to know."

"Well." Christa ran her free hand through her short dark hair. It shone in the light from the street lamps. "My parents don't believe it's a real career, but I really think I'd be a good chef. I love cooking in a way I've never loved anything in school. There's an art to it. My parents don't get that."

"That's awesome." It really was awesome. I'd never known anyone who wanted to be a chef. "Is that why you're helping Señora Suarez at lunch?"

"Yeah. It's been cool, learning how to cook the way she does. Back home, I usually do the grocery shopping and cook dinner at home since my parents work so late. In middle school I used to look up recipes and watch videos so I could learn how to make different things. Then I started inventing my own recipes. My parents always say the food I make is re-

ally good, and I get awesome responses on Instagram when
I post the photos."

"That's so cool. The only thing I can make is pancakes, and
half the time I burn them."

Christa laughed. "Maybe I can teach you sometime, now
that you'll actually consent to eat food that isn't toast."

I grinned. "That would be fun. Maybe when we get back
home."

"Yeah, maybe." Christa's voice sounded far away.

"So you'd rather be a chef than a photographer?"

"I think so?" She shrugged again. "I really want to do both.
Right now, photography feels more like a fun thing to do and
cooking feels more like a thing I want to do all day and forever. But who knows what I'll think in a few years? I hate the
idea of having to choose."

"Do you have to?"

"Not this second, but it's tricky because to be a chef you
have to go to a special culinary school. It's not something you
can just major in at UMD or wherever. But it also kind of
doesn't matter because my parents wouldn't let me do either.
They want me to go to an Ivy League school and major in
science or business or law. Or something else I'd totally hate.
Just as long as it sounds fancy to their friends."

"Have you told them that's not what you want?"

"No. I know what they'd say."

"Technically you don't need their permission once you're
eighteen. You can do what you want. That's what Drew's
doing."

"I need their permission if they're the ones paying." Christa
stared down at the ground in front of us.

"Oh. Yeah, I guess."

I squeezed Christa's hand. Then I realized—wait.

I was holding Christa's hand. Out in the open, where any-one could see.

I dropped it, fast.

Then I realized something else. I'd been holding Christa's hand. And Christa had let me.

She must've just realized it, too, because she was staring at me, her eyes wide.

"I, um." I tried to distract her. "I have no idea where we are."

"Me, neither." She turned around to look. I stared at her hand where it hung now by her side. I couldn't believe that happened. "Oh, wait. We've come almost the whole way back. We're not that far from the dorm."

"Oh. Um…" Suddenly I felt the weight of the backpack on my shoulder. With everything else that had happened, I'd nearly forgotten about my trip to the health center that afternoon. "You know, I never even went into the dorm. I haven't seen the rooms or anything. Do we need to get a key or something?"

"I have it." Christa pulled something out of her purse. A plastic hook with a white card and a small metal key hanging from it. It seemed like the key to more than just a dorm room.

"Should we go back, then?" I said.

"Yeah, yeah, okay, let's go back."

We headed down the path, walking faster than before. I thought about taking her hand again but I didn't want to press my luck. Besides, soon we'd be seeing people we knew.

Except, somehow, we didn't. The campus was full of peo-ple, but none of them were faces I recognized. Christa and I were nothing but two girls in a crowd here. No one stared at me for being black or for being my father's daughter or for being the one the lesbo rumors were about.

It was exhilarating, being out here. So much so that I said

what I was thinking without even worrying about how it would sound to Christa. "You know, we're talking about the future, about what we want to do, and for me it's always felt as if the future is so hypothetical. I've never had the chance to actually try any of it. It's the same thing with being bi. That's always felt like a theory to me, too. Now suddenly it's all changing."

I could feel the heat rising in my face as I trailed off. But I didn't regret what I'd said.

"I…" Christa's eyes were focused in front of us, on the dorm looming larger the closer we got. "I know what you mean."

"Well, you're closer to the reality of it than I am. You already know what you want your career to be. And you're already, you know…" I wanted to say that she'd already hooked up with girls before me—not to mention the whole boyfriend-back-home thing—but that felt like going too far. "You're living your full life."

She laughed. "Sure I am."

"Anyway, that's part of what college means to me, I think. A fresh start. So I can really start trying things. Figuring out who I actually am."

"Yeah." Christa nodded. We were almost at the dorm now. "I get that. Except college is still a long way away."

"Yeah, that's true. I don't want to sit around waiting for things to happen, either."

"Same here."

As Christa let us into the front door of the dorm with her plastic card, she turned to smile at me, and I felt this weird, awesome rush of happiness that seemed to come out of no-where at all.

I smiled back as wide as I could.

We got in an elevator to go to the sixth floor, just the two of us, and I couldn't help it. I kissed her, right there. She laughed and kissed me back.

The doors opened too fast, spilling us out into a hallway with dingy industrial carpet and flickering florescent lights. Christa led me down a hall, explaining how she'd already stashed her stuff in our room and warning me that the space was tiny. She unlocked the door and I followed her in, flicking on a desk lamp that cast the room in a dull gold glow. The walls were white painted cinderblock, the two twin beds were made up with beige blankets that looked decades old and the window was covered in a thick gray curtain that looked so stiff I was afraid to touch it.

It was beautiful.

Christa was here, and she was all mine. For tonight, at least.

I dumped out my bag onto one of the beds, pulling out the box of dental dams and the rubber gloves. Christa must've seen all this stuff before, so I didn't want her to think I thought it was a big deal, having protection with me. Wait, *barriers*. That was probably what Christa was used to calling them.

I was still sorting through my stuff when I felt Christa's hand slipping around my waist from behind. I closed my eyes. It was like being in the guest house in Mudanza. Except here, we had all night, and a room that was all ours.

Christa kissed my neck. I turned around slowly. She linked her arms around my back as I leaned in to kiss her. Her lips were soft and warm. I melted into her, our tongues slipping together, her body pressing into mine. I wanted so much in that moment.

We stumbled. The backs of my knees struck the side of the bed and I fell backward, laughing and pulling her on top of me.

"Hey," she said, reaching under me. Something was poking into my back. "What's this?"

"Oh, yeah." I reached back. It was the box of thirty-six dental dams. "I got some stuff. You know, barriers? For if we need them, I mean."

"Oh." Christa took the box of dental dams and sat up. I sat up, too. My shirt was rumpled. I tugged it down. "So this is—barriers?"

"Yeah, um." I felt awkward now. I wished the light were dimmer. "Dental dams and gloves. I went and got them from the campus health center. And the drugstore."

"Dental dams and gloves," Christa repeated. She picked up the box of gloves and held it out, too. "Okay."

My face flushed. I could hear my voice creeping higher and higher as I said, "They're for if we, um, want to go further? You know, ever? I just figured we should be prepared, right?"

"Oh. Yeah, sure." Christa turned over the box of dental dams and started reading the instructions. "Ohhh, okay, I get it."

Hmm. "You've used this stuff before, right?" I asked her.

"Oh, yeah, totally." She picked up the package of gloves and peered at it. "I mean, I think I have. Well, okay, maybe I haven't, actually."

"Oh." I frowned. "So you just…you didn't use anything?"

"No. I mean. I guess it, um, never came up."

"What do you mean, it never came up?" If Christa had been having unsafe sex, maybe she and I shouldn't go further after all. "You…did it without using anything? Like with Madison? Or your other ex-girlfriends?"

Christa blushed. "No. I mean, I've never, um. Never needed to."

I shook my head. "I don't get it."

Christa sighed. "Look, I've never. Um. You're the only one I've gone this far with. Okay?"

Oh.

Ohhhh.

She'd never—

So that meant—

Christa hadn't done it before. The same as me. Well, she hadn't with a girl, at least.

So that night, when we were hooking up and I sort of, well, steered things toward third base—that was the first time she'd ever even done that?

And I'd gone and gotten the dental dams and the gloves. Christa hadn't even thought about it until now.

All this time I'd been thinking I was following along after her. Did this mean *I* was the one being followed?

Did she even want to do this, or was she only here because I started it? I hoped she didn't think I was a slut or anything.

"But you have with Steven, right?" I said.

She looked quickly from side to side. "Um. Not really."

Oh my God. She *did* think I was a slut.

"Okay, well that's cool." I started gathering up the dams and gloves. "I mean, never mind about that stuff. I only got it, you know, in case. It's not a big deal. I mean, whatever."

Christa shuffled over closer to me. She took my hand, but I didn't look up to meet her eyes.

"No!" she said. "Don't. I mean, I'm glad you got it. You don't need to put it away. I think it's cool. Safety is really important. I definitely want us to be totally safe."

She pulled my hand up to her lips and kissed each of my fingers.

My chest pounded. I raised my eyes to meet her gaze. Her face was flushed bright pink. She was so pretty.

"I'm not—" I swallowed. "I mean, I've never done anything like this, either. I haven't done anything at all, really. Especially with a girl."

"That's cool, too." She pressed her lips to my fingers again.

I closed my eyes. "It's good that this is new for both of us. It makes it special."

I hadn't thought about it that way, but she was right. It did feel special. *She* felt special.

This was special. What we had. What we did.

My eyes were still closed. I leaned in, resting my cheek on her shoulder. She held my wrist up to her face and kissed the inside of it where the skin was thin and sensitive. I shivered. She kissed down my wrist to the inside of my elbow. Her lips were warm and light against my skin.

"You feel so good," she whispered, just as I was thinking the same thing.

I giggled and kissed the side of her neck, right at the slope of her shoulder. I could feel her pulse under my lips.

She was real. Solid.

She wanted to be with me. And I wanted to be with her. I *wanted* her.

I kissed her cheek, her jaw, working my way around. I wasn't really sure if this was what I was supposed to do, but she sucked in a breath, so she probably liked it. When my lips met hers, she kissed me so hard I fell backward onto the bed. I would've laughed, but everything had suddenly grown serious.

Christa fell with me. Even after weeks of making out, it was still so amazing, the interplay of lips and tongues and limbs. She ran her hands up and down my sides, my stomach, my breasts. I squirmed happily and looped my arms around her, pulling up her shirt to run my hands over her bare back. She moaned, exactly the way girls did in movies. I could feel it vibrate in my throat as we kissed, and it made me moan as if I was in a movie, too.

We pulled off our shirts and fumbled to unhook each other's bras. Hers was shiny and black and looked amazing. We touched and kissed and frantically moved against each other. I dipped my fingers below the waistband of her shorts and she made these noises that made me never want to stop.

Her hand was between us, reaching down. My heart was pounding so hard I thought it would jump out of my body. She undid the zipper on my shorts and then she was reaching down, her fingers sliding into my underwear. This was faster than we usually went, but I didn't care. I wanted fast this time.

She hesitated. Then she pulled back, her whole body lifting off me. It was awful. I didn't know what I'd done wrong.

I propped myself up on my elbows, my head spinning as she leaned over the side of the bed. I was about to ask what was going on when I heard a rustling sound. She was opening the packages. Ohhh.

She pulled out a purple latex glove and rolled it onto her hand. It was funny, and I giggled because it looked like she was getting ready to do the dishes. She giggled, too, at first. But then she rolled back on top of me and pulled off my shorts, and then her hand was between my legs again, and we weren't laughing anymore.

She kissed my lips and touched me through my underwear. I kissed her back. Her nipples felt like pebbles under my palms. She reached for the waistband of my underwear and tugged it down slowly. I sucked in a breath. We'd never done that before. Taking off underwear made this feel really serious. Official.

She pushed my underwear halfway down my thighs. I felt crazily exposed. It was a good feeling and a not-as-good one at the same time. I felt self-conscious, but I also wanted to kiss her more. I wanted to everything her more.

She slid her hand up the inside of my leg while we kissed. My heart was pounding harder than it ever had, all nervousness and anticipation and basically every other feeling I'd ever felt combined into one overwhelming sense of desperate need.

Then she touched me, and I seriously thought I might explode.

I'd thought the glove would be weird, but it just felt smooth and warm and good. Almost too good. She kissed my neck and my breasts while she touched me, and I arched up into her mouth and made sounds that weren't words and weren't moans, either. I didn't know what they were. I might've been embarrassed, except we were way past the point of embarrassment now.

She moved her hand back, and then I could feel her fingertip pressing right there. My face was on fire. We'd never done this before. Her finger pressed more, and more, and then it was inside me. Only the tip, but it was so much.

I squeezed my arms tight around her back, my nails digging into her shoulder blades. She slid her finger farther in. It didn't hurt, but it was so intense it was hard to breathe. I wound my hand up the back of her neck and into her hair, twisting the strands around my fingers.

She moved her finger deeper, and it was so much, nearly too much. A new current was pumping through us, from her into me and up through my entire body.

I cared about her so much. More than I could ever imagine caring about anyone.

She started to press deeper, and I grabbed her elbow to stop her there. She must've thought I wanted her to stop altogether, because she pulled her hand all the way out, fast. I gasped at the shock. I'd wanted it to last longer.

She peeled the glove off and tossed it over the side of the bed. I could barely move. My heart was still pounding so hard.

"Are you okay?" She leaned over me, frowning.

I nodded.

"Was that all right?" She bit her lip.

I nodded again and finally found my voice.

"Yes." I tightened my arms around the small of her back, pulling her to me. "Yes, it was perfect."

She ducked her head. I propped myself up on my elbow and kissed her. I could feel her smiling against my lips.

My heart was slowing down, but I still felt so warm. I loved the way she felt against me. Like she was all mine.

We rolled over until I was on top of her, and right away I reached for the zipper on her shorts. She was breathing so fast. I undid the zipper, then ran my hand up and down her thighs. She made a high-pitched noise that I loved. I wanted to touch her everywhere.

I peeled her shorts down, then her underwear, leaving them partway down her thighs, the way she'd done to me. Her hips squirmed on the bed, and I looked down at her, fascinated by her body. I'd never seen her like this before. She was amazing.

I found the package of gloves on the bedside table and fumbled for one. It took me forever to roll it on, and the glove kept bunching up together. Christa had slipped the glove on so fast it had seemed sexy, but I felt like I was ruining everything.

She didn't seem to mind, though. She lay on her back with her eyes closed, her hand running up and down her rib cage.

God, she was hot.

I finally got the glove on and moved back down to her. Seeing her this way was so interesting. She didn't look so different from me, except that her skin was lighter.

She made little moans and grunts as I moved my fingers over her, rubbing lightly. Touching her with the glove, with no underwear between us, felt different from when I'd touched her before. I had more control now. I didn't feel quite so nervous.

When her moans and grunts started coming faster, I reached down farther between her legs and found the right spot. Somehow, it surprised me a little that her body worked exactly the same way mine did, even though it should've been obvious. I pressed the tip of my finger in, moving as slowly as I could.

She gasped. I nearly pulled back, but then I remembered how it had felt when she'd done this to me, and I stayed where I was. I waited a minute, then pressed in deeper, and she gasped again. It was amazing, seeing her react this way to something I was doing.

I pushed in farther, waiting for her to stop me. She didn't. Was I hurting her? It didn't look that way. Her eyes were closed, but her whole body was pulsing. My finger was halfway inside her. I pulled it back a little, then pushed it in again. Her eyebrows creased together, and she made a low sound.

Then she grabbed my wrist so fast I jumped and pulled my hand away from her. Her face creased. What had I done wrong?

"I'm sorry, I'm sorry," I said. "Crap, I'm so sorry."

Her eyes were still closed, her face still creased. "It's all right."

"Did it hurt? What did I do? I'm sorry! I swear I'll never do it again."

She shook her head. Her breathing came in heaves. "It's totally fine. It was just—a lot. Come here."

She pulled me by my shoulders. I leaned down against her, my face pressed against her chest. Her chin rested on the top of my head.

I didn't understand what had happened. Everything had been going perfectly at first. Next time I'd have to go slower, more gently.

Or maybe she'd felt the same way I had when I grabbed her elbow. It hadn't been bad. It had just been—wow.

I peeled the glove off carefully and tossed it over the side of the bed. I thought about how we'd look if you saw us from the ceiling—two mostly naked girls with a couple of damp rub-

ber gloves below them, as if we'd been performing surgery—
and I giggled.

"What's so funny?" Christa's words sounded funny, almost slurred.

I smiled and kissed the top of her breast. "I was thinking
about how if somebody saw us, they'd think we were, you
know, doctors, or something. Because of the gloves."

She didn't say anything at first. Then she started laughing.
Her body shook under me.

"Yes," she said. "Doctors. That is *totally* what they would
think."

I started laughing, too.

We held each other, and we laughed. Everything about the
world seemed so absurd right then.

And I felt that same rush of happiness again.

This time it didn't go away.

CHAPTER 18

IT WAS THE HAPPIEST I'd ever been.

Christa and I were sitting side by side on the bleachers in a massive football stadium while Christian rock blared across the speakers. The band was on a stage in the middle of the field, playing an endless song about following the Lord into the wilderness. Giant screens showed the musicians droning into microphones with their eyes closed. The close-ups were so extreme we could see their nostril hairs.

And I was so, so happy.

I barely noticed the band. All I could focus on was the feeling of Christa's finger moving up and down my arm, hidden under the cardigan we'd draped across our shoulders like a blanket.

That morning, she'd drawn a tiny heart on the inside of my wrist with one of her markers. Her hand kept drifting back to it now. Every time she touched me on that spot I had to force myself not to start beaming like a fool.

All day, I'd wanted to do nothing but touch her. When we'd woken up together, her head cradled on my chest, it had felt like perfection. I didn't want to move an inch. But eventually I had to because I needed to pee. Then before I was even out of the bathroom (by the way, having a real bathroom after three weeks of outdoor showers was *amazing*), Gina and Olivia were knocking on our door shouting for us to come help make breakfast. Christa was dressed in a flash and out the door, so I followed her to the dorm's tiny kitchen where she found eggs, cheese and frozen vegetables in the fridge and somehow put together a feast for ten of us. Everyone else raved about the food, but all I wanted was for them to go away so I could pull Christa into my lap and bury my face in her neck.

By then, though, it was time to get ready for the Bible festival. When we got to the stadium, Christa and I found places in an area of the stands where we didn't know anyone, and for an hour, we pretended to listen to the concert while we took turns tracing patterns on each other's arms under Christa's cardigan.

Our movements had gotten more and more elaborate. At the moment, I was pretty sure Christa was trying to spell out letters on my forearm, but I had no idea what she was saying. The very idea that she was touching me was enough to make me shiver.

The song finally ended and the lead singer announced that it was time for a prayer. Reluctantly, I pulled my arm away from Christa. I bowed my head and closed my eyes, listening to the rustle of thousands of other people doing the same thing. The singer called on God to help us keep our minds open that we may receive His guidance during the festival today. He went on and on about it, until I got the sense he loved the sound of his own voice more than he loved our lord and savior. I played a David Bowie song in my head to drown it out. When at last he said amen, my hand stretched back to meet Christa's reaching fingers as we all echoed the word together.

Even though the prayer was over, the singer was still talking about sharing our faith with others and nurturing our personal relationships with Jesus. Maybe it was totally blasphemous, but right then the only relationship I wanted to nurture was with the girl sitting next to me.

I waited until the band started playing another song, a slow one, before I slid my fingers along Christa's arm. She slumped lower in her seat and covered her smile with her free hand. I skittered my fingers up past her elbow to the inside of her biceps. She giggled and squirmed. I faked a shiver in case anyone was looking and pulled up the cardigan to cover our shoulders. We were both wearing the same T-shirt everyone else at the festival was wearing—it was light blue and said I'M FINDING MY FAITH in fluorescent green letters across the front—and I'd already memorized exactly how those letters looked spelled out across Christa's chest. I had to force myself to face forward as I slid my hand all the way up the inside of her arm until my fingertip was resting where the edge of her T-shirt met bare skin. She didn't move a muscle as I dipped my fingertip under the fabric, a fraction of an inch, then farther, until I was tracing my finger down around the outside curve of her breast. I held my breath the whole time.

After a few seconds I didn't dare keep going, so I pulled my hand away and straightened up in my seat. My face felt so warm I was sure I must be giving off a signal to the entire stadium, but no one turned to look my way. Christa, still slumped down in her seat, wound her fingers into mine and squeezed my hand tight.

The band played a dramatic drumroll then and the singer yelled, "That's it for us, you guys! Now you have a break for lunch, but come back at one o'clock because Pastor James is going to lead you in an awesome workshop on finding your truth!"

Everyone stood up at once. I didn't want to look weird, so I leaped to my feet. So did Christa, her face bright red. Her cardigan and our purses tumbled to the ground. I bent to pick them up, trying to smooth my braids out at the same time. I'd never felt so flustered. I didn't even want to think about how I looked when I stood back up and came face-to-face with Jake.

"Uh," he said, glancing back and forth between me and Christa. "Hey."

"Hey." I pushed my hair back again. Had he seen us fooling around? Would he say anything if he had? "Where are you sitting?"

"Down there." He pointed several rows below us. Good. "I saw you guys when we were getting up. Did you like the show?"

"Sure," I said. "Whatever. Did you?"

"Nah, I can't stand these guys." Jake jammed his thumb in the direction of the stage as we stepped aside to let people past us. "Give me Jars of Clay any day."

I nodded, trying to look as though I knew the first thing about Christian bands and wondering if Jars of Clay sounded anything like David Bowie.

"Anyway, so I've been getting about a million questions about the debate." Jake was trying to act nonchalant, but I could tell he was at least slightly annoyed at me for being MIA all morning. "I've been trying to find you. We've got a lot to figure out and only a few days before it's supposed to happen."

"Right." I sighed. I hadn't thought about the debate since I got off the bus yesterday. "The debate."

"Can we talk over lunch?" Jake pointed at the stadium gates. "There are food trucks outside with about eighty different kinds of tacos."

I glanced at Christa. "Want to come eat?"

"Nah." She brushed a strand of hair behind her ear. "I need to find a computer. Lots of Instagram to do after three weeks offline, and I want to write some emails, too."

"Okay, cool." I turned to Jake. "Can I come meet you in five minutes?"

"Sure. I'll get a table."

I followed Christa down the steps and out of the stadium, waving at the people we knew. We filed out through the gates with the crowd.

"Will you come meet us when you're done?" I asked her. "I want to make sure we can sit together during the next session, too."

Christa bit her lip. "Do you think that's really a good idea?"

At first I thought she was seriously worried. Then she started giggling, and I laughed, too. I wanted to take her hand again, but I resisted. "Who do you need to email?"

"My parents, mostly. They're really annoyed we haven't talked at all. And I should write to Steven."

Of course. Steven.

I glanced at the phone in Christa's hand. She hadn't been on it that much since we'd been down here. I'd thought she and Steven would be texting all the time. "How's he doing?"

"He's good." Christa wouldn't meet my eyes. "He might go back to Milwaukee at the end of the summer. That's why I want to write to him, to see if he knows for sure what the plan is."

"Whoa. Milwaukee? That's really far."

"That's where he used to live. His grandmother's sick, so they're thinking about going back."

"You mean for a visit, to see his grandmother?" I wondered why she didn't just text him to ask.

"No, they might move, for real." Christa kept walking, unconcerned, as if she was telling me the list of taco flavors.

"Wait, so does that mean you'd—" Were she and Steven going to break up? I didn't want to say it out loud. If you tell a wish, it won't come true. "What would that mean for you and him?"

She shrugged. "We'll figure it out. Anyway, it's just a maybe. Don't worry about it. You need to go meet Jake and do important debate stuff."

She smiled at me out of the corner of her eye. I felt myself smiling back. I was physically incapable of not smiling back at this girl, apparently.

"Okay. Let me know what Steven says."

"I will."

I wished I could kiss her goodbye, even though we were only going to be apart for an hour or so.

When I got to the taco trucks, I expected to find Jake sitting by himself, but instead he was in the middle of a group of girls. Gina was there talking to Hannah and Olivia. Once I sat across from Jake with my paper plate full of tacos covered in cheese, onions and guacamole, I realized another girl had joined them. Lori.

"Hi, Aki," she said.

I set down my food, trying not to look at her. It was startling to hear her say my name. Startling and...actually, kind of nice. As though maybe the world was going to right itself again after being upside down for so long. "Yeah. Hi."

"Lori and I were talking about debate plans," Jake told me. "She has some great ideas."

"Really?" I didn't mean to sound skeptical. Okay, maybe I did. I took a big bite of taco, smearing my lip with guacamole in the process.

"Really," Lori said, ignoring my tone. "For one thing, I think the debate needs to be a whole afternoon, not just an hour after vespers. Otherwise there's no way you'll get through all the speeches on time."

"But we're supposed to be working during the day." Even though Jake and I had made up the whole plan just the day before, it felt like Lori was interfering. Like she thought she knew better than us. "The chaperones aren't going to let us take off a whole afternoon."

"Yes they will. I talked to my aunt. She said we're ahead of schedule on the fence and they were going to give us Friday afternoon off anyway."

I glared at her, trying to think of something to argue back with. We were still fighting, right? "You talked to her before you asked us? That's not okay."

"Jake said it was fine." Lori's voice was cool.

I turned to frown at Jake, but he just looked tired.

"I wish you two would get over whatever issue you have," he said. "I know girls are always dramatic about every little thing, but—"

"Shut it, Jake," Lori and I said in unison.

I couldn't help giggling. Lori did, too.

I quickly made myself stop. I wasn't just going to pretend things were normal between Lori and me again. Besides, she still needed to end things with Carlos, pronto.

"Also," Lori added, "I think we should have a vote after the debate's over. Have everyone tally up where they stand on all the issues."

"That would be cool," Jake said. "We could share the results with the conference delegates."

"Actually," I said, an idea forming in spite of my annoyance, "maybe we could have two votes. One before the debate and one after. So we could see how many people change their minds when they hear the arguments."

"Hey, that would rock," Lori said. Jake nodded vigorously.

It turned out all of us had a lot of ideas. Gina and the Harpers Ferry girls, too. Jake wrote it all down, filling a notebook he'd bought at the campus bookstore with our plans and ideas. By the end of lunch, we'd agreed that Jake and I would be masters-of-ceremonies during the debate, so we'd be in charge of introducing everyone, and that Lori, Gina, Hannah and Olivia would help with the setup.

I didn't love the idea of MCing—I hated public speaking,

after all—but Jake flat out refused to do it by himself, and anyway, I wouldn't have to actually talk that much. All I had to do was say some people's names every couple of minutes. My own speech on health care would be a lot harder, but I'd put off thinking about that for now. Instead we spent most of lunch coming up with ideas for how to run the event to make sure all the debaters would have a fair shot at making their case.

It was weirdly fun, planning it all out. In fact, except for my time with Christa, that taco lunch was the most fun I'd had since I'd left Maryland.

Our break was over, so I gathered up everyone's trash and carried it over to the recycling bins at the edge of the picnic area. When I turned around to go back to the stadium, I saw Lori watching me from the table. We locked eyes. For a second I thought she was going to come over. Maybe she'd apologize for being so obstinate. Or maybe I'd apologize to her, for real this time, for what I'd told Christa.

Then her aunt Miranda called my name, waving, and all bets were off. Miranda was walking straight toward me with a determined look on her face.

There was no way this was going to be good.

"There you are, Aki!" Miranda fanned her face with a flyer for that morning's concert. It had a big picture of the singer, his hands bent in prayer. He looked like just as much of a tool in the photo as he had on the big screen. "I've been trying to get you alone so we could have a talk. Since you promised to come find *me* the other night."

Her voice was pointed, teasing, but I didn't want to deal with her right now. "It's lovely to see you, Aunt Miranda."

"Enough of that. I'm going to cut right to the chase with you, Aki. We've always been honest with each other, isn't that right?"

"Uh." I shoved my hands in my pockets, twisting my wrist

to make sure the heart Christa had drawn on my arm was covered. "Yeah, of course."

"Good. Because I'm going to be frank with you. I've gotten the sense that you've been exploring your sexuality this summer, and I want you to know, I'm here anytime you need to talk. No judgments, just straight talk. Well, in a manner of speaking." She tittered.

Exploring my sexuality? Oh, God, was I *that* obvious?

"I don't know what you mean, Aunt Miranda," I said, trying with every ounce of energy I possessed to keep a blank face.

"It's all right, honey. As I said, no judgments."

"That's great, but—" I edged around her. "There's nothing to judge. I mean, I'm not—doing anything."

She nodded. "Of course you're not. Listen, baby, I know it's tough when you're away from home. I know you miss having your momma to talk to. Your daddy, well, he's your daddy. It's not the same. But since you can't talk to Momma right now, I want to make sure you understand you can always talk to Aunt Miranda."

God, she was so embarrassing. I was so tempted to say, "You're not *my* aunt, you know." Instead I put on my best fake smile and said, "Thanks. I definitely will if there's anything I need to talk about."

"Good." She nodded again. "I know when you're in high school, a lot of the time it feels as though you need to have everything figured out right away. But I'll let you in on a secret. Us adults, most of us *still* don't have it all figured out. So when you're struggling with something, well, I want you to know that it's okay to struggle."

Aunt Miranda was such a hippie-dippie. "Okay. Thanks."

"All right. I now release you from the burden of talking to me." She laughed again. "I know you've got someplace better to be."

She was right. Everyone else was already in the stadium by now. If someone had taken my seat next to Christa, I was going to have to kill them. "See you later."

I ran down the path toward the stadium entrance, but as I did, I couldn't help glancing back at Aunt Miranda. She was watching me, her lips pursed. I wondered how much she knew. I wondered if she'd ever so much as kissed a girl herself. Maybe. She'd never gotten married, and she'd probably been even more hippified in her youth.

Either way, I wished she didn't know. I had to work on being less obvious.

"Aki. Hey."

I sighed and turned around. I knew that voice better than anyone's. "Hi, Lori."

I glanced toward the gate. There were only a few other people still out here. All I wanted was to go back into the bleachers and sit next to Christa. But Lori had a look on her face that meant she absolutely must say something. "Sorry about my aunt. Was she being nosy?"

"Oh my God. It was so embarrassing."

"I know. She's getting worse. She asked me the other day if I was thinking about 'losing my virginity.'" Lori made air quotes, giggling. She was acting almost normal. It was strange.

"What did you tell her?" I asked.

"First I told her the truth. Just to see the look on her face." Lori snickered. "Then I told her I was only joking."

"Wait. What truth?"

Lori only raised her eyebrows.

"Lori." I stared at her. "Did you really—with Carlos?"

"Well. I mean..." Lori's smile faltered. "That was the plan, right? A summer fling?"

"Lori. He's *married*."

Her smile was gone now. "You don't get to judge me."

"I'm not judging you, I'm only—" I stopped. "Okay, you know what? I am judging you. You seriously want this to be how you remember your first serious relationship? With a guy you barely even know, who you can't tell anyone about, who couldn't be with you for real even if he wanted to?"

Lori's face froze. "You're one to talk."

I sucked in a breath. "Shut up."

"No, *you* shut up. Look, it doesn't always work out for everyone exactly how it does for you, all right? I know all you care about anymore is yourself and your little wannabe-girlfriend, but out here us regular people are doing the best we can, okay?"

My little wannabe-girlfriend?

"Um, all right." I crossed my arms over my chest. "Why did you come over here to talk to me? Earlier I was thinking maybe you'd finally gotten over yourself, but clearly that's not the case."

"I don't remember, but whatever it was, I've definitely changed my mind. Have a nice life."

She turned to go. I'd never felt so frustrated.

"You have a nice life, too!" I yelled after her. She flipped me off without looking back.

In that moment I couldn't remember anything I'd ever liked about Lori.

But I couldn't let her get to me. That was what she wanted—to get under my skin. She wasn't going to win this one, though. I'd put her out of my mind for good.

Besides. I had other things to think about.

CHAPTER 19

THAT AFTERNOON LASTED about fifty million years.

Christa and I sat together in the bleachers again, but this time instead of listening to a concert we had to pay attention to some minister. He'd preach for a while on the big screens, then make us divide into groups and do activities. One time we had to role-play talking to a friend at school about how Jesus would save them. At our churches back home we didn't really do these kinds of things, so it was hard to take it seriously. Christa and I wound up in a group with Rodney and Sofía. We spent the whole time making up our own lyrics to the songs the band had played that morning. Rodney changed the lines to the song about following the Lord into the wilderness so they were about following the Black Panther into Wakanda, and we were all laughing so hard we almost got in trouble with the chaperones.

All afternoon I longed to touch Christa, but the lights were too bright. There was too much movement around us. I wished all of it would disappear until there was no one but us.

When the last activity finished and the minister led us in

a final prayer, my mind chanted instead, *Almost. We're almost finished. Almost ready for tonight to start.*

Then the minister said, so slowly I wanted to throttle him, "Amen. Praise be to God. Now you're all invited to join us for a barbecue supper on the—"

By then everyone was already jumping out of their seats, Christa and me fastest of all. The idea of barbecue made my stomach rumble, but I wanted to be alone with her more than I wanted food.

"Should we try to meet up with people?" I asked her as we pressed through the crowd surging down the aisles. "Are you hungry?"

"Nah. Let's just head back."

It was exactly what I was hoping she'd say.

The stadium wasn't that far from our dorm, but the campus was big, so it was still a hike. The lawn was packed with people, the way it had been the night before. This time I didn't stop to look around, though. I was on a mission.

Christa must've felt the same way. She was walking just as fast, her purse swinging from her hand. She'd tied her cardigan around the handle, so her arms were bare under the sleeves of her T-shirt.

She was so pretty. She kept looking over at me and smiling as we walked, and I kept smiling back.

I wanted to jump up and down when we first caught sight of our dorm, then again when the elevator doors opened onto our floor. While Christa fumbled around for the room key, I wished I could kiss her right there in the hallway. I hated having to worry about stupid things, like people seeing us.

As soon as we got inside, though, the waiting was over, and everything was perfection. I kissed the back of her neck while she was still locking the door behind us. She turned around, grinning, and kissed me back. I was so wound up I couldn't think straight. I pressed her back against the door, wrapping my arms around her waist.

"Come on," she whispered, taking my hand and pulling me toward the bed. That was when this room became our entire world.

A thousand years ago, when I first met Christa, I used to think of everything we did as something for the tally. I used to have all these different labels. First base. Second base. Hooking up. Whatever.

It was all about checking things off a list. Sometimes I didn't even think about whether I was ready for them or not. All I cared about was going forward.

That seemed ridiculous now that I knew what it meant to be with someone and have it really matter. It wasn't about what you did or how far you went on a stupid imaginary list. What mattered was what you felt.

Tonight, I wanted to feel everything. Tonight, I was ready.

I followed Christa, watching the way her body moved as she walked. I loved the curves of her hips and her legs. She turned around, caught me looking at her, and gave a self-conscious shrug. She leaned back, laced her fingers through mine and kissed me softly on the lips. I kissed back just as softly.

We sank onto the bed. I ran my hands up and down her back and sides, feeling the warmth of her skin through the fabric of her T-shirt and denim skirt. She kissed me all over my face, her lips trailing down to my neck, down to the neckline of my T-shirt.

We kissed, and kissed, and then she broke off and pulled my shirt over my head. I reached for the hem of her skirt, summoned my courage and pulled it all the way up. She wriggled out of it and tossed it aside, throwing her T-shirt off with it. She lay on her side in her bra and underwear. Matching white lace. I stared at her. I couldn't believe how beautiful she was.

Before I knew it was happening, I'd said it out loud.

"I can't—" My lips caught on the words. "I can't *believe* how beautiful you are."

"You are, too," she whispered, reaching for my shorts. I let her unzip them and pull them down. I kicked them off and tried not to feel embarrassed as she looked at me. My underwear wasn't as nice as hers, but she didn't seem to mind. She ran her hand up and down my side lightly. It tickled. I tried not to laugh.

She kissed my breasts over my bra. I rolled onto my back, and she leaned over me, running her hand over my stomach and down to my hip. I slid my hand under her bra. She made a sound somewhere between a *hmm* and a *mmm* that made me want to never stop touching her.

Christa kissed my neck and unhooked my bra. I slipped out of it, then I unfastened hers and pulled it off, too. We held each other, skin to skin, breath to breath.

"I kind of can't deal with how I feel right now," I whispered. This time, too, I hadn't meant to say anything before I spoke. I dipped my head into the crook of her shoulder so she wouldn't see how flushed I felt.

"I know exactly what you mean," she whispered.

I pulled back and looked at her. There were tears in her eyes.

I couldn't believe this was real. I couldn't believe this was my life right now.

I leaned in to kiss her, tasting tears. I kissed across her cheek to her ear and down to her neck. She clasped the back of my head to press me against her.

I kissed her breasts, moving my hands up and down her sides, her hips, her legs, squeezing her gently through her underwear. She squirmed against me, pressing up into my hand. I tugged her underwear down, bending to kiss her stomach.

She was shaking. I was, too. I pulled her underwear down past her ankles and she kicked them off.

She was naked underneath me. I'd never felt anything like this. The incredulity, the apprehension, the desperate need for *more, more, more*.

I kissed her stomach down to her hip. She was shaking so hard I could feel the mattress rocking below us. My hand trembled as I reached over to the desk.

I found the box of dental dams and pulled one out. It was sealed up in some sort of wrapper, so I tried to rip it. It wasn't easy. My hands were shaking, too. But I got the wrapper open and a thin, soft sheet of what looked like plastic or rubber came out. It was flat and light pink, but I could see through it. I was expecting something closer to a condom, but this was much simpler. I could see how it was supposed to work, though.

I was more nervous than I'd ever been in my life as I moved back between Christa's legs. She'd bent one knee up off the bed a little. She was so astonishingly gorgeous.

I spread out the dam. The instructions said to hold it in place with my fingers, so I did that, and then I lowered my lips to her.

Touching her through the dam, I quickly realized, wasn't so different from touching her through her underwear, except that I was using my mouth instead of my fingers. The dam tasted like smooth thin rubber with a very faint twinge of plasticky fruit, but I forgot about that fast as Christa's hand clamped onto the back of my neck.

I didn't know what exactly to do, so I just moved my tongue and my lips around, trying different things. She wound her fingers through my braids, the way she did sometimes when we kissed. But this was so, so different from kissing.

Because this was it. Maybe what we'd already been doing qualified as sex—I didn't know—but I knew for sure that this was the real thing. For so long I'd wondered if this would ever really happen for me, and what it would be like if it did.

Then I stopped thinking. I lost track of time. My whole world was Christa.

Eventually, I figured out that there were some things I did that elicited new sounds from her, and some that made her tug on my hair until it hurt. I figured that was a good sign, so I tried to do those things more often. She started breathing faster. I kept doing what I was doing, wondering how I would know when it was time to stop.

Then, right when my jaw was starting to ache, she pulled back. I climbed up, crumpling up the dam like a tissue and tossing it over the side of the bed.

Christa's chest rose and fell sharply as I lay down beside her on the pillow. She leaned over to kiss me, but I felt weird kissing her on the lips after that, so I kissed her neck instead.

We rolled over to lie on our sides, facing each other. I'd never felt so close to her. Before I had time to think about that, though, Christa was tugging my underwear off, none too gently. Then she was moving down, kissing my breasts and my stomach, rolling me onto my back.

Things got kind of hazy after that.

I remember her kissing me, her lips running over my stomach and my thighs. I remember her reaching toward the box on the desk and fumbling with a wrapper. I remember how shocking it was, the first time I felt her mouth on me. How it seemed so strange, the idea that she was choosing to do this, to me, out of all the people in the world.

I didn't know how long it lasted. It was a mixture of every feeling there was. Affection and tension and boldness and awkwardness and freedom and anxiety and pure, straight-up joy. I was ready to explode from it all.

I couldn't believe I was lucky enough to have this, all of it, all at once.

When my heart started to slow down a little, I shifted down on the bed until I was lying next to her. She slid over to lie on my chest, the reverse of how we'd spent last night. Somehow I felt even closer to her now than I had then. Two days before I wouldn't have thought that was possible.

I wondered what else I'd been wrong about.

PART 5

Breakdown

CHAPTER 20

I WAS POSITIVE everyone would be able to tell.

As soon as I left the dorm room, it was as if there was a spotlight shining on me. As if all the built-up feelings from last night were spilling out of my mind and radiating out through my skin.

But so far that day—through our whirlwind of packing up the dorm, the early-morning chapel service the chaperones dragged us to and the hours we'd already spent on the bus—the only person who'd looked at me differently was Christa.

She was two seats up next to Rodney, but she kept twisting around to look my way. I met her gaze as often as I dared. Usually, after a few seconds, one or both of us would start giggling and she'd twist back around. Then a few minutes later we'd start all over again.

I reached back, rubbing the spot on my shoulder blade where she'd drawn three more tiny hearts that morning. I'd drawn a matching set next to her belly button. That way our shirts would cover them up, but we'd always know they were there.

It was a quiet ride. There were a few people being obnoxious at the back of the bus—unsurprisingly, it was Nick, Paul, Tyler and their crowd—but everyone else spent the first half of the ride on their phones. By the time we'd crossed the border into Mexico a collective resignation had swept through the bus as, one by one, our phones stopped working, and eyes started drifting closed.

I was sitting with Jake again. He was telling me about all the secret parties that'd happened in various dorm rooms late last night. He'd hung out in Gina and Lori's room with a bunch of people from our church's youth group, and now he kept asking me questions about Eric, our youth group president. I got the sense he was interested, but he never came right out and said so, so I was saved from having to break the news that, in addition to being older, taller, better-looking and more boring than pretty much any guy at our church, Eric was as straight as they came.

"I didn't see your brother, though," Jake said. "He didn't even come into our room last night until I was already asleep. Then he tripped on the carpet and woke me up. It's a good thing I've been sleeping on the floor of a church with twenty other guys for the past three weeks or I'd have had a heart attack."

"Sorry," I said. "Drew's a giant klutz."

"Where do you think he was all night?"

I shrugged. I seemed to barely even know my brother at this point.

Jake kept talking, but I tuned out. It was so bizarre to think that only a few hours ago I'd been naked in bed with Christa, and now I was sitting here on a bus as though nothing had changed.

I was dying to tell someone. There was always Jake, but... he was a guy. He wouldn't get what a big deal this was. Plus, I was pretty sure he'd never done it, so he might be embarrassed.

The person I really wanted to tell was Lori, but after what happened yesterday it looked as if things between us were permanently over. Apparently I was on the market for a new best friend. Maybe Christa should take her slot. After all, "friends" would be our only option once we got back home.

It sucked, but being Christa's friend would be better than being her nothing.

"Hey, I wanted to ask you something." A white guy from Jake's church whose name I couldn't remember was suddenly kneeling in the aisle next to my seat. "Did you have anyone sign up yet for gun control?"

Oh, right. The debate seemed a lot less exciting this morning than it had during our big planning session the day before.

"Which side?" I asked as Jake reached for his notebook.

"The hunters' side," the guy said. "These gun control people have never seen what a daggone herd of deer can do to your garden."

Jake chortled in his seat. I wondered if everyone in West Virginia felt that way about deer.

"No one's signed up yet, Luke," Jake said. "I'll put you down."

"Thanks, man." Luke reached over me to whack Jake on the shoulder in that way guys did sometimes. Jake smiled. I wondered how often guys used to whack Jake on the shoulder before he started hanging out with girls so much.

"How many sign-ups does that make?" I asked him.

Jake turned to the schedule we'd scribbled down yesterday at lunch. "Almost twenty. We should really figure out how long we want everyone to talk for. Pretty soon we're going to have to start cutting people off from adding new issues."

"Hey, Olivia." I leaned between the seats to get her attention. She was sitting right behind Jake and me, next to Gina. "Want to look at the debate schedule with us?"

"Sure." Olivia leaned out into the aisle.

"I think we should open with gay marriage," I said. "That's probably going to be the easiest one."

"We still don't have anyone signed up to argue the pro side, though," Jake said.

"Then you should do it," Olivia said. "You haven't signed up for anything yet, have you? You'd do a better job than anyone else here."

"She's right." I nodded emphatically. "You'd be great. I mean, this whole thing was your idea."

Jake cleared his throat. "I thought I'd do the opening welcome. As master of ceremonies."

"I can do that." I wasn't going to let him make excuses. "I'll do the intro and then hand it over to you for the first debate."

Jake's forehead creased. "I thought you didn't want to talk first. Because of your public speaking fear."

Oh, right. That had seemed like such a big deal before. "Whatever. It'll be easy. I'll go, 'Hi, welcome, our first debate is on marriage rights,' and hand it over to you."

"Seriously, Jake." Olivia's smile was earnest. I had a feeling I wasn't the only one who'd suspected Jake wasn't straight. "You'll be fantastic. Almost everyone here signed your petition. They'll all be cheering you on."

That got Jake's attention. "Maybe. I'll think about it. Let's leave that blank for now."

We worked on the schedule for a few more minutes. Then Olivia wanted to start writing her speech, on insurance coverage for birth control, so she moved up to the front of the bus where it was quieter.

It took Jake and me almost the entire bus ride to get through the rest of the list. We barely noticed as the landscape changed outside our window and some of the people who'd drifted off to sleep started opening their eyes and stretching. We were trying to figure out when to announce the results of the final vote when I felt someone poking me in the arm.

I turned around, ready for another sign-up request. Instead, someone shoved a phone in front of my face.

On the screen was a picture of me and Christa. Kissing. Our eyes closed, our mouths wide open, up against the wall of the church in Mudanza during our first week there.

I stopped breathing. I felt invaded. Violated. Like someone had snuck into my room at night while I was sleeping.

"Where did you get that?" I tried to grab the phone, but the guy holding it snatched it away. It was Nick. His eyes were cold and hard.

"It was you, right?" Nick slipped the phone into his back pocket. His voice was low. Most of the other people around us were still asleep, but Jake was watching and listening, his eyes wide. "You told your daddy on us?"

"I—" I swallowed. There was no point denying it. Besides, I didn't want to lie. Nick and his friends were the ones who'd done something bad, not me.

"Tell him you were wrong," Nick said, still in that weird low voice. "That you didn't see what you thought you saw. Unless you want me to send this to the whole church email list."

He pointed to the phone in his pocket.

Oh, God. The Holy Life email list. My parents were on that. *Christa's* parents were on that.

"Seriously?" Jake whispered to Nick. "You so had it coming."

"They called my dad," Nick muttered. "Do you have any idea what he's going to do to me when I get home?"

"That isn't Aki's fault," Jake muttered back. Part of me wanted him to shut up—I could fight my own battles—but mostly I was glad he was talking, because I had no idea what to say.

"I'm not kidding," Nick whispered. He was looking at me, not Jake. "If you think I am, wait. You'll find out."

No one had ever looked at me with so much hate.

"How'd they get that photo?" I asked Jake, my voice shaking, as Nick walked back down the aisle.

"Uh, well." Jake rubbed the back of his neck. "I think it was actually one of the Rockville girls who took it. People were kind of, um, passing it around for a while. Sorry. I didn't want to be the one to tell you."

"Oh, my God." I buried my face in my hands.

"What I want to know," Jake said, "is how they found out you were the one who told on them."

"Huh." I looked up. "Good question. I only told you and—"

And Christa.

Christa, who'd been friends with those guys since they were kids.

She wouldn't have. Not after everything that had happened that weekend.

But...maybe if she didn't *mean* to...if it only slipped out... the way it did when she told Madison about Lori...

I wasn't her girlfriend, after all. She didn't have to be loyal to me over her friends.

But, man, did it ever hurt that I couldn't count on that.

Dad stood up and called for the bus's attention, jerking me out of my thoughts. I'd been sure Dad would know what had happened as soon as he saw me that morning. But when we'd gathered in front of the dorm for breakfast all he'd said was, "Hope you've had a good weekend, Aki."

He sounded exactly the same as when he asked me how school was back home. He was trying to be an attentive dad, but he couldn't care less what answer I actually gave him.

Mom would figure it out when I got home next week, though, I was certain. I'd have to figure out what to say. I didn't know which would freak her out more—the idea that I'd had sex, or that I'd done it with a girl.

"Welcome back to Mudanza, folks," Dad called from the front of the bus. "We're getting back late thanks to that line at the border crossing, so we're going to hurry straight to dinner. After that we'll have a special extended vespers to talk about everything you learned during the festival, so make sure you come ready to share."

Everyone groaned, me most of all. Extended vespers meant I wouldn't have time with Christa before we had to be back at the church. I wouldn't be able to ask her about what happened with Nick.

Maybe that was okay, though. I could use some space to think.

I climbed off the bus with Jake and joined the line trudging toward the food, but before I could make it ten feet, I felt a hand tugging at my elbow. I turned, afraid to face Nick again.

"Hey, Sis." Drew was at my side, his face tight. "I need you to come help me."

"Okay." I didn't ask questions. I didn't know what Drew wanted, but I could tell it was serious.

He led me toward the Riveras' house, walking so fast we were nearly running. For a second I thought about telling him what had happened last night, but I held back. I wanted to tell someone, but not my brother. And definitely not when he was on such an intense mission.

"I decided you were right." Drew's words were so clipped I had to strain to hear him. "I've gotta get this over with. Like a Band-Aid."

"Get what over with?"

But I figured out what Drew had in mind when I saw Dad up ahead. He had a bag over his shoulder and was about to go through the Riveras' back door.

Drew called out to him first. "Hey, Dad, hold up!"

Dad turned around. His face paled. "What's wrong, Drew? Aki?"

"Nothing's wrong." Drew was nearly panting when we caught up to Dad. He hadn't played basketball since he left high school, and he must've gotten out of shape. I hadn't noticed until now. "I have something I've gotta tell you."

Dad looked back and forth from Drew to me. His face was still. "Of course, son."

"Yeah, so." Drew looked at me, too. I shifted my weight from one foot to the other, anxious, waiting. This was going to be awful.

Finally Drew said it. "I'm going to— Dad, just so you know, yesterday I went to the ROTC office and told them I want to join the army."

Dad didn't move. His face was as still, as pale, as it had been when Drew and I first ran up to him.

"It's only," Drew went on, when Dad didn't respond, "college isn't really the right fit for me. I want to do something different, and the army, it's perfect. I'll just join for a couple of years. They can give me training to get a really good job when I get out, maybe in a tech field or something. Or maybe by then I'll want to go back to school, or—"

Drew stopped talking suddenly. I followed his gaze. Dad's eyes were closed, and he was paler than ever.

He had that same frazzled look I'd seen a few times earlier that summer. And his hands were shaking.

No—all of him was. His whole body quivered.

I'd never seen my father this way. It was scary.

"Daddy? Are you okay?" I stepped forward, then threw my arms around him. That was what he and Mom always did whenever Drew or I freaked out about something.

At first, Dad didn't react at all. Then, after a long, frantic minute, he patted the back of my head, gently. "There, there, sweetheart. It's all right."

"What's the matter?" I drew back. His face was still pale, but his eyes were open and gentle. "Dad?"

He didn't answer me. Instead he turned his focus to Drew. My brother looked almost as pale as Dad did.

"Dad?" Drew's voice croaked on the word. "I—I don't—"

"Young man." Dad pulled away from my embrace, leaving one firm, reassuring hand on my shoulder.

He was using the voice he used to lecture us. Low, heavy, as though he was measuring every word. I exhaled slowly. This was the Dad I knew.

"You're over eighteen," he told Drew. "Which means that, legally, this is your decision to make. But there is a piece of information I should have shared with you, and with your sister, too, before now. All I ask is that you listen to what I have to say before you make this decision."

Drew swallowed. It was strange to see my brother looking meek now that he was even taller than Daddy. "Yes, sir."

Dad turned to me. "Aki, do you recall the photo you found in my bag, of your uncle Andrew?"

I nodded, lost.

"I know it must have been strange for you, seeing that photo," Dad went on. "You haven't seen any pictures of your uncle Andrew since you were a little girl, have you?"

"No." I paused. "Wait, that's weird. Why don't we have any up at the house? We have photos of everybody else in the family."

Dad cleared his throat and turned back to Drew. "Well, that's because my memories of your uncle are complicated. I've been thinking of him more and more this summer, especially with some of the recent news reports we've seen. You see, Andrew was only a boy when he died—he was nineteen, the same age you are now, Drew—and there's a lot he didn't get to do. That's why it hurts to see his face and remember how short a time he had here."

God, Dad was right. That was incredibly sad. When my uncle died, he'd only lived four years longer than I had right now. What would I do if I only got to live four more years?

"That's why it's important to me that you kids have the opportunities Andrew didn't." Dad's eyes were locked on Drew's. "And it's crucial that you both have a strong relationship with God and with your faith. It's the only way to achieve true happiness when you're grown."

Drew nodded, waiting to see where Dad was going with this.

"But there's something else you don't know about your uncle." Dad's lip trembled, but he kept talking in that low, calm voice. "I've always told you that he died of cancer. Well, I'm ashamed to admit it, but that was a lie. I found the truth too painful to share—but that's no excuse. We must always face the truth. I should've learned that lesson by now."

"Dad." Drew swallowed. "You don't have to—"

"Yes, I do," Dad interrupted. "You see, son, your uncle and I made a plan when we were in high school. I was one year older than him, and we decided that as soon as we were both old enough—as soon as your uncle turned eighteen—we would leave school together and enlist in the air force. We wanted to be fighter pilots, you see. We believed that only when we were wearing our new uniforms would our lives truly start."

I bit my lip. I was struggling to believe all of this—Dad had always told us he loathed the military and everything to do with it—but I could sort of understand that last part. About waiting for your real life to start.

"Well," Dad went on, "we were still a year away from Andrew's birthday when we made that plan, and by the time it was approaching, I'd had second thoughts. I'd started college, and I'd met your mother, and suddenly the idea of becoming a pilot didn't hold the same appeal for me that it had in high school. When I told your uncle I'd changed my mind, he was furious. On his eighteenth birthday he walked straight into a recruiting center. A little over a year later, he was killed in the Gulf War."

I was watching Dad's face as he talked—his slow, patient delivery, the same way he gave sermons at church—so I didn't look at Drew until Dad was finished. When I did turn to face my brother, he was shaking, too.

We'd never known our uncle, but still, tears sprang into my eyes at the thought of him walking into that recruiting center all alone. Just like Drew did yesterday.

"I swore afterward that I would do everything in my power to support peace." Dad's eyes were still locked on Drew's. "Because there is no reason for anyone's brother or sister, or son, to put their life on the line for someone else's politics. And I assure you, Drew—and you, too, Aki—that's all wars are. The very worst kind of politics."

Drew was shaking harder than ever. "You never told us."

"I know, son, and I'm sorry, but—"

"All these years." Drew was yelling now. I could feel the strength of his fury. It scared me. "You *lied* to us. *You.* You're a *minister.* You're our *dad,* and you *lied* to us."

Dad's eyes widened. "Son, that's not—"

"You *lied!*" Drew rocked from side to side where he stood, his hands balling into fists. "I can't *believe* you!"

Then he turned and half ran, half stumbled toward the street. When he reached the pavement, he took off in a flat-out run back toward the old church.

Dad stared after Drew. He was still shaking, too.

I couldn't stay here. I ran after my brother. "Wait! Drew!"

But I was too slow, or he was too fast. He'd seemed tired before, but now he was running at full tilt, and his legs were a lot longer than mine. "Wait! Please, wait for me!"

But too soon he was out of my sight. He must've passed the church and kept on going.

I slowed, my breath coming in gasps. Up ahead, I spotted something familiar.

My suitcase. The one I hadn't seen in three weeks. It was lying against the side of the church, next to a dusty red pickup truck.

Carlos was standing next to it.

He waved. "Aki! I'm sorry it took us so long, but we drove into Tijuana yesterday, and here it is!"

And maybe it was because I was mad at Dad or Drew or Nick or even Christa. But in that moment, my hatred for Carlos surged up all at once until it consumed me.

I couldn't believe he had the nerve to act as if everything was normal. As if he wasn't having a disgusting affair with my underage former best friend.

I'd promised Lori I wouldn't say anything. But—ugh, the man was *repulsive*. If I kept quiet, it could go on forever.

Someone had to do something.

Besides, I knew what it meant now to be with someone you really cared about. Carlos was cheating Lori out of experiencing that.

I ran up to him, the adrenaline still surging through me. I didn't know what I was going to say, but the right words would come when I got there, I was sure of it.

Before I could open my mouth, though, Lori grabbed my arm.

"Gracias," she said. "Thank you, Carlos."

Carlos looked from me to Lori. His smile wavered slightly.

"You're welcome." He tipped his hat to me, then Lori. Then

he stuck his hands in his pockets and walked away, glancing back over his shoulder at us as he went.

"Wait!" I started to call. Lori held her hand over my mouth. I pushed her away, but it was too late. Carlos was out of earshot.

"You can't keep doing this." I jerked out of Lori's grasp, grabbed my suitcase and hauled it up. It was dustier than when I'd seen it last. "If you don't end it, I'm going to tell someone. I swear. You can't *do* this, Lori. It isn't right."

"I know." When I looked back at her, her lower lip was trembling. "It isn't."

"Then what on earth are you doing it for?" I heaved the suitcase up the church steps. It was incredibly heavy. I could barely remember what I'd packed.

My breath was starting to even out. I couldn't process everything that had just happened. My dad—my brother—my uncle, God, my uncle.

I couldn't think. All I could do was lug my suitcase across the dark, deserted church, not caring when I bumped into people's stuff, when I stepped on the boys' strewn sleeping bags.

Lori followed me and watched in silence as I dropped the suitcase next to my sleeping bag with a final heave. When I turned back to her, she was crying. Full-on, tears-running-down-her-face crying.

"I'm not," she said. "I didn't."

"You didn't *what*?"

"I didn't do anything," she said. "With Carlos. I made it up."

"You—what?"

I couldn't process this, either.

Why would she say something like that if it wasn't true? And the way Carlos had looked at her just now—

Wait. He'd looked at me, then at her. With his forehead wrinkled up, as though he was confused.

He hadn't looked guilty. He'd looked lost.

He'd thought *I* was acting weird. Because I didn't thank him for going all the way to Tijuana for my suitcase. Instead I'd stood there, glaring at him.

Lori really *had* made the whole thing up.

"Why?" My anger surged all over again. "Why would you tell me that?"

Her tears were noisy. The messy sounds echoed in the empty church.

"Because it's embarrassing, okay?" She blew her nose on her sleeve. "Everybody else has stuff going on. *You've* got stuff going on. And I'm just sitting around, waiting by myself. I guess I wanted to have stuff going on, too."

"Even if it was something you made up?" It seemed so obvious now, that she'd been lying. I couldn't believe I'd bought it. But Lori and I had never lied to each other before.

Lori shrugged, her tears coming faster. "I didn't know what else to do."

"Why?" What was happening? Why were so many things wrong all at once? "Because of the stupid fling pact?"

"No, it's not that." Lori scrubbed at the tears running down her cheeks. "It felt like—like I've been waiting forever for my real life to start. I thought maybe if I started acting as if something was happening, something really would."

Oh. That—I could sort of understand that.

"But it's not like there's a rush," I said. "We've got lots of time to start our real lives."

She blew her nose again. "These *are* our real lives. Besides, you've been in a *massive* rush ever since we got here. You and that girl went from zero to sixty in a day."

"No we didn't!" I shook my head furiously.

Then I stopped to think about it.

I'd met Christa three weeks ago. Then, this weekend, I'd had sex with her.

That was never how I'd thought it would go. When Lori and I used to talk about our first times, with our first serious boyfriends—and it was definitely always *boy*friends back then—we always thought we'd be with a guy for a long time first. "Not until you've been on, like, fifty dates," Lori had said once, while I nodded along. "Not until you've gone out wearing a fancy dress and he's brought you roses."

We were kids then. We didn't know what we were talking about.

Still, though.

I'd never thought it was possible to feel about someone the way I felt about Christa. Yeah, it had only been a few weeks, but they'd been a *really intense* few weeks.

And despite all that...what Christa and I had wasn't serious. It couldn't be. Sure, it felt that way sometimes, but she was already serious with somebody else.

That thought twisted in my chest until I pushed it away.

"Okay," I said. "Maybe I get it. Kind of. But please tell me you wouldn't do this in real life. Carlos is old. He's *married*."

"God, no." Lori shuddered. "I was kind of offended you believed me, actually."

"Okay, good." I looked at my sneakers. "And I'm sorry I told Christa all that stuff. I can't believe she told Madison. She feels really bad about that now, by the way."

Lori looked away. "I know that stuff shouldn't matter, but it does. I hate knowing people are talking about me."

"I know what you mean."

"Yeah. If it helps, though, no one's really talking about you and her lately. At least not from what I hear. You guys are old news."

"Not anymore." I told her about what Nick had done on the bus. Lori's face paled.

"He's not going to—" She swallowed. "Oh, my God. He wouldn't really, would he?"

I shook my head. "I don't know. I hope he's bluffing."

"I mean, that's a seriously awful thing for him to do. I knew he was pissed about you getting him in trouble, but—"

"You did?" I frowned. "Has he been going around talking about that?"

"Yeah, they have, some." Lori's words came out in a rush. She looked really worried. "But I can't believe Nick would seriously threaten you that way."

"Yeah, it would be really bad. If he seriously sends that photo around, Christa's parents will see it, and that would be awful for her."

"Ugh. I'll try to see what I can find out, okay? Jake might know something, too. He always knows what's going on."

I nodded, grateful. From the way she was acting, Lori must think we were friends again. I was glad. She couldn't un-say the things she'd said—but then, neither could I. And the truth was, I needed my best friend back.

"Can I tell you something else?" I asked her, glancing around again to make sure we were totally alone.

"Sure, what?"

In a rush, I swore her to secrecy, then told her what had happened with Drew and what Dad had just told us. By the time I was done, I was blinking back tears again.

"Oh, my God." Lori's mouth hung open. "I'm so sorry. That's terrible about your uncle."

"It's weird. I don't even know how to think about it. He died before I was even born. But I can't even register what this means. I can't believe my parents would keep this a secret. For my whole *life*, you know?"

"Yeah. For real."

We were both quiet. I was feeling so many different things, all at once.

"Also, um…" I covered my face with my hand. Even with everything else that was happening, my brain kept pulsing, *You had sex last night. You had sex last night. YOU HAD SEX LAST NIGHT.* "On a totally different subject, can I tell you some, um, news? From this weekend?"

Lori's lips turned up into a huge grin. "You and her did it, didn't you?"

I winced. "Guilty."

Lori clapped her hands and laughed. "I knew it!"

I let out a tiny giggle. "Am I that predictable?"

"Kind of. I mean, two nights in a dorm? And you guys didn't show up to a single party. Hello, what else could've possibly been happening?" She grinned. "So what was it like? Did it hurt?"

"I don't know. I guess it did a little, but not that much. I mean, we're both girls, remember?"

"Oh, right. I guess it only hurts a lot if there's a guy involved."

"I guess. Does it always hurt, though? Or does it depend on if the guy is, you know, big?" I giggled again. Giggling with Lori felt amazing after everything that had happened.

Lori's face turned pink. "I don't know! Anyway, quit changing the subject. Tell me details!"

I laughed. "It was just really nice. She's incredible, you know? It was so sweet. Like we were closer to each other than we'd ever been before."

"Oh, gag me," Lori said. "Don't talk to me about *sweet.* Talk to me about the sex!"

I laughed. "What do you want to know?"

"I don't know." She fidgeted. "What do lesbians do, anyway? Did you actually use those dental dam things?"

"Um. How do you know about those?"

"Whatever, I have Google."

I gaped at her. "You Google lesbian sex tips?"

"I Google lots of things."

I grinned. "The dental dams actually weren't bad. Tasted kind of weird, though."

"Ew!" Lori clutched at her chest as if she was going to puke. "It's so gross to think about *tasting* it."

I rolled my eyes. "Well it's gross to think about tasting a guy's, you know."

"Oh, really?" She raised her eyebrows high. "What, so are you totally a lesbian now that you've done it with a girl?"

"No, I'm still bi. I'm only saying, the idea of having oral sex with a guy is gross when you actually think about it *that* way."

Lori made a face.

I decided to change the subject. "No one else knows yet what happened."

"Your dad couldn't tell?"

"No! I was sure he would, too."

"That would be so weird if he could. I mean, your parents don't even know you're gay. I mean, bi."

"Yeah." I didn't want to think about that right now, either. "I had to go to the health center on campus to get dental dams. It was so embarrassing."

Lori howled with laughter. "They let you take them?"

"Yeah. I mean, they aren't cigarettes. There isn't a law about them or anything."

Lori laughed even harder. "Can you imagine if there were? If they had a bouncer in the health center checking IDs?"

I put on my best gruff voice. "Excuse me, young lady, it is

highly inappropriate to engage in lesbian safer sex activities without your parents' written permission!"

We both nearly died laughing. There were tears at the corners of my eyes.

I couldn't believe it. I'd really done it. Everything was different now.

I was different now.

I'd always wondered what my first time would be like. Usually I'd pictured it with a guy. Someone cute, who wore nice clothes and held my hand a lot. I'd thought we'd go into a dark room with a big, soft bed, and the guy would pick me up and carry me over to it. I'd envisioned myself wearing a fancy dress and the guy taking it off me slowly.

Come to think of it, when I'd pictured my big Day of Doing It, it had never involved *me* doing much of anything. Instead my faceless boyfriend did all the work while I lay there and enjoyed it. Also, in my fantasies I'd usually skipped over the actual sex part and cut to later when we were lying in each other's arms, cuddling.

Real sex had been different. I definitely hadn't skipped any parts, and I hadn't wanted to, either. There had been no being carried around, and no boyfriend, for that matter.

And I'd definitely done way more than just lie there.

The only part I'd gotten right in my daydreams was the lying in each other's arms afterward. That part had been awesome. But so had the rest.

Being with Christa was way better than being with some generic well-dressed boyfriend, even if she didn't bring me flowers. The *who* mattered a lot more than the *what*, across the board. I hadn't had sex with a guy yet, but I was pretty sure I was right about this. How you felt about someone was way more important than, like, parts.

"Everything okay?" Lori said.

"Yeah. Sorry, I spaced out for a second."

"No worries. Um, so can I ask you something? I'm only, you know, curious."

"Sure." Now that Lori and I were friends again we had a lot of missed time to make up for. "Of course."

"Did you and Christa say you loved each other before you did it?"

I paused. Part of me wanted to say yes. I wasn't going to lie to Lori after everything that had happened, though.

"No," I said. "She has a boyfriend, remember? This thing with me and her isn't about that."

"Then what's it about?"

"It's a summer fling." I shrugged.

"You don't talk about her like she's a summer fling. You talk about her like you *lurrve* her."

I could tell Lori was trying to be funny, so I laughed.

"Do you think it makes a difference?" she said. "Having your first time be with someone you aren't, you know, in love with?"

"I—" Suddenly, my throat closed up.

Breathe. Breathe. It's all right, it's only a question. Just breathe.

I stumbled over my words as I tried to force out an answer for Lori. "I... Wow. I guess I, I mean. I don't know. I don't have anything to compare it to. It...it was pretty awesome the way it was, though."

Lori nodded. "I guess that's what matters."

"Right," I said.

I didn't know if I really meant it, though.

Lori's question had kind of hurt my soul.

CHAPTER 21

"ADIÓS, AH-KI," JUANA called as she ran after the other girls. The pink-and-white ribbons I'd hot-glued onto her new barrettes streamed after her in the breeze.

It was such a relief to see her playing like she used to. I didn't know what had happened about the guitar, exactly—the adults must have done something, but they hadn't said anything to me. Either way, I was glad Juana had started to smile again.

I'd wanted to make the ribbon barrettes in our first week here—who doesn't love ribbon barrettes?—but Lori said we should save them for the end. It turned out she was right, because the girls got obsessed with the glue gun as soon as they saw it. Every time I set it down on a blanket, someone would snatch it up and start gluing her fingers together with glee. Now that the lesson was over they were running off with glue all over their hands, their clothes, even their faces. I cringed at the thought of Señora Suarez's face.

"Do we have any glue left at all?" Lori asked as we gathered up the leftover barrettes.

"Maybe a little?" I checked the gun. "Enough to do the bead rings tomorrow at least."

Lori smiled. "Remember those barrettes we made in sixth grade? The music notes with the pink and black sequins? Mine was supposed to be a treble clef but it came out looking like a disco alien. I think that was the first time I ever used a glue gun by myself."

"It was mine, too. I got glue all over my jeans. I tried to hide them so my mom wouldn't get mad, but later she found them at the bottom of my closet stuck to a pile of old magazines. She took away my phone for two weeks."

"I got glue in my *hair.* Remember? I tried to get it out with peanut butter but we only had the chunky kind and my whole head was a congealed mess. You had to come back over and it still took hours to get it out."

"Oh, wow, I'd forgotten about that!" I laughed. "That was so gross. Anyway, hey, listen, you go back in. I'll finish cleaning up."

Lori looked around at the glue spots and ribbon fragments strewn across the blankets. "Are you sure?"

"Yeah. You've been doing most of the work this whole time. I've got to make up for it."

"Okay." Lori didn't need more convincing. She waved as she walked back toward the work site. Being friends with Lori was way better than being in a fight with her.

She and I had analyzed every detail of everything that had happened with Christa. (Well, not every *single* detail—there were some very specific parts of our weekend in Texas that I was keeping to myself. But we'd talked about all the really big stuff.)

Lori's theory was that Christa was on the verge of breaking up with Steven for real. For me. I acted as though I didn't care either way, but I was almost desperate she was right.

But something else was bothering me. Something I hadn't told Lori *or* Christa.

It had been a day and a half now since I'd had sex, and I still felt kind of, well. The same.

I'd thought crossing that particular threshold would trigger some kind of shift in me, but I still seemed to be regular old Aki. Albeit a version of Aki who knew a lot more than she did before about how to have sex with a girl.

It wasn't what I'd expected. That's all.

I shook the blankets until I had a little pile of ribbon pieces. I was scooping them into a baggie so we could save them for our next project when I heard footsteps walking toward me.

I recognized those footsteps right away. I'd heard them every day since I was born.

"Sweetheart?" Dad loomed over me. "Can I talk to you about something?"

I looked up. He'd taken off his baseball cap, and his face was grave.

Oh, God. Had Nick already sent out the picture? If Christa's parents found out—

Oh, God. Oh, *God*.

"Aki? Are you all right?" Dad squatted down next to me and felt my forehead. "You look shaky."

"I'm fine," I choked out.

Did he know what had happened in Texas, too?

My parents had never said I wasn't allowed to have sex. Drew had sex in high school. They must've known that, right? I mean, they weren't delusional.

But this wasn't only about me having sex. This was about me liking girls.

Was I ready for my dad to know that?

Did it even matter if I was?

"You sure you're all right?" Dad looked worried. "Here, let me help you. Are you taking all this back to the church?"

"Yeah," I said as Dad bent down to gather up the blankets. "Thanks."

I climbed unsteadily to my feet with the glue gun and supplies. Dad rolled all the blankets into a bundle and lifted them onto his shoulder. The pile of blankets was a lot bigger than his head, so it made for a pretty funny sight.

He wasn't acting like he was mad at me. I started to calm down a little.

"Everyone's talking about your debate on Friday," Dad said as we walked. "Do you think you have everything you need?"

"Hopefully." We started down the road to the church, dirt kicking up around our sneakers. "Thanks for getting Reverend Perez to let us use his courtyard. The only thing I'm stressed about now is my speech on health care. We've been so busy organizing everything I haven't had a chance to write it."

"Well, you already know your material," Dad said. "That gives you a leg up on the others."

"I guess."

"You know, I'm very impressed with how you've gotten the kids here to focus on this." Dad switched the blanket bundle from his right shoulder to his left. We were almost at the church. "I'd been worried they all saw this trip as a purely social experience—making new friends, that sort of thing— instead of taking time to reflect on their spiritual journeys and the importance of the work we're doing here. But now instead of talking about who likes who, I'm hearing kids your and Drew's age talking about how the church should approach important social justice issues. And as far as I can tell, that's your doing. I know you've missed having music in your life, but I think there's a lot to be said for taking up worthwhile new interests, too."

I smiled and dropped my head as we climbed the steps. "It was really Jake who started it."

"Nonetheless." Dad dumped the blankets in an empty corner of the room. He was sweating. "You can tell Jake I'm quite pleased with the pair of you."

"Thanks." I was still embarrassed.

"Now then." Dad fanned his face with his hand. "There's something I want to ask you. It's a little, well, delicate."

Oh, no. He *did* know.

Should I deny it? Tell him the photo was faked?

Maybe I should tell him about Christa's boyfriend. He could check with Christa's parents and know I was telling the truth. Christa would probably appreciate that.

Except if I did that, I'd just be lying again.

Oh, God, oh, God, oh, God...

"It has to do with your brother." Dad cleared his throat.

Oh. I was somehow relieved and also...not. "What's up?"

"You see, well..." Dad's eyes fixed on the stack of blankets. "I know you and Drew tell each other things you don't tell your mother and me sometimes, and that's fine." He looked up at me. I swallowed. "But after what he said the other day, I'm hoping you'll tell me if there's something bigger going on with him. You know, besides this—this idea of his."

I swallowed. "Have you asked him?"

Dad shook his head. "He's been avoiding me since we talked. I know he's still angry with me, and I understand that, but I'm afraid there's something he's not telling me. It's in a parent's nature to worry, after all."

I sat down on the blanket pile to buy some time. Dad sat next to me. The blankets sank under his weight until we were basically sitting on the floor, but I didn't complain.

Dad was right. He and Mom always worried about us. It was annoying how they demanded to know every single thing that was going on in our lives.

Dad especially was obsessed with giving advice. I didn't

know if it was because he was a minister or just because he was a dad, but he always tried to act as if he understood everything. Like he was hip to the teen speak or whatever. Any time he tried it with me I always ended the conversation as soon as possible.

But this—Drew leaving us, doing the one thing that would break Dad's heart—this wasn't some high school drama. This was a serious life decision. Drew *needed* our parents' advice this time. And Dad didn't know what Drew had told me in the airport that day—that he was failing out of school.

It would be so easy to tell. Let it all spill out and let my father figure out how to deal with it, the way I'd done with Juana's guitar.

But my brother had kept my secret. I had to keep his.

"Give him time," I said. "If there's something going on, he'll tell you."

Dad studied me. I met his eyes and kept my lips firmly sealed.

"All right, then." Dad dusted off his jeans and stood up. "Oh, and before I forget, tell your friends to be careful if they go out after dark. Someone tried to break into the Riveras' guest house last week. They didn't take anything, but it was clear someone had been inside, so they put a new lock on the door. But you should all watch out. You never know who's around at night in a town like this."

"Oh, um…" I swallowed again. "Okay, thanks. I'll tell people."

Dad started toward the door.

He was just stepping over the threshold when I stood up, too.

I couldn't do this any longer.

"Daddy?" He turned around, his face solemn and resigned,

as if he'd known I'd call him back. "There is something I need to tell you. It isn't about Drew, though."

"Oh?" Dad's face was neutral. Unreadable.

"Yeah. I—" I closed my eyes. I had to just say it. "I'm bi. I mean, bisexual."

God, it was so hard saying the word *sexual* to my dad. It was so hard saying any of this.

"Oh, sweetheart."

I opened my eyes. Dad's face was still a mask. I couldn't tell if that was a sympathetic *Oh, sweetheart* or an aghast *Oh, sweetheart*.

"I didn't know if I should tell you." I swallowed. Then I swallowed again. My throat was tight. "And Mom. I didn't know what you'd think."

Dad didn't answer right away. In the dim light, I could see his face changing ever so slightly.

Maybe this had been a mistake. Maybe Christa was right to keep secrets.

Maybe Dad couldn't handle this. Maybe this really was crushing him.

"Sweetheart," Dad said. "Baby girl. Of course you were right to tell us."

I burst into tears.

I didn't even feel it coming on. One second I was standing there, holding it together fine, and the next I was a complete wreck.

Dad had his arms around me before I'd even seen him move. Hugging me tight, the way he used to do when I was little, rocking me back and forth. Except now I was almost as tall as he was, so instead of crying into his stomach I was crying into his shoulder, my tears soaking his sweaty T-shirt.

"Sweetheart, it's fine, it's all just fine." He stroked my braids softly. "You know all your mother and I want is for you and your brother to be happy. We love you, and we know you'll find someone you love someday, too. All we care about is that whoever that person is, they're just as proud of you as we are."

I sniffed and pulled back. "Really?"

"Really." Dad squeezed my arm while I wiped at my face. "This isn't—well, you know, your mom and me, we're a different generation. We didn't grow up knowing about this kind of thing the way you and Drew did. But times are different now, and we knew there was a possibility our kids might, well, turn out differently than we did. You can talk to your mother more when you get back home, but trust me when I say that we both support you, and we love you no matter what."

I wiped my eyes again. The tears were still falling. God, I was so embarrassing.

"Does this have anything to do with why you and Lori have been fighting?" Dad squeezed my arm again. "I know you two have always been very close, so…"

"So…?" I brushed the tears away. He rubbed the back of his neck and looked away. "What, you think *Lori* and me—"

I broke off, laughing. Dad looked more confused than ever, which only made me laugh harder. At least I'd managed to stop crying.

"No," I said between giggles. "Lori and I had a fight, but it didn't have anything to do with me being bi. We're okay now."

"Oh, all right, then." Dad rubbed his forehead. "Well, I'm glad you two made up. I've always liked her."

"Me, too." I hiccupped. I'd had as much laughing and crying as I could handle. "I probably look awful. I'd better go fix myself up."

"You look mighty fine to me." Dad patted my arm again. "I'll see you back at the work site. And, sweetheart, I'm glad you told me about this. Now I feel like I know my daughter a little bit better."

That nearly made me start crying again. "Thanks, Daddy."

I watched him walk down the steps, his hands in his pockets, his head down.

I wiped my face again and pulled back the curtain to the girls' half of the room. My suitcase was up against the wall where I'd left it yesterday. I fished inside it for a mirror.

For the first time in three weeks, I was wearing my own clothes. I'd thought I'd miss wearing Christa's, but having my own stuff was actually fantastic. It felt like I was finally in my real skin for the first time all summer. Maybe since before that.

I pulled out a compact and stared at my reflection. I didn't look as bad as I'd expected. I'd wiped away the tear streaks on my face. Behind them my eyes looked bright and open. I looked awake. I looked alive.

In Texas, with Christa, I'd done something I'd never done before. It was fun. It was special. Afterward it seemed like I'd taken the most important step I'd ever take in my whole life. Certainly the biggest step I'd take this summer.

But it wasn't. Not compared to what just happened. I'd done something this afternoon that had *truly* changed my life.

I was still shaking. Still reeling from how nervous I'd been. But I didn't need to be nervous anymore.

In fact, I couldn't imagine ever feeling nervous again.

"We can't do gun control right after the war." Lori took a big bite of rice and beans, then held her hand in front of her mouth as she talked. "We should put something in between that isn't, you know, violent."

"Let's move up climate change, then," Jake said. "We can put global health at the end. Are you cool with going last, Aki?"

"Sure." I flipped through the notes under my dinner plate. I'd been wolfing down the vegetables the church ladies had made us. I was going to miss this food when we got back home. "At this point the only time I'm going to get to write my speech is while the rest of the debate is happening, so that plan sounds perfect, actually."

"Come on," Lori said. "You still have four days. You'll be fine."

"But I haven't even *started*. All I have are notes."

"I've barely started mine, either," Lori said. "And I have to argue something I'm morally opposed to. I'm totally beating you in the procrastination Olympics."

Jake couldn't talk because his mouth was full of toast, so he gestured emphatically toward his chest. Finally he swallowed. "I'm beating you both. I've totally given up on writing my speech. I'm going to wing it."

"I don't believe that for a second." I waved my fork at him. "All that research you did before we even decided to *have* a debate? You're going to be über prepared and make the rest of us look like losers."

"Nah, just Lori," he said.

"Hey!" Lori kicked him under the table. Jake nearly choked on his toast.

"Hi, Aki," a soft voice said behind me.

I twisted around to face Christa. She was wearing her fedora with a white T-shirt and jeans that were so long they bunched around her ankles. No one else could rock a T-shirt and baggy jeans the way Christa could.

"You look nice," she said.

I smiled and glanced down at the dirt and grime covering my clothes. I'd spent the day working on the ditch for the fence, and since I tended to sweat a lot while digging, I felt pretty disgusting at the moment. But if Christa wanted to say I looked nice, I wasn't going to argue with her.

"Thanks," I said.

An awkward silence descended. There was so much I needed to say to her, but I couldn't do it here.

"So." She looked from side to side, then whispered, "See you later? The usual place?"

"Uh." Lori and Jake were almost certainly eavesdropping on us. Others might have been, too. I climbed to my feet and steered Christa a few feet away from the picnic tables. "It turns out that's not a good idea anymore."

"Why?" Christa's face fell. "Don't you—want to?"

"It's not that." Crap. We *really* couldn't have this conversation here. I motioned toward the back of the house, and Christa followed.

"We can't use the guest house anymore," I said once we were a safe distance away. "The Riveras figured out someone was in there."

Christa's eyes widened. "Do they know it was us?"

"No, thank God. They think somebody broke in or something."

"Wow. That was close." Christa shivered. "Where can we meet up tonight, then?"

"I don't know." We'd rounded the corner of the house. There was nothing but pink-painted walls to one side of us and a gorgeous setting sun to the other.

I had to tell her. Even if telling her meant losing her.

"Christa, I—I told my dad."

Her mouth dropped open. "You—what?"

"I didn't say anything about you," I added quickly. "All I told him was that I was bi. I—I guess I came out to him."

"Oh my God." Christa clapped her hand over her mouth. "He's seen us together. He'll figure it out. Oh my *God*."

"He won't, I promise. He thought I was having a thing with *Lori*, of all people."

I'd thought that would make Christa laugh. Instead she

started shaking. "Can you tell him it's not true? Tell him you changed your mind?"

"What?" I stared at her. I couldn't believe this. "Changed my *mind*? I don't want him to think this is only a phase or something. Look, this is a *good* thing, me telling him. He was really nice about it. I don't know—I think it kind of brought me and him closer."

Christa shook her head fiercely. Her eyes were wide and bright. "I can't believe you did this. I can't believe you didn't ask me first!"

"I didn't need your permission." My face was getting hot. "I was telling him about *me*, not you. And I hated lying. Don't you? Especially lying about something that's such a big part of you?"

"I don't have a choice!"

"Everything's a choice." The words were spilling out of me rapid-fire. "I hate to break it to you, but you like girls. We now have serious evidence of this fact. I don't get why you're fine gaying it up with me and Madison but it'll be the end of the world if anyone else gets even the slightest hint."

There were tears in Christa's eyes. "You don't understand. My parents will *kill* me. They'll never let me leave home to go to college. They'll never let me do *anything*."

"Why does everything have to be about *your* parents?" My hands balled into tight fists. "Why do they get to be in charge of *my* life? If by some insane coincidence my coming out to my dad means *your* parents find out, you can always trot out old Steven and prove your heterosexuality. You could hook up right in the middle of your living room floor while they watched if they didn't believe you."

I was out of breath by the time I finished talking. Christa stared at me, her chin quivering.

The worst part was, now I was picturing her and Steven hooking up on Christa's living room floor.

"Is that what this is really about?" She wouldn't look at me. "Are you punishing me because of Steven?"

"*Punishing* you?" God, I couldn't believe her. "This has nothing to do with Steven. Or you! I told my dad because I wanted to tell my dad!"

"But—"

"I'm not trying to punish you for anything. If there's anyone who should be punished, it's me. I knew you had a boyfriend. I knew what I was getting into."

My breaths were coming heavily. I didn't even know what I was talking about anymore.

"Then give it a rest." Christa shook her head. "You don't have to be so melodramatic."

"*I'm* being melodramatic? I was having a *fantastic* day until I started talking to you!"

I waited for her to snap something back at me.

Instead we stared in silence. Each waiting for the other to bend. I certainly wasn't about to be the first.

"By the way, I know you told Nick I'm the one who turned him in." I crossed my arms over my chest. "He's blackmailing me. Did you know that? He has some picture of you and me and he's threatening to send it out to the Holy Life email list."

"What are you talking about?" Her eyes were wide. "I didn't say anything to Nick. What picture?"

I didn't know whether to believe her or not.

I shut my eyes and scrubbed my hands over my face.

Maybe I should've talked to her before I told my dad. But she still had no right to be mad at me.

"I don't know why I'm even getting so riled up about this." I couldn't look at her. "This whole thing between us is no big deal to you, since you're already taken, right? Well, it's no big deal for me, either. Do you even know how this started out? It was a stupid pact I made with Lori the first day here. We said we were both going to have a summer fling. There was a hookup tally and everything. And I won, by a lot. So thanks. That's all I was ever going for."

I looked up at her then. It was so hard, seeing the pain on her face.

I never wanted to hurt her. I never wanted *anyone* to hurt her.

"Fine," she said after a minute. "You got what you wanted. You can have a fantastic day tomorrow, and the day after and the day after that and forever after, and you can do it without me."

I could've snapped *Fine!* back. I could've said, *No, please, don't say that. I'm sorry.*

I didn't do either of those things.

Christa turned around and walked away from me. Off into the trees and the fading sun.

I didn't call for her to stop. She didn't look back.

Just like that, it was over.

CHAPTER 22

"BUT WHAT DO I say at the *beginning*?" The panic was plain on Gina's face. "Do I start with 'Hi, my name is Gina and I'm here to talk about climate change'? Or do I launch straight into telling everybody why Brian's wrong?"

A dozen people had asked me some version of this question already. If our phones worked I'd have sent out an FAQ so I didn't have to deal with this stuff. Instead I kept my eyes on the index card where I was copying my notes and said, "Jake and I are introducing everyone. You can launch straight into your argument."

"But how am I supposed to argue with Brian when I don't even know what he's going to say? Shouldn't he have to show me his speech first?"

"That's not how debates work. You have to think on your feet."

Gina looked even more terrified than she had before. I sipped my hot chocolate and tried not to let my impatience show. The debate was only a few hours away. I'd gotten up early that morning so I'd have time to transcribe my notes for my health care speech onto the cards I'd borrowed from Jake.

It was the only chance I'd get to work on my own speech all day. After breakfast we had to finish putting the fence up, and after that Lori and I would teach our last jewelry class of the summer. Then we'd run over to the Perezes' house to set up before everyone else got there. There were exactly zero minutes in the schedule to spare, but even so, all through breakfast I'd done nothing but answer questions from way-too-nervous people.

This debate that had started as a random idea had suddenly become an epic event that everyone was taking very, very seriously. The people who'd signed up to speak seemed to be realizing that if it didn't go well they could wind up looking pretty dumb.

"Don't stress about it." I spotted Lori motioning to me from across the room, so I tucked my index cards into my pocket and got up to join her. Gina followed me.

"All you have to do is make sure you know what arguments you're going to use," I told her as I started to roll up the blankets for our class. "Remember, you have a built-in advantage. Most people will go in agreeing with you that climate change is an actual thing that we need to fix."

"For real," Lori said. "Meanwhile, Madison has to go out there and argue against gay marriage. Which is supported by 95 percent of people our age or something."

"That's true." Gina looked slightly comforted.

"Aki?" a guy said. I peered past the blankets. It was Rodney. "Can I ask you a question?"

I sighed. Even though Jake and I had planned this whole thing together, somehow I'd become the person everyone pounced on with their questions about all the nitpicky details. Whereas Jake had become the guy who sat in the corner and freaked out at the prospect of making a speech in front of everyone.

Not that I wasn't freaked about that, too. I just wasn't quite as freaked as Jake. I understood, though. He was terrified to get up in front of everyone he knew and talk about gay politics. Being closeted did that to you.

Besides, I was kind of into details. They reminded me of math, or music, where things were logical and orderly.

"Sure, if you'll help carry some blankets." I pulled half the blankets off my pile and gave them to Rodney. He slung them over his shoulder as if they were nothing, so I gave him one more and led him down the steps. "What's up?"

"I need an extra minute," he said. "I practiced my speech and it came in right at four."

"Can't do it. Everyone gets three minutes and that's it."

"But I've got this awesome conclusion. The rest of the speech won't work without it. Here, I've already got it memorized, I'll do it for you now and you can tell me what you think. I'm going to wind up with a bunch of statistics about attacks post-Ferguson and then I'll say—"

"You can't have an extra minute!" I stuffed the rest of my blankets in Rodney's arms. He took them and stepped back, his eyes wide. "We don't have time! Besides, it isn't fair if you get more and no one else does."

"Come on, Aki, all I need is—"

"No!" I stamped my foot in the dirt. Rodney took another step back. "If we're even one minute over, the whole schedule's off! Go rewrite your dang speech!"

"Whoa, there, Sis." Drew's hand fell on my shoulder. "You stressed at all?"

"I wouldn't be stressed if people would listen to me!" I yelled.

Rodney nodded rapidly. "Three minutes. Got it. Uh, where did you want these?"

I pointed to Lori, who was laughing from behind her hand and climbing the hill to the work site. "Follow her."

Rodney scurried off. When I turned, Drew was chuckling, too.

"Oh, can it," I said. "Have you come to ask me a dumb question like everyone else?"

Drew held up his hands. "Hey, man, I have my orders. Passing out ballots for the voting. Far as I can tell I got the best job there is. I'm the only one who doesn't have to write a speech."

"Good for you." I wished I had a blanket to throw at my brother, too.

"Uh, so." Drew started walking toward the work site. I fell into step beside him. "I do have a question, but it's not about the debate."

"Yeah?"

"Yeah. I wanted to know, uh, if you'd told Dad about, you know."

Oh. I wondered how he'd found out. "Yeah. I couldn't keep it secret anymore. You were wrong about his reaction, by the way. He was actually surprisingly cool about it."

Drew stopped walking and ran a hand over his eyes. He looked as though he was on the verge of tears. "He was?"

"Yeah. It was really okay. I know you thought it would crush him, but actually he told me he was proud of me, and—"

"Wait." Drew cut in. "What are you talking about?"

"What are *you* talking about?"

We both got it at the same time.

"Oh, no, no, I didn't tell him anything about you," I assured him. "He asked me if something was up with you, but I didn't tell him. I only—"

"You told him about *you*." Drew gazed at me. I couldn't tell if he was disappointed or impressed. "And he took it okay? Really?"

"Yeah." I told him what Dad had said, about him and Mom being of a different generation. "It was actually kind of awesome. I'm glad I talked to him."

I didn't add that telling him had cost me Christa. I was trying so, so hard to not think about that.

"That's awesome," Drew said. "I'm really happy for you."

"Thanks." I gave Drew an awkward hug and refused to think about how much I'd wanted her to say those exact words.

"So," he said. "Since you told him, I guess that means this lesbian thing—it's for real?"

"I'm not a lesbian. I'm bi." I'd forgotten that I never got a chance to really talk to Drew about this. He rolled with it, though.

"Oh. Okay, then. But the bi thing, is that definitely for real? You think you'll stay this way?"

I sighed. "Drew. You sound so dumb when you say this kind of stuff."

"You know what I mean."

I did, actually.

It was getting confusing. I forgot sometimes how I was supposed to feel. Like, maybe I'd see a guy from far away and think he was hot. But then I'd think, *Wait, I'm with a girl. I'm not supposed to think guys are hot anymore.*

I liked Christa so much I figured I really shouldn't be interested in anybody else, boy or girl. Except that *she* was interested in someone else already, so what did that mean?

Then I'd remember that either way, I was bi, so it was okay. But then I'd get confused again. Because even if Christa wasn't really my girlfriend, didn't the fact that I cared about her so much mean I *shouldn't* think anyone else was hot? Or did it mean that I could think guys were hot, but not girls? Or the other way around?

Of course, none of that mattered now. Christa and I weren't together anymore. But that didn't make it any less confusing.

Sometimes when I couldn't sleep I'd go over all this in my head. Would I be this confused for the rest of my life? What about when I was an actual adult? I'd picture myself all grown-up and married to some faceless person, and still just as lost as I was now.

It used to be that whenever I pictured my grown-up, married life, I was always married to a faceless guy. Now, though, I usually saw myself with a faceless girl. Did *that* mean I was gay now? Or gayer than I used to be, at least?

Were bi people always supposed to be *exactly* bi? Did it have to be fifty-fifty, or could it be, say, sixty-forty? And could it be different percentages on different days? I'd had a thing with a girl, so did I have to go out with a guy next? And now that I'd had sex with Christa, was I supposed to go have sex with a guy?

I kind of didn't want to have sex with a guy. Not right now, anyway. Did that mean I didn't like guys as much as girls?

Maybe I just wanted to wait until the right moment to do it with a guy. Maybe I took sex with guys more seriously than sex with girls.

Except I didn't really want to have sex with a girl right now, either. Unless that girl was Christa.

I glanced over at Drew. I could talk to him about a lot. Not this, though.

So all I said was, "I don't know. I've still got a lot to figure out."

He nodded. "You know I'm on your side, right? I mean, maybe it seemed kind of weird at first, but I'm totally fine with it, really. I think it's great that you like her so much. And she seems to really like you."

God, those words. He had no idea how it felt for me to

hear those words. My heart was slowly falling down in pieces around my feet.

"Thanks," I said. Drew was being sweet, even if he didn't really get it. "And, hey, I think you should tell Dad everything. About what happened last semester and all. He might not react the way you expect."

We were almost at the work site. Dad was at the far end of the fence line, hammering something into the ground with a shovel. Even from this distance we could see the sweat pouring down his face. I hoped I didn't get sweaty during the debate. I was going to be standing up in front of people an awful lot that afternoon.

"Talk to him," I said. "Don't agonize about it anymore. Be totally honest and you'll feel better. I definitely did."

Drew's eyes fixed on Dad.

"Maybe." Drew looked at his feet, then back at me. "Okay. I guess I can't really put it off. Thanks, Sis."

I didn't think he'd actually do it, but the next thing I knew he was walking toward Dad, calling out to him. Dad leaned on his shovel, looked up and waved at Drew.

I looked away before anything else could happen. When my eyes shifted, though, they landed on Christa.

She was working on the other end of the fence, holding a pole steady while one of the other girls hammered it into the ground. She was wearing yoga pants and a purple tank top. She'd pinned her hair out of her face with a dozen different sparkly clips. Even from this distance, she looked adorable.

It still hurt, physically, every time I saw her. Usually I looked away.

This time I didn't want to.

"Yo. Hey." A hand was waving in front of my face. On instinct I reached up to swat it away, like a fly.

"Hey." Madison pulled back her hand, laughing. "You don't have to take my arm off. I've been calling your name forever."

"Oh. Sorry." She was holding a stack of papers. I braced myself for another debate question.

"No worries. You looked rapt." She nodded toward where Christa was pulling her hair back into a messy ponytail. "Anyway, I wanted to ask, is there a break between speeches? Meaning, if I want to talk about something Jake says in his speech, do I have time to make notes before I go up?"

"Nope." My eyes stayed fixed on Christa. "We wanted to put in break time but we had too many speakers. If we put time between each person we'd wind up going until midnight."

"Okay." I could feel Madison watching me as I watched Christa. "I guess it doesn't really matter that much. I'm already arguing something I don't even agree with, so I'm screwed no matter what. Remind me to never volunteer for anything again, will you?"

I tore my eyes away from Christa. I'd never really looked at Madison closely, except to stare daggers in her direction.

"I thought you said something about not all gay people wanting to get married?" I said.

"Queer people. And, yeah, that's true, but it doesn't mean marriage shouldn't be *allowed*. I might not want to get married, but that doesn't mean *you* don't."

I swallowed. It was weird, the way Madison was talking to me. As if we were the same.

I'd spent so much time resenting Madison that I hadn't really thought about what it must be like to be her. She was the only out gay person on this trip, as far as I knew. She must've been out to her parents, too, since she didn't seem to mind the chaperones hearing her talk about gay stuff.

That was a pretty big deal, now that I thought about it.

"Hey, so, um…" I studied Madison's face. She was studying me, too. "Can I ask you something?"

"Sure. I just asked you something."

"Right, so." I cleared my throat. "Do Christa's parents know you guys are friends?"

Madison laughed. "Not anymore. I'm not exactly welcome in the Lawrence household. You know she's totally closeted, right?"

I nodded. I couldn't imagine Christa's parents being cool with her hanging out with a girl who wore T-shirts that said Gay by Birth, Fabulous by Choice.

"But not totally," I said. "Only with her parents, right?"

"Mostly, but even so, she's weird about it. Last year we went to Youth Pride in Dupont, and it was awesome and fun, and she got those pink hair streaks she wears all the time and she was taking tons of photos. But then someone we didn't know tried to take a photo of *us* and she flipped out."

I sighed. "She's always afraid something will get back to her parents. They're really conservative, right?"

"Yeah. I mean, that's the thing. You know those people you hear about on the news, who kick their kids out of their house for being gay or trans or whatever? Well, I thought those people were only in, like, Kentucky, but then I met Christa's parents. And…maybe they wouldn't go *that* far, but honestly, if I were her I wouldn't take any chances, either."

God, I was horrible. So many times, I'd acted as if Christa was just being paranoid. I looked at my feet.

"My parents were cool with it from the beginning, though," Madison went on. "Back in middle school, the first time I went to Youth Pride, they came with me. My mom even ordered a shirt that said I Love My Gay Kid."

"Wow." That explained a lot about Madison. "That's so amazing."

"Yeah. I mean, they're still hella annoying, but when it comes to that stuff, I guess they're pretty cool." Madison pushed her glasses up on her nose. "Anyway, listen. While we're talking. I want you to know that we're good, you and me. I wasn't sure about you at first—I couldn't tell if you were really into chicks or if you were just using my girl for target practice—but you seem okay. So, it's too bad it didn't work out for you and her, but if you ever want to hang out once we get back home, that could be cool. There aren't that many girls like us around."

My head was spinning. She'd thought I was *using* Christa? For *target practice*?

"Girls!" Aunt Miranda was shouting. "Madison, Aki! Grab a shovel, we've got a lot to finish today!"

"Coming!" I yelled back.

"Let's text on Sunday, okay?" Madison said as we jogged back toward the ditch. "So we get each other's numbers. If you want to go to Youth Pride next year, maybe we can hang out."

"Okay." I still wasn't sure what to do with all the information Madison had just given me.

She was sorry it didn't work out with Christa and me.

Was that what Christa told her? That we "didn't work out"?

I hadn't spoken to Christa since she'd walked away from me on Monday night. I'd been spending most of my time with Lori and Jake, planning the debate. They'd both noticed that I suddenly had a lot more time free, and they'd started asking if something had happened with Christa. Finally, on Wednesday, I told Lori an abbreviated version of the story and asked her to tell Jake. They'd both been really understanding, which only made me feel worse. I'd hoped for at least a little bit of shock and outrage on my behalf.

We were flying back home the day after tomorrow. After

that, Christa and I would never see each other again. I should probably go ahead and delete her from my phone.

None of this was supposed to bother me. I'd set out to have a summer fling, and that's exactly what I'd done. Sure, it had been a big deal when it was happening, but would I still think that a year from now? Or five years from now?

By then I'd have a whole new life. I'd barely even remember what Christa looked like.

Except I couldn't imagine ever forgetting her face.

And I didn't want to.

CHAPTER 23

"PUT IT UNDER the window. No, the *middle* window. No, more to the right. No, that's not—never mind, I'll do it."

I took the chair from Jake and positioned it directly under the Perezes' back window while he huffed behind me.

"Hurry up, you guys," I said as Gina and Olivia snickered. "We've only got a few minutes before people show up. This place looks crappy."

We hadn't been able to find anything that remotely resembled a podium for the debate. Reverend Perez had offered to detach the lectern from the church and haul it over, but that seemed mildly sacrilegious so we told him not to worry about it. Instead we'd brought one of the big living room chairs outside and positioned it with its back to the crowd. If someone was standing behind it, and you squinted, it kind of looked podium-like.

"Way to be a bossypants, Aki," Gina said. But she started moving chairs again.

"For real," Jake said. "Don't you think you're taking this all a little seriously?"

"Like you aren't. How many drafts of your speech did you write again?"

"Only three." Jake paused. "Or maybe four, I don't know. I only wrote two drafts of the intros I'm doing for each of the other speakers, though."

"Right." I moved the chair another inch to the left. I still needed to write my intros. I hadn't had time. People kept asking me questions.

"Aki, I have a question." I turned around and groaned in relief when it was only Lori. "Who's in charge of counting up the ballots and comparing them? You guys are supposed to announce the results a few minutes after the last speech ends, right?"

"Uh." I pulled a sheaf of notes out of my pocket and flipped through them. The last speeches—mine and Lori's, on global health—ended at eight thirty. At eight forty we'd compare the results from the first round of voting against the votes that came in after everyone had heard the speeches.

"I guess. Hmm." I hadn't actually thought about this. "I guess I'll count them up?"

"You're not going to have time." Lori shook her head. "You can't do everything yourself, you know. People are going to come up and talk to you after it's over, the way they keep doing now. Oh, and someone needs to count that first set of ballots, too."

"Crap. Everybody's already got their jobs. Jake is giving the closing speech, and you're in charge of crowd control and—"

"I can do it," Drew said, making me jump. I hadn't heard him come in. "I'm already passing out the ballots, so I'll gather them up and look at them really quick after."

"But you hate math," I said.

Drew gave me the look he reserved for when I'd just said something particularly obnoxious. "Even I can add, Sis."

Lori and Jake laughed.

"Sorry," I said.

"Don't worry about it. Hey, I know you're busy but can I steal you for a second?"

I didn't have a second, but I followed my brother through the courtyard gates anyway. He stopped at the same place where Christa and I had talked that first night. So much had changed since then. I felt like a different person now.

"I talked to him." Drew tucked his hands into his armpits.

"You told him the whole story?" I hadn't been sure if he'd really go through with it. "What happened?"

"He, ah…" Drew tilted his head and scratched the back of his neck. "Well, he didn't actually *yell* about the grades thing, but I could tell he wanted to. There was definitely some sputtering involved."

I smiled. Drew was being funny. That was a good sign. "What did he say?"

"Well, it took a minute for it to, I think, absorb. So he was quiet at first. That was the scariest part, the waiting. Then he said he was disappointed, but I was an adult now and it was up to me to decide how to deal with my own mistakes. He said we could talk more about what my different options are with Mom when we get home on Sunday."

That was better than I'd expected, honestly. "Are you okay with that? Talking to Mom?"

He shrugged. "I guess."

"But you're going anyway? To join the army?"

He stared out past my shoulder into the empty hills. "Probably? I need to think more. I haven't signed any papers yet. Dad said if I wanted to wait a while to decide, maybe I could take off school for a semester or two, get a better job back home. He said he and Mom could maybe help me out with an apartment. So I guess I'll see. I really just need—look, something's got to change, you know? I can't keep going the way I was. I need to figure out what to do next. Get this funk out of my system."

Drew lowered his chin, and our eyes met. For a second we were kids again. I remembered the time I fell off the see-saw on the church playground and the other kids pointed and tittered at me. Drew came over and pulled me up, and right away everyone stopped laughing.

I hugged my brother. Fiercely. After a second, Drew hugged me back. He was one of the only people around who was still taller than me, and his chin rested on my head as he said, "Sis, I appreciate the support, but I think people are looking for you inside."

"Oh. Crud." I pulled away and turned back to the gates. At least twenty people were standing around while Olivia and Gina rushed frantically to set up. Aunt Miranda was hauling four chairs at a time and calling for Olivia and Gina to move faster.

"Drew, go!" I shoved him in the shoulder. "Help them—now!"

He laughed and mock-saluted me. "Aye aye."

I moved fast on Drew's heels. Before I'd even made it through the gates, it started again.

"Hey, Aki, I have a question."

"Aki, where's this supposed to go?"

"There you are, Aki—all I need is this one thing."

There were so many questions I could barely keep track of who was asking, let alone who was coming in, but the courtyard was fuller than I'd ever seen it before. I must've lost track of time as I tried to answer everyone because it was a complete shock when Jake asked me, "Hey, should we start? It's a couple of minutes past."

Almost everyone was sitting down by then. Drew had a big pile of already-completed ballots jostling in his baseball cap from the first round of voting.

We hadn't even started and already we were off schedule?

"Oh. Uh, yeah." I gestured for the latest question-asker to go sit down. "We'd better hurry."

"Wait." Suddenly Lori was there, tugging on my sleeve, her eyes wide. "First I have to tell you something. Outside."

"Now?" She had to be kidding.

"Now." She dragged me through the gates.

Behind us, the crowd was turning around to talk to each other in their seats. Dad stood along the back fence, looking at his watch.

"Okay, so first of all," Lori said, her voice low so the others wouldn't hear us, "I'm really, really sorry. I had no idea this would happen."

A pain gnawed at the bottom of my stomach. "You're sorry for what?"

"I, um. It was me who told Nick you turned them in."

I gaped at her. "You *what*?"

"I'm so, so sorry!" She really did look like she felt awful. "I didn't know he'd do this. It was after that fight we had in Texas. I was just so pissed at you, and he was ranting on the bus about how much trouble he was in with his parents and how awful his dad is to begin with, and it sort of—I don't know. I couldn't help it."

"I cannot believe this." I pinched the skin between my eyebrows. "You—seriously, I can't *believe*—wait. Why are you telling me this now?"

"I heard—um, a rumor." Lori looked as if she might cry. "Just now. The Harpers Ferry girls are talking about it. Nick and his friends are going to slip you a note after the speeches start. He's saying you have to tell your dad, before the debate's over, that you were wrong and it wasn't them you saw that night. You have to get him to say he'll call their parents and tell them, too."

"Seriously? *Tonight?*"

She nodded. "If you don't, he's going to stand up in the middle of your speech and show that picture to everyone."

I swallowed. That would destroy Christa.

"He's bluffing." I wished I totally believed that. "He has to be."

"I hope he is." Lori patted my arm awkwardly. "Seriously. I am *so* sorry."

As though her being sorry helped anything.

Maybe I'd been wrong to think everything with Lori was back to the way it used to be. Maybe that could never happen. Not after everything that had changed this summer.

"What are you going to do?" Lori said.

I had no idea. "I guess I'll figure it out when I get in there."

I pushed past Lori and hurried through the gate. I didn't think about what she'd said or how late we had to be running now. I just walked straight up to the makeshift podium.

I looked at Dad as I passed him, but I didn't stop.

Maybe Nick was bluffing. Maybe not. Either way, there was nothing I could do about it. I wasn't going to lie. Not for him or for anyone else.

Then suddenly I was in front of the whole group saying, "Hello. Thanks so much, everyone, for coming."

I said thank-yous to the chaperones and the Perezes for their help getting the debate organized while I took in the sight of the crowd. No wonder the courtyard had looked so full. *Everyone* was here. Every single person and every single chaperone from all three youth groups. Plus Reverend and Señora Perez, the Riveras, the Suarezes, Carlos and Alicia, other church ladies I recognized from our dinners, Juana and the rest of our jewelry class, the girl who worked at the computer shop where I'd done my research... People were even standing behind the neat rows of chairs, filling every available spot.

They'd all come out just to see this? To see *us*?

And I hadn't even had time to get nervous.

As I kept talking, there was one face in the crowd that drew my eye again and again. Christa was sitting in the second row

next to Rodney. I couldn't read her expression. I wondered
if she'd heard the same rumors Lori had, about Nick's threat.

"Each speaker has a strict time limit of three minutes," I
told the crowd, tearing my eyes away from Christa. "My dad's
timing everyone and he's not going to hesitate to cut you off,
so don't bother cheating, you guys."

People laughed as Dad held up his running watch and
pointed to it menacingly. I glanced at Christa again. She was
smiling, too.

"Every issue will be debated in the same order," I said. "First
the side arguing in favor of the proposed resolution, then the
side against it. Our first issue is item number twenty-one on
the conference's agenda, the 'Resolution to Recognize All
Marriages through Official Church Doctrine.' So I'm going to
hand things off to our first set of debaters—Jake Spotswood,
who's arguing in favor of the resolution, and Madison Richmond, who's arguing against."

Jake stood up, notecards clutched in his hand. I stepped
back from the podium-chair and joined Dad leaning against
the fence. Jake's fingers were white at the knuckles, but his
face looked distinctly green.

"Hello. Ah." Jake cleared his throat once, then twice. Dad
held up his stopwatch. Jake saw him and gave a small nod.
"Hello. I'm here to tell you why you should vote in favor of
the resolution on marriage equality." He cleared his throat
again and glanced down at his notecards. Then he looked up,
took a long breath, swallowed and tossed the cards into a messy
pile on the chair. He looked straight at the crowd. "Frankly,
it's self-evident. As people of faith, it's our duty to love everyone, the way God loves everyone. There's no reason why
any one group is less deserving of love—either the love of a
church community, or the love of a family—than any other."

Wow. Jake always sounded smart, but this was a whole new level.

The crowd ate it up. He kept talking, using his now notecard-free hands to make a lot of excited gestures. You could tell how much he meant what he was saying. If I wasn't already on his side, I would've been by the time he made it to the two-minute mark. I could see people nodding along, even the guys from his church who'd given him a hard time when he first started circulating his petition.

"Finally…" Jake's time was almost up. He was starting to turn green again. "I wanted to close by saying that, um. Well. The reason I think the delegates should recognize same-sex marriages is because of everything I just said. And also because, well, I might need one of those marriages myself someday."

After that, it was so silent it was almost scary. Jake stood in front of the crowd, staring from face to face. Everyone stared back at him.

Then someone started clapping. I thought it was Lori, but it was impossible to tell because immediately someone else started clapping, too. Then more joined in.

There were people who didn't clap, but not many of them. Next to me, Dad was clapping so hard I was afraid his hands were going to fall off. I stuck two fingers in my mouth and whistled the way my mom had taught me. Then I dared to glance at Christa. She was clapping, too. Discreetly, with her hands below the seat in front of her.

Jake grinned. Then he charged toward me, walking right past his own empty seat on the front row.

"Congratulations!" I squealed. "I didn't know you were going to do that!"

"Yeah, neither did I." Jake might have been hyperventilating.

"Congratulations, young man." Dad shook Jake's hand. "That was quite a speech."

"Thanks, sir." Jake nodded, his face greener than ever. Then he turned to me and lowered his voice to a whisper. "Aki, I can't go up there again. You're going to have to do the rest of the introductions."

"What?" I whispered back. Madison was already climbing to her feet to give her counterargument. One of the guys from Harpers Ferry came over to us, clapped Jake on the shoulder, and handed me a folded piece of paper that looked like a ballot. "I can't. I don't know what to say."

We'd planned to take turns introducing each topic. After Madison was done, Jake was supposed to introduce the next resolution, on marijuana legalization.

"I need—" Jake seriously looked ready to pass out. "I've got to sit down, okay?"

"All right, all right." I pushed him into an empty seat. Only then did I realize he'd tossed all his notes into that messy pile on the chair. The introductions, too.

"Well, Jake's speech is basically impossible to follow," Madison said from the podium. "I think we can all agree what he just did was awesome, right?"

More cheers and applause. I fished through my pockets to find the schedule. After marijuana legalization, Rodney was talking about the police having access to military gear. How was I supposed to pivot from pot-smoking to such a serious issue?

"But this is a debate," Madison said when the cheers died down. "That means we're supposed to argue for and against every issue on the table, and I think every perspective deserves a fair hearing. So here we go."

I stuck the schedule back in my pocket. The ballot the Harpers Ferry guy had handed me fell out. Except, I saw now, it wasn't a ballot. It was a note.

The note from Nick. The one Lori had warned me about. Oh, *crap*.

This was real. He wasn't bluffing.

I shoved the note deep inside my pocket and tried to force it out of my mind.

Madison launched into her speech. The strange thing was, she sounded almost as convincing as Jake. She used notes, but only to read quotes from judges and from what other church organizations had in their bylaws. She didn't try to say we should be morally opposed to gay marriage, but she said the church could take some incremental steps, like allowing ministers to officiate at same-sex weddings that didn't take place in churches, before we went whole hog. She talked about how not all gay people—actually, she called them "queer people"— wanted to get married, either legally or religiously, and how it was important not to equate the movement for marriage rights with the movement for fairness overall.

"After all," she said, "it might be legal for me to get married once I turn eighteen, but there are a still a lot of states where I can get fired from my job tomorrow for being who I am. And my trans friends back home are looking at some terrifying statistics on hate crimes. We can't let marriage distract us from solving the urgent civil rights issues still facing the whole LGBT community."

People clapped for Madison, but not the way they had for Jake.

"Well done," I whispered under the applause as I passed her on my way back to the front.

"Thanks," she whispered back. "It was an interesting challenge, at least."

"The next resolution we're going to talk about," I said from the podium, glancing down at my schedule, "is number thirty-nine, the 'Resolution to Support State Laws Removing Penalties for Use of Non-Lethal Substances.' Um, that means legalizing marijuana, in case it wasn't clear."

People laughed. I stood up a little straighter and introduced the debaters, then went back to the fence next to Dad.

I watched the crowd more than the speakers this time. People seemed to be actually following along with the arguments. Even Juana and the other kids were paying attention.

Not Nick, though. His eyes were locked on me.

I had to do something. If he wasn't bluffing, he could ruin everything for Christa.

The pot legalization arguments ended and I walked quickly toward the front, glancing down at my notes. The last speakers had talked about the disproportionate police enforcement among young black men for marijuana use, so I went with that, using it as a lead-in to introduce the segment on police using military equipment.

Then I stepped back to watch Rodney's speech. It was great, even without the extra minute he'd begged me for. Like with Jake, you could tell he was really passionate about what he was saying.

Everything went so fast after that. I got more and more anxious as the night crept closer to the end. Not because of the introductions—they were easier than I'd expected—but because of the way Nick kept glaring at me.

When we'd first decided Jake and I would MC this thing, I'd thought I would embarrass myself every time I got to the podium. It turned out, though, I didn't have time to stress about what I was saying. Whenever I went up to the front, people in the crowd smiled at me. They even laughed at my feeble attempts at jokes.

It was starting to get dark, and people were settling into their seats. This wasn't only politics, I realized. This was entertainment. There was no movie theater in Mudanza, but there was the Aki-and-friends show.

I got into the groove of introducing each topic as I went.

I stopped looking to see what was coming up next and paid closer attention to each argument as it was happening. I tried not to think about my speech on health care that kept getting closer—and with it, Nick's threat.

Rosa gave her speech on immigration in both English and Spanish, translating each sentence as she went. She got big cheers, and I clapped, too, but even though I was ridiculously impressed by what she'd done, I was too consumed with worry to listen closely. By the time Brian was finishing his speech on climate change, my stomach was tied in eight hundred different knots.

I was up next. It was all about to happen.

"Hey, Dad," I whispered to him as the crowd clapped politely for Brian's closing. "Wasn't Brian's speech terrific?"

I glanced toward Nick, and sure enough, his eyes were glued to me and Dad. I had to keep talking so it would look as if I was really telling him what Nick wanted me to say. "For real. I thought he was fantastic. He totally convinced me, you know? Did he convince you, too?"

"Sure, sweetheart, he was pretty good." Dad was looking at his stopwatch.

"No, I mean seriously." I grabbed his arm. He looked up at me, alarmed. I prayed it would be enough to convince Nick. "He made me understand the issue in a way I never did before."

Dad looked down at my hand on his arm. "Sweetheart, you're about to give your speech so we can talk about this later, but if that young man really convinced you that the rights of corrupt businesses are more important than the right of your children to have breathable air, then, well, I might need to have a talk with your science teachers when school starts up again."

Oh. Hmm… I'd have to backtrack on this later.

But Nick was still watching us. Was that enough?

It would have to be. I was out of time.

"Sure," I said to Dad. "Time for me to go give a speech now."

"Good luck, sweetie," Dad said, pulling his arm out of my grip and patting my shoulder. "You'll be terrific."

Nick had turned back around in his seat. I tried to breathe easily, but my notes were clutched in my hand as tightly as Jake's had been in his.

If Nick didn't buy it, I was so screwed. *Christa* was so screwed.

As I made my way back toward the front, the audience buzzing in low voices, someone stepped in front of me. I was sure, at first, it would be Nick. But it was Christa.

"I have to tell you something," she muttered, her voice low.

I stopped walking. Was she here to tell me I should give in to Nick's demands?

Maybe she was right. After everything that had happened, she still meant so much to me. And this would mean so much to her.

But I couldn't. I was done lying. Even for her.

I stepped around her, my heart thudding in my chest as I reached the podium. I forced a smile, relaxing into the patter I'd used to introduce every round before.

"So," I said, "our next topic is resolution fifty-one, in support of—oh. Sorry, you guys, apparently I'm up here introducing myself."

I didn't look toward Nick or Christa in the crowd this time, but the others laughed, shifting comfortably and fanning themselves with the final ballots Drew had just passed out. At the back fence, Aunt Miranda gave me a lazy thumbs-up.

And I realized Nick and Christa weren't the only problems I had.

The crowd was *too* comfortable. The rapport I'd been building all night was going to work against me now that I had to talk about something serious. This was my one chance to convince people that they should support this issue that mattered so much. I had to change things up.

I started by shifting my stance. I let go of the podium and let my notes fall down on top of Jake's. Then I stepped around to the side, so everyone could see my whole body—I was wearing a long, light blue dress that actually fit me, because it was actually mine—and held my hands out, the way our lead pastor did at church when she was getting ready to start a sermon.

It seemed to work. People sat up straighter in their seats. I swallowed down the anxiety that kept pulsing in the back of my throat.

"I'm here to tell you," I said, "why the conference delegates should vote yes on the 'Resolution to Support Health Care Aid to Developing Nations.'"

A few people shifted in their seats again. The name was boring. Why did these things have to have such boring names?

"That's a pretty dry title for something that could make a huge difference in the lives of thousands of people," I said. "It could even save lives—maybe thousands of them—but only if people get behind it."

Now the crowd was paying attention again. I kept talking, my voice growing steadier with each word. This wasn't how I'd written the speech, but my notes were out of my reach now. Besides, I knew what I wanted to say.

"This resolution is about helping countries that are having trouble getting enough health care and other resources to their people. Here in Mudanza, we're only a few hundred miles from the US, but the whole town only has one part-time doctor. That means when someone gets sick, it could take them weeks to get treated, no matter how badly they need it. And that's only if they can afford to pay for it, and if the clinic happens to have the medicine they need."

A few people from our group glanced around at the local families standing in the back. The locals didn't react, though. Their eyes were on me.

"It's not only Mexico, either," I went on. "The nation of Angola, in Africa, has the highest rate of child death in the world. Half the kids born there die before their fifth birthday. There are nonprofit organizations that can help them, but only if enough people support the work they're doing. That's where our churches come in."

Every eye in the courtyard was locked on me now, and no one was laughing anymore. I took a breath before I delivered my final punch. I'd rehearsed this part a hundred times in my head.

"We call ourselves Christians. Well, if you read the Bible, it's very clear that it's our responsibility as followers of Christ—and as human beings—to do what we can to help others. That's why I'm calling on you. This resolution is asking us to look outside ourselves, outside our immediate personal needs, outside our own communities, and think about the lives of others in the wider world around us. That's the Christian thing to do. And it's the right thing, period."

That came out sounding more melodramatic than it had in my head.

Even so, people clapped. Lots of them. I let myself smile for the first time since I'd started my speech.

Members of the audience smiled back at me. Some of them were even reaching for their ballots to scribble things down, which they weren't supposed to do yet, because the other side hadn't presented their case.

Oh, right. The other side. I had to introduce Lori now.

Wait. Wait! This meant I'd made it through the whole speech.

Either the covert whispering session with my dad had done the trick, or Nick really *had* been bluffing.

I grinned and stepped back behind the podium, to signify that I'd switched roles.

"Now," I said, "here to tell you why everything I just said is wrong, please welcome Lori Smith."

The crowd chuckled. As she approached the podium, I could see Lori's hands clenching and unclenching.

I studied my own hands as I took my spot on the wall next to Dad. They were steady.

I looked calm. I *felt* calm.

How had that happened? I'd been a nervous wreck before every school presentation of my life.

"Great job, sweetie," Dad whispered.

"How'd I do on time?" I whispered back.

Dad held up his watch so I could see. "Two and a half minutes. You could've kept going."

"Nah," I said. "No use talking just to fill the space."

Dad clapped his hand on my shoulder. "Well said."

Lori started her speech. It was hard for me to pay attention with the adrenaline surging through me, but from what I could tell, she was actually pretty good. The arguments she was making were totally wrong, of course, but I could see some people in the audience nodding along as she talked about how we should focus on solving the problems that were close to us before we tried to take on the whole world. I didn't see why we couldn't do both at the same time, but I still clapped when she was done to show that I was being magnanimous.

"All right, everyone," Drew called when the clapping subsided. "You know the drill. Stick your new ballots in the hat so we can compare them against the vote from the beginning of the night."

Everyone was talking at once as they filled out their ballots. Even the chaperones and the local families seemed to be voting. People were talking about what the speakers had said, or trying to convince their friends to vote one way or another. None of them seemed to be talking about a scandalous photo of Christa and me, though, so I thanked God for that small gift.

It was so weird to think we'd done all this. Only a few weeks ago, everyone thought Jake's petitions were a big joke. Me included. Things changed so fast sometimes.

"Aki," someone said. I turned, expecting another question. Instead it was Christa, holding out a ballot and looking straight into my eyes.

With her standing in front of me, I expected everything else to stop mattering. To float to some distant corner in the back of my mind, the way it used to.

Instead it all collided. I was splitting into pieces. My brain wasn't big enough to hold Christa and everything else that was happening all at once.

Then she said, "Can we please talk? Soon?" and it got even worse.

All I could do was stare at her. I couldn't imagine my mouth forming actual words.

"Aki." Dad's voice this time. "Your brother needs you."

I took Christa's ballot from her hand and spun around. Drew, Jake and Lori were standing by a table on the far side of the courtyard, pulling ballots out of Drew's hat and pressing them down flat. I strode up to them and added Christa's ballot to their pile.

"We're still counting these up, but I've got the tally from the first round of voting over here." Drew handed me a crumpled sheet of paper as Lori and Jake sorted through the second-round ballots. "Check it out."

I blinked down at the list, trying to forget the stricken look on Christa's face. Drew had listed everything out by percentages. Before the speeches, gay marriage had gotten 55 percent support, lower than I'd expected. Ending the war had gotten about 50 percent, too.

My heart sank further when I saw the numbers for global health. Only 20 percent had voted yes. How was that even *possible*?

"I think we've almost got the numbers for the new round." Drew jotted something down. "You going to announce the results?"

I glanced at Jake and Lori.

"This is all you," Jake said.

"Everyone out there loves you," Lori said. "You should be the one to wind things up."

People in the crowd were standing, stretching, chattering. A few of them looked over toward the gates. I had to tell them the results now before they started filtering out.

"Okay." I grabbed the list from Drew. There was no time to read the numbers from the second round of votes. I strode back toward our trusty chair-podium and yelled, "Hey, everyone, I have the results!"

People stopped moving toward the exits and turned to face me. It was dark out, but the lights from the house cast a warm glow across the group. Half of them were standing behind the no-longer-neat rows of chairs my friends had set up.

Christa was at the front of the crowd. I wondered what she'd wanted to tell me. Though I wasn't sure I really wanted to know.

"I'll go in the same order as the speeches." I looked at the first vote and broke into a grin. "The marriage equality resolution had 55 percent of the vote before the debate, but now it's at 80 percent."

"Woo-hoo!" Drew yelled. Other people laughed and clapped. Jake was beet red at the back of the group, but he was smiling bigger than I'd ever seen him smile before.

I went down the rest of the list. Not one issue had the same results on both sets of ballots. The debate had changed at least someone's mind on every single topic. For some, it had changed a lot. On the war, only a few votes had moved—I guess people already felt pretty strongly about that one way or another—but on the police equipment resolution, more than half of the no votes had changed their minds. Rodney had made a really powerful case.

The global health resolution was last. I was already grimacing for a bad result.

"And finally, on international health care," I said, "before the debate, support for the resolution stood at 20 percent. Afterward—"

I stopped. I stared down at the number. That couldn't be right. Could it?

"And after the debate." I swallowed. "It's at 65 percent."

My dad led the applause this time, but the others joined in fast.

How had this happened? I hadn't said anything in my speech that wasn't self-explanatory.

But everyone was clapping, and smiling. *Something* had happened.

I'd changed people's minds. I'd taken something that was so obvious to me it didn't even need to be explained and, somehow, I'd explained it.

Drew must've been right. Not everyone thought the same way I did. Not until I convinced them to.

Christa was clapping and smiling in the front row. I was overwhelmed with that weird breaking-apart feeling again.

I'd thought this whole summer would be about her. About me and her, together. But maybe it was possible to have more than one majorly important thing happening at the same time.

Maybe there actually *was* room in my brain, in my life, for all of it.

I said thank-you and goodbye to the crowd. They clapped again. For me, I guess. My face hurt from smiling so much.

We filed out of the courtyard and into the open air. It was another gorgeous night. Maybe gorgeous nights were all they had in Mexico.

People kept coming up to tell me about how much fun they'd had. Everyone who'd given a speech—even the ones who'd been mega nervous before they went on, and even the ones who'd lost the vote—were talking and laughing now. It was so strange that standing in front of people and talking about something that was important to you could actually be fun.

The chaperones and families drifted off toward their houses. Dad gave me a hug before he left. Even Reverend Perez came up to say he thought I'd done very well. Everyone else started walking in little groups toward the church.

I hung back. Waiting.

Soon enough, when almost everyone else was gone, she was there, looking radiant in a green polka-dot sundress.

"I wanted to tell you something," she said.

I was feeling too many different things to smile at her. "What?"

She stared into my eyes, then dropped her head. She wasn't smiling, either.

"I lied to you."

CHAPTER 24

"YOU LIED?" MY head was buzzing. "When? About what?"

"Everything." She looked miserable. "I understand if you never want to talk to me again."

"Just tell me." Had she been lying about liking me? Had she been pretending, when I'd been taking her seriously the whole time?

Did she know I'd lied to her, too?

I wanted to disappear. Melt away into the dark Mexican sky.

"It's bad." Her hands shook. "You're going to think I'm horrible."

"I won't think you're horrible. Please just hurry up and tell me."

Her head was still bent low. I could barely see her face. "I made it all up."

"Made what up?" I could barely choke out the words. "Did you make up how you felt about—me? Is that it?"

"What? No." She glanced up, confusion flashing on her face. Then she hung her head again. "I made up Steven. I don't really have a boyfriend. The truth is, I've *never* had a boyfriend. Or a girlfriend, either. It was only—I didn't want you to think I was boring. But in reality I'm the most boring person ever."

"You've never..." I took a step backward, trying to make sure I understood. Steven wasn't really her boyfriend? "What about Madison? Isn't she your ex?"

"Not really. We never actually went out. All we did was kiss a couple of times, and people found out, and it got blown way out of proportion."

I thought about all those times I'd stared at Christa and Madison, worrying. Christa had definitely made it sound as if they'd been a couple.

She'd done that on purpose.

"Is Steven even a real person?" I shook my head. "Or did you invent him completely?"

She twisted her shoulders to one side. "He's sort of real. I mean, there was a guy named Steven I had a crush on in Milwaukee when we visited there once. I haven't seen him since we were kids, though. That's why I made up the thing about him moving back. I was trying to think of a reason for me to break up with him, but—"

"But you made that up, too." The pieces were falling into place. "I've never had a real boyfriend, either, much less a girlfriend. Do you think *I'm* boring?"

"No!" She looked up. Tears dotted her cheeks. "You're the opposite of boring. That first night, you seemed so cool and sophisticated. You seemed to know exactly what you were doing, and I... I don't know. I wanted you to think I was cool and sophisticated, too."

I laughed, even though a massive cloud of anger was still taking up most of the space in my brain. "I thought *you* were the cool, sophisticated one. I had no clue what I was doing that first night."

"Yeah, well." She laughed, too, though she didn't sound

amused. "I didn't know—I mean, I didn't think it would be a big deal. I figured we'd never see each other again after this, so I might as well try out being somebody else. Then I got to know you, and I realized—I liked you too much. I wanted you to know the truth. But by then it was too late."

I tried to take that in.

Now I felt guilty more than anything else. I'd lied to her, too. About the stupid pact. About applying to MHSA. About being a musician, even though I seemed to think about speeches more than songs now.

Her lie had been different from mine, but I wasn't sure it was any worse.

Lori had lied, too. For that matter, so had Drew, when he hid everything that was happening last year at school. And even Dad had lied to us about Uncle Andrew for all those years.

Was no one ever straight-up honest? Was it even possible to be?

"I'm so sorry." She wiped her eyes. "I'm the worst person ever."

"You're not the worst person ever." I had to tell her the truth now, whether I wanted to or not. And I did want to. "I lied to you, too. I should've told you about that dumb pact I made with Lori. The thing is, I stopped thinking about that pact after the first week. And I promise, it definitely wasn't the reason I wanted to be with you, not ever."

Christa looked up. Her eyes were bright.

"But that's not all I lied about."

Oh, God. I didn't know how to say this. There weren't any words that would make it better. Lying to Christa hadn't seemed like a big deal that first night, when she was a cute girl with a pink streak in her hair and a flirtatious smile, but now she was so much more. Now she was kind of my everything. "The truth is, I haven't played my guitar or sung or done anything with music except listen to it in more than a year. I auditioned for that school you wanted to go to, MHSA, and they wouldn't let me in. I was so devastated, I quit music altogether."

"God, that's awful." Christa looked aghast. "They're total tools for not letting you in. They probably got the paperwork mixed up or something."

I couldn't help laughing, even though there were tears sprouting from my eyes. "But I lied to you. You said you thought artists were so much better than everyone else, and I didn't want you to know I'm not an artist. I'm not anything special. I couldn't even get into some dumb public arts high school."

"But you *are* an artist." Christa shook her head at me. "Even if you don't play anymore, you've got art in your soul. Music is still a huge part of your life, even if you just listen now. Plus, that speech you gave tonight, about health care? And this whole huge event you organized? There's definitely art in that."

I was crying harder than ever now. I couldn't talk about this anymore.

"Am I the only one you told about Steven?" I asked her, scrubbing at my cheeks. "Or is it a story you tell a lot of people?"

She looked away again. "My parents were the first."

Ohhhh. "So is this whole thing about you not wanting them to know you're bi?"

Christa stared at me, her chin quivering.

"You—you *are* bi, right?" My frustration was flaring again, but at the same time, a new thought crept into the back of my mind.

Christa had never actually told me she was bi. I'd just assumed.

Maybe I shouldn't have. After all, people had been making the wrong assumptions about me all my life.

"I've been into girls and I've been into guys." Christa shrugged. "So, yeah, I guess. Sometimes I think *pan* might be a better word for me than *bi*, but either way. And yeah, part of it is me wanting to make sure my parents don't suspect. Not that it's really been an issue, until you came along."

That made my chest feel a little fluttery, but I ignored it. "So you made him up for them, then trotted him out again for me."

This time she met my eyes. "You've got to understand. My parents think I'm a completely different person than you do. Not only because of—you know, that. It's everything. With them I'm quiet, I'm sweet, I go to church, I do my homework, I want to go to a good college and be a rocket scientist or whatever they've dreamed up for me. But when I'm with you, I'm—well. Me."

"Except not the real you." I shook my head. "All summer you've been someone you made up."

Tears flowed down her face.

"I don't want to make things up anymore." I was still crying, too. "I'm sorry. I should've been totally honest with you about everything, from the beginning. But there have been so many lies going around this summer, and none of them have done anyone any good. I'm done with lying."

"Me, too." She sniffed. "I mean, I still have to lie to my parents, but I'm not going to lie to you, not ever again. I didn't think it would be this way. When we met that first night, I thought, well, maybe something will happen here, but it won't be anything serious. I didn't think you'd like me enough for that, and I thought it could be fun to, you know, maybe have a friend-with-benefits kind of thing this summer. I'd always wanted to do that. I thought it would be with a guy, though."

I shifted. Her thinking back then sounded a lot like mine had been. "So what changed?"

"Everything." She wiped her eyes again. "I didn't think I'd feel—I mean, I hadn't thought everything would be so *real*."

I nodded. I knew exactly what she meant. "I've never felt anything like what I've felt with you."

For a long moment, we looked at each other, not speaking.

Then she blushed and looked away. "That's why I had to tell you the truth. After—what happened in Texas, and you telling your dad. Suddenly everything seemed different. Now we're leaving in two days, and I don't know what I even want anymore. Except I knew I couldn't handle never seeing you again. And I couldn't deal with you not knowing the truth."

I nodded softly.

"That's what I thought, too, at first." There was no anger left in me now. If there had ever really been any. "I figured if anything happened it would be really short-term. Honestly... I'm only really realizing this now, but deep down, I think I didn't believe I could really like any girl *seriously*. I thought if I tried it once, I'd get it out of my system."

Drew said that, too. About getting a feeling out of his system.

"You wanted an experiment." Christa nodded.

It sounded bad when she said it that way. I shifted from one foot to the other. "Is that what you thought, too?"

She shrugged again. "When I kissed Madison before, I was definitely thinking *experiment*. I wanted to see what would happen. If it would be different from kissing a boy."

"Was it?"

"Not really." She blushed again. "Kissing *you* was different, though. But I don't think that was because you're a girl."

Oh. *Oh.* "Kissing you was different, too."

She paused for a long moment, watching me.

"I meant what I said before," she said then. "I've always

been the real me around you. I lied about having a boyfriend, and I guess about Madison, too, and I wish I hadn't. But other than that, I was realer with you than I've ever been with anyone. You're basically the only person who knows the real me."

I stayed quiet. What did you say to something like that?

She'd lied to me. But now she was standing here crying, saying she was sorry.

I believed her. She'd made a mistake. I made mistakes all the time. I'd lied, too.

And what she'd said...about the way she felt about me...

At first I'd thought Christa seemed cool, and pretty, and fun. Now she was this entire complicated person, with good parts and bad. Just like me.

And I actually cared about her *more* now that I knew all that. A *lot* more.

So much I'd already forgiven her for lying. So much I wanted to hold her hand and never let go.

"Was this what you were trying to tell me during the debate?" I asked her. "Right before my speech?"

"Oh, no. That was something else." She let out a short laugh. "I was going to tell you about Nick."

"Right. Nick. You heard about that, too?"

"Yeah. Ugh, I'm so sorry I was ever friends with him. He's turned into a complete loser."

"Well, whatever he had planned, it didn't happen. I tried to trick him and I guess it worked. I let him see me talking to my dad and he didn't follow up on his stupid threat, so..."

"Oh, good." Christa exhaled. "They totally did it, you know. They broke Juana's guitar. I got them to admit it."

I sucked in a breath. "You did? How?"

"I talked to him right before the debate started." Her lip quirked up into a half smile. "I reminded him how we'd always been friends, and I told him what he was planning was a really awful thing to do to a friend. He started looking like he felt really guilty. Then he said it wasn't *my* fault you turned him in, so instead of standing up in the middle of your speech and showing the photo to everyone, he'd go up to your dad and just show it to him, so you'd see from the podium and freak out. He acted as though he was doing me a favor."

Wait. What? This whole time I'd been so worried Nick was going to ruin Christa's life.

I shook my head again. "So what happened?"

"I told him he could screw his favor. I said he was a complete loser and he needed to own up to what he'd done. He'd trashed some poor kid's guitar and if he got in trouble for it, that was his own stupid fault."

Wait. Did that mean— "Does that mean you'd already believed me, that he did it?"

"Yeah." She nodded, as though it was obvious. As though it didn't mean the whole world, knowing she'd believed me over her friends, after everything that had happened. "I didn't think you'd say that if it wasn't true. That's not the kind of person you are."

I smiled a little. "So you convinced him?"

"Yeah. I knew how important this debate was to you. I wasn't going to let him mess it up. Also, I might've implied that if he said one word to your dad, I'd make sure everyone at church *and* school knew exactly what he did to that guitar. Even if he showed that picture to my own parents."

Wow.

This was all too big. Too scary. I was feeling way too many things all at once.

"All right. I have an idea." I took a step toward her and wiped my eyes. We were so close I could see the tear streaks on her face gleaming in the light from the house behind us. "We fly out the day after tomorrow. We both wanted a summer fling, so that gives us one more day to give it a shot. Are you up for it?"

Christa looked confused again. "What, you mean—what?"

"I mean." I swallowed and tried to think. "I mean, let's go back to the way things were, just until we leave Mexico. Well, not *exactly* how they were, because there's nowhere for us to, you know, have any real privacy. But we can be together anyway. If you want to."

"Starting now?" She wiped the corner of her eye.

"Yeah, starting now." We were so close it was nothing for me to reach for her hand. Nothing for me to thread our fingers together and swing our arms gently at our sides. Nothing for me to reach up and brush a tear from her eye. "But we'll have to keep a watch out for coyotes."

That made her laugh. I hadn't realized how much I'd missed that sound.

I led her over to the row of trees that lined the little valley we'd snuck off to all those weeks ago. We sat with our backs against the widest trunk, our fingers still linked, both of us still drying our eyes.

We sat there, and we talked. We talked for hours.

We talked about our families—her parents' rigid expectations, my parents' subtle hints that sometimes felt like just as much pressure in their own way. We talked about school and our friends and church and how weird it was to be raised according to beliefs we weren't sure we even understood. We talked about the future—the strange idea of high school as a finite thing, and the even stranger idea that there were whole worlds, whole lives, waiting for us afterward that we couldn't even glimpse yet.

"I think you should be honest with your parents," I said. "I mean, maybe not about all of it, not at once. But start with just one thing. Maybe tell them you want to think about culinary school.

You've still got two years left before you have to go anywhere, so if you tell them now they have time to get used to the idea."

I thought again about Drew. If he'd told our parents last year he was thinking about the military, the conversation between him and Dad might've been completely different.

And if Dad had told us the truth about Uncle Andrew, maybe Drew wouldn't have wanted to enlist in the first place.

If Christa and I had been honest with each other all summer— and Lori, too—we could've spared each other so much pain.

All summer I'd thought what I wanted most was to have a fling. To have my first girlfriend, my first real relationship. To have sex for the first time.

To test my theory. To start living my real life.

Well, I'd done all that. And I was glad I had. It had been a lot of fun. I'd learned a lot, too, and not just about dental dams.

But none of that mattered as much as being honest with the people I cared about. I wanted that a lot more than I wanted to check stuff off some arbitrary to-do list of experiences.

"If I tell my parents, they'll be devastated," Christa said.

I understood. The truth was awesome, but it was also terrifying.

"This summer has been dangerous for me," she went on. "I've gotten used to being the me I am here. When I go back there, I'll have to go back to being the me they know."

"You're basically living a double life."

"Kind of." She reached into her hair and unclipped the pink streak, smoothing it out against her thigh. "I'm living a double life here, too, though. On the one side I'm the whacky girl who wears fedoras and makes up bizarre stories, and then when I'm with you, I'm just…me."

I thought about that. "But you made up bizarre stories for me, too."

"But I didn't want to. Not after I really got to know the

real you. Now I don't want there to be anything between you and me that isn't real."

I sucked in a breath.

"Well, you should try being real with your parents, too." I didn't want to badger her about this, but it was important. I'd only started to understand just how important it was now that I'd talked to Dad. "Not about everything, and not all at once if that's too much. But college is a big deal. You should tell them what you really want."

Christa tipped her head onto my shoulder. "I'll think about it. If I'm going to come clean about something, maybe it should be this. College and careers and all that stuff—I mean, it's important, but it doesn't feel as much like a part of me as you do."

I squeezed her hand. God, it felt so good to touch her.

"What about you?" she said. "What do you want to do? In, you know, the future? Are you really done with music for good?"

"I don't know." I looked down at our clasped hands. "About any of it. I think I might want to pick up my guitar again when I get home, but if I do I'm only going to play for me, for fun. Not for lessons or anything. I used to want to grow up and be Prince, playing every single instrument there was, and singing and dancing and writing music and generally being a badass, but I think I'm kind of over that now."

Christa laughed. "You're already a badass. And you can always come back to it later on if you decide that's what you want."

I laughed, too. "The one thing I think I do know for sure, though, after last weekend, is that I definitely want to go away for college. Not live at home the way Drew did. I want to be part of a community. My school now is so tiny, and I like the idea of being part of something bigger, where you can get lost in the crowd if you want to, but everyone's there for the same reason as you—because they want to learn." I laughed again. "I'm sorry, that sounds so cheesy."

Christa smiled. "Maybe, but who cares? You've got to be honest with yourself about what you want."

I got quiet again. She was right.

I only had one more day with Christa, and I wanted as much honesty as we could muster.

"Do you think," I began, then paused. "I mean, speaking of, you know, the future. Do you think you'll, maybe, get married someday?"

She took a minute before she answered. "I think... I don't know. Maybe? It seems so far away it's hard to even think about."

"I know what you mean." I stared off into the distance. "Lately I've been wondering... I've been thinking of myself as bi because I've been into guys and I've been into girls. But will I *always* be this way? Or will I decide someday, you know, that I'm actually a regular lesbian or whatever?"

"Or that you're straight?"

"Well, after this summer, I kind of can't see myself only liking guys. But, I guess, maybe? Someday? Anything's possible, right?"

Christa was quiet for so long I wondered if she'd fallen asleep. Then she said, "I wonder about that stuff, too."

"You do?" I leaned around to look at her. "What did you say before, about maybe being pan? Does that mean *pansexual*?"

She half smiled. "Yeah. Sometimes I think that word is perfect for me, but other times, I'm not even sure I completely get what it means."

"Me, either. I've heard it before, but I'm not really sure how being pan is different from being bi."

"I think it's saying that you can be attracted to anyone—guys and girls, but also people who don't see themselves as guys *or* girls. Anyone at all, really."

"Huh. I don't think I've met anyone who doesn't see themselves as a guy or a girl."

"Not that they've told you about, anyway."

"Oh." I'd never thought about that. "Wow. Well, but can't you be bi and still be into, you know, everyone? Potentially?"

"Yeah, I think so. Also do you know there's this thing called biromantic? Or homoromantic or heteroromantic or whatever. The idea is that you can be romantically attracted to someone, but that doesn't mean you're necessarily *sexually* attracted to them. That you could be biromantic but heterosexual, or vice versa."

My head was spinning. "That's—wow. That could actually change some things for some people I know." Or for me, even. I knew I was into Christa in both ways, but what about the guys I'd kissed before, the ones I wound up feeling mostly meh about? Maybe I was bisexual but homoromantic. Or the other way around.

"For me," Christa said, "I've had crushes on more girls than guys over the past year, but sometimes I'll still see a guy I think is hot, and I'll try to figure out *why* I think he's hot. Is it because he looks girly? Or is it because I like guys the same way I like girls? Also, I used to be into more guys than girls, but then I wonder if that's only because, you know, society *expects* me to be into guys, and when I was younger I didn't know to question that."

"Yeah, I know what you mean." I squeezed her hand. "The thing is, I've wanted all along to figure this stuff out as soon as I possibly could. But lately I've thinking more like—there really isn't a rush, right? We've got time to make sense of it all."

"You think? I always thought most people already knew about all this—you know, whether they were gay or straight or bi or whatever—by the time they got to be our age."

"I used to believe that, too, but now I'm not as sure. I mean, if you think about it, people used to not realize they were gay until they were really old and already married to straight people. That's the way it was for, like, Eleanor Roosevelt."

"Yikes," Christa said. "That would suck."

"For real."

We grew quiet again. Thinking. Wondering.

Then, after a long moment, I realized there was something I wanted to do. Needed to do.

I turned to face her. To break the silence.

I smiled at her. She smiled back.

"I never told you my favorite song," I said.

She laughed. "I knew you had one!"

"I'm sorry. I guess that was another lie when I told you I didn't."

"It's all right. What is it?"

Instead of answering her, I took out my phone and pulled it up. While the song was loading, I stood up and held out my hands, pulling Christa to her feet beside me. When the song began, I closed my eyes and started to dance.

I'd never danced in front of anyone. I'd never shared this song with someone, either. I'd thought it would be embarrassing, and it kind of was—but more than that, it felt as though I was opening myself up for her. Letting her see a part of me. Because I wanted her to.

"I know this song," she said after the first few notes had played. Her hands tugged at mine. She was dancing with me. "Prince, right?"

I nodded. It was Prince's best song of all time. The best dance song of all time, too. "This is 'Kiss.'"

We danced together under the stars. I kept my eyes closed, but I could see her anyway. I could feel her.

The pulse and pound of the music ran through us as her finger traced the edge of my jaw. Turning me to face her.

I opened my eyes. She was looking right at me, her eyes soft and warm, the music still thumping through our bodies.

She kissed me. She kissed me, she kissed me. Our lips parted and danced together, lightly, exploring each other again for the first time.

I'd never felt anything like this before. Not even in our Texas dorm room. Here, the sun shone down on us, even in the dark night.

I'd been spending my whole life trying to figure out where I was supposed to be, *who* I was supposed to be, when I was supposed to be right here. Kissing her.

We separated slowly as the song ended, our lips drawing apart, our foreheads drawing together. I linked our fingers again—our hands had come apart somehow, had wrapped themselves around our backs, our necks—and, slowly, I pulled her against me.

It was late. I didn't know how late and I didn't want to check. I wanted to keep Christa at the center of my world, even if it was only for a little longer.

"So what happens tomorrow?" she asked as we turned back toward the church.

"I don't know. What do you want to happen?"

"More of this." She squeezed my hand.

"Let's do it, then."

"But what about—you know. Everyone?"

"We'll figure something out."

She squeezed my hand again. I squeezed back.

I felt almost ready to burst again, from feeling too many things at once. Except this time it was a good feeling.

But I hated that I only got to feel it for one more day.

CHAPTER 25

SOMETHING SHARP POKED into my back. I blinked
foggily at the ceiling high overhead as I dug around to find
the offending sharp thing—a sleeping bag zipper. Whoever
put their bag close enough to mine that I wound up sleeping
on the zipper was in for it once I was awake enough to complain. It was our last morning in Mexico, and in a couple of
hours we'd be on a bus for the airport, but that didn't mean
one of these annoying girls could get away with—

The girl next to me rolled over until her face was only
inches from mine. I had to shake myself fully awake before I
believed it was really Christa.

She was smiling at me, still mostly asleep, stretching in her
sleeping bag with her eyes half-closed.

Then I remembered.

The night before last, Christa and I had decided to start
again. That this thing between us could last right up until we
climbed onto the bus for Tijuana.

I didn't want to think about the bus, though. I wanted to
remember yesterday.

We'd spent the entire day side by side. We watched each

other silently during breakfast, smiling secrets at each other over every bite. We spent the morning together at the work site, helping to finish installing the fence. After that we had the afternoon off, so we went into town. We went to the computer place first, then bought tacos from a street vendor and sat in the plaza in the middle of town, talking.

Now that we weren't lying about anything, we had more to say than ever. I wanted to tell her all my stories, and I wanted to hear hers. For the first time, we talked about our past relationships (or lack thereof). Christa told me how she'd wound up kissing Madison—once on a dare and once on a sugar high—and I told her the story of the college girl who gave me my thirty-six dental dams. She broke her no-selfies rule and took a photo of the two of us with our arms around each other, giggling up at the camera. I broke my no-singing rule and let out a few bars of the cover version of "When Doves Cry" that I'd been working on since I was ten.

We talked and laughed and smiled until the sun got low in the sky. The only time we touched was when our hands brushed by not-quite-accident as we were getting up to leave.

I'd thought it would be torture, spending so much time together but not being able to really touch, but it was actually a fantastic afternoon. I felt closer to her after that than I had in Texas. Back then, it had still felt like we were holding something back. Probably because we were.

We sat together at dinner and vespers, too. Vespers was twice as long as usual because we all had to go around and say what we were going to miss the most about being here. Some people got pretty emotional. A few girls cried, and even my dad looked choked up when he talked about how he was going to miss the local families he'd gotten to know and how even with the language barrier we were all part of the larger church family. I looked over at Juana, who was resting her head on her mother's lap, and I got kind of choked up, too.

Jake said he was going to miss vespers. Most people laughed at that. Brian coughed and muttered something under his breath. I couldn't make out what he said, but Jake must have because his face paled and his eyes dropped. Some of the other guys laughed, but Drew gave them the stink eye and slapped Jake on the shoulder, muttering, "Don't worry about them, dude. We've got your back."

When it was my turn I said I was going to miss the food and that I'd never go to Taco Bell again. People laughed. It was weird to say that sitting next to Christa, though. I'd miss her with a ferocity I couldn't even fathom yet.

Christa said she was going to miss the idea of making a difference and helping others every single day. I was surprised, because I'd never heard her talk that way before. As she spoke, she wiped at her eyes, and I realized I was doing the same thing.

After vespers we went back to our spot by the tree. We didn't talk at first. We just sat and watched the branches sway and the stars gleam. I don't know how long we were there—maybe an hour—before Christa started murmuring.

"I decided something. During vespers."

"What did you decide?" A niggling feeling of hope sprang up in me. Did she want to throw our one-day fling plan out the window? For us to be together, even once we got back home?

"I'm going to tell my parents I want to go to culinary school." She nodded firmly. "And that I'm a lot more serious about cooking and photography than I'll ever be about law school. Plus... I'm telling them I broke up with Steven. It isn't the whole truth, but it's a lot closer than I've been."

I squeezed her hand. I let myself feel disappointed, but only for a second. "I think that's an incredibly brave decision."

We kissed.

In the beginning we'd kissed hard and fast, trying to squeeze as much as we could into the time we had. Now, when we had hardly any time left, our kisses were slow, almost lazy. We touched each other with a warmth and lightness we hadn't bothered with before.

When it was time to go back to the church, we decided wordlessly to move our sleeping bags together. As I lay there, waiting to fall asleep, it was the first night I hadn't felt the hard, unforgiving floor beneath me. Instead, I was only conscious of the warmth of Christa lying next to me.

We didn't even touch. It was just the knowledge that she was there. The sound of her breath. The shape of her in the dark.

That morning, I watched as she slowly opened her eyes. She frowned, sighed and closed them again. I smiled and nudged her arm with mine.

At first she winced and turned away. Then she saw me and widened her eyes. "Oh!" She clapped her hand over her mouth and started giggling.

I giggled, too. Then I felt something wet on my pillow and realized I was crying at the same time.

I didn't ever want this to end.

I wished we could skip straight to college. I wished we could have a whole world to ourselves. Even if that world was just a tiny, dingy dorm room.

But we'd already decided today was the end.

"What's wrong?" Christa whispered. My eyes were still leaking tears.

"Nothing," I whispered back. I sat up quickly. "We're behind. Everyone's packing already."

I wiped my eyes and reached toward the foot of my sleeping

bag for my clothes. Most of us changed in our sleeping bags. It was easier than waiting in line for the bathroom.

There were some things I would definitely not miss about Mexico.

Once I'd wriggled into jeans and a T-shirt, I climbed out of my bag and rolled it up so I could shove it into my duffel. Next to me, Christa was packing silently. I was about to say something to her—maybe *Don't forget the shirt I borrowed*, maybe *I'll miss you*, maybe *Let's just try emailing when we get back and see how it goes?*—but before I could open my mouth, my dad was standing next to me.

"You almost ready, sweetheart?" He surveyed the stuff strewn around my sleeping bag. It should've been abundantly clear that I was *not* almost ready.

"Actually, Dad, I wanted to ask you something."

"And I wanted to tell you something. Let's go get you some hot chocolate."

I caught Christa's eye, gave her a tiny smile and followed Dad outside. The church ladies had set up breakfast for us right out in front of the church with coffee and hot chocolate and bread. I poured myself a mug and picked up a roll.

"What's that?" I asked as Dad licked the flap on an envelope.

"A donation from Holy Life of Rockville, to help the congregation here finish up the rest of the construction." Dad tucked the envelope into his pocket. "I've got to remember to give it to Reverend Perez before the bus leaves."

"Oh, whoops. Were we supposed to finish the whole thing while we were here?"

Dad chuckled. "Er, no. The youth program is more of an outreach effort than a true construction team. This donation, though, is an offering from the Rockville congregation. They offered to compensate Señor Suarez for his guitar, but he refused to take it. So they decided to give the church this gift instead."

"Oh." I hadn't even thought about how much that guitar must have been worth. "Poor Señor Suarez."

"I think he's just relieved his daughter isn't so broken up anymore." Dad patted the envelope, making sure it was still there. I did the same thing whenever I put something in my pocket. "I understand you had a lot to do with that."

I smiled. "Juana's awesome. I'm going to miss her."

"I think she'll miss you, too."

I took a breath, then launched into my question.

"I did some research," I told Dad, trying not to sound nervous. "It turns out there's a thing where youth group members can petition to be junior delegates to the convention. They can't vote, but they can go to all the events and hear the speeches and stuff."

Dad smiled and sipped his coffee. "That's true."

"Do you think maybe I could go? As a junior delegate, I mean?"

Dad's smile widened. "Junior delegates need to be elected by their congregations."

"Then maybe I could run for it, or whatever? The thing is, I want to know more about how this stuff works. I mean, not only at church, but in the world. Especially when it comes to things like foreign aid and health care. I've been thinking—I have some free time now that I quit my music lessons, so maybe I could do that. Help out a group that's working on that stuff. Maybe I could help them start a new project to work with immigrants. Or I could start my own group, maybe. Oh, and I'm going to start paying better attention in Spanish class, so I can learn to speak it for real. Maybe I could come back down here next summer to volunteer on my own. Or I could go somewhere else where I could help." I took a breath. "I don't know. I guess I need to figure it out."

Dad took another sip of coffee. "I think those are all fine ideas, Aki."

"The thing is, I want to *do* something. You know? Not just talk about it."

He nodded. "You may want to think about exploring a career in public health policy. A friend of mine from college got his master's in that. You'd also be an excellent doctor. Or a lawyer or a politician. And you'd certainly be a fine community activist. Quite a few of those jobs involve making speeches, and we know now how good you are at that."

I smiled and tucked my hair behind my ear. "Doesn't everyone hate doctors and lawyers and politicians?"

"You'll change their minds." Dad tugged on one of my braids. I squirmed and pulled away. "By the way, sweetheart, I know you were upset when you didn't get into that school, but I hope you won't give up on music altogether. You can still enjoy it even if you don't want to make it your career. I remember how happy you used to look when you sang in the youth choir at church, and I know the choir directors miss having you there, too."

Wow. Dad had almost made it through the whole summer without guilt-tripping me about that.

I nearly said something sarcastic, but then I stopped myself. He'd been so nice about me coming out. The least I could do was answer him for real.

"I still love music." I thought carefully about how I wanted to explain this. "I don't think I want to major in it for college or anything, but when I get home I was thinking about playing guitar again. Just for fun. I guess I could think about choir, too, but no promises. I think I need to try different things instead of obsessing over just one the way I used to do."

Dad nodded. "Fair enough. Anyway, sweetie, you know you've got plenty of time to decide on all of that. No need to be thinking about college majors yet. For now, though, when we get back home, I'll show you the forms to fill out to apply to be a junior delegate. Then if you get accepted, you can come to the conference with me and see exactly how exciting all of this voting and speech-making can be."

I grinned. "Am I totally a dork?"

"Don't worry, I won't tell your brother." Dad set down his coffee cup. "Now, I wanted to tell you about my own plans for the conference. I've made some decisions about these resolutions."

I wasn't sure I wanted to hear this. If he was voting against health care—or, worse, against gay marriage—that was going to hurt. "I thought it wasn't up to you. I thought the church committee had to decide and then you'd vote whichever way they picked."

Dad nodded. "Well, that's true, but I can make a case to the committee. They'll take what I have to say into consideration."

"Oh." I wondered why Dad hadn't told me that before. "So what are you going to tell them?"

"A lot of different things, on a lot of different resolutions. There are far more of them than you covered in your debate last night, of course. But there was one I'd been wrestling with before we came down here, and that was the international health care plank. I knew we should support people in developing countries, of course—that was part of why I wanted us to make this trip. I'd still been uncertain about the resolution, though, because there are so many folks back home who need our support, and we only have so many resources to go around. But your speech last night, sweetie—well, you convinced me. You really did. Everyone on the planet is a child of God, not only the people in our own neighborhoods. So I'm voting yes."

At first I didn't think I'd understood. "Because of what *I* said?"

"That's right." Dad smiled so big I worried his face might break.

"But it was so obvious! I didn't say anything new."

Dad chuckled. "It's obvious to you, because that's how you see the world, but it's not obvious to everyone else until you persuade them to look at it that way, too."

I felt another tear forming in the corner of my eye. God, how embarrassing.

"By the way, I'm voting yes on the marriage resolution, too," Dad said. "I'd already made up my mind on that one, but if I hadn't I certainly would have after what you've told me this summer."

"I—" I didn't know what to say. "I didn't make a speech on that one."

"You didn't have to. You being you is enough."

I hugged him, moving so fast I nearly spilled his coffee. He hugged me back, his hand thumping on my shoulder.

"Also?" I said, while he was still clasping me tightly. "That photo you carry around of Uncle Andrew? I was wondering, could we maybe put it up at home somewhere? To remember him better?"

Dad released me partway, his hand still holding my arm. His eyes were bright and locked on me. "Well, sweetheart, if that's something you want, we can talk about it when we get home."

"Okay." I swallowed at the thought of going home.

"I'm glad we got to spend some time together down here." He let go of my arm and took a step back. "We'll have a lot to tell your mother when we see her tonight."

"Will we ever." It was strange to think I was going to see Mom so soon. I wanted to see her—I wanted to see my room and my friends and my cat, too—but I was so used to life here now. To hot chocolate for breakfast. To talking about church politics as though my opinion mattered.

Most of all, to seeing Christa's smile.

Dad looked at his watch. "You'd better get a move on with that packing. The bus will be here any minute."

"Oh, right. Crud." I put down my mug and jogged into the church. Dad was right—nearly everyone else had already finished packing. My pile of stuff was alone in the middle of the floor. Someone had wheeled my suitcase over to it. On top of my suitcase was a piece of paper, folded in half. I opened it and read the note.

I went to help Rodney pack stuff up outside. See you on the bus!
Christa

She'd drawn a little heart by her name. I was so happy to see that heart I didn't even mind that she'd gone off somewhere and I wouldn't see her until the bus ride.

Except...when we got on the bus, this was all over.

Oh, well. I guess it already was. Standing next to each other while we packed wouldn't have meant much.

Still, though. Every minute, every second even, counted for something.

I shoved my stuff into my suitcase and my duffel, not bothering to pay attention to what went where. I was tying the duffel closed when I heard the sound of the bus crunching on the gravel outside. There was no avoiding the inevitable.

I hauled my stuff out and joined the throng. Lori was at the edge of the group, loading her suitcase into the bottom of the bus. I joined her and put my stuff next to hers.

"You doing okay?" Lori was the only person I'd told about the arrangement Christa and I had made.

I shrugged. "It's only the worst Sunday of my life, is all."

"Sorry." She hugged me. "Want to sit together on the bus? We can play Candy Zone the whole time. You can't be stressed when you're playing Candy Zone."

I was really, really glad Lori and I were friends again. It wasn't the same as it had been before—it probably never could be—but that didn't mean I didn't need her. "Sure."

Even though things were different between us now, in some ways, they actually felt more natural. As though we'd become *better* friends now that we were being totally honest with each other.

It felt that way with Dad, too. And Drew, actually.

And Christa. Her most of all.

I'd started this summer wanting to *do* something. I thought that meant an experiment. I'd wanted to have my own little separate world with Christa. But that had been impossible until we'd stopped hiding parts of ourselves.

Now, though, Christa and I really did have our little world, and it was amazing. The truth was, though, Lori and I had a world of our own, too. We had years of history, of understanding each other, that no one got but us.

Dad and I had our own world now, too. We understood each other in a different way than we had before. It was the same with Drew. And it was even true, now that I thought about it, with Jake, and some of my other friends.

Except—

I didn't want all of those worlds to be separate. We were all in one big world, together. It was a lot more fun that way.

Lori and I climbed onto the bus behind a group of guys

who were yelling out a countdown until they could go to the airport McDonald's. On my way down the aisle, I passed Aunt Miranda. She was trying to shove someone's Hello Kitty backpack into the tiny overhead rack.

"Um, hey." I leaned over so she could hear me. "Thanks, you know, for what you said that time. You were right, it turns out."

Aunt Miranda leaned out from behind the backpack. Her hair was frizzy around her sweaty face, but she smiled. "I'm so glad to hear that, honey. Remember, anytime you need to come talk to me, even once we get back home, you do that."

"Okay. Thanks again."

I found two seats for Lori and me near the back and slid in by the window. I tossed my jacket onto the seat next to mine while Lori stuck her purse in the overhead rack. Before she was done, a shadow appeared over me.

"Hey, um, can I sit with you?" Christa pointed to the seat I'd saved for Lori.

"Oh. Um." I stared up at her. We'd agreed that once the bus left Mudanza, our fling was officially over. If we sat together on the bus, what did that mean?

The thing was—I didn't really care what we'd agreed. Or what it meant.

I wanted to sit next to Christa on this bus ride. I wanted to get as much Christa time as I could out of this life.

I glanced at Lori. She mouthed "Go for it!" and gave me a thumbs-up behind Christa's back. I managed not to laugh.

"Okay." I nodded. Christa slid into the seat without another word, glancing at me with a split-second smile and reaching into her purse for her headphones.

We didn't talk during the ride. All we did was listen to music, separately. It was cold on the air-conditioned bus, so I spread my blanket out over my lap, but Christa stared out the window, not even glancing in my direction. I tried to play a game on my phone, but I gave up after half an hour and settled for staring out the window, too.

It was a constant struggle not to cry.

This was it. These few hours were all we'd ever have again.

The bus was rolling into the outskirts of Tijuana when I felt it. A slight pressure on the inside of my wrist. Sliding up to the top of my hand.

I was so startled I nearly yanked my hand away. Instead I looked down.

Christa was still staring out the window, but her fingers were stroking mine. Lightly. Under my jacket.

We weren't supposed to be doing this. Even where no one could see.

Had Christa forgotten the plan? Would this make it even harder when we had to walk off the bus and act as though we didn't know each other?

Whatever. Screw it.

I slid my hand into hers, linked our fingers together, and squeezed. Christa turned toward me, biting her lip. She squeezed back.

This time I didn't bother to wipe my eyes. There would be more tears where these came from.

After ten minutes of hand holding and silent tears, the bus turned onto the airport ramp. The chaperones yelled for everyone to stay in their seats until the bus stopped, but no one listened. I scrubbed at my face with my free hand and tried to breathe deeply so the tears would stop.

I waited for Christa to pull her hand free from mine. She didn't. She was crying, too.

We sat still and silent while everyone around us clambered to their feet and gathered up their stuff, the bus buzzing with excited conversation.

Aunt Miranda yelled that we should all assemble at the departure boards right inside the terminal while the chaperones got our suitcases. Everyone moved forward except Christa and me. I waited for the separation to come, for the forward momentum we couldn't avoid.

"I've been thinking," Christa whispered. I could barely hear her over all the shouting and talking. I leaned in carefully. "And I think I... I don't..."

"You don't what?" Even through my whisper, my voice shook.

"I don't want this to be over. Not today. Maybe not ever." She squeezed my hand again. "But only if that's what you want, too."

I closed my eyes. I didn't know the word for what I was feeling right then. *Elation? Relief?*

Love, maybe?

"That's what I want, too," I said. "That's so completely and totally what I want."

Without thinking, I leaned in to kiss her. But she was thinking, and she leaned back.

"I'm sorry." I wanted to sob.

She shook her head. "No, *I'm* sorry. I—I can't do that. I'm sorry, I just can't."

"Okay." I squeezed her hand. "But *I* have to."

Christa didn't say anything at first. Then she nodded.

"I get it," she said softly. "I wish I could, too."

"But we can be together. I mean, it'll be hard, but I want to do the hard stuff if that's what it takes."

She squeezed my hand so tightly I thought it might burst open.

I slid my free hand into my bag and pulled out a marker. It was one of hers. I'd lost track of how many things that I thought of as mine now were really Christa's.

"I need your help." I told Christa what I wanted her to do. When I finished explaining, we were both laughing, and brushing away tears at the same time.

"Okay." She dropped my hand to reach for the marker. "Hold still."

It only took a minute—which was a good thing, since Aunt Miranda was glaring at us from outside the bus—but when it was done, I realized I was terrified.

"You're really going through with this?" Christa popped the cap on the marker and tucked it back into my bag.

I nodded. "I care so much about you. I want everyone to know that, but if I can't tell them, then at least I want them to know *me*."

We were the last two people off the bus. Christa walked in front of me. My heart was pounding harder than it ever had in my life as we climbed down those steps into the throng of people.

They were going to see it. *Everyone* was going to see.

The first person I spotted looking our way was Jake. His eyes locked on me, and his mouth dropped open. Then he grinned.

Someone else, one of the guys from his church, saw Jake looking and followed his gaze. He nudged the guy next to him and gestured toward us.

Soon everyone was staring at me, pointing, whispering. I looked around for Dad but he was bent over grabbing stuff from under the bus.

People were starting to walk toward the terminal, so we walked, too. Christa drifted into the crowd, smiling at me as she went. I smiled back, the nerves rolling under my skin.

On the front of my T-shirt, Christa had drawn a tiny rainbow. Below that she'd written, in letters so big no one could miss them, "HI! I'M BI!"

I saw Lori as I approached the sliding glass doors. Her eyes widened. Then she came up to walk alongside me. My nerves started to cool down the tiniest bit.

When we passed through the glass doors, every eye in the group was fixed on me. Drew gave me his patented half grin. Most of the others were smiling, too. Jake and Rodney and Sofía and Gina and everyone—everyone I'd ever known, it felt like. Even Dad was there, glancing my way with a soft smile and a bemused nod.

I could see Christa up ahead, standing in front of the destinations board. I went up to join her, Lori on my other side, looking up at the ten-foot high screens listing what seemed to be all the places in the world. Sydney. São Paulo. Honolulu.

I glanced over at Christa. She glanced back at me, still smiling. Then I turned to read the names. All the places I could go someday.

And I could. I really could.

I could do anything. All of us could. We were only as limited as we let ourselves be.

Our future was wide open. And the future started today.

★ ★ ★ ★ ★

ACKNOWLEDGMENTS

THIS BOOK, YOU GUYS.

Our Own Private Universe is the book I've wanted to write ever since I knew I wanted to write books. And it's the book I wish I'd had when I was a young-adult reader myself.

But it took a ton of time and work—by way more people than just me—to get this book into the shape it's in now that you're holding it. (Or reading a digital version of it. Or virtually experiencing it, if you're reading this in the future and by now we all read books via brain implants or what have you.)

I have to start by thanking my amazing editor, T.S. Ferguson. T.S., I don't know how many girl-on-girl hookup scenes you'd edited before this book came across your desk, but I know you didn't blink an eye and dove right in when I sent you *Our Own Private Universe*, and the book is all the better for it.

And my agent, Jim McCarthy. I keep sending Jim queer books of all stripes, and he keeps helping me figure out exactly what to do with them. I can't imagine navigating this strange career without Jim there to illuminate the murky path.

Thank you so much to the rest of the Harlequin TEEN team for helping my books find their place in the world, including Natashya Wilson, Michael Strother, Gigi Lau, Mary Luna, Siena Koncsol, Shara Alexander, Amy Jones, Bryn Collier, Evan Brown, Ashley McCallan, Olivia Gissing and Rebecca Snoddon.

So many thanks to my incredible critique partners, beta readers and awesome friends, who were a huge help as I developed the early drafts of this book (some of which were so different from the final version that they took place in an entirely different country, so thanks, guys, for helping me figure *that* out along with all the rest)—Anna-Marie McLemore, Justina Ireland, Miranda Kenneally, Jessica Spotswood, Andrea Colt, Kathleen Foucart, Tiffany Schmidt and Caroline Richmond.

Thank you to Darcy for being my inspiration every single day, even if it will be quite a few years before you're old enough to read this book.

And thank you, most of all, to Julia. For everything, always.

*Turn the page for a sneak peek
at Robin Talley's next novel*
Pulp
*a stunning dual-narrative story of two gay teens,
one in 1955 and the other in present day,
connected by the power of storytelling.*

Monday, June 27, 1955

JANET HAD MADE a terrible mistake.

Two weeks ago, when she'd written the letter, she'd still been flush with her discovery. She hadn't been thinking clearly.

But her mother was always telling her she was rash and reckless, and Janet had finally proven her right: it had only been *after* the postman had already whisked her letter away that it occurred to Janet that a reply could come at any time. That it would be dropped into the family mailbox alongside her father's Senate mail, her mother's housekeeping magazines and her grandmother's postcards from faraway cousins. That anyone in the family might reach into the mailbox, open that letter and see who'd been writing to Janet. And that they could realize precisely what that meant.

So Janet had spent every afternoon since she'd mailed the letter perched by the living room window, listening for the postman's footsteps on the walk.

Each day, when she heard him coming, she leaped to her feet and tore out the front door. Sometimes she beat him there

and burst outside while he was still plodding up the steps to
their tiny front porch. On those days, she forced a smile and
held out trembling fingers to take the pile of letters from his
hand.

Other days she was slower, and stepped outside just as he'd
departed. Those days she pounced on the stuffed letter box,
flinging back the lid where Jones Residence was written in
her mother's neat hand.

Then there were afternoons like this one. When Janet was
too late.

She'd made the mistake of getting absorbed in her reading, and when she heard the slap of brown leather filtering
through the window glass she'd told herself it was only the
next-door neighbor, a tall commerce department man who
left his office early in the evenings and never looked up from
polishing his black-rimmed glasses.

Her eyes were still on the page in front of her—it was one
of her father's leather-bound Dickens novels; Janet's parents
had been after her to read as many classics as she could before
she started college in September—when the mailbox lid clat-
tered. Before she realized what had happened, her mother's
high heels were already clacking toward the front door. "Oh,
there you are, Janet. Was that the postman I heard?"

Janet bolted upright, the Dickens spilling from her lap. She
bit back a curse as she knelt to pick it up, smoothing back the
bent pages as her mother frowned at her. "Really, Janet, you
must take more care with your father's things. And what *is*
that getup you have on? You know better than to wear jeans
in the front room, where anyone walking by could see you."

"Sorry, ma'am." Janet tucked the volume under her arm
and stepped past her mother, narrowly beating her to the door.
Janet was an inch taller than Mom now, and her legs were still
muscled from cheerleading in the spring.

Janet jerked open the front door and slid her hand into the mailbox before Mom could intervene. Three letters today. Janet tried to angle her shoulders to shield the mail from her mother's view.

The first two letters were for her father, in official government envelopes with his address neatly typed on by their senders' secretaries. The third letter bore Janet's name.

It had come.

A short, sharp thrill ran through her as her fingers reached for the seal. Would this be the day everything changed?

Two weeks ago, she'd discovered that slim paperback in the bus station. That very night, she'd read every page and found herself so enraptured, so overwhelmed, that she couldn't help writing to its the author. Now here it was—a reply. The author of that incredible book had written a letter just for Janet.

But Mom was still standing right behind her. Could Janet slip the letter into her blouse without her seeing?

"What's gotten into you today?" Mom reached over Janet's shoulder and plucked all three letters from her hand. Simple as that. "What's this one with your name?"

"It's nothing." Janet ached to snatch the letter back, but forced herself to breathe instead as Mom tucked her finger behind the seal. Everyone in the family had always felt free to open Janet's mail. She was eighteen years old, but still a child in their eyes.

She'd have to think of a lie quickly.

The letter had been addressed to Janet by mistake. That was what she'd say. Whoever had sent it must have found her name on some list of recent high school graduates.

No, of course Janet couldn't possibly imagine what the letter might refer to. She'd never heard of any "Dolores Wood" or "Bannon Press." As a matter of fact, the letter could be a

cleverly disguised Communist recruitment tool. For safety's
sake, they really ought to burn it before the neighbors saw.

Though the idea of burning that letter, before she'd even
had a chance to read it, made tears prick at Janet's eyes.

"Oh, it's from the college." Mom withdrew a single sheet
of paper from the envelope and scanned it. "It isn't important.
Only a packing list."

"The college?" Janet hadn't even glanced at the return address on the letter, but there it was. The letter was from Holy
Divinity.

Janet couldn't believe she'd been so foolish.

"Well, you won't be needing this." Mom tucked the letter into the pocket of her apron. "They must send it out to
all the new girls, without regard for which will be moving
into the dorms."

Janet nodded, hoping her mother couldn't hear her heart
still thundering in the silence.

"Are you all right?" Mom frowned again. "You look
flushed. Your father and I had planned to go to the club for
dinner, but if you need us to stay home—"

"It's nothing, ma'am." Janet shook her head, but she could
feel blood rushing to her cheeks under her mother's scrutiny.
"I, ah—I have to get ready for work or I'll be late."

Mom's frown deepened. "I didn't realize you were working tonight."

"I am." Janet wasn't. Another stupid, rash thing to say. Now
what could she do? Put on her uniform and show up at the
Soda Shoppe, ready to trot milkshakes out to station wagons
on her night off?

To put off that decision, Janet dashed past Mom into the
row house and ran up the narrow wooden stairs, her foot-
falls echoing behind her. Dad was always after her not to run
in the house, saying it would disturb her grandmother's rest,

but Dad wasn't home. Besides, Grandma always said it did her heart good to hear a child scurrying about the house and that Dad should shut his cake hole.

Janet reached the second-floor landing and threw open the door of her small bedroom, the hot air hitting her like a steaming kettle. The room was the same as always—the bed neatly made with its delicate pink spread, the flowered wallpaper that was starting to peel around the edges after a decade of Washington summers, the round mirror over her dresser with photos tucked into the frame. They were school portraits of her friends, mostly, plus an old yearbook photo of Janet and Marie in their cheerleading uniforms with pom-poms at their hips, their bent elbows lightly touching.

That photo was Janet's favorite.

Marie, her soft hair framing her dark-rimmed glasses and always-gleaming smile, had been Janet's best friend all through school. They'd done everything together, sitting side by side in every class and lunch period. In junior high they'd been the only two girls to enter the science fair at the boys' school, growing mold in carefully labeled jars and winning a red ribbon for their trouble. In high school they'd practiced their cartwheels and splits on the football field, giggling every time they fell onto the grass and making up silly variations to the official St. Paul's cheers. Janet had never been happier than when one of the chants she made up provoked a fresh bout of laughter from Marie.

Marie was a year older than Janet, though, and after she graduated Janet's senior year had been lonely indeed. Marie had spent the year off at secretarial school, learning to type and take stenography and do other important things while Janet sat in Latin class again, wearing her childish uniform blazer and holding out her palm for the nun to strike when she forgot a conjugation.

That morning, eager to hear her voice again, Janet had tried to call Marie, but she was out, as usual. Janet had been forced to leave a terribly awkward message with her mother instead. Mrs. Eastwood had always seemed to think Janet was somewhat odd, and she could only have made that impression worse with the way she'd stumbled through the quick call.

She'd tried to explain that she was only calling to ask about Marie's job search. Now that she'd finished her business classes, Marie had been so busy with applications and interviews they hadn't seen each other in two weeks, and Janet was desperate to talk to her again.

Most of all, she longed to tell Marie about the book she'd found. Janet couldn't wait to hear what she thought of it—even though she could probably guess. Despite their shared memories, Janet knew Marie probably wouldn't want to remain her friend once she knew her secret. No normal person would.

Still, Janet had made up her mind to tell her. There was no one else she could talk with about this. Certainly no one in her family. If her parents ever found out… Janet didn't dare to think of it. Marie was the only one who might be willing to listen.

Janet broke her gaze from the glossy photo and knelt on the floor next to her bed. She lifted the pink spread and in a single, practiced move, slid her hand between the mattress and bedframe until her fingers reached the cracked paper spine. She checked again to make sure the bedroom door was fully closed before carefully withdrawing the book from its hiding place.

She really ought to find a better spot for it. The weight of the mattress had not been kind to the binding. The cheap glue had already started to come undone, and a few of the pages were loose, but Janet tucked them back into their proper place. She sank onto the rug between her bed and the wall, where she'd be out of view of anyone barging in, and gazed down at the book's cover.

Its background was a deep, glaring shade of red. That color was what had first caught Janet's eye when she'd spotted the wire rack full of books at the Ocean City bus station. It had been surrounded by similarly glaring paperbacks—detective fiction, gangster stories, the sorts of books you saw certain men reading on the streetcar. The sorts of books her father dismissed with a sniff as trash.

But it was the drawing, the strange image that stood out starkly from that palette of red, that had held Janet's eye for far longer than it should've.

The book's cover showed two girls, neither much older than Janet herself. One girl had blond hair and one brown. Both had long, dark eyelashes and full, red lips. The dark-haired girl perched on a bed in the foreground, her legs long and slim, her skirt pulled up above her knees. Her green blouse was un-buttoned far enough to show a hint of pale slip beneath and a curve of bosom above. The blonde girl stood farther back, dressed in nothing but a white nightgown that clung to her curves and a pair of deep brown stockings, the hems at the thighs fully visible below her shockingly short gown.

The dark-haired girl sat twisted around on the bed, so that the two girls' eyes met. The blonde's lips were parted, as though to speak to the other girl.

Or, perhaps, to kiss her.

Janet blushed at the thought, as she did every time. Though she knew well enough that within the book's pages the girls *did* kiss, and even more besides.

Janet had only glanced around the bus station for a tiny moment before she slipped the book under her blouse. It still mortified her to remember that she'd stolen it. The price on the cover was thirty-five cents, and Janet had had two dollars

in her purse, but she couldn't imagine showing her purchase
to that smirking boy behind the cash register.

That novel was the only thing Janet had ever stolen in her
life. She'd read it straight through that first night, and she'd
stared at the cover in secret every day since.

Yellow letters above the drawing screamed the book's title,
A Love So Strange. Smaller black text below read, "A world
spoken of only in whispers, where women enjoy twisted pas-
sions. Betty knew it was wrong…but she was powerless against
her unnatural attractions."

At the bottom, in the smallest type on the cover, was the
author's name, Dolores Wood.

Janet had read each of those words more times than she
could count. Still, whenever she gazed at that cover, her eyes
were pulled to the illustration. To the girls' eyes where they
met across the room. To the shapes of their bodies in their
skimpy clothes.

Janet pressed one finger into the dip in her lower lip. Her
breathing had grown heavier.

She'd never imagined there was a word for the strange feelings she'd had so many nights, alone in her bed, in the dark
silence of her room.

Lesbian.

The word made her shudder. But it sent a tiny shiver down
her spine, too.

Janet had never understood, not until she turned the thin
brown pages of Dolores Wood's novel, that other girls might
feel the way she did. That a world existed outside the one
she'd always known.

It had never occurred to her that life could be different from
what had already been set out for her. Ill-fitting uniforms and
nickel-sized tips at the Soda Shoppe. Her parents pausing in
the dining room to listen to the guarded phone calls Janet

made in the kitchen. Solemn history and mathematics lessons taught by stern-faced nuns. Then, someday, an equally solemn wedding to a faceless man, and a future spent baking solemn casseroles for solemn, faceless children.

Janet had never thought books like *A Love So Strange* could be written, let alone published and sold, right in the middle of a public bus station. She'd never imagined that some girls might really *do* the sorts of things Janet had only furtively imagined in those brief, solitary moments between waking and sleeping.

Reading *A Love So Strange* had made Janet remember some things differently, too.

The way she and Marie had talked and laughed while they'd practiced their cheers. The way they'd touched, lying side by side on Marie's back porch while her parents were out on warm summer afternoons.

The way Janet would trail her fingers along Marie's bare arm after she'd pointed out some item in a magazine. The way Marie would smile and wait several moments before she drew her hand away.

When Janet thought of kissing a girl, the way girls kissed other girls in the pages of Dolores Wood's book, she always thought of kissing Marie. When she thought back to Marie's smiles on those lazy afternoons, she wondered if Marie might feel the same way, too.

If Janet could only show that book to Marie, it could change everything.

Still, she should never have sent the letter.

She'd been so foolish, to dream of writing a book of her own. To scrawl out that letter with all her silly, immature questions for Mrs. Wood. To address it to the publisher listed on the book's cover and drop the envelope into the letter box, as though it were as simple a matter as sending in for a catalog.

Downstairs, she heard the front door open, then close again. "Janet! Come back down!"

At the sound of her mother's voice Janet scrambled to her feet, shoving the book back into its hiding place. She winced as she felt the cover bend. "Coming, ma'am!"

Only then did Janet remember she'd said she had to work tonight. Mom would wonder why she hadn't already changed into her uniform. She tried to think of another lie—she'd checked her schedule upstairs and realized she wasn't working that night after all; there, that one was simple enough—but all thoughts of lies and excuses left Janet's mind when she reached the bottom of the staircase and saw Marie in the foyer, smiling at a now-apronless mom and fiddling with the strap of her purse.

A delicious thrill ran through Janet all the way to her toes. She wished she'd thought to reapply her lipstick.

Marie looked as she always had, with each dark curl in place, her glasses polished to a gleam. Yet she looked older than usual, too, somehow. Her suit was neat, the skirt perfectly tailored where its hem fell around her calves. The jacket was a matching blue flannel, and the string of pearls her parents had given her for her eighteenth birthday was wound around her neck.

Janet had never seen her friend look so much like a real grown-up. A lovely grown-up, at that.

"There you are, Janet." Mom turned from Marie with a lingering smile of her own. Janet's mother had always been fond of Marie. She talked about her using words like *stable* and *settled*. Especially when she sought to admonish Janet.

Janet ignored her and bounced toward Marie. "I'm so glad you came! I have so much to tell you."

"It's been ages, hasn't it?" Marie's smile was wide enough

to match Janet's own. "I'm terribly sorry I missed your call this morning. I was at an interview."

"An interview." Janet nodded, her eyes drifting down to Marie's neat suit. She felt herself flushing deeper. "Of course."

"I've been so nervous." Marie smiled, and fumbled again with her purse. "It's wonderful to see you, though."

"Marie has the most exciting news." Mom held out a hand, ushering them into the living room. She didn't approve of dawdling in the foyer. "I'll bring you girls some refreshments."

Mom left for the kitchen, where she could still overhear every word they said. Even so, as Janet and Marie took seats on the sofa, Janet leaned in close and said, "I was just looking at our photo from the cheerleading squad last year. I remember that as if it was yesterday."

"Do you?" Marie smiled. She looked even more sophisticated from this distance. "It seems like a hundred years ago to me."

Janet's smile began to fade.

"There we are." Mom set down a tray of chocolate chip cookies and two glasses of milk, sitting primly in the armchair opposite the cold brick fireplace. "Marie, I simply can't wait one moment longer to hear what Janet thinks of your news."

"Well, then, what's your news, Marie?" Janet wished Dad were here, so they could smile together at this ostentatious etiquette. Mom treated every visitor like President Eisenhower.

Laughter sparkled behind Marie's eyes, too, but, ever demure, she didn't let it reach her lips. "I've been offered a job, just today. I'm going to be a typist at the Department of State!"

"Marie!" Janet clapped her hands. "That's marvelous! That's the kind of job we all dreamed of having, do you remember?"

"Of course."

Any sort of government work had seemed glamorous to the girls of St. Paul's Academy. Their mothers had all gone to work as "government girls" during the war, of course, but they'd retired once the men came home. These days only the most elite girls, those capable of passing stringent tests and maintaining the highest personal decorum, were hired to work as government secretaries and typists. Janet's own distant ambition, of studying journalism in college and working for a newspaper or magazine someday, was far less exciting.

Working for the State Department was perhaps the most prestigious government position of all, surpassed only by working in the White House itself. At the State Department, a girl might meet a famous ambassador or foreign film star. Perhaps there might be a need to travel overseas, to take dictation for an important summit in Paris or Rome, or even some far-flung country like China.

It was all temporary, of course. The true goal, spoken of only through happy whispers over cafeteria lunches, was to meet a government man with an impressive job of his own, perhaps one with a title like *director* or even *undersecretary*. Once you were married, you'd leave your job to set up housekeeping so you'd be ready when the children came along.

Of course, it was far too early for Marie and Janet to think about any of *that*.

"Well, I'm not surprised," Janet said, still beaming. "Didn't you have the highest marks of all the girls coming out of school?"

Marie cast down her eyes. "Thank you, Janet. I was hoping we could go out tonight to celebrate, but your mother said you're working."

"Oh, no, I'm not. Let's go celebrate!" When Mom raised her eyebrows, Janet hastily added, "Sorry, ma'am, I was confused about my work schedule earlier. Let's go, Marie—if we leave now we can catch the streetcar pulling in."

Marie rose instantly, nodding toward the untouched milk glasses. "Thanks so much for the refreshments, Mrs. Jones."

"Of course." Mom's plastered-on smile stayed firm as she eyed Janet's plain blouse and jeans. "Marie and I will wait here while you change."

Janet longed to be out the door, but her mother was right. Janet rarely wore much makeup, and most days she preferred button-downs and Bermudas to frills and fashion, but regardless, no restaurant in Georgetown would let her in for dinner wearing pants. "I'll be fast, I promise."

She ran upstairs, exchanged her jeans for a simple plaid skirt and stockings, and ran back down. Mom eyed her again, probably wishing Janet had at least taken the time to run a comb through her short blond curls, but all she said was, "You girls have a lovely evening. Marie, please do send your mother my regards."

"I will, ma'am, thank you."

Janet grabbed her purse, took Marie by the arm and pulled her out the door before her mother could launch into a new round of pleasantries. The streetcar was already clanging as it approached the end of their block, and the girls had to run. Marie's high heels made her stumble, and Janet, in her ballet flats, was faster. She stepped onto the wide streetcar platform and held out her hand to help Marie aboard as the car pulled out, both girls laughing so hard the driver admonished them with a glare as they started north up Wisconsin Avenue.

It was exhilarating to be going out without her parents on the spur of the moment this way. Janet was certain Mom wouldn't have allowed it if she'd been with anyone but Marie, and flushed with pleasure at the thought.

"I thought we'd go to Meaker's for dinner." Marie squirmed through the crush of after-work passengers, struggling to keep her footing as the car lurched forward. A man in a fedora

reached for her elbow to steady her, nearly dropping his cigarette.

"That sounds perfect." Janet smiled at the man until he released Marie's arm.

The two of them made their way to the back of the car.
Janet couldn't stop herself from staring down at Marie's clothes.
The perfect fit of her suit. The way she stood gripping the
ceiling strap, with one heel turned out to steady herself as the
streetcar rocked over bumps. The shape of her legs, so pretty
in her stockings. It reminded Janet of—

The book. It reminded Janet of the picture on the cover of
A Love So Strange.

She swallowed and tried, again, to make herself breathe.

"Are you all right?" Marie peered at Janet unsteadily as the
streetcar swung beneath them.

"I'm fine." Janet had never felt finer, in fact.

"You're sure?" Marie pointed ahead. "Meaker's is just another block, but we can catch the car going the opposite way
if you need to go home."

"I don't want to go home." As they reached their stop, Janet
hopped past Marie down to the sidewalk, glad to feel earth
beneath her feet once more. She wasn't quite sure what type
of place Meaker's might be, but she didn't care. "We have to
celebrate, don't we?"

Marie smiled and took Janet's arm. "We certainly do."

The restaurant turned out to be a small, quiet place on a
side street off Wisconsin, with worn white tablecloths and dim
lamps hanging overhead. The girls were seated right away,
and Marie ordered for both of them, smiling up at the waiter
with a poised nonchalance Janet envied.

Marie was so strong and composed. She showed none of
the clumsy awkwardness Janet always felt. It was a lucky thing
Marie had wanted to celebrate with her.

Janet smiled fondly across the table as two drinks appeared in front of them. She recognized the glasses from her parents' cocktail parties. "What are these?"

"Martinis." Marie smiled and lifted her glass. Janet imitated her, trying to look equally refined. The waiter hadn't said a word about identification, so he must've thought the girls looked older than their eighteen and nineteen years. No one here at Meaker's, it seemed, had realized Janet was nothing but a plain schoolgirl. "My father always orders them on special occasions."

Janet took a swallow. The drink was cool, with a hint of spice. It tasted very adult. She could picture the girls in *A Love So Strange* sipping such a drink alone in their apartment one evening.

Marie asked about a friend from high school she hadn't seen lately, and soon they were caught up reminiscing about their high school days. Before long, Janet's glass was empty and a fresh drink had taken its place. She wasn't sure exactly how much time had passed, and she couldn't quite remember what had just been said that had made her laugh so hard. All she knew was that Marie was laughing, too. That was all that seemed to matter. Their food had arrived, but Janet had barely eaten. Marie's pot roast and potatoes were in a similar state.

"So this fellow Mom wanted me to go out with tonight," Marie was saying, as she took another sip, "he's a college man in town for the summer. Dartmouth. His uncle works with Dad at Treasury, and he's a dreadful bore—"

"How do you know he's a bore?" Janet interrupted. "Have you met him already?"

"No, no, but you know how these college men are."

Did she? This was the first time Janet had heard Marie talk about college men that way. Or was it merely the first time

Janet had noticed it? Had Dolores Wood's book changed the way she saw everything, all at once?

"In any case," Marie went on, "Dad's up for a promotion—that's why they've been going to the club so often—and so Mom thinks I ought to go out with this Harold Smith fellow, since his uncle would be Dad's boss if he gets the new job. But I told Mom I didn't want to go out with some strange man. I said I wanted to go celebrate with my best friend instead. Mom huffed and puffed, but what could she say in the end? Soon I'll be earning my very own paychecks, and she and Dad won't have any say over what I do."

"Really?" Janet hadn't thought of that. "Won't you go on living with them, though?"

"Well, sure—unless I were to move in with some of the other State Department girls, I suppose. A few of my business school classmates invited me to share an apartment, but I didn't have a job yet so I had to tell them no. Wouldn't that be magnificent, though? Not to have to follow anyone else's rules? To be able to go out whenever you chose, with whomever you wanted?"

Janet nodded, but in truth she couldn't imagine such freedom. Until she'd read *A Love So Strange*, her dreams had only extended so far as a college dorm. It seemed a lovely idea, though, to be away from her family's watching eyes.

In a dorm, of course, there were still strict rules and curfews. Living at Holy Divinity, only a mile or so up Wisconsin Avenue, might be even more restrictive than living at home. At least in the house Janet was allowed to use the phone when she chose, provided Mom, Dad and Grandma didn't need to make a call.

"I must admit, I'm a bit nervous." Marie bit her lip, and Janet forgot all her musings about college and apartments.

Her hope flared bright. Could Marie be nervous for the same reason as Janet?

"What will everyone in the office think of me?" Marie gazed down into her drink. "What if I don't keep up with the other girls? What if my boss expects more of me than I can do?"

Janet tamped down her disappointment. "Oh, you don't need to worry about that. You had the highest marks of anyone in your class, remember? Besides, they're all bound to adore you. How could they not?"

Marie smiled up at her, yet she still looked bashful. "That's kind of you to say."

"I'm not being kind. I'm being honest. You're perfect, Marie."

The words were out of her mouth before Janet could think about how they sounded. Now she felt bashful, too.

Yet Marie didn't look embarrassed as she held her gaze across the table.

Neither of them spoke, but something passed in that shared look that Janet could not have named. It buzzed through her with an energy she'd never known.

Unless that, too, was solely in Janet's imagination.

The waiter came to take their empty glasses, inquiring if they needed anything else. His eyes were on Marie and she answered for them both, in a voice so grown-up Janet couldn't believe she'd ever found cause to be nervous about anything. "No, thank you. I suppose it's getting late."

The waiter left, and Marie withdrew a few bills from her purse and tucked them under the glass. Her every movement was mesmerizing. "We ought to catch the streetcar. Your mother will be worried."

"Oh, forget my mother." Janet laughed and climbed awkwardly to her feet, holding the table to right herself.

Marie laughed, too, and followed. On the way out of the restaurant, she took a matchbook from the front desk and slipped it into her purse with a smile. Janet grabbed one, too, giggling.

The sidewalk was dark under the burned-out streetlight as the girls stumbled outside, the pavement grit caking under their heels. Up ahead, on Wisconsin, people were walking quickly along the sidewalk, but out here there was no one out but the two of them.

"I'm glad you didn't have to work tonight after all." Marie tucked her arm into Janet's as they began to walk. "This afternoon, the very instant the man at State told me I'd gotten the job, I knew the only person I wanted to celebrate with in all the world was you."

Janet closed her eyes, tasting the words.

If she were Sam, the main character from *A Love So Strange*—if she had Sam's courage, her knowledge of girls, her understanding of the world—she would kiss Marie. Right where they stood.

Sam didn't bother with waiting. She went after what she wanted.

Of course, even Sam wouldn't dare kiss a girl out in the open darkness, where anyone might see them. But maybe they could move somewhere out of sight. Duck beneath the awning of the shuttered corner shop, perhaps.

Sam would've said a clever line, too. Something witty and alluring.

Janet opened her eyes.

She meant to think of something clever. Really, she did. In the end, though, the words that came out were, "Um... let's go over there."

Marie didn't seem to mind her abruptness. Her eyes were bright, her answer quick. "Yes, let's."

They hurried around the corner and stood, silent, their eyes locked on one another's. Janet could no longer think about books or jobs. She couldn't think about anything but Marie and that look they'd shared across the table.

She closed her eyes. And all at once, there in the darkness, it was happening. It was real.

Janet was kissing her.

It was madness. She knew it was madness, because in that moment Janet could not have prevented herself from kissing Marie if all the world had tried to stop her. And so it was some time before she began to understand that Marie was kissing her back.

She could scarcely breathe. In all the world, there existed nothing but Marie's lips on hers. Marie's hair, soft under her hand. Marie's body, pressed so close Janet could feel the seams in her flannel suit.

"Hey!"

The girls sprang apart, four feet of space materializing between them in an instant. There was no way to tell where the shout had come from.

Who'd seen them? Would her parents find out? Already, before Janet had even truly found out for herself?

"Is it the police?" Marie whispered. Janet hadn't even thought of that.

"Hey!" The shout came again. This time, it was punctuated by a round of laughter from high above. A girl's laughter.

Whoever had shouted, it wasn't the police.

Janet tilted her head back, looking for the source of the sound. Next to her, Marie did the same.

They both saw it at the same time. A girl, framed in an open window. An apartment two stories above the darkened store.

A man leaned into the window frame. The girl ducked out

of his way, still laughing, holding a bottle of beer. The girl's eyes were locked on his.

She hadn't seen them.

Only then did Janet feel the full weight of relief crashing down around her.

She lowered her gaze, locking eyes with Marie. Marie's breathing was rapid, but her smile danced behind her glasses. The madness had touched her, too.

The sound of the streetcar made Janet's heart beat faster. It was late, and the next car may not come for some time. They'd have to dash for it.

She longed to take Marie's hand—that was what Sam would've done—but she didn't dare. Instead, they turned and ran in a single movement.

This time, Janet didn't beat Marie to the curb. This time, they stayed together.

They climbed onto the sparsely populated car and took seats side by side. They didn't dare to touch, but they watched each other carefully. After another moment, they began to laugh.

Janet waited for her heart to slow, for normalcy to retake her mind. Yet as long as she waited, it never came.